WHY DID HE DIE?

LOUISE BRODERICK

Published 2023 by Lavender and White Publishing.

Email info@lavenderandwhite.co.uk

Typesetting, layout and design Lavender and White Publishing.

www.lavenderandwhite.co.uk

ISBN: 978-1-7393049-1-1

Other books by Louise Broderick

Romance:
Trainers
Winners
Millionaires Are A Girl's Best Friend
The Derry Blake Boxset

Crime:
After – Sometimes The End Is Just The Beginning
Where Is My Daughter?

Non-fiction:
Plot. Write. Sell.

Writing as Jacqui Broderick:
Pony For Free
The Unwanted Pony
The Cat's Whiskers

Dedication

To the incredible friends who, long after they should have given up on me ever finishing this book, kept asking when it would be published, especially, Stephanie who bravely read the first version, Bridget and Trish.

Acknowledgments

I love writing the acknowledgements piece as it means the book is finished and about to be released. With '*Why Did He Die,*' I've been waiting nine years to finish it. The book was originally written in 2014, with a completely different title. It was the first crime novel I had ever written and was pretty dire, but it gave life to my DI Grace Tallis. Stephanie, the brave structural editor of that early version gently pointed out to me glaring plot holes. Life somehow got in the way of the book being finished, thank goodness. While the book was on ice I went to university and completed a Masters degree in Writing. I had intended to do the rewrites of this book during the course, but another idea hatched and I wrote '*After – Sometimes The End Is Just The Beginning.*' This book, I reasoned, would be the next in the series. However, I shelved '*Why*' when I got the urge to write '*Where Is My Daughter?*'

That published it was time to rewrite, 'Why Did He Die?' This took rather a long time, as it was more of a job than I had realised it would be. Over the years I have come to know my detective, Grace Tallis, she's not the same in 2023 as she was in 2014 and so the book has had to reflect her changes as well as those of the murder she is investigating. At times I wished I had scrapped the book and started from scratch as I rewrote almost every line and scene. It would probably have been easier, but I'm always learning and hopefully this book will be worth the effort.

The book is set in the far west of Cornwall, where my paternal grandmother lived and a place where I have spent much of my life. I have, for my own purposes, taken huge liberties with the county and with Penzance.

Contents

Chapter One

JUNE 2017

There was something jaunty about the way the grass growing over her grave danced and swayed. He liked to know she was beneath it; she was his favourite.

Jago Carey stood in the pale moonlight beside the bedroom window. The only sound was the gentle breathing of Zara, his sleeping wife. On the nights when sleep would not come, he would ease himself out of bed, look out over the beautiful acres that belonged to Park Hall and remember.

He eased open the window, leaning out into the cool air. The pastureland beyond the house was bathed in the silvery light from the full mid-summer moon. In the brightness from the moonlight, he could see the corner of the field, close to the stable yard where her body lay. He breathed a long sigh of pleasure, lips curving into a smile.

His mood changed instantly as a movement caught his eye. Out of the dark shadows cast by the stable wall a large, shaggy black and white dog appeared. 'Bastard dog,' Jago hissed.

As he watched, the dog trotted purposefully across the field to her grave and began to dig frenziedly, long tail wagging. Jago's jaw clenched in temper as the dog unearthed a strip of something dark. The animal tensed itself, leaning back, tugging.

The dog had hung around all the previous day. No matter how many times Jago had driven it off it returned relentlessly to the same corner of the field. He'd thought the vicious kick he had given it the previous evening had sent it on its way. Yelping it had bolted. It was back again now, drawn irresistibly to the same spot.

Silently he pulled on a pair of jeans and a tee-shirt, walked quickly downstairs and slipped out of the house.

The stray dog didn't take any killing – one quick blow to the side of its head with a shovel. It had been so focused on digging, flinging clouds of dry earth over its muscular shoulders, it hadn't even noticed him coming. In the pale pre-dawn half-light Jago could see the dog had succeeded in unearthing a section of plastic sheet. He glanced at his watch; the numbers clear in the florescent light. Just after four. He had plenty of time. No one came to the stables before eight and Zara would sleep until he brought her a mug of coffee.

Jago seized the dog's front legs and dragged its still warm and twitching body out of the way. He returned to the spot where the dog had been digging and pushed the bloodied blade of the shovel into the dark earth. She had to be moved. If one dog had been attracted to the grave, there would be others.

He worked slowly, moving the soil cautiously as though she would feel the metal blade if he touched her remains with it. With almost reverent movements he levered off the first level of turf from around her grave.

The exposed earth was dark, glistening damply. He wiped the back of his hand against his nose as the foul stench of rotting flesh hit his nostrils. He turned, opening his mouth to suck in a lungful of clean air, before resuming his task. The brown earth was sticky, each shovel full heavy in his hands. Gradually he heaped up the earth at the edge of the long narrow hole.

'Fucking dog.' Jago scowled. Without the dog's keen nose, poking into what wasn't its business; he wouldn't have to be digging her up. She could have remained in her corner of the field. He could see her grave from most of the rooms on the field side of the house. The best view was from his office, where he could lean back in his leather chair and relive the memories.

The sticky earth gave way to drier, more crumbly soil. Deep in the ground was the long bulky bundle he was searching for. The slow but relentless onset of daylight illuminated an elongated, narrow shape. Crouching down he reached into the hole to let his fingers brush the rolled-up plastic and the stained ropes knotted at intervals along the bundle. He eased one leg into the hole, pushing his foot into the moist soil beside the plastic wrapped shape. He bent, using one hand to brush the remainder of the loam away.

The plastic sheet was cool beneath the damp heat of his fingers. He rocked backwards, hauling the bundle towards himself inch by inch. The silence was broken by the sound of the plastic scraping on the soil, loud even above the laboured sound of his breathing.

Sweat trickled down his back, soaking the fabric of his tee-shirt. Panic began to set in. He was taking too long. He re-doubled his efforts. A moment later, with a loud scrape across the surface of the soil, the cumbersome bundle slid free.

Jago rocked back onto his haunches, panting, his muscular forearms and thighs on fire with the effort and urgency of his task.

He paused then, letting his breathing return to normal, rubbing his aching muscles with earth-stained fingers. He checked his watch; it was too early for anyone to be in the stable yard. Still though, he lifted his eyes to scan the fields that surrounded him.

A delicate wisp of mist was rolling slowly across the valley floor, in front of the wooded slopes, grey tendrils, gliding silently across the short, cropped grass. The wooded slopes beside the fields were becoming visible as the early morning light began to highlight the green shapes.

Behind where he crouched, the old sandstone farm buildings formed a quadrangle beneath faded slate grey roofs. From within the stables came the sharp, scrape of metal against concrete as one of the horses got to its feet, iron shod hooves scattering the straw bedding seeking grip in its effort to rise. The noise startled him, every nerve and sinew tense with the apprehension of discovery. Long moments passed. He could hear his breathing, loud and ragged. He got slowly to his feet, heart pounding, the dim thud audible through layers of bone, skin and his sweat drenched tee-shirt. Even the sound of his throat, as he swallowed, seemed ear splittingly loud.

Jago forced himself to relax, his nostrils flaring as he pulled cool air into his lungs. Gradually his heart slowed, he no longer could feel its tattoo against his rib cage.

Holding a blood splattered front and back paw Jago lifted the dog and flung it into the hole. It landed with its head back, tongue still lolling from its dangling jaw. Without pausing for breath Jago shovelled the earth back into the hole, covering the dog's corpse.

The task complete Jago tucked a hand into the rope that bound one end of the bundle and began to pull it closer to the buildings. In the stables he heard another horse get to its feet in alarm. He expected at any moment for the bedroom window to be flung open and Zara to look out demanding to know what he was doing. He began to jog, his heels catching the plastic, he stumbled, panic making him clumsy. 'Fuck,' he breathed a sigh of relief as he reached the corner of the stone built stable block. He was out of sight of the house. Leaning over he put his hands on the burning muscles of his thighs, waiting until his laboured breathing returned to normal. There was no time to waste. He jogged back across the dew damp grass, fetched the shovel and began to dig, muscles pumping, his shoulders on fire with the effort. Although his watch said only five it was fully light, already the mid-summer temperature beginning to climb, the mist rapidly disappearing.

The hole complete, he tossed the shovel to one side and stood, finally relaxed enough to contemplate the plastic wrapped bundle that lay at his feet.

A slight smile tugged at the corners of his mouth. She had been the best so far.

He unwrapped the rope gripped one corner of the plastic sheeting and gently eased it open. There was a ripping sound, like the two edges of Velcro being pulled apart as the surfaces separated. On the inside edge of the plastic a dark patch cracked, the dry surface splitting into a myriad of pieces. Dark flecks tumbled to the mist dampened earth between his knees.

The sudden stench that hit his nostrils made him recoil, sending him sprawling backwards. He heaved, an involuntary reaction to the vicious wave of rotting flesh. He got to his knees choking, fighting back the acid bile that stung the back of his throat. Despite his efforts a bubbling yellow stream of liquid exploded from his mouth. Breathing through his mouth he turned back to his task, desperate to see his handiwork again.

There was nothing left of Catherine Marshall. The young woman whose last breath he had witnessed was now a revolting mess of ooze. Most of her long blonde hair, encrusted with blood the last time he had seen it, had been engulfed by the rotting flesh of her scalp. The strands had sunk, tangling into the mound of putrification, a single, thick blonde strand, still clung to a wrinkled cap of skin.

He reached forwards and cautiously twisted his fingers into the strand, not wanting to touch any of the rotten flesh. He remembered how silky it had felt when he had gripped it.

One limb, or what was left of it, soft, sickly green meat clinging to yellowing bone slid gently towards him, the bony claws of fingers coming to rest inches from his knee. A coil of blue nylon rope was still looped around what had been her wrist. There were more coils around what was left of her other wrist and her ankles.

With the back of his hand Jago wiped at the beads of sweat that had broken out on his forehead as the memories made him harden beneath his jeans.

She had been so thrilled that hot afternoon when he had invited her for a cold beer. So trusting. So naïve. Like the rest of them.

Jago smiled, remembering the way her face changed as he had locked the door. Her delight had turned to confusion, anger and then naked fear, when she glimpsed what lay ahead. She had been desperate to live, still hopeful she would get away.

'Let me go, please…' she had begged, 'I'll do anything you want.'
'You will.' He had smiled.

She had fought the hardest of them all. Later, he had realised she was no longer fighting, or moaning. Her body was limp against the bed frame, her blue eyes staring fixedly at a point somewhere beyond the window.

No one had come looking for her. She was another nobody with nowhere to go and no one to care about her.

Jago got stiffly to his feet, aching with tiredness at his early morning exertions. He was irritated now, annoyed by the stray dog, at the bother of having to unearth her corpse and rebury it.

The sound of a horse whinnying broke his reverie. Pulling the plastic over Catherine Marshall's stinking corpse he rolled the bundle into hole he had dug. It lay at the bottom, a featureless lump. Working fast he shovelled damp loam into the hole, covering the tangled mass of plastic, bones and rotting flesh. The hole filled he put the chunks of turf back, treading them carefully into place. Later he would cover the grave with the unused, old show jump wings that had accumulated behind the stables over the years. She was safe here, tucked away from sight. 'Bye Catherine,' Jago shouldered the shovel and turned towards the house. If he hurried there would just be time for him to shower before he made Zara her morning mug of coffee.

Chapter Two

'It will take you literally five minutes,' Zara Carey's voice had a strident, insistent edge. 'All you need to do is replace a broken bracket on the shelf in the groom's accommodation.'

'I'll do it later.' Her words took him back to the moment it had been broken. Catherine Marshall's head had snapped it from the wall when he had flung her against it. He could still hear the screws ripping away from the wall, the thud as it hit the ground and see the fear in her eyes.

'I've been asking you to do it for the last nine months.' Zara's fingers hovered over the delicate container filled with makeup brushes of assorted sizes and shapes until she found the one she was looking for. 'Why must I always have to nag at you to get anything done?' She dusted powder over her cheeks, looking in the mirror to assess her work.

'I said I'll do it.' Jago brushed at a dusty mark on the knee of his jeans. He longed for the moment when he could watch her Range Rover disappearing down the drive. For a moment his thoughts drifted back to the early morning and reburying Catherine Marshall's corpse. His arm and leg muscles ached with the effort.

'I can't get a builder to come in just for a minor job like that.'

'No need. It's on my to do list.' There was a hint of sarcasm in his voice. He met her grey eyes in the mirror. The light pouring in through the window emphasised the harsh lines around her mouth that even limitless amounts of botox and filler could not erase. Nothing she did could disguise the fact she was aging faster than he was. The five years between them was became more apparent every day.

'I was out at six this morning sorting out the ditch over in Home Meadow. I've a full day ahead. But I will do it.' Jago dropped his eyes.

'I'm getting sick of reminding you.' She liked to have the final word. Zara applied a slick of bright lipstick, rubbing her lips together before sitting back to admire her handiwork.

Jago moved towards the window, screwing up his mouth in a parody of her expression, mocking her, knowing he was out of her line of sight. If ever a woman needed taking down a peg or two it was her. He liked to imagine the expression on her face if he twined his fingers into her blonde hair and slammed her head against the wall.

'How the hell did the shelf get broken in the first place?' Zara dropped the lipstick in her makeup bag and pushed her fingers into her hair, fluffing up the blonde strands. 'What do they do in there?'

Seeing her sharp glance Jago smoothed all trace of amusement from his face as turned towards her. 'No idea.'

She turned to face him; her long fingers entwined in her lap. Despite the expensive hand cream she applied liberally, she could not disguise the age spots that were beginning to appear. She looked, in the unforgiving sunlight, every one of her forty-three years. There was no brushing Zara off when she was in one of her demanding moods.

'What are you doing today? What else have you got to do?' Her voice held the headmistress tone that set his teeth on edge. He watched her lips move over her neat, white teeth as she repeated the words, slowly enunciated the sentence as if he were deaf, or simple. Above her white spots of light danced on the wall from the sunlight reflected on her diamond rings. With a barely disguised sigh Jago sank down on the edge of the bed. 'Sam Green is coming to shoe a couple of horses. Michael Alderton is due at some stage. One of the breeding mares looks slightly lame. I want him to check her out. I've got to keep my eye on Simon O'Connor, for a gardener he shows very little interest in doing anything that involves getting his hands dirty. He'll have his feet up in the wood shed if he gets half a chance. And there's all the usual horse owners and pupils, Ruth Watson will be here, Miranda Dawson, Tamara Grey too I imagine. There's only Issy to help with the horses.'

'Hmmm,' Zara stood, pressing her face closer to the mirror as she ran the tip of her index finger along the line of her bottom lip, making sure no lipstick had bled into the lines around her mouth. 'Shame you can't stop the grooms leaving.'

The bed creaked as Jago got to his feet. 'When will you be back?'

'Sometime this afternoon, later probably. I need to call into the Truro shop. There's a new line come in. I need to make sure the manageress displays the evening dresses properly. Then I'm meeting Caroline for lunch. I've no idea how long that will take. You know how it is when Caroline and I get together.'

'Yes. Well have fun. Sorry but I need to go.' Jago itched to be away from her. He moved to the window and looked out, beside the stables there was nothing to show the earth had ever been disturbed. To one side beyond the walled garden, he could see into the quadrangle of the stables, the pale stone the colour of butter. Horses, their eyes bright with intelligence, looked out over stable doors which were painted annually in an elegant blue. Behind the stable yard was the car park, vehicles were already lined up on the gravel. He recognised each of them. The pale grey Porsche that belonged to Tamara Grey. Beside the expensive vehicle stood Miranda Dawson's Mercedes. The other car was an old Mazda sports car, a tired relic that Ruth Watson had recently started to turn up in. Simon O'Connor's ancient Ford Ranger truck was parked at an odd angle. As he watched Simon's batty Springer Spaniel got to its feet and walked a circuit of the machinery in the bed of the truck before settling down again.

Jago bent to drop a light kiss on the top of Zara's head. Her hair smelt of expensive shampoo and the hairspray that kept the strands in place, 'Have a good time.'

The bedroom stool creaked as Zara stood up, her eyes meeting his. 'I intend too. Off you go, look after your ladies.'

Silently Jago, held her gaze, before he dropped his eyes.

Slamming the front door behind him he ran lightly down the pale stone steps.

He crossed the lawn, shoulders relaxing as the tension left him. There was delight to be had in a whole day without Zara. Letting himself into the walled garden he whistled a jaunty tune, the day stretched before him, hours of Zara-free pleasure.

'Alright?' Jago started as Simon, the gardener who had been crouching in the depths of the herbaceous border suddenly got to his feet.

'Fine thanks,' Jago recovered his composure, irritated by the younger man's contrived cockney accent. He'd come to Cornwall from one of the better areas of London, choosing to live like a hippy in one of the caravan sites that were dotted around the green lanes of the county. When he wasn't working on one of the gardens of the countless second homes in the district Simon spent his time in the sea, perfecting his surfing.

Jago breathed in the scent of lavender and the first of the roses. 'Please do the lawns sometime today.'

Ignoring Simon's mocking incline of his head Jago pushed open the gate into the stable yard which was already a hive of activity. Issy the groom, red-faced with effort shoved a muck laden wheelbarrow across the yard. 'Make sure you scrub out the water buckets properly,' Jago said as he passed her.

'I am still doing the work of two you know,' Issy retorted.

'I know and you are an absolute saint.' Jago slapped her ample bottom. The placid girl had been working at the stables since she'd left school ten years previously, cycling from her home in the village every morning.

A large Nissan truck crunched steadily over the gravel into the yard. 'Sam,' Jago greeted the muscular farrier as he got out. 'We've a busy morning for you.'

Sam nodded, hauling his equipment out from the back of the truck. 'Line 'em up and I'll do 'em.'

'Simon or Issy will give you a hand if you need it. I'll chat to you later.'

'Excuse me.' The female voice was cold, dripping icy contempt. As the sound of iron shod hooves rang out over the stone flagged stable yard Jago stood to one side. A tall, handsome dark horse was being led towards him by a blonde woman.

Jago grinned, amused by the obvious tension in the taut line of her shoulders and the fixed expression that could not disguise her beauty.

'Morning Miranda, how is Elite?'

'Fine, thank you,' she snapped in a tone that did not encourage conversation.

He turned to watch her lead Elite across the yard towards the mounting block a thin smile playing at the corners of his mouth. He hadn't forced her into investing in the Spanish property development any more than he had compelled her to buy Elite. The stupid bitch blamed him when she lost all of her money. He knew how she was making a living, someday soon he was going to answer one of her online adverts.

'Morning Ruth,' Jago nodded in greeting watching as she led her chunky grey horse, Badger out of his stable. The stiffness of her back and shoulders amused him. She blamed him, of course. She had thrown herself at him and then was surprised when she lost everything when her husband had found out about the affair. She'd come crawling to Jago, expecting him to leave Zara, set up home with her. Another stupid bitch. She stayed because of the prestige of Park Hall. They all did.

Jago watched her go. She pushed Badger into a trot, following Miranda and Elite. As she turned the corner in the yard and was lost from sight Jago snorted in derision. Leaving Zara had never been on the cards, Ruth should have known that from the start.

At the far side of the stable yard one of the half doors stood open, a chain across the opening, preventing the horse from going out while allowing easy access to the handler. He crossed the yard with an easy loping stride.

Tamara was brushing her black and white horse, Lanson. She started as Jago leant over the stable door. 'Good morning.'

She straightened up, her knuckles white as they gripped the brush. 'Morning,' her gaze was focused at a point along her horse's back.

'How are you today?'

Her face was pale, her mouth taut. 'Do you need to ask?' she turned to face him, dark eyes blazing above the livid patches of colour that had flashed on her cheeks.

Jago ducked under the chain into the gloom of the stable. He ran a hand along the horse's muscled neck, his eyes locking onto Tamara's.

'You know you enjoy it.' Jago dropped his voice to a whisper.

She shook her head. 'No. I don't.'

'Oh, but you do. You love deceit, pulling the wool over everyone's eyes.'

'Jago, I've had enough. I won't do it anymore. Please leave me alone.'

'You haven't had enough until I say so.'

'Fuck off.' Her blue eyes blazed beneath sharply arched eyebrows.

Jago stood, watching her. Seeing the furious red blush rise in an ugly tide, flooding her neckline. He cocked his head, listening as a car drove into the stable yard. 'I'll say when you've had enough.' Bored with baiting her Jago, dropped a cool hand on the top of her arm, feeling the fiery heat that burnt there. He grinned, moving in a leisurely fashion to duck beneath the chain as he left the stable.

'Ah, Michael.' Jago walked across the yard, as the vet eased his long legs out of his Land Rover. 'Good to see you.'

The vet did not reply, instead hurrying to the back of the vehicle to pull out the handful of equipment he would need.

'Sorry to call you out. I know how busy you are.' Jago raised his eyebrows as he met the man's eyes, seeing the discomfiture there.

'The mare is this way,' Jago led the way across the yard, listening with amusement to the vet's jerky breathing. Another person he could bait.

Chapter Three

While the yard hummed with activity Jago made his way back to the house. He pulled the front door shut and leant against it, listening for the sound of any activity that would indicate Zara had unexpectedly returned, or the cleaner was working. A moment later, confident the house was empty he released a long sigh of guilty pleasure. Zara, he knew would likely be gone for most of the day. His time was his own. He bounded up the stairs into one of the spare bedrooms. He pressed a concealed lever beneath the antique dressing table, releasing a panel at the back. He eased himself between the wall and the solid bulk of the dressing table, slid his hand into the concealed compartment and closed his fingers over a mobile phone. A moment later he was walking slowly back downstairs, the phone held lightly in his hand.

He rummaged in the vast fridge, shifting the piles of healthy vegetables and salad Zara insisted they ate. Humming softly to himself he sucked an index finger before trailing it into the bowl of fruit salad Zara ate most mornings for breakfast. He stacked a plate with cheese and ham, grabbed a token tomato from an open container and shoved the fridge door shut.

Slathering mayonnaise and mustard onto two slices of bread, he fashioned himself a doorstep sandwich, before sitting in front of the table and levering the heels of his boots onto the pine surface in a gesture of defiance.

With one hand clamped around the sandwich he used the other to scroll through the contents of the phone, deftly flicking his thumb to open a file. While he knew the contents of the file by heart, he looked at the photographs at every opportunity. He selected one of the images, biting into the sandwich as he enlarged the image, zooming in on the girl's eyes. He loved what was visible in her eyes, the fear, the anger, the despair. He had taken the photograph as she was half turning towards him, when she had realised what lay ahead. There were others, taken as she lay dying, and dead, with the light fading from her eyes, but none gave him as much pleasure as this one.

The sandwich finished he shoved the plate away, sliding his boots from the table-top. He selected another of the photographs in the phone. Glanna Pendrick. It was a blurred image, taken from a newspaper article, coverage of the crimes of his hero Eddie Hammett. Twenty years after his death the image made him feel close to his mentor. It was a privilege to continue the work that Hammett had started.

Only the avoidance of Zara's sharp tongue if she realised he hadn't mended the shelf in the groom's accommodation drove him back to the stable yard. It was a wrench to have to replace the phone and leave the silence of the house, where he could be alone with his memories.

The yard still buzzed with activity. 'Still here Michael?' Jago raised his eyebrows in askance at the vet who was watching Issy run across the yard dragging one of the mares behind her.

'I had to go off to an emergency. I'm just back to look at this mare and then I've to give Tamara's horse Lanson his 'flu booster shot.'

'Hopefully you won't have any other emergencies,' Jago turned away, smiling at the vet's sharp look at his sarcastic remark. He walked away; he didn't have to look at the vet to know his face would be flushed with embarrassment. He knew all about the supposed emergencies the vet went too. Emergencies that usually involved meeting a certain man.

'Trot her back towards me, Issy.' There was a note of tension in the vet's voice.

'Plenty for you to do, Sam.' Jago ran a hand over the back of the horse the farrier was working on.

'Yep,' Sam's voice was muffled as he bent over, almost beneath the horse's belly.

'I'm sorry, I should have made you a mug of coffee. Everything goes to pot without Zara here.'

'S'okay,' Sam fumbled with the rasp he was using on the horse's hoof, dropping the heavy metal implement which clattering across the yard.

At the far side of the stable yard, Tamara, Miranda and Ruth had returned from their ride. Their horses were tied in the shade of the building while the women washed the sweat off them. Ruth had spilled water down her front, the fabric of her teeshirt clung to her body, highlighting the shape of her underwear. 'Good ride ladies?' Jago sauntered towards them.

'Yes, thank you for asking,' Tamara's voice dripped hatred.

'Fine, thanks.' Ruth's echoed Tamara's.

'Lovely.' Miranda straightened up from sponging water over her horse to glare coldly at him.

'Issy looks like she could do with cooling off,' Jago watched the chubby girl puffing her way towards him with the lame mare.

'Michael thinks she has a bruised sole.' Issy came to a stop beside Jago.

'Well, he's the vet.'

'I'm just going too…'

'Just get on with it,' Jago snapped. Issy's puppy-like eagerness to please irritated him.

Bored Jago left the stable yard and made his way up the sandstone steps at the back of the yard into the groom's accommodation, above the main stable block.

At the top he emerged into a long space under the eaves of the building which made one large airy room. A bed occupied the far end. Closer to the entrance was a small kitchen. On the opposite side of the room was a sofa and a coffee table. A television hung from the wall. When the groom's accommodation wasn't occupied Jago found himself drawn time and again to the room. Apart from giving him a respite from the liveries on the yard, he loved reliving what happened in the room.

Zara was currently interviewing candidates to fill the vacancy left by the last groom. She'd done a bunk, disappearing one night a few weeks previously. Jago puffed out his cheeks, sighing. Stupid bitch, there had been no need, she wasn't in any danger from him. He'd despised the girl, but she had been a good worker. The yard was too much for Issy on her own. Zara needed to hurry up and find a replacement, before Issy got sick of doing all the work and threw in the towel as well.

Jago lowered himself onto the sagging sofa, positioned against the back wall. It had been in one of the many reception rooms in the house before Zara had replaced it, deeming it good enough for the groom's accommodation. It had seen a lot of use since then.

At the far side of the room a wooden shelf rested at an awkward angle. One of the supporting brackets had collapsed in Catherine Marshall's desperate struggle for life. Afterwards Jago had tidied up the books and china ornaments that had fallen. He'd stacked the books on the floor beneath the shelf and swept the broken ornaments into the bin.

He slid his eyes over the room. A wide double bed stood in the centre of one wall, the delicately flowered cotton duvet out of synch with the deeds that usually took place on the feminine fabric. The wooden bars of the headboard were scratched and scuffed, from the ropes that had been frenziedly jerked against them in a vain attempt to escape. He had a sudden vision of Catherine Marshall's last breaths. Her limbs had twitched compulsively, her eyes had fixed resentfully on his. He had taken photographs of her then, fascinated as the movement slowed and finally stopped and the light in her eyes faded to nothingness. Jago smiled at the memory of Catherine Marshall when she had realised what was going to happen, her face a mask of shock and fear, her eyes darting around the room. She had still hoped she could get away. Right to the end.

Jago tore his eyes unwillingly from the scuff marks.

It was impossible to sit still, while those thoughts whirled in his mind. Jago got to his feet, he wandered around the room, trailing his fingers over the bed. He ought to mend the shelf, Zara would whine again if he told her he hadn't done it.

The temptation of the cold beer stacked in the fridge was too much. It was after lunch and Zara wouldn't be back from seeing Caroline until later. He kept the fridge well stocked. It came in handy. He opened a can.

Footsteps sounded on the steps outside the door. 'Hello,' Jago turned, as someone came into the room. 'This is a turn up for the books,' Jago grinned, leaning back against the windowsill and taking a leisurely sip of his beer. The ice-cold liquid hit the back of his mouth. He let it trickle down his throat slowly, savouring the bitter taste. The dust, floating upwards from the stables below, danced lazily in the shafts of sunlight that came in through the low windows.

'So... What can I do for you?'

The silence lengthened. 'Beer?' he said, as much to break the silence rather than a polite gesture. When no reply came, he moved to the fridge, opening it and pulling out a beer.

As he swung the door shut there was a bang, that reverberated through his brain. His head felt as if it were lifting from his body, stars danced in front of his eyes, there was a rushing sound as the floor came up to meet him. He forced his eyes open, seeing a face, looking at him quizzically, he yelped at the stabbing pain in his arm and then darkness closed in to enfold him.

The pain in his head was intense. He was aware of a groan. It took him a moment to realise the noise came from himself. He was uncomfortable, he needed to move. His eyelids felt too heavy to lift. Slowly he became aware of his surroundings, the warm afternoon sunlight on his skin, the faint sound of someone else's breathing. Arms aching, he tried to shift position. That was when he discovered he couldn't move. Consciousness rushed in, the awareness that he was spread eagled on the bed. He forced his eyelids open, blinking against the sunlight shining straight into his face. He jerked at the ropes that secured his arms to the bed frame, digging painfully into his flesh. From the discomfort in his ankles and thighs he knew they were fastened in the same way.

Wincing at the pain, he raised his head, watching the silhouetted shape of his captor. His breath caught at the back of his throat as he realised the clothes he had been wearing were heaped carelessly on the chair beside the bed.

'Very funny,' he said, annoyed at the uncertainty in his voice. 'You can let me go now.' He twisted his head, glancing at the rope that held his wrists. His circulation was struggling to pump blood upwards to fingers that were tingling painfully. The bleakness of his situation was not lost on him. How often had he sat in that chair watching some young woman struggle, helpless in the knowledge she was trapped.

'I thought you liked to play games.'

A glimmer of relief swept through him. A game. A spot of revenge. How he would make them suffer when they inevitably let him go.

It was then that he saw it. A knife, coming slowly, but relentlessly towards him.

'No. No. No. Don't. Please. Don't hurt me. Let me go. Please let me go.' His voice was high with panic. He panicked, jerking, wrenching at the ropes, beyond all pain and sensation other than the need to free himself.

'I don't think you'll be playing any games again.'

Sunlight flashed on the knife blade as it bit down. A bloody mass was shoved into his gaping mouth. He tasted blood, semen, urine, felt the liquid warmth on his thighs as blood pumped from the wound. He took a gasping breath, struggling to force air into lungs emptied by the scream. The bloodied lump of flesh heaved backwards by the suction forcing itself into the back of his throat, choking him.

The knife flashed again, beyond all effort now he could only watch as it bit into the flesh of his belly, travelling swiftly downwards. He was vaguely aware of the warm sensation as his guts spilled out in a heaving mass, cascading over his legs.

Chapter Four

As a career move Cornwall had been a mistake. A brief few weeks into a new posting and already Max Wilton hated everything about the county and the end of civilisation station where he was now based. Max glanced disdainfully at the bitter tepid brew that passed for coffee, the pale coloured liquid oozed from beneath the ill-fitting lid of the takeaway cup. As he turned his eyes back to the road a black and white wall of movement blocked the narrow highway. He swore, slamming his foot on the brakes. His low-slung sports car which pre-dated the niceties of anti-lock braking skidded side-ways on the muddy surface, coming to a halt just metres behind the hairy hind quarters and swinging udder of the last of the cows.

'Dammit,' Max, surveyed the remnants of his coffee, now soaking into the rubber casing around the gear stick, surely there was a law against animals wandering the roads when people were trying to get to work.

The overall clad farmer accompanying the bovine herd turned to glare balefully at Max.

After what felt like an interminable time the road cleared, the last of the herd shuffling slowly into a muddy gateway beyond which Max could see green fields stretching into the distance.

Max, biting back the tirade that was on the tip of his tongue shoved the car into gear and drove on.

A short time later he was steering in between the tall stone gate posts, set into a high stone wall around the perimeter of the Police Station and easing his car into a narrow parking spot.

Max slammed the car door shut and turned with a sigh to look at the imposing grey stone building that housed the Penzance Police Headquarters. He loathed Cornwall. He had been looking for a simpler life, somewhere away from the stress and strain of life in the Manchester Police force. He'd had a vision of being able to walk in the countryside, learn to surf, perhaps even take up fishing. Instead, he'd instantly hated the silence, the mud and damp and the steady laid-back colleagues he worked with.

He tapped the screen of his phone as he walked towards his office, surreptitiously checking on the countdown app to see how many days remained until he could comfortably hand in his notice. He'd installed the app just two days after he had started work. Two years he reckoned, before he could finish here, get another posting and head back to something closely resembling civilisation. Back to where he belonged. 568 days. He swiped the face of the phone blanking out the depressing information.

Max strolled into the building. Years after the smoking ban it still smelt of tobacco as if the institution cream coloured walls had absorbed years of discarded cigarettes and exhaled smoke. Long forgotten posters advertising police association dances and family barbeques fluttered in the breeze from the open door.

In the early evening, when he was due to start his shift, the air in the office was filled with the day's accumulated meaty odour of the numerous Cornish pasties that had been consumed. In the far corner, Pete Brooks had his feet up on his desk and was tucking frenziedly into a pasty, 'Chicken tikka,' he announced between mouthfuls.

Max felt the watchful eyes of the detectives on him as he crossed the room to his desk. He was, and he suspected always would be, an outsider. Anyone not born within the western tip of the country was apparently viewed with the greatest suspicion.

'Good day?' Pete queried, moving his hand to catch spraying pasty crumbs.

'Great thanks,' Max nodded, unwilling to share the story of his failed surfing attempt. The vision of deftly surfing a big wave that had inspired his move to Cornwall had proved elusive. He had spent a miserable, cold, damp few hours up to his neck in water trying in vain just to kneel on a bucking surfboard. Standing on it in the wash of a giant wave seemed an impossible feat.

The hours that would make up his evening shift lay ahead, depressing in their dullness. There was the inevitable mountain of paperwork that was generated by the small-time rural crime. Instead of finding his less stressful than dealing with tough inner-city crime, Max found the laid back, steady approach to solving crime irritated him immensely.

'Wilton,' Edward Farrell, the desk sergeant appeared in the office doorway. He was a huge bear of a man, the generous fold of his double chin spilt over a shirt collar clearly a size too small for him. He planted shovel sized hands firmly on either side of the door frame.

'Steve Cooper wants a word.' Farrell's eyes were lit with a barely controlled excitement that spoke of something more interesting than the usual sheep rustling and shop lifting crimes that trickled into the station.

'Been a naughty boy then?' Lowena Rowe, the solitary female detective in the office, glanced up from the newspaper she was surreptitiously reading. Max shrugged, his lowly place as the odd one out in the station meant that he didn't feel comfortable flinging back the banter. The locals here liked to dish out the lip, but they didn't like to take it in return.

DCI Steve Cooper's office was located at the back of the building. As always with top ranking officers his desk was positioned in front of the window, so the light shining through shone straight into the eyes of whoever was unfortunate enough to be hauled into his office.

Cooper's office was no different, although Max suspected the momentary blinding from the window gave the DCI the chance to shove the newspaper he was reading into his desk drawer.

'Yes Sir?' Max waited.

'Here's one for you,' Cooper said, waving a piece of paper in Max's direction, 'Something more like what you are used too.' He turned the corners of his mouth down firmly to demonstrate his clear distain for all things beyond the Cornish border.

'Murder... Park Hall.' Max, already used to zoning out while listening to Steve Cooper rambling about rural petty crime, came abruptly back to the present. He struggled to arrange his face into a mix of attention and dispassionate commitment, finally something more interesting than the treacle slow mire of West Country crime.

'There's been a body of a man on the premises. Found about an hour ago.' Cooper waved a sheet of paper in his direction. 'I'm going to partner you with Tallis on this one. I think you'll be a good team. This will be a bit more interesting for you.'

Cooper glanced at the doorway, before bellowing, 'Where the hell is Tallis?'

'Annual leave,' The desk sergeant's face appeared in the doorway, 'Back the day after tomorrow.'

'Well, you had better find her, Wilton.' Cooper snapped, 'I need her back here.'

'Yes sir,' Max backed hastily out of the office, turning he found his face buried in Edward Farrell's shirt front.

'Park Hall is near Blackthorn Farm.' Farrell ran a hand through what was left of his hair. 'That bastard...those young women...' Farrell thrust his jaw forwards. Max watched as the muscles beneath his face contracted with tension.

'Tallis worked on that one.' Even twenty years after the perpetrator of the horrific crimes had jumped to his death when cornered by the police, the case was still talked about and Tallis's name mentioned reverently. Max shook his head, impressed. Finally, he was going to meet the woman who had solved the case. Tallis. She had been the reason he'd chosen Penzance out of all the Cornish places he could have picked. Max tried and failed to hide the grin of excitement that split his face. Steve Cooper had picked him out to work with DI Tallis. This murder, a dead body found at a farm couldn't be as interesting as the case Tallis had solved, but working with Tallis could be a great boost to his career.

'Where will I find DI Tallis?'

Farrell leant over his desk and quickly scribbled directions onto a notepad, 'She's not answering her mobile so you'd better go and find her. Here's her home address. It's Long Meadow Farm, out on the coast.'

Farrell grabbed Max's suit sleeve and steered him towards a large scale map on the office wall. 'Here,' he said pointing an ink-stained finger at the map.

'Got it,' Max said, heading back outside, before punching the address into his car's navigation system. He screwed the paper into a ball and threw it into the passenger footwell.

He set off, leaving the town behind as he headed out into the countryside. A murder. Max hadn't been immune to the air of excitement that hung over the office.

'Turn left in two hundred metres,' intoned the impassionate voice of the navigation. Max slowed the car, unable to see any turning in the thick hedge that bordered either side the road. 'Turn left,' the voice intoned. Max braked again as a narrow opening appeared in the greenery. He steered through the seemingly impenetrable barrier and out onto a wide, straight track that led down a gentle slope across fields towards a tangle of farm buildings, beyond which stretched an impossibly blue sea.

At the end of the track was a wide stretch of concrete around which were stables, their doors all gleaming with fresh paint. Hanging baskets spilling over with summer flowers, swayed gently from hooks above the doorways. Off to one side was a sprawling two story stone farmhouse.

At the other side of the yard behind a dark wood fence, stretched a wide expanse of flat sand, dotted here and there with show jumps that looked to be an impressive height even to Max's uneducated eye. In the centre of the sand arena an enormous black horse was leaping and plunging on the end of a long rope held by a slender, jeans clad red-haired woman. For a moment Max watched fascinated. The horse looked huge, powerful and utterly terrifying, its muscles rippling, snorting as it bucked and plunged. The woman trod an inner circle, calmly walking while the horse plunged.

Max picked his way across the concrete yard, skirting around a pile of horse dung. His leather shoes were not made for this type of conditions, they were more suited to the sunshine and pavements of the Italian city they had been made in. Cautiously he clambered the fence around the sand arena, dusting off the wood first to make sure he wouldn't get dirt on the sleeves of his pale grey jacket. 'Hello!' When there was no reply Max waved to attract her attention. The horse spooked, shying away from him, galloping across the arena. The woman, hauled on the rope, leaning back to stop the horse. When it was back under control she glanced in his direction. 'Have you no bloody sense?' Long strands of wavy auburn hair had escaped from their clasp and blew across her face. Max took in long, toned legs, a neat shapely butt, and a long narrow waist.

'I'm looking for DI Tallis,' Max said.

'Well, you've found me.' Her voice was filled with irritation. She tugged gently on the rope, the horse slowed his pace, coming gradually to a walk and finally to a standstill.

'Max. DS Wilton, I'm from Penzance nick, I transferred from Manchester a couple of weeks ago. Living in Truro.' Gingerly he eased himself down from the fence.

'Bit quieter here normally than Manchester I imagine.' Her eyes raked over him, sparkling with amusement.

'I thought so but looks like I was wrong. There's been a body found. Somewhere called Park Hall. Steve Cooper wants you to be SIO. You're not answering your phone. He sent me to tell you.

A cloud flashed across her face, similar to the one he had seen on Edward Farrell. 'Okay, you told me.' When Max didn't move, she glanced at him quizzically. 'Tell him I'm on my way. You can head back to Penzance.'

'I'm not going anywhere. Steve Cooper wants me to be your DS.'

Chapter Five

'I see.' Grace said in a tone that was hard to read. 'Park Hall, that's next door to Blackthorn Farm.' She put a slender hand on the horse's neck and patted it before walking across the arena towards Max. Now that the horse had stopped its headlong flight Max could see how big it was, yet beside her it was quiet and docile.

Max moved hurriedly out of the way, half afraid of the unfamiliar creature. He stumbled on an uneven patch of ground. 'Careful,' she said her eyes dancing with some amusement.

'I'll have to shower first… get changed, it will only take a few minutes.'

As she spoke a tall man with a mass of curly dark hair came towards the arena, a terrier trotting at his heels. Max saw the older man's eyes rake over him.

'Kaden. DS Wilton.' Grace said by way of introduction.

Kaden slid an arm possessively around her waist.

'I've got to go.'

'Fuck's sake. Can't they manage without you? This is supposed to be your holiday,' he took the rope and whip from Grace. 'You'll be gone over supper time, I assume.'

'Yes. Something's come up.' Grace said wryly.

'We're supposed to be getting this place straight.' Kaden glared at Max as if it was his fault.

'I'll be back as soon as I can.' Grace was already walking towards the house.

'Nice house,' ventured Max as the uncomfortable silence between him and Kaden lengthened.

'Not that Grace will get much chance to enjoy it.' Kaden's voice was filled with irritation.

'Goes with the job, I guess.' Max shrugged.

'Rachel,' Kaden shouted as he walked across the yard. A tall, dark haired young woman hurried out of a stable and took the horse from Kaden, who stood in the yard glaring with undisguised hostility before walking in the direction of the house.

The front door stood open. Inside Max could see an ancient looking kitchen, battered pine units were set above a chipped countertop. The stable yard clearly had taken priority when Grace and Kaden had moved in. A dying bunch of flowers occupied the centre of the kitchen table. Whatever Grace did in her spare time it didn't seem to involve domesticity.

A few moments later she returned, wearing jeans and a white shirt, her auburn hair damp but tucked neatly into a long plait down her back. She shrugged her shoulders into a tweed jacket. 'Let's go.'

There was no sign of Kaden or Rachel as they walked back to the stable yard. Grace glanced around with a sigh of regret. 'You'd better follow me,' she said, flinging open the door to a Land Rover as Max lowered himself into his car. She was at the top of the farm track before he had managed to turn his around, the car's low slung suspension grating on the bumpy surface.

Max had to drive to the best of his Advanced Driving Course limits to keep up with the Land Rover as she swung it around the bends with a deftness that belied its steady appearance.

Max followed Grace across country, narrowly missing overshooting a driveway as she turned her vehicle into it. A wide concrete lane followed the contours of the land. A moment later Max caught sight of their destination, Park Hall. He had an impression of a vast house, surrounded by buildings of butter coloured stone which nestled like a jewel amongst the gentle folds of the Cornwall countryside.

They reached a firmly closed gate, behind which a pinched, cold looking PC caught out by the cold evening breeze, hunched his shoulders against the constant whip of the wind.

'Sorry, the stables are closed today,' he said from between teeth firmly clamped to stop them shivering.

'DI Grace Tallis,' She flashed her warrant card at him and gestured at Max, 'DS Wilton, I'm SIO.'

'Oh, sorry Ma'am. I'm seconded from Truro.'

The constable unlatched the wide wooden gate and swung it back to let them drive though. Once in the wide expanse of stable lined yard it was obvious where their destination was. The blue and white tape of the police cordon fluttered in the wind marking off a wide area. At the foot of a set of stone steps which led to an open, smartly painted blue door, another constable stood with a clip board, carefully detailing everyone who came and went.

At the far side of the yard a group of people were huddled together watching the proceedings.

A moment later clad in rustling, paper suits Grace and Max made their way up the stone steps towards a low hum of noise.

Grace entered the room first taking in the body on the bed and the hive of activity around it.

Their arrival brought the work to a pause, the officers drawing back from the bed, each glancing in their direction, heads nodding in acknowledgment.

'Oh Christ, poor man.' The words were out of Grace's mouth before she had chance to check them. The face of the dead man was a mask of pain and shock.

'Nasty one.' The police photographer said, leaning in towards the man's mouth and the bloody scrap of flesh that dangled from it.

Beside him worked Mark Lowther, the pathologist, his work case open, revealing plastic bags and containers.

Grace took a stride towards the corpse before stopping, pausing in the centre of the room. 'Is there a bathroom anywhere?'

A collective titter of amusement ran around the room, the SOCOs brought in from Truro the nearest city, hardened to bloody scenes, were amused by her reaction.

'Yes, Ma'am,' This way,' One of the white suited figures came towards Grace and took her arm.

'Not for me,' she shook him off angrily, nodding her head towards Max who, his face a peculiar shade of green, was slowly sliding down the wall he was leaning on, 'for my Sergeant. Can someone take DS Wilton outside and give him a hot cup of tea, plenty of sugar please.'

Grace ran her hands through her hair in an impatient gesture of annoyance at the assumption that she, as a woman, would be unable to stomach the gruesome scene she had to deal with. 'Yes Ma'm,' there was a scuffle of boots on the wooden floor. Grace didn't need to turn to imagine the rush to escape the room. Any one of the young grey faced SOCOs would have been only too glad to have to escort the deathly pale Max Wilton downstairs. Grace swallowed hard, fighting against the nausea that bubbled within her. She was glad of the mask that covered her face, but even that could not disguise the smell of faeces, urine and fear.

A moment later, Max was forgotten, as was her annoyance at being called in to work before her leave had finished, and at the men who had assumed it would be her who felt faint. All faded as her attention focused on the room in front of her. The white suited SCOs were taking photographs, cataloguing the scene. Around her a low buzz of conversation hummed, punctuated periodically by the sound of laughter. Grace could imagine the jokes, gallows humour, anything to lighten the mood.

She strode across the room on the raised metal plates that had been laid down to keep unwanted footprints from disturbing the evidence. Blood, huge droplets splattered the dusty wooden floor, pooling beneath the bed. She looked at the dead man's face, his eyes wide open, staring, head thrown back, his mouth open, his expression one of fear and pain.

More than pain… of utter agony. At the crown of his head she could see tufts of blood soaked hair, from the head wound that had presumably been what had initially subdued him. From between lips drawn back over a line of red stained evenly shaped teeth jutted a bloody scrap of flesh.

'Is that…?' Grace began, this was a vision she would struggle to forget.

'Yes,' the pathologist said with the careless nonchalance of one used to dealing with blood and gore on a daily basis, 'His penis, someone cut it off and stuffed it in his mouth.'

The severed penis was not the worst of the man's injuries. His stomach had been cut, sliced open with a very sharp blade. Someone had sliced downwards, deep into the flesh, the skin opening likethe zipper on a jacket, spilling his internal organs. The man's bowels and small intestine, gleamed dully in the shaft of light which shone in from the window, the flesh tinged a grey-green. The coils spilled out, between the man's outstretched legs, heaping in his lap like some huge snake.

He had been tall, even sitting up his legs were still a long way down the mattress. His wrists and ankles were secured to the bed frame with strong rope. He had fought for survival; Grace noted the bruised and bloody flesh on his wrists and ankles.

'This is Jago Carey,' Grace whispered, a man she knew, if not personally, but of. He was an event rider, well known and successful. She blinked trying to clear her vision, making sure she took in everything about the crime scene. This murder had taken time, and planning.

Jago, she knew from local gossip was a womaniser. Could his wife have killed him in anger? Perhaps an angry husband – someone strong enough to force the man onto the bed, someone strong willed and determined to kill Jago Carey. Anyone with half a heart wouldn't have been able to stomach seeing him in agony.

'What can you tell me?' Grace directed her voice to Lowther.

'Well, he's dead. That much I can tell you.' His voice was BBC English, humourless. He offered Grace a gloved hand and then retracted it equally quickly.

'Time of death?' Grace tried again,

'Sometime within the last few hours.'

Grace turned away from the bed, watching the SOCO's work, photographing the scene, cataloguing and recording.

'Any murder weapon been recovered?' Grace asked.

'No, not yet, although officers are outside searching now. The wife has just come back, she'd been out with a friend.'

Grace nodded, 'Make sure his phone goes off to be checked. That might throw something up.'

'Tea ma'am,' a young, fresh faced female police officer handed Grace a mug of tea.

Grace took it gratefully, glad of any distraction. She glanced quickly around the room, there were no signs of a struggle, everything was calm and ordered. The dead man certainly hadn't been concerned about his safety when he entertained whoever had killed him. A beer can lay opened on the coffee table.

What was he doing in the groom's accommodation rather than in his own home, Grace pondered, peering out of one of the low windows. Beyond the dusty glass she could see the stable yard, a dozen or so horse's heads looking out, curious at the unusual activity. At the far side of the cobbled yard a group of people stood, women, young and not so young were huddled together, tissues clutched in hands, one, her head bent was visibly shaking as she cried. Beside them, three men, shuffled their feet, hands thrust deeply into jacket pockets. Beyond the stable yard was the house, covered in wisteria and the deep red leaves of a Virginia creeper. Inside the house, was his wife. Grace struggled and failed to put a name or face to her.

Her life had just altered forever. Had she changed her own life, deliberately? Had she been driven to commit this heinous crime by her husband, through his chasing other women, or through his treatment of her? Was she a criminal or a victim?

The mortuary assistants hovered in the doorway, trying to look inconspicuous, waiting until the pathologist had finished his work. Eventually Mark Lowther stood up slowly as if his back ached with the effort of bending over the body. 'I can't do any more until I get him to the mortuary,' he said, gesturing at one of the assistants. The white clad figures moved forwards. Grace saw one pause as he got the full view of the body, wondering at the problem of how to get Jago Carey, plus all his exposed innards into a body bag.

Chapter Six

Outside the fresh air had never felt so good. Grace and Max sat on a sandstone step halfway down the flight that led to the scene of Jago Carey's death. On each step a riot of flowers bloomed in a selection of wooden tubs and earthenware pots. Pale pinks of Carnations battled for space with the brightly coloured purple heads of Lobelias. It was a scene utterly at odds with the devastation that lay just a short distance above them. Grace sucked in a deep breath, trying to rid herself of the lingering odour of death. Beside her Max's face still had a green tinge.

Grace turned as Mark Lowther emerged from the doorway. The young WPC standing beside the door offered Lowther her arm as he battled his way out of the paper suit. He shrugged it off to reveal faded, ripped jeans and an ancient AC/DC tee-shirt.

Finally freed he ambled down the steps.

'Any thoughts?'

Mark sat down between Grace and Max. Grace spotted the look of wry amusement as he glanced at Max who was still fighting to control the rising tide of bile that threatened to expel itself from his stomach.

Mark puffed out his cheeks, raking his hair back off his forehead with long, pale fingers before shaking his head slowly. 'All I will say,' he turned down the corners of his mouth, 'Is that someone really hated him.'

'Mmmm,' Max made a noise of agreement.

'I would say I'll know more when I've got him back to the office but the cause of death looks pretty obvious. Anyway, I'll chat to you later.' He unfolded his long limbs and ran lightly down the steps.

'Nice bike,' Max chanced speaking. They watched as Lowther packed his equipment into the bike's panniers, shrugged his arms into a leather jacket, buckled his helmet, got onto the sleek looking machine and powered it into life. With a cheery wave of a gloved hand, he steered the bike out of the yard and onto the driveway that led to the road.

As the notes of the engine faded into the distance Max levered himself to his feet. 'Sorry Ma'am. Something must have disagreed with me.' His eyes did not meet hers, his tone quiet and sheepish.

'Boss, Chief, Tallis… anything but Ma'am please, makes me feel like the queen, or a brothel keeper.' Grace smiled, tilting her head on one side to look at his pale face, 'Dead bodies will generally do that,' she touched a hand to his arm, 'It will get easier…. Unfortunately.'

Max nodded, the colour slowly coming back to his pale cheeks. 'I've seen plenty. Just not like that.'

'Okay now?' Grace asked gently. 'We've got a lot of work to do.'

'Yes, I'm fine.' Max shook his head in disbelief at the way his body had betrayed him. He'd seen enough dead bodies over the years to not let the sight of blood get to him. Just none as deliberate and brutal. He followed Grace as she headed towards the stable yard where the prospective witnesses stood, their faces pale, all eyed fixed on the building where Jago's body lay. Max lengthened his stride to keep up with her.

The Crime Scene Manager met them halfway across the yard. 'His wife arrived home about an hour ago, family liaison are with her now. She's been told her husband is dead.'

'Thanks, I want to talk to the witnesses first.'

'Who found the body?' The Crime Scene Manager consulted the paperwork on his clipboard.

'Simon O'Connor, the gardener. He's in a bit of a state. Would have had a shock finding someone…like that…'

Grace crossed the yard, letting her eyes rove over the group of people waiting for her. Was the murderer amongst them? She was aware of each person gazing with open curiosity at them.

'Who are they?'

'They keep horses here. Miranda Dawson,' the Crime Scene Manager discreetly directed his pen in the direction of tall, elegant blonde who appeared to be in her mid-thirties. 'On her left is Ruth Watson.' He indicated a slightly older woman with dark blonde hair. 'And Tamara Grey.' Grace nodded, glancing at the tearful petite blonde who also looked to be in her mid-thirties. His pen moved once more, indicating a younger woman standing apart from the others, 'Issy Jordan, his groom.'

'And the men?' Grace let her eyes move over the three men who leant awkwardly against the building. 'Vet, Michael Alderton, Sam Green, farrier,' Grace recognised the smartly dressed grey-haired vet. Beside him stood the stocky figure of the farrier Grace knew from horse events. Sam Green shifted his weight from boot to boot as if he could not contain his pent up energy.

'And lastly Simon O'Connor, the gardener who had found the body.' The Crime Scene Manager lowered his clipboard. Simon sat apart from the group, his back against the stone building, raking shovel like hands through a tangled mat of sandy-blonde hair. To Grace it was obvious he was the one who had found the body. There was a tortured look in his eyes, something that told her he had seen a vision of hell up in the room where Jago had been killed.

'How long are we going to have to stay here?' Tamara Grey disentangled herself from the group and addressed Grace.

'I'm sorry, but we do need to talk to you all, individually. It may take some time. Please ring your homes and tell anyone you need to that you'll be late.'

'I still have calls to make.' Michael Alderton followed in Tamara's wake. 'There's a cow...'

'I'm sorry,' Grace put up her hands to silence him. 'This takes precedence. Please bear with us. We need to talk to you all and we are trying to arrange somewhere comfortable to do that.'

She ignored the murmur of annoyance as she moved away from the group to crouch beside the trembling form of the gardener. 'Simon, I'm going to have to interview you along with everyone else, but can you tell me what happened.'

Simon drew a long breath. '|I was supposed to have been clearing one of the flower beds, I wanted to check with Jago that everything was to come out. Simon swallowed hard, continuing with obvious difficulty, 'I went up to the groom's accommodation. Jago did paperwork in there sometimes rather than going back to the house.'

Grace wondered why he preferred to be in the dusty loft rather than in the beautiful home he shared with his wife.

'I shouted his name,' Simon's skin had a grey tinge. 'There was no reply,' Simon continued, 'So I went up to see where he was.'

'And then what?' Grace asked gently.

'I walked up the steps,' Simon said, eyes clouding as he recalled the moment he had entered the building, 'then I went in...'

'Take your time,' Grace said gently, the scene that Simon had discovered had been horrific. It was traumatic enough to turn the stomachs of experienced coppers so there was no wonder the man was in a state. There was a long pause while Simon seemed to gather his thoughts and composure.

'Then I could see...' his words faded into silence before he whispered, 'I could see he was dead.'

Grace touched the man's shoulder lightly. 'That must have been horrible for you.'

She moved away, turning to the Crime Scene Manager. 'I'll see the Jago's wife before we do the other interviews.' Grace and Max walked silently through the walled garden to the house, both aware that Jago Carey had trod this very path a few hours before. Their footsteps crunched on the gravel forecourt outside the house. A uniformed police officer, recognising Grace, smiled tightly in their direction, before pushing open the front door.

Inside a wide, stone flagged hall was dominated by a circular table, topped with a huge bowl of flowers. Max's leather soled shoes clattered on the stone flags, beside him, Grace's trainers were silent. They followed the low hum of voices to a room at the far end of the hall.

Grace tapped lightly on the wooden door, pushing it open. 'May we come in?' Without waiting for a reply, she stepped into the room, holding the door for Max to follow her. They entered a vast wood panelled room, light streamed in from huge windows that overlooked an expanse of garden. Outside she could see borders crammed with flowers lining a lawn that stretched down to wooden fencing, behind which horses grazed.

Zara Carey, Jago's wife sat, utterly immobile in the centre of a large, faded leather chesterfield sofa. She had the coldest eyes Grace had ever seen.

Michelle Dolan, the young family liaison officer sat, shoulders hunched, on one side of the sofa. She had been given the unpleasant job of telling Zara her husband was dead. Michelle glanced towards Grace. Her face was filled with desperation and fright at the situation she'd had to deal with. Grace shot a small smile in her direction, seeing the young officer's tense shoulders sag with relief that someone older and more experienced was finally there and going to take charge.

Zara's eyes, the expressionless grey of a Great White Shark, fixed themselves on Grace's face. The hair at either side of a razor sharp parting was a glossy natural looking dark blonde, there wasn't a trace of grey or dark roots showing. 'What happened to Jago?' she demanded.

Grace hesitated. Zara finally dropped her eyes, staring fixedly at a patch on the Indian patterned rug that broke up the expanse of polished wooden floor.

'I'm so sorry Zara, Jago was murdered.'

Zara's blonde head jerked upright, two spots of bright colour burning on her high cheek bones. 'Murdered?' Zara's voice trailed away.

She slumped back into the deep upholstery of the leather sofa, staring ahead, immobile except for her hands, her fingers chaffing in a distracted movement against her palms. They were long, pale, elegant fingers, the nails unpainted but glossy, the whites immaculate, certainly not those of someone who spent their lives messing around with horses. Instinctively Grace covered her own hands, her nails were broken and ragged.

There was nothing to do but wait until Zara processed the information and they were able to continue the interview. Grace let her eyes rove unobtrusively around the room, taking in the dark wooden panelling and the deep red, heavy velvet curtains. The furniture was all dark wood, antique, she presumed.

Zara let her head fall back onto the back of the sofa, her eyes moving between the two detectives. She took in a long breath, the delicate slope of her breasts rising. The pink tip of her tongue flickered briefly over her glossy lips. 'Murdered? You mean someone shot him or something?'

'We won't know fully until after the post mortem,' Grace neatly sidestepped the question. 'When did you last see him?'

Zara wasn't stupid, Grace knew she must realise she was the prime suspect in his death. She would have seen enough television shows to know the relatives were the most likely candidates. Wives, girlfriends, lovers, black widows, their heartbreak hiding a catalogue of crimes against the men who had hurt or slighted them.

'This morning. He had a busy day planned. Plenty of women to keep him amused.' Her tone was that of someone who has gotten used to or accepted their husband's infidelity. 'There were rather a lot of them.' Zara added, her fingers still twisting compulsively against the white palms of her hands. 'Where was he? Who found him?' Her hands curled into tight fists. Her neck and cheeks flamed with colour.

'Your husband was found in the groom's flat above the stable yard by Simon O'Connor, your gardener.'

'He was supposed to mend a broken shelf in there.'

'Where have you been all day?'

'I was out, working. I run a chain of boutiques, but I'm sure you know that already. Afterwards I had lunch. With a friend, Caroline Salter.'

Grace got slowly to her feet, 'Thank you, could your friend collaborate that?'

'Oh God, I know what you're getting at.' Zara released a snort of derision. 'I. Did. Not. Kill. My. Husband,' her mouth twisted into an angry snarl, 'I suggest you look at his girlfriends, or their husbands.'

Chapter Seven

Grace sucked in a deep breath of horse and hay scented air, glad to be away from the fraught atmosphere of the house.

'What do you think, boss?' Max fell into step beside Grace as they walked back towards the stable yard.

'She has a point. Our victim was well known for his philandering.' She released a sigh at her own choice of word. 'There's going to be a lot of leg work looking at everyone Jago had a connection with.'

Police vehicles still filled the stable yard car park.

'Going to be a late one, Max,' Grace said as Pete came across the yard towards them. 'Boss, we've arranged for an interview room to be put to one side at the Rankin Arms Hotel, it's about a mile down the road from here.'

'Cheers Pete.'

The grizzled detective withdrew a pack of cigarettes out of his jacket pocket. His face arranged itself into a hangdog expression, 'I'd imagine they're all itching to get home.'

'We'll be as quick as we can, I want to talk to them while everything is fresh in their minds, no point in going all the way to the station. Easier to do it close by.'

A private room had been organised at the Rankin Arms. The bar hummed with noise as tea and coffee and plates of sandwiches were brought out. Everyone who had been on the yard at Park Hall turned to look, as Grace and Max walked in, Pete at their heels. A deathly silence fell over the room.

'Good evening.' Grace began, letting her eyes rove around the expectant faces. Grace was aware that with all probability amongst them was someone who really did not want to be there, someone who knew a lot more about Jago's death than anyone else. 'Thank you for giving up your time, I appreciate you are all busy, so we will make this as quick as possible.' She swept a hand towards Max, 'DS Wilton and I will interview you all individually. At this stage we are just taking witness statements to see if anyone saw anything that might be of any relevance.'

There was an angry buzz of noise as people glanced at each other, grimacing with barely concealed irritation.

'Can I be first?' Tamara Grey stepped forwards, 'I need to get home.'

'Don't we all.' Ruth Watson's voice was filled with a sarcasm that was directed at the glamorous blonde.

The resident's lounge had been put into use for the interviews. It was a room whose beauty was at odds with the reason for their being there. The late evening sunlight poured in through French windows that looked out on herbaceous borders filled with colour. The room, used for residents to relax, had two deep, comfortable looking sofas arranged facing one another beside a fireplace.

Tamara Grey followed Max and Grace into the room. 'Please take a seat, Mrs Grey.' Grace indicated one of the vast sofas.

'Sure,' Tamara still wore a pale green pair of jodhpurs and brown leather boots. She sat opposite the detectives, extending slender legs across the beige expanse of carpet. Her leather boots, Grace noticed, were rimmed with sand from the menage.

Grace pulled a notebook out of her jacket pocket, out of the corner of her eye seeing Max do the same. 'Mrs Grey, Tamara. As you know we are interviewing anyone who had a connection with the yard to see if they saw anything during the time Jago was killed. Perhaps something you saw might have felt irrelevant but could be crucial to our enquiry.'

'I wasn't at the yard,' Tamara said, 'I was out riding.' She began to twist an intricately carved wedding ring around a long, pale finger. Her nails, Grace noticed where immaculate, long and beautifully painted. Tamara clearly wasn't one who did much mucking out, or housework for that matter. Hardly surprising, she was so beautiful any man would treat her as a prize.

Tamara pressed her lips together as if she would never speak again.

'Okay,' Grace said, 'Where did you go?'

'I left the yard at just gone twelve,' Tamara began, speaking as if she were reciting a passage learned from memory, 'Ten past, I think it was, I rode up the lane and into the woods, quite by chance I met Ruth and Miranda. We were out until gone four. When we got back Jago's body had been found. I can assure you I had nothing to do with his death.'

Grace nodded slowly. Tamara, she thought, had spent a long time working out what she was going to say.

'I need to go, I have to get dinner organised, my husband is waiting for me.'

'Mine too,' Grace sighed as Tamara stalked from the room.

Miranda Dawson came in next, she sat down stiffly, her face a blank mask. 'I am glad he's dead,' she whispered, not raising her head from an intense study of her fingers which lay curled in her lap. She released a long breath, then, as if it took an immense effort, she raised her head and met Grace's eyes with a cold stare, 'but I didn't kill him.'

Beside her Max smiled, 'That's what they all say,'

Miranda relaxed slightly, as if tight straps holding her shoulders had been released. 'I can imagine they do,' a hint of a smile turned up the corners of her mouth.

'Could you tell us what you were doing today?' Grace asked.

Miranda brushed a strand of blonde hair behind her ears with long fingers. Her nails, Grace noticed were bitten down to the quick, somehow out of keeping with her immaculate makeup and toned body. She wore a pair of jeans with an oversized checked shirt hanging loosely over them.

'Riding,' she said, leaning back into the depths of the sofa and regarding them both with a challenging gaze. 'I rode along the coast bridlepath nearly to Penzance. I stopped at one of the beachside cafes for ice-cream. The girl serving brought out a bucket of water for Elite.'

'That was kind of them,' Grace smiled, watching Miranda's leg which was jumping with tension.'

'I go there quite often,' Miranda said. 'On my return I caught up with Tamara and Ruth. We finished our ride together. When we got back Jago's body had been found and the police were there.

'Presumably they'll remember her at the beach cafe.' Max looked up from writing his notes as Miranda left the room, closing the door quietly behind her.

Grace nodded, all the alibis made for lots of hours of careful checking, which could all amount to nothing, while all the time the killer was making distance between themselves and the crime.

Ruth Watson came next. She was the oldest of all the women, her beauty obvious beneath a careworn exterior. She walked elegantly into the room the leather heels of her riding boots tapping on the wooden floor. She sat down in front of Grace and Max, before regarding them coolly.

'As you know we are interviewing everyone who was on the yard at Park Hall today.'

Ruth's grey eyes moved slowly from Grace to Max and then back again, her face impassive. 'I was out riding.'

'Where did you go?' Max asked, pen poised above his notepad.

'I went out onto the cross country course, with Badger, my horse.' Ruth's voice was low pitched.

'How long were you gone?' Grace asked irritated by Ruth's apparent lack of desire to help or cooperate. She was clearly going to make them drag every word out of her.

'At least three or four hours. I got back just after his body was found.

I went onto the beach afterwards I met up with Miranda and Tamara, then we all rode back through the woods.'

'That's very helpful,' Grace noted on her pad, before looking at Ruth with a smile, 'Thank you. If there is anything else we will be in touch.'

Ruth inclined her head before getting up and sashaying out of the room.

'Can I come in? Issy Jordan's face appeared around the side of the door.

Grace and Max watched her walk across the room, treading lightly. 'My boots, this nice carpet.' Issy's steady voice was heavy with a local accent. 'I'm filthy,' she sighed, brushing ineffectively at her jeans clad ample bottom with grubby hands, succeeding only in scattering shavings and hay dust onto the carpet.

'What was your routine on the yard today?' Grace leant forwards, trying to reassure the nervous young woman.

'I helped dad with the milking, then I…'

'We only need to know what you did at Park Hall,' Max interrupted her.

'Oh,' Issy's bovine face flooded with colour. 'Well, I mucked out the stables. Rode a few of the youngsters. I went home for my lunch, I helped Sam, the farrier with some horses, then after I worked on some ponies that are being trained. There's a nice one, real kind he is, but he's nervous.'

'Okay, thanks.' Max's pen flew over his pad trying to keep up with Issy's headlong torrent of words.

The vet, Michael Alderton came in next. Grace knew his reputation as being very good at his job, although, like the Sam Green, the farrier, she had never used his services. He eased the fabric of his trousers upwards before lowering himself onto the sofa and sitting down. 'I was with Jago first thing, then I had to go off to an emergency. When I came back, he was dead.'

'You were the last number he called.' Grace raised her eyebrows quizzically.

'Of course. He's often on the phone to me. I am…,' he paused, correcting himself, 'was Jago's vet for the last ten years.'

She heard the momentary pause, in Michael's words, a hairsbreadth of hesitation.

Michael studied the pale carpet beneath their feet, his head turned to one side. 'He'd rung me to discuss a horse that was lame,' he said, raising his head slowly to meet Grace's eyes.

Grace nodded, 'That's fine, thank you for your time. Please send the farrier in.'

Sam Green stalked into the room his shoulders stiff with tension. He sat down as far away from them as he could, his eyes flickering around the room, looking everywhere but at the two detectives. 'We'll make this as painless as possible, Grace said, pointedly.

Sam couldn't be further from the fictional brawny blacksmith, he was short and wiry, with a shock of dark hair. His dark good looks weren't lost on Grace.

'We are talking to everyone who was on the yard this morning. You were one of them.'

Sam let out a sigh of annoyance, 'I'm a farrier, he had a yard of horses, he was always ringing me about one or another of the horses losing a shoe.'

'Yes, I understand,' Grace, paused, watching Sam. 'We just need you to account for your movements today.'

Sam sniffed loudly, 'I was trimming the hooves of a bunch of Jago's mares and battling with some half wild youngsters he'd never bothered handling. Took me and Issy four hours. Still haven't got to the other calls I was to make.' Sam met Grace's eyes, his brown eyes holding a challenge. 'Jago was a bastard; it was only a matter of time before someone gave him a good hiding.'

'This is slightly more than a hiding,' Grace said, trying to control her temper. Jago, probably had been an out and out bastard, but that did not give anyone the right to kill him.

'Fair enough,' Sam's demeanour had the arrogance of someone who is used to dealing with the police and held no fear of them.

'Just Simon O'Connor left, Boss.' Pete came quietly into the room as Sam left. 'He's pretty shook up still.'

Simon's face still held the grey pallor Grace had seen on Max just before he fainted. He sat down, his scratched, work worn hands visibly shaking.

'Sorry,' he raised his hands in a bewildered gesture. 'I wasn't expecting…' He was well spoken, his accent from London, Grace guessed. A posh boy kicking against the traces.

'Why did you go to find Jago?' Max watched Simon's legs jumping beneath his faded jeans.

'You've already asked me that,' Simon glared at Max. 'I needed to ask him about the flower bed. He was often in the groom's apartment. He found it easier to work up there, do some paperwork. He'd sometimes get his head down, have a sleep. When I went in, I thought he was having a nap and then…' Simon leant forwards, suddenly, his eyes wild. 'You think I did it?'

'We have to interview everyone.' Max put his hands up in a stop gesture.

'I didn't. I couldn't kill anyone. Not even a bastard like Jago.'

The hotel foyer was deserted by the time Grace and Max emerged. All that remained of the people they had interviewed were empty coffee cups and outside, hanging in the air a trail of dust left by their speeding cars.

'What now boss?'

'Home. I'll meet you at the mortuary in the morning.' Grace rubbed her temples which were taut with tension. 'Odd how they can all alibi one another.' Grace shook her head. 'Pretty convenient don't you think.'

Chapter Eight

'I'm going home. We can't do anything more here today,' Grace nodded in Max's direction by way of a goodbye, as she got into her Land Rover. There wasn't much of 'today' left. The interviews had taken a long time.

At the exit of the hotel car park Grace steered her vehicle to the left. Max she knew, would turn in the opposite direction, towards Truro, the capital of Cornwall.

So late in the day she had the road to herself, the headlights of the Land Rover illuminating the ribbon of road as it wound between the Cornish hedges and walls. Instinctively she braked as a pair of eyes, picked out by the lights, shone from within the depths of the undergrowth at the side of the road. A moment later a fox darted in front of her, jumped nimbly onto the top of the wall beside her and was gone, swallowed up by the darkness.

She shuddered, involuntarily. The fox had crossed onto land owned by Blackthorn Farm which neighboured Park Hall, Jago's home. Twenty years on from the case that had been the beginning of her career, she often found her thoughts drifting back to Eddie Hammett, the man who had taken and killed a series of young women. Only the bravery of one, who escaped, freed by Hammett's daughter, Mia, had brought the case to a close. Somewhere along this road, Susie Carne had shoved her way through a hedge as Hammett pursued her and had been rescued. He was dead now. He'd committed suicide when the police had closed in on him.

Hammett's daughter, Mia Lewis lived on the farm now, along with her grandmother, Nan. Tragedy seemed to stalk Mia; her boyfriend Tom had been reported missing two years ago. His vehicle had been found on the coast road; the assumption was that he had committed suicide by jumping into the sea from the cliffs.

Grace pushed her foot onto the accelerator, feeling the lumbering vehicle pick up speed, this road gave her the creeps. She would, Grace knew, have to interview Mia, see if she had seen anything, or if she knew anything about Jago and the people on the yard that would be relevant to his death. That was an interview she was not looking forward too. She hated the place, the very fabric of the Blackthorn Farm seemed filled with foreboding, it felt as though it had soaked up the pain and trauma of Hammett's victims.

As she drove her thoughts turned to the people who were on the yard at Park Hall. One of them probably held the key that would solve the case of who murdered Jago Carey. Was it Zara, his wife, driven to commit a dreadful crime by his philandering? Was it one of the liveries, the women who seemingly had such golden lives? Or Issy, the gentle young woman who cared for the horses. Or was it one of the men? The farrier, gardener or the vet? One of them had to be guilty, unless a random stranger had come across the fields and attacked Jago. The thought seemed highly unlikely.

The tragedy aside, she loved the enormity of the puzzle, the challenge of discovering who had killed Jago and bringing them to justice.

At Helston she turned off the main road onto the Lizard peninsula. At this hour every house she passed was in darkness. On either side of the road the inky blackness stretched out, blanketing out the countryside. She inhaled a deep breath, feeling the tension leaving her body. She was home now, safe. She could relax.

What an introduction to life in Cornwall Max had experienced. She should have been enjoying another few days leave if this crime hadn't been committed. Four more precious days with Kaden.

Her thoughts miles away Grace almost missed the entrance to Long Meadow Farm. She slammed on the brakes, feeling the huge vehicle judder in protest as she brought it to a more leisurely pace and turned into the driveway. In the daylight the fields belonging to Long Meadow Farm stretched in every direction. They had been a great selling point for her and Kaden and one which had kept the tourists from buying the farm as a holiday home.

A short distance up the rutted track she stopped in front of a square, two story house. A single light burned in one of the windows. Grace got out of the car, feeling the sense of relief wash over her.

Through the inky darkness of the night she could hear the waves pounding on the beach at the far end of the farm land she and Kaden had owned for the last four months. She breathed in air filled with the tang of the sea, mixed with the hay and horse scent of the stables.

Despite her tiredness, Grace leant against the Land Rover, letting the heat from the engine warm her back. 'You are so beautiful,' she whispered, looking at the old house. She had known, from the moment Kaden had brought her here that this was where she wanted to make her home. Kaden had found the farm, spending hours trawling around the local estate agents and driving around the country lanes.

The purchase of the farm was the culmination of years of hopes and dreams. They'd got together almost twenty years ago, the attraction that had crackled between them finally coming to a head one evening. They'd been inseparable ever since.

Gradually they had bought bigger and better houses, starting with a small terraced one in Marazion. Buying the farm had been a natural progression. They'd used every bit of their savings, plus money inherited from both sets of parents to purchase the old farm with its surrounding land and buildings. The plan was to renovate the old house and for Kaden to open a livery and training yard. The house, although restored structurally and given a new roof, was still a wreck. It would take time and money to turn it into a beautiful home. In the meantime, every penny and spare moment would be poured into making the equestrian facilities perfect.

She let herself into the house. Inside, the kitchen was filled with boxes, still waiting to be unpacked months after they'd moved in. The oven hummed quietly in the background. Grace opened the door, wincing as she pulled out the solid looking remnants of the meal Kaden had saved for her. She scraped the rock-hard pasta and Bolognese sauce into the bin.

From further inside the house came the faint sound of the television. Grace picked her way past more boxes, along the hallway and into the lounge.

Kaden lay asleep on the sofa, his head crooked at an uncomfortable looking angle on the arm of the sofa. His beloved terrier, Soda lay curled in the crook of his arm. Soda glanced guiltily at Grace, knowing well she wasn't allowed on the furniture.

Grace let her fingers gently touch one of Kaden's tangled dark curls, the hairs on his temples were shot through with a faint smattering of grey hairs.

'Kaden,' Grace said softly.

'Mmmm,' he stirred sleepily. 'You're back.' He opened his eyes, smiling at her, as he reached out to enfold her in his arms.

'I'm home.'

'How did it go?' his voice was slurred with sleep.

'Okay, I assume you heard who had died.'

'Yes. Fuck.' He was wide awake now. 'Who would want to kill Jago Carey?'

'I don't know yet.' Grace closed her eyes trying to blot out the image of Jago's ravaged body. She let herself be pulled into the warmth of his body, feeling the stress leave as she nestled into the safety of his arms.

* * * * *

'Good night Mr Max,' the diminutive owner of the Chinese takeaway held the door open to let Max out. What did it say about his lifestyle Max wondered as the door closed behind him, the wind chimes jangling merrily in the night air. He'd been in Cornwall for such a short time and already he was such a regular at the takeaway the owner knew his name.

He walked down the deserted street, past shops long closed for the day. He let the heavy bag swing gently, the grease seeping from one of the containers to stain the brown paper.

Above the noise of his leather soles on the cobbled street the cathedral clock a few streets away began to chime the hour. A single long note echoed out over the already silent city. The first hour of a Wednesday morning and there wasn't a soul around. In Manchester the city would still be heaving with people.

As he walked, his mind drifted relentlessly back to the crime scene and the horrors of Jago's body. What an idiot Grace Tallis must think he was, fainting like it was his first murder scene.

This morning he had been doubting his decision to move to the remote county. There had, since he had arrived, been a countless stream of dull, inconsequential crimes, nothing to keep his attention focused. Within a few hours that had all changed.

Grace, he knew would be having the same thoughts as him, why had Jago been killed? Who hated him so much they felt his death was the only way out? He had experienced plenty of deaths in Manchester even violent gun and knife crime, but nothing had prepared him for the scene he had witnessed today. It had been calculating, someone had taken great care to plan the man's death. Jago seemed to have trusted them, let them get close to him. Or were they wrong in thinking that, had it been just a random death, a robbery gone horribly wrong and set out to look like something more? He itched to know what had happened and knew, with Grace, he had a partner who was as determined as he was to find the culprit and bring them to justice.

Max reached the end of the street and turned onto a broad tree lined road flanked at either side by tall Georgian houses. As had become his habit since moving to Cornwall he paused a few houses away from his own. This was, he knew, the best part of the move. In Manchester a home like this would have been an impossible dream, here, prices meant he could afford this fabulous house, found via an internet search. As soon as he had made the initial trip to see the house, he had fallen in love with it. He drank in the splendour of the building, wide stone steps leading up to a front door, painted in what the estate agent's brochure had described as aubergine. A wide fan of glass framed the top of the door. The house soared upwards, all three stories of it, with a basement below the level of the street. He had intended, when he bought the house, to rent out part of the house, convert the attic to a bedsit, but in the end he glorified in the space he had to himself. He had been torn, daily, between his realisation that he was unsuited to working in a small rural force, with the love of his new home.

The door swung open into a wide, stone flagged hall. There was a lot he wanted to do to the house. He intended to furnish it by trawling auctions and antique shops looking for pieces that took his fancy. Downstairs he planned, one day, to take out the ancient and inefficient kitchen and put in a new one. He had a vison of cream painted woodwork, marble surfaces.

He dished the takeaway onto a plate and headed up to the lounge, revelling in the silence of the house, the only sound his shoes on the wooden flooring. He snapped on the vast wide screen television he had treated himself too and settled back into the sofa.

He dipped his fork into the gently steaming food, the rice mingling with the noodles of the Chow Mein and running gently into the deep red of the sweet and sour sauce. He brought the fork slowly to his lips; bile rose swiftly into his throat as images of the crime scene flashed into his mind. Panic stricken he put the plate down on the coffee table with a clatter and dashed, hand over his mouth for the bathroom where he wretched until his stomach muscles ached.

Chapter Nine

The room was so silent Grace could hear her heart beating. Everyone's eyes were fixed intently on her. Slowly she pulled the pale blue folder across the desk towards herself, the flimsy cardboard making a scraping noise on the wooden surface.

Grace's long fingers splayed over the cover of the file. She paused, reluctant to open it and reveal its contents. There was a sliver of dirt in the corner of one of her nails, it had escaped the ministrations of the nail brush when she had showered. Before coming to work she'd helped Kaden and their groom, Rachel muck out the stables. The pride and joy she had previously felt in the beautiful old property had been spoilt by the horrors of Jago's death. Grace had spent a sleepless night, her mind churning with everything she had to do to make sure the case was solved. She'd been glad to come into work and get started.

Someone shifted in their seat, another coughed, the air filled with expectancy. She could not put off the moment any longer. Grace opened the folder, revealing the photographs of Jago. They were the last ones that would ever be taken of him. The images had taken from every direction, showing the remnants of his last, horrific moments on this earth.

Grace sensed the atmosphere change, becoming charged. There was squeaking of chair legs against the floor, as her team of detectives shifted, sitting upright, focused.

Grace fanned out the images, unwilling to look at the close-up bloodied details of Jago's horrific injuries. She selected three, one of Jago's stricken face, his head wound clearly visible, she looked for a moment at his shocked, terrified expression, his eyes, wide and unseeing. The other was a shot from a distance, his ravaged body lying amidst the crumpled bed linen. The final one showed the gaping wound in his abdomen, his flesh, livid, bright red, his entrails an artist's palate of greys and browns.

She turned, pinning each one briskly onto the white board behind her and then turned to face the team she had selected. They watched her expectantly. Grace knew that each had a fire of determination burning deep within them. She could see their longing to get started, the drive to delve into Jago's life, and that of everyone who knew him. They were ready to do everything necessary to find out who hated him enough to kill him.

'So, thoughts…' Grace let her words hang in the air, watching their expressions.

'Wife sick of him playing around,' Pete Brook's voice came from his preferred position at the back of the room.

'Angry husband,' Ron Austen spoke next.

'Overkill,' Max said, leaning against the wall halfway down the room, 'He trusted whoever did this. Trusted them enough to let them get close enough to knock him out.'

Grace ran a finger down the bridge of her nose, shaking her head slowly, 'No one seems to have noticed anyone strange on the yard.

Equally no one seems to have seen anyone go into where Jago was found. Did someone surprise him, bash in his head without him knowing anyone was around.'

Max made a grunt of agreement, 'Maybe.'

Grace let the silence settle around the room again, watching her team's faces as each mused over the possible scenarios.

'Let's get to work then.' She noticed her DCI, Steve Cooper slip quietly into the room and stand, arms folded over his shirt front, watching the proceedings.

'Pete, can you check alibis.' Grace mentally ticked off the assignments. 'Has his phone been gone through yet?' She scanned quickly around the room.

'Not yet, Boss.' Max shook his head.

'That needs to be done.' Grace noted the task on the white board. 'Phone records. Who is checking those?'

'Me,' Rowena Lowe ran her hands through her hair, smoothing back the dark strands.

'Have a look at his computer, see if that yields anything,' Grace looked at Ron who nodded in agreement.

'Have a look at his record, see if anything flags up. Are there enemies we need to be aware of?'

'On to it.' Mike Smith, a detective seconded in from Truro spoke.

'We'll meet back here at six for a run through, see what we've come up with.' Grace thrust her mobile phone into her pocket, 'I'm off to the mortuary. Max, you come with me.'

The mortuary stood behind the main hospital. The long, single story, pebble dashed building was hidden behind a screen of high laurel shrubs as if the planners had felt it was best to keep it hidden.

Mark Lowther was at his desk when they arrived, a steaming coffee and cheese roll beside him. Max's stomach churned as he glanced at shelves crammed with specimen jars. At the far end of the echoing room a blackboard was neatly divided into sections reminding Max of a class at school, except for the headings, which listed various body parts and their weights. A wide glass window looked out onto the white tiled cutting room, where, on stainless steel tables, sheeted discreetly, lay the shapes of bodies.

Max felt sour bile rise in his throat, yet again and swallowed hard, determined not to let himself down again by passing out. He was relieved to see that Grace had been equally affected by their surroundings her face had a pale, yellow tinge. A sheen of sweat glistened on her brow, sticking tendrils of chestnut hair to the skin.

'Just finished with your customer,' Lowther took a large bite of his roll and chewed vigorously. 'Come on through and have a look.'

Grace glanced at Max as he hastily disguised a whimper of horror by turning it into a cough.

The pathologist lifted the sheet from Jago's body. Beneath the thick green cover, the corpse had been straightened, cut, delved into and then put back together again. A brown tag bearing his name hung limply from one of his big toes, Jago's eyes, once staring and horror filled were now closed.

The mortuary assistants had closed his mouth erasing the rictus of horror. Although his face had been smoothed and straightened, the trauma of the pain and anguish of his last moments remained, deeply etched into the planes of his face.

'Your suspect did half my work for me,' Lowther grinned drawing the sheet back further. The gaping wound out of which Jago's intestines had spilled had been neatly sewn back together. The bulging mass of intestines had been removed. 'You can see, he was in good shape, very fit.'

Grace nodded, looking at what had been up until a few days ago the tanned and toned torso of Jago Carey. The ridges of muscles remained on a belly, marred by the staples that held his abdomen together.

'Was he cut open before he died?' Grace asked, nodding towards the now closed wound in Jago's stomach.

'Oh yes.' Lowther looked at Jago as though he was an exotic specimen of immense interest. 'This was what killed him, but not quickly, shock, blood loss, that did the trick.

He would have had plenty of time to know what was happening to him.' Lowther pulled the sheet lower to revel the springy mat of Jago's pubic hair and the bloodied scrap of skin that was all that remained of his penis. 'If that hadn't caused his death, this would have.'

'What about these?' Grace let one finger hover close to the deep, raw looking injuries on Jago's wrists. Now that the body had been removed from the bed and the rope bindings taken off, she could see closely just how deep the wounds were.

Lowther nodded, 'See how he fought to free himself, that is how these abrasions were caused. He was fighting for his life no doubt.'

Max glanced away from the corpse, wishing he were anywhere but here. The mortuary windows were frosted glass, but through them he could see the green, blurred outline of a tree, moving slowly in the breeze. He longed to be outside, where the air was fresh and where he didn't have to look at this terrible sight.

'What can you tell me?' Grace straightened up and took a step back as though she could not wait to distance herself from the stainless-steel slab and the pale, rigid form on it.

'Cut was from the bottom of the rib cage downwards, a single slash. Whoever did it had drugged him, presumably to stop him thrashing around.' Lowther stared intently at Jago's corpse. 'He had eaten, prior to death, about an hour before. Lunch presumably. I'd say it was a sandwich, some kind of meat and salad,' the pathologist moved away from the body to a table where he picked up a specimen bowl, swilling the contents around while looking at them intently. He took a deep breath over the bowl, 'And a beer.' Lowther picked up a specimen jar, 'This is his missing appendage.' He seemed to delight in their discomfiture, swirling the glass jar around so that the liquid spun, catching the light. Suspended within was an unidentifiable piece of flesh. 'Hacked off, I'd say your suspect was right-handed, held the penis in one hand and hacked with the other.'

'Poor bastard,' Max shuddered a short time later as they emerged into the warmth of the sunlight, both taking gasping breaths of fresh air.

They drove away in silence, each lost in thought.

'Settling in?' Grace broke the silence, shaking her head at the banal question. Jago's death was so horrific she desperately wanted to talk about something other than his suffering.

'Yes, Boss, thanks.' He couldn't tell her the reality, how he hated the openness of the countryside, the deserted back lanes, the slow pace of life.

'I imagine it's very different down here from what you're used to.'

'You could say that.' Max grinned, turning to catch the quick smile that flashed across her face.

'How could you not love all of this?' Grace eased the Land Rover to a slower pace as the lumbering form of a caravan blocked the road in front of them.

Max held his breath as a moment later she accelerated, the hedge crashing against the side of the vehicle as she steered it past the caravan. He wiped sweat dampened hands on the front of his trousers, seeing her grin as she noticed his action.

'Park Hall,' Grace turned the Land Rover off the road, they were back to business. Max recognised the driveway. They'd come at it from a different direction. Police vehicles still littered the stable yard, blue and white crime scene tape fluttered in the breeze.

'Anything of interest been found?' Grace asked the Crime Scene Manager, striding across the yard towards him. 'Murder weapon?'

He shook his head. 'Not yet, we'll keep going. We can get divers and a dog team out here if we need too.'

Grace stood beside Max in the sunlight, watching the teams working, searching every inch of the yard and stables.

Hours later, they returned to Penzance. The office buzzed with noise and activity.

Grace stood beside the whiteboard, as silence gradually fell on the room.

'Phone records?' she looked towards Rowena.

'There's nothing on his phone, Boss, no text messages, no numbers that seem to be calling on any regular basis, except for those who we've accounted for already, liveries at the yard, his pupils that kind of thing.

'Keep digging, something might come to light.'

Pete spoke next. 'Nothing showing up anywhere else yet, he's no Police record, not even a parking ticket.'

Grace thrust her hands into the pockets of her jeans, 'Anything on the alibis of the people who were on the yard? Who saw anyone going to the groom's flat? Who had a reason to kill him?'

'Still checking,' Ron's reply.

'There's nothing more we can do tonight, until we've proper records and more information come through,' Grace said. 'I think we should knock off now and meet up again at eight tomorrow. Anyone fancy a beer?'

There was a murmur of agreement. The noise level grew, heads nodding, smiles widening. Grace led the way out of the building to the local pub. 'On me,' She caught the barman's eye. It would do the team good to have a beer or two, bond, keep their spirits up before they began the long slow slog of proper detective work, digging and poking and slowly uncovering layer after layer of Jago's life, exposing it as brutally as his killer had. Something she hoped would also reveal who had a motive to kill him.

Chapter Ten

'Calm down. Relax. Breathe,' Michael Alderton forced dog and disinfectant scented air into his lungs. He had to stay calm, not disintegrate into a quivering heap. It was essential he stayed focused, carry on as normal, as if the filthy bastard who had tried to ruin his life had not just been found dead.

Michael pulled the cover off the long, fine hypodermic needle and brought it slowly towards the rubber seal on the small vial of anaesthetic. His hands felt like they were made of wood, stiff and unyielding. The bottle and syringe flipped suddenly from between his fingers. There was a long, slow moment while he juggled, catching them briefly before they bounced, hitting the surgery floor and shattering into a myriad of tiny pieces. The liquid spread over the tiles, the strong anaesthetic odour assailing his nostrils.

'Shit!' He grabbed a handful of kitchen roll and crouched down, scraping the slivers into a heap. The liquid soaked into the paper, turning it from a pale blue to a dark indigo.

'Here, let me,' Sally McKenzie, his brusque, Scottish veterinary nurse brushed past him and began to sweep the debris away. Michael struggled to his feet and leant against the work surface watching her solid, shapeless form as she cleared the mess away.

'All done,' she said a moment later, getting to her feet and meeting his gaze.

'Thank you, Sally,' Michael nodded, letting his eyes slide away from her piercing blue ones. 'I can manage now.' Get a grip, he told himself sternly. He had to rein in his emotions, not let them rule him. Everything had to appear utterly normal. Could Sally see how shaken he was? Did she know what was on his mind? There was something perceptive about her gaze. She had to know something was wrong. That was his third accident of the morning. Michael could feel Sally's eyes following him as he took another vial of anaesthetic out of the store and filled a second syringe with fingers that trembled visibly. It was not the best way to be when preforming the delicate surgery needed to spay the beloved tabby cat of his best client, a fussy, elderly lady.

He selected a CD of soothing classical music and put it into the player. It helped, the notes blocking out much of his relentless mind chatter. He forced himself to concentrate. One more operation and he was finished. Later he could think about how to explain his lie. The police were bound to find out. He had seen enough police dramas to have no doubt about that. The problem was, he had no alibi – or at least not anything he could easily explain – especially if Julia were to find out where he had been the afternoon Jago had died. So many years, so many lies.

He should, by now have built up a sound business that would have let him walk away from Julia and live the life he really wanted. But still he clung to her, and their dead marriage – she seemed to have no idea. Of course, her money helped. Or rather her father's money.

Michael knew he wasn't a businessman. It was hard to force money out of people when they didn't have it. How could he refuse to operate on a sick animal when the owner cared so much about them?

And then of course there was Danny, their son. It would be hard to walk away from him. So, Michael continued weaving his tangle of lies.

Incredibly Carl had seen straight through him. Michael had known from the moment he had met Carl he understood. Had he seen the longing in Michael's face? Had there been some spark of recognition in him as their eyes met. Whatever it had been that night Michael had felt compelled to remain in the hotel bar as it slowly emptied. He had sat in the far corner away from the bar, watching as the customers left, until just he and the handsome man remained.

From then it was only a matter of time until Carl was calmly walking beside him to the room Michael was occupying on the second floor. They had been silent, their shoes padding softly on the thickly carpeted hallway. Michael had opened his room door, gone in, painfully aware of Carl behind him. As it had closed the two men had stood apart, quietly regarding each other. Then Carl had taken a step forwards, closing the gap between them.

Michael knew there was no going back, in that moment he had become the man he had always wanted to be. He had been surprised at how easy it was to lie. How simple it was to conceal an affair.

Julia had never suspected. He hated everything about her. Her body repulsed him, soft and curvy, her clothes clinging to the curves of her stomach and breasts. He loathed the way her long, wavy hair billowed and whipped around her face. Even the warm, spicy smell of her, revolted him. How could he have told her that he preferred Carl, his body, taut beneath a plain white shirt his hair, short, swept back from his face. He hated the feel of her hand in his, her fingers warm and delicate. Carl's larger, cool ones felt far, far nicer beneath his.

An evening with Carl was fun, taking about football, cricket, anything other than work. All the time feeling the undercurrent of sexual tension, the thought of what was to come later, when they were alone, in hotel rooms or back in Carl's studio flat over-looking the river at the far side of town.

Michael had thought that the out-of-town restaurant was safe. A place he and Carl could meet in peace.

Michael hadn't known that Jago had spotted him. Or that he had immediately worked out that their companionship was more than just a business meeting. How triumphant he had been. The revelation had taken Michael completely by surprise. 'I know what you do.' Jago had hissed in his ear as he was vetting a horse Jago was selling to a client. The horse, a beautiful big bay eventer seemed slightly lame. Jago's soft voice had shattered his concentration.

He had turned to look at Jago, seeing his eyes dancing with amusement, a facetious grin splitting his face. 'You and your… friend.'

'I have no idea what you are talking about.'

'I think you do. Did you have a good dinner the other night?' Jago had said, suddenly, jolting Michael with the malice in his voice.

'Yes, thank you,' Michael felt the panic rising in the pit of his stomach and yet hoped against hope that Jago had seen him at dinner with Julia and was making a polite social enquiry.

'The Grenville is a nice quiet spot, isn't it?' Jago had leant against the stable door. Michael forgot all about the horse that was trotting towards him. 'Perfect for le liaisons dangerous,' Jago had smiled, drawing back his lips from a row of even white teeth, and leaving Michael in no doubt as to what he meant. His eyes had been cold, calmly appraising Michael, watching for his reaction.

'I guess so,' Michael had been still desperately trying to keep the conversation light, not to admit to anything. Jago may have seen him with Carl, but he had no proof that anything was going on.

'I've just sold this horse to America… for a lot of money,' the malevolance in Jago's voice was clear. Maybe, just maybe if he gave the horse a clean bill of health he would forget about seeing Michael with Carl. The threat was clear.

'Good,' Michael said, hearing the slightly higher note of tension in his voice, 'Let's hope he does well for his new owner.'

The threat went away. The horse went to America.

Michael wanted, as he often did, to switch off the part of his brain that felt any emotion he had wanted to forget all about Jago, forget the undercurrents of tension that existed in his own life and just focus on the things that were important. His son and Carl, the love of his life.

One evening, Michael was doing the evening surgery. Thinking that all histhe clients had gone and would be finished soon, he went into the waiting room for a final check around. Jago sat, in the centre of the line of chairs, seemingly engrossed in an ancient copy of Farmers Weekly. 'Been back to the Grenville recently?' he had said softly, putting down the tattered pages of the magazine and regarding Michael with eyes as cold as a shark's. His intention was clear. He was going to make Michael squirm over the knowledge he had gained 'I'm sure you wouldn't want Julia to know about your new friend,' was all that he had said. It was enough to make Michael's world crumble.

Julia had never suspected. Of that he was sure. Her life, and that of Danny had ticked along its usual lines. Michael dealing with client's emergencies while Julia lived her seemingly perfect life. He had, as always, come home late after a long day at the surgery, or dealing with emergencies. She had never known, or at least never questioned where he was – and how could a detour to see Carl possibly make any difference to her? Of course, it would have if she had known that her husband was sleeping with another man, someone he was deeply in love with. It would have meant the end of their marriage and their life. The traditional Cornish farmers would never have wanted to give him business.

Carl struggled to understand the relationship Michael valued so much had to remain a secret.

Jago was the one to benefit from their love. And from keeping it hidden. Turning a blind eye to horses that were not as sound as they should be was the price Michael had to pay to buy his silence. The threat was never made. Jago didn't have to do that. His smug face, and twisted smile were enough to let Michael know what the result would be if he didn't comply. Jago had had known exactly what was going on. Somehow, he had seen through the shabby veneer of Michael's life, the sham marriage, He had taken that knowledge and used it to torment Michael, to take the pleasure he had found with Carl, and made it shabby and filthy.

At first it hadn't mattered. He had been so enamoured with Carl, so thrilled at his new life and at finding a soulmate it hadn't mattered. A horse could easily lame itself while being transported. Michael's opinion of its soundness was just that, an opinion.

Gradually he began to resent the hold Jago had over him. He hated himself for being at Jago's beck and call, for not calling his bluff. Jago knew too much and that was very dangerous. He found himself becoming more and more resentful of the bastard who was holding him hostage. The anger at Jago had built up until it became a wild, caged animal that he could no longer keep contained. The hold he had on Michael needed to end. Enough was enough.

Unfortunately, Jago's death meant that the police were going to start delving into his life looking at his alibi. The fear of discovery tormented him. He'd told the police he had left Park Hall, that an emergency had come up. How long would it take before they discovered he had lied? That detective, Grace Tallis, her eyes seemed to have the ability to see right into the depths of his soul. She had known he was lying; he was sure. But she couldn't prove it. He would stick to his story. The notes of the music washed over him, bringing him back to the present, soothing his jangling nerves slightly. He tightened his grip on the scalpel. The sharp tool felt unfamiliar in his sweating fingers.

It was a cat, for heaven's sake – just a simple spaying operation – not brain surgery.

Blood oozed from the wound he had created, the sides, pulled back revealed the cat's innards, glistening in the bright surgery lights. Humans and animals were the same, blood and guts. Jago had been conscious when he had been cut open. The guts spilling over his thighs, the pain must have been unimaginable. Michael found himself picturing Jago in his last moments. He had deserved it. Michael was glad that he was dead, glad that he had died screaming in agony.

Chapter Eleven

'Answer the phone. Issy. Answer the phone,' Tamara Grey drummed her fingers impatiently on the black marble kitchen work surface. Patrick would be back any time now. Alive with tension she moved from the kitchen, into the hall, her heels tapping a tattoo on the wooden floorboards and on into the vast open space of the lounge.

Why the hell hadn't the stupid cow activated the message service on her telephone? Tamara thought, sinking down on one of the stone steps that encircled the sunken sitting area of the lounge.

Even in her stressed state Tamara couldn't help but admire the room. The elegant, modern house had been built in the grounds of the original Brennan Hall, burned to the ground in a drug fuelled rage by a previous owner during the 1970's. Light flooded through tall windows, giving glorious views of the gardens that Capability Brown had worked so hard to create.

Finally, the phone was answered. 'Hello,' Issy's voice was filled with her puppy-like eagerness to please.

'Issy, it's Tamara,' she spoke quickly, trying to hide any note of urgency in her voice. 'Something has come up, I have to go away for a few days, so I'm not going to be riding. Could you make sure Lanson goes out into the field every day and put him on the horse walker so he doesn't lose any fitness.'

'Yes, of course,' Issy was quietly professional. 'You are probably better staying away from the yard anyway,' she continued, 'The place is still full of police.'

Was there a slight edge to her voice? Was Issy implying Tamara knew something about Jago being killed? If Issy suspected her, did the police as well? Had they seen through her fragile alibi? Tamara's mind turned in rapid loops. Should she say more? Would doing so be incriminating? Or should she ignore Issy's insinuation? In the end she plumped for coldly innocent with an edge of abject horror, 'Yes of course it would be. They must do their jobs. Find out who killed Jago. Not me anyway,' she forced a laugh, aware of its brittle note.

'I don't know who would have wanted to kill Jago,' Issy's voice broke. Even over the telephone Tamara could tell that she was crying, 'He was so good to me, such a nice man.'

'Yes, he was,' Tamara stood, walking out of the lounge. She glanced at herself in the ornate mirror positioned on the wall closest to her. The face that stared back at her was coldly composed. The face of a liar.

'Are you going anywhere nice?' Issy was fishing for information.

'Just seeing friends.'

'Have fun then.' Issy answered, shortly, sulky that she hadn't managed to get Tamara to say more about her plans, 'I'll look after Lanson.'

'Thanks, just keep him fit, please.' Tamara replied, eager to end the conversation, 'I'd really appreciate that.' She ended the call. The less said the better, then she couldn't be caught out in a lie. Something she had learned the hard way from Jago.

'Tamara?' Jago had given a snort of laughter, a few weeks after she had moved her new horse to the exclusive livery stables at Park Hall. 'It was plain Mandy last time I saw you.'

A jolt of electricity had shot through Tamara, she could feel her cheeks burning as she looked at the man who owned the stables. He had been so charming to her when she had first brought her horse to the yard.

'My, you've come a long way.' He moved to stand close to her horse, one hand clutching its reins so she could not ride away. While her body reeled with shock he had put a cool, possessive hand on her thigh. 'You were at Buryford Secondary School.'

Speechless, Tamara stared at him, grim realisation that she had been caught out slowly dawning.

'I was two years above you. I'm very hurt you don't remember me.' His voice had been barely above a whisper. His eyes had locked onto hers and held them.

School had been a grimy red bricked building of a soul-less northern industrial town. She had not connected Jago, the glamorous superstar rider with the nameless, gangly, spotty faced teenager she had vaguely known about. He had a reputation for ambushing the younger girls and covering their breasts with his clammy palms.

'When did you become Tamara?' his hand had remained on her thigh, the fingers inching slowly upwards. 'What happened to common little Mandy?' An amused smile had twisted the sides of his wide mouth.

Tamara had dug her heels into her horse's sides, trying to ride away, but Jago had held the reins tightly, stopping her.

'I er...,' Tamara stammered. She didn't remember the precise moment she had ditched the name Mandy and become Tamara. She had always known that, as Mandy, a girl from the back streets of a northern town she was not going to get far in the world. The reality of her childhood had been a cold, damp, cramped house. Her father had been a lumbering, dull man who slipped from job to job as often as the rain battered through the grimy streets. Her mother had been a quiet, nonentity of a woman who cow tied to everything her husband said and who clearly thought that her daughters should do the same.

But Mandy had wanted more than a job in a factory and a home in one of the back-to-back terraces. As soon as she could Mandy had packed the best suitcase she could find and headed south, to the bright lights and better future of London, reinventing herself on the way. She had become Tamara, naming herself after a character in a book she had enjoyed. Creating a new past for herself had been easy. To everyone in London, she was Tamara, the daughter of aristocratic parents who had tragically been killed in a car crash. She invented a distant relative who had brought her up and spoke of a childhood which consisted of posh schools and trips abroad. Eventually the lies had become so real she had almost believed them herself.

A job in PR had led her to Patrick Grey, heir to a hotel fortune built by his father with a chain of exclusive boutique premises that stretched from Scotland to the south coast.

Patrick was perfect, good looking and wealthy. Tamara couldn't believe her luck when he had asked her to move into his elegant Chiswick house. She had been over the moon when he had inherited his parent's home in Cornwall and suggested they move out to the west country. Patrick spent a few days a month in London, but otherwise was content to let a management team run his business while he enjoyed a semi-retirement. Life was blissful. In Cornwall Tamara had everything she had ever wanted, a beautiful house, flashy car and what had once seemed an unattainable dream – a horse of her own – kept at livery – so that she could train with one of the best event riders in the country.

It had never occurred to her that Jago Carey, the event rider and owner of the livery yard, was the horrible boy from her school days. Back then she hadn't even known his name. The gangly boy had morphed into something far more glamourous, tall and extremely good looking. He was still hateful though. He had loved every second of seeing her squirm when he announced that he knew who she was.

'It will be our little secret... Mandy,' he had said, looking up at her, his face a mask of pure sadistic pleasure. She knew then that he would hold that over her forever, and that she would always be looking over her shoulder, waiting for the moment when he told her secret to the world.

'Of course, I don't have to tell anyone if you make it worth my while,' he had said, maliciously. She had soon discovered what he meant – as if he didn't have enough women throwing themselves at him willingly, he wanted her.

She belonged to Patrick. Jago had taken her unwillingness to stray and made sure that she did. She was never certain if he enjoyed her repulsion more, or the fact that he was getting one over on Patrick.

'You are rotten to the bone,' she had said, when the full realisation of what he meant had sunk in. She had no choice, but to go along with him, trust him when he said he wouldn't tell Patrick. Just a little fun for him on occasional afternoons, he had smiled, told her how he had wanted her when they were at school. He took great pleasure in possessing what he could never rightly have.

She had torn herself apart with worry. Desperate to hide the truth from Patrick.

If he had known where she originally came from, he probably wouldn't have cared. But her lies had got her into the circles he moved in and once she had fallen in love with him there had been no going back. To explain to him who she really was would have meant risking losing him. How could he trust and respect someone whose very existence was a tissue of lies.

Rather than leave her alone, once she had given in, Jago taunted her, reminding her constantly of the treacherous path she had trodden and how easy it had been to get her into bed. She had thought that she was protecting Patrick, and her life with him and yet it had dragged her into a living nightmare from which she could not escape. The tangle of lies became deeper and deeper. Lies about where she was when Jago sought out her company. Patrick, filled with trust had never seemed to suspect her duplicity.

This would be the last piece of deceit. Once today was over she would go back to her life, try to forget what she had done.

Patrick must never know she had travelled to the next county to destroy the life growing within her, or what had happened on the day of Jago's death. How she would come to terms with what she was doing was something she put out of her mind. They longed for a child and looked forward to the day she got pregnant. She was mid-thirties now, the chances of having a baby were lessening.

She had covered her tracks well telling Patrick she was going to Exeter for a shopping expedition. Not to kill a child. He would have had no reason to suspect that anything was any different, or that anything had ever happened between her and Jago.

All that mattered now was to make sure no one ever knew what she had done. Her tracks were covered, of that she was sure, Patrick had no need to think she was doing anything else other than shopping. She hated deceiving him. Tamara's stomach heaved. She dashed hand over her mouth to the downstairs bathroom and vomited a stream of bitter, yellow bile.

Two hours later Tamara was on the outskirts of Exeter, she steered her car into the driveway of an elegant Georgian house. She ignored the woman, dressed in a long flowing patchwork skirt, gamely clinging to a pro-life banner who glared pointedly at her. The woman's ginger dreadlocks bounced gently in the breeze. Was the child she was about to destroy Jago's or Patrick's? Tamara had no way of knowing. But in case it was Jago's, conceived in one of his horrific sessions, the child had to be destroyed. All evidence of her infidelity had to go. Nothing must remain of her deceit.

The receptionist was cool and polite, she could have been checking in for an appointment at an elegant spa, not checking in for an operation that would effectively kill a child. Tamara put that out of her mind. There would be no more lies once this was over. She would start her life over.

Jago was dead. He had no power over her any longer. And she was glad. He had died in agony, in a horrific way. He had been cruel, vindictive and spiteful. He deserved everything he got.

Chapter Twelve

Ruth Watson pushed the front door shut with her bottom. 'Owww,' she winced, her palms stung with the weight of the grocery filled plastic bags. The skin, when she dropped the bags onto the kitchen worktop was red, scored with deep lines where the handles had dug in. She stood for a moment, letting out a long, heartfelt sigh, not of relief to be home, but for the awfulness of her surroundings. The worst thing was the smell. The odour of stale garlic and fried fish lay heavily in the still air of the cramped flat.

Rubbing her palms together Ruth shoved open the window above the stained stainless-steel sink. From below the spicy aroma of curry did battle with the fishy odour, the two small mingling into a nauseous mixture.

The nylon overall she wore was heavy and itchy against her skin. The urge to strip off the hated, sweaty uniform was too strong. Abandoning her shopping, Ruth hurried along the short corridor that led to her bedroom, shedding her uniform into a crumpled heap onto what the estate agent's literature had described as carpet. The dusty, faded fabric was an indeterminable colour that could have once been red, or orange or any shade in between. She eased sideways into the cupboard sized space the estate agent had called an en-suite. Ruth kicked off her knickers, she had lost so much weight the tiny scrap of silk, slid easily from her hips.

The shower let out a pathetic stream of water as though it couldn't be bothered to make the effort to travel through the pipes. At least it was hot. She scrubbed her body with a natural sponge, lathering pools of expensive shower gel into it, before scrubbing at her skin. Expensive skin creams were now beyond her meagre budget, but the shower gel was a favourite. Something she wouldn't give up.

Once showered, Ruth pulled on a dressing gown before unpacked the shopping, wiping the shelves of the cupboards before the tins and packets went in. She might live in a hovel but at least it was a clean one.

Her task completed she reached with relief for the bottle of wine she had bought and filled a cut glass goblet to the brim, before curling up on the sofa. The wine was a treat, something she looked forward too at the end of the week. Her limit was one bottle, drunk over the weekend. It was no longer the expansive brand she had loved, but it did the trick, putting a blurry edge on her life.

Settled, she switched in the television, a vast flat screen, one of the few possessions she had managed to keep hold of, smuggling it out of the house a few days before she left. Neil, blind in his fury, had either not noticed, or had not cared enough to protest. Ruth flicked through the channels, there seemed to be nothing on but screeching reality shows and sobbing obese people. She settled on the news; the local roundup had just begun.

She recognised the backdrop immediately, the beautiful lines of Park Hall with its pale stone façade. She watched the red-haired lady detective from a few days ago being interviewed by a glamorous looking female reporter. Wine slopped from Ruth's glass as she reached for the remote, increasing the volume. She watched transfixed. What did the police know about Jago's killer?

As the report came to an end, Ruth picked up her drink. 'Cheers, Jago.' She raised her glass towards the screen. 'You deserved all you got.' She was glad he had suffered. Ruth held him totally, utterly responsible for what had happened to her.

'Red wine? Gin?' Two hours later, Ruth's older sister Claire leant over the bar, a twenty-pound note in her hand, demonstrating her utter determination to pay for the round of drinks.

'Wine please. You don't have to pay. I'm not a pauper.'

Claire spun to face Ruth, her eyebrows raised. 'Well things aren't exactly rosy for you either, are they? There was a certain smugness in her sisterly concern. Claire had the perfect life, while Ruth's had gone so spectacularly wrong.

The barman poured the wine, catching Ruth's eye. 'Merlot okay for you?

'Fine.' Ruth said shortly, ignoring the flirtatious tone in his voice, she never wanted to have anything to do with a man again. Ever.

Claire paid, then spinning on the heels of her very elegant shoes she headed across the room to an empty table. 'The man that died, is he the one...?'

'Yes,' Ruth twisted her glass, watching the liquid swirl, catching the light, turning into a myriad of colours.

Claire's eyes widened. 'You didn't...?'

'What do you think?' Ruth filled her voice with sarcasm.

'Of course not. You couldn't have hated him that much!' She released a peel of near hysterical laugher. 'I hope you've got a good alibi.' The laugher died and Claire regarded Ruth solemnly. 'Were where you when he was killed?'

'Riding, with some other women.'

'That's convenient.'

'I suppose it is.' Ruth closed her mouth with a finality that she hoped would make Claire realise she wasn't going to be drawn any further on the matter. 'Can we change the subject. Please.'

Claire's mouth twitched, her eyes raked over Ruth until she spoke again, '*Work* good?' Claire's emphasis on the word showed exactly what she thought of the menial role Ruth now performed.

'Great,' Ruth repeated, hearing the tension in her voice. Was *great* a word that could be used to describe stripping urine-stained sheets from beds, sweating in the airless heat.

'Enjoying life in your apartment?'

'Yes, it's lovely, very cosy.' Cosy really wasn't the word she would use to describe her dingy, claustrophobic flat. Lovely it certainly was not. It was on the cheap side of town, surrounded by takeaways and pubs, her neighbours were either students or rough looking drunks.

Claire gazed intently at her thumb nail, examining the blood red nail varnish with deep intention.

'Would you go back to Neil?'

Ruth fought to swallow a mouthful of wine.

'I wouldn't imagine for a moment that he would have me back,' Ruth's snort of derision caught the attention of the couple sitting on the adjoining table.

Ruth pulled a wry face. Neil had well and truly moved on. She hadn't seen him since *that* day, but she could see how happy he was from his social media account, which he hadn't bothered to make private even though he had unfriended her rather rapidly.

She found herself unable to stop herself tracing his progress from heartbroken cuckold to new man. His online status had gone from 'married' to 'single.' Happily single, it soon transpired as she watched his posts of party pictures and holiday snaps. It was as if their relationship breaking up gave him a new lease of life. Ruth had hoped he regretted their break-up as much as she did. Quite clearly, he did not.

Gradually a woman began to appear in the posts, a willowy looking blonde, with a mane of straight ice blonde hair and a stunning figure. She gradually moved from the periphery of the images to finally to stand beside him. It was then only days until his relationship status changed to "in a relationship with Gilly Blackwell." And days after that before Ruth found it impossible to stay away from her rival, wanting to know everything about the woman who had replaced her.

Three glasses of wine later, Ruth waited for the inevitable. She saw

Claire scratch at an imaginary itch on the back of her wrist and use the movement to surreptitiously glance at her watch. 'Oh, it that the time?' She wasn't even good at feigning surprise in her eagerness to put some distance between them. Ruth longed to say something sarcastic about getting back to her husband and cooking his dinner. The truth was she missed that part of life, the routine of unwinding together at the end of the day. Now there was no one to chat to about the day – not that working in a nursing home was something she wanted to admit too, let alone discuss with anyone.

Claire drained her drink, put the glass delicately on the table, swung her bag onto her shoulder and scrabbled in her pocket for her car keys. 'Right. Better go.' the Mercedes logo on her keyring waved jauntily in Ruth's direction, reminding her of all she had lost.

They parted with a brief hug, before Claire turned and walked rapidly away.

Ruth watched her weaving through the groups of drinkers until she vanished from sight.

She cupped her fingers around her almost empty glass and regarded her nails, the polish was chipped, the cuticles ragged, from their immersion in hot water and chemicals. With a sigh Ruth stretched out her legs, hooking a heel into the wooden strut of the bar stool. The boots, an expensive brand, were now looking decidedly past their prime. Once she would have not considered wearing anything as old. That was then, now there was no choice. Why had she turned her back on the security of her marriage to Neil? It was a question Claire had asked time and again.

At the far end of the bar a couple caught her eye. The man was doing something on his phone, the woman engrossed in what looked like a crossword in the newspaper. Closer another couple stood at the bar, their legs woven together, locked in conversation. As Ruth looked the girl put her head back and laughed at something her partner said, her eyes dancing with amusement, twirling a strand of hair around her finger.

Life with Neil had been like a tepid bath, dull and uninteresting. Of course, she had the security and a wonderful lifestyle, but there was no spark. Jago had seemed to sense the empty hole in her life. He was everything Neil wasn't, attentive, good looking and very, very sexy.

Having a horse was something that she had always longed for. To Neil, buying her one was no big deal, no doubt he wrote it off as a business expense. They had found Badger through a friend of a friend. For Ruth, it was love at first sight. Keeping him at livery was the only option though as there was no way she could keep a horse at the luxury apartment she shared with Neil. Park Hall, she had been told, was the best place.

Jago ran the yard and trained a succession of ladies who wanted to improve their riding skills. He was a brilliant teacher, kind, patient and very good at getting his message across.

Ruth rusty from long years of not riding, felt herself beginning to improve under his careful tutelage. One afternoon, after a lesson, she had led Badger into his stable. Jago as usual followed her in to help unsaddle the big, powerful grey horse. As she undid the girth Jago slid the saddle into his arms. He crossed towards the door as she moved in front of the horse to sponge down his sweat stains. They met in the middle. 'Sorry,' Ruth moved to the side. Jago however did not move. He put down the saddle and stood still. She waited, knowing what was going to happen, the inevitable after the tension that had been building up between them. Slowly he moved to kiss her. His lips were soft on hers, his hand moved to twine into her hair, his body moving against hers in a way that made her forget everything she had with Neil. One kiss and she was lost.

It was the first of many stolen moments in the stable after riding and then longer moments in the bed in the groom's apartment above the stable yard. Later came dinners out and even nights away. Neil did not even seem to notice. Or so she thought unti,l one night, letting herself quietly into the apartment after an evening out with Jago, Neil met her in the hallway.

There was something about the stillness in him that set alarm bells ringing. 'Have you had a good night?' he asked softly. He had never asked before, never seemed remotely interested and Ruth sought desperately to remember where she had said she was going.

'Lovely, thank you,' she said, buying time.

'You know you reek of sex?' he said quietly. And that had been the beginning of the end.

Jago, when faced with the knowledge she was single, very quickly side stepped out of the relationship. She had begged him to stay with her, pleaded for him to leave Zara. In response he had just laughed. Now she knew to Jago their relationship had just been a bit of fun. A typical bored, lonely housewife she had been easy prey to his slick charms. For that brief firework of attraction Ruth had paid the ultimate price. Her fall had been quick and as brutal as the life she now lived. A grotty apartment was all she could afford, paid for by a job as a care assistant, the only job she could get. She clung to Badger, as she clung to all the other hopes, that Neil might take her back, or that Jago would want her. And so she stayed, hating Jago more and more each day for what he had done to her. It bought her great pleasure to know he was dead and that he had died screaming and begging.

Chapter Thirteen

Miranda Dawson rested her forearms on the top of the fence which surrounded the glorious pastureland that belonged to Park Hall.

'I'm glad he's dead, Issy.' She laid her head on her arms and sighed. For a moment the two women stood in silent contemplation, looking at the horses, grazing peacefully. Beyond the paddocks the gardens, surrounding the house, were in full bloom. The blue and white of the police cordon tape clashed with the pink and purple heads of the delphiniums and the pastel shades of the roses. Behind the women, two days after Jago's death, the stable yard was still full of police.

Miranda glanced at the girl beside her and then looked away into the middle distance. Two horses grazed side by side at the far end of the field in front of the centuries old house which slumbered on regardless of the trauma going on around it.

'You don't mean that. You can't,' Issy's long pale hands gathered up the mass of dark curly hair that clouded around her face and attempted to pull it into the bright pink hair band she wriggled off one wrist.

'I do,' Miranda pushed herself away from the fence and stood upright. She rummaged in the pocket of her quilted waistcoat and pulled out a packet of cigarettes which she waved in Issy's direction. She took one and moved to the stone bench which rested in the shelter of the wall that bordered part of the gardens. Issy pulled a lighter from the pocket of her jeans and offered it to Miranda. 'What did you do the day he died?'

'It's not important.' Miranda met Issy's eyes.

A bee droned in the distance. Miranda released a long plume of cigarette smoke which mingled with the sweet scent of the honeysuckle and jasmine which sprawled over the wall.

'Please tell me you didn't kill him.' Issy was shook her head, dark eyes roving over Miranda's face.

'He deserved to die. He was a bastard.'

'But after everything he did you stayed here.'

Miranda snorted, her voice bitter. 'I stayed because I wasn't going to let him think he'd won.'

'I love Elite,' Issy said a moment later, breaking the tense silence that had fallen between them. 'He's such a beautiful horse.' Issy gazed longingly down the field at the two horses. Elite grazed side by side, with Lanson, Tamara Grey's stunning piebald. The horses picked at the short-cropped grass their faces almost touching. The sun sparkled on coats which were glossy with good health and grooming.

'Thank you.' Miranda dropped her head, focusing on her brightly polished leather boots. She exhaled a sigh of cigarette smoke. Elite was beautiful, but really it was madness to keep him. She should give him up, be sensible. 'I ought to sell him really, I can't afford him.' But even as she spoke she knew she would never give him up. 'I loved Elite from the moment I first saw him.'

She pictured the moment the huge horse box carrying Jago's new event horse had pulled into the yard. Everyone had stopped to watch the arrival of the horse Jago had spoken so proudly about. Even the other horses seemed to stare in awe at Elite as he was led down the lorry ramp.

Elite was jet black, he stood almost seventeen hands high and had been bred in Ireland. He was the perfect mix of Thoroughbred and Irish Draught. He had competed in Ireland and then been bought by Jago to event.

As Jago had predicted, Elite been the ultimate eventing machine, fast across country, accurate over show jumps and magnificent in the dressage arena. While everyone who kept their horses at Park Hall admired the huge horse from afar, Miranda had fallen head over heels with him. Her own horse, Dunmore, an elegant chestnut, who was a brilliant eventer, seemed to pale in comparison beside the majesty of Elite.

Miranda spent hours watching Elite. She had been thrilled when Jago he had asked if she wanted to ride him. After that nothing else mattered, her own horse was forgotten. Her heart and soul went into the magical Elite.

When Jago had asked if she was interested in buying Elite she had no hesitation in saying yes, even though he had asked an eye-watering price. But that didn't matter– all that mattered was that he was hers. She was going to ride him every day and compete on him. He was magical across country, as if he truly had wings, and there wasn't a fence he couldn't jump. Dunmore was the deposit for Elite and was sold on by Jago for a teenager to event.

'How stupid I was?' Miranda drew deeply on the cigarette, burning it down to the filter, 'Paying £40,000 for a bloody horse. A fool and his money are easily parted, my father used to say.' Miranda ground the butt of the cigarette viciously beneath the heel of her boot.

She'd been blinded by her desire to own Elite and her intoxicating friendship with Jago. She had just inherited half of her father's estate, enough money for her to invest in a business, to set her up for life. 'Jago saw me coming a mile off. First the horse then he asked me to be his partner in what he called an *amazing* business idea.' She raised her fingers in the air mimicking semi-colons around the word amazing. 'Everything has gone now.'

Miranda met Issy's eyes, hating the sympathy she saw there.

Jago had woven his web, sucking her slowly into a dream of huge profits from a property development scheme. She'd ploughed the remains of her inheritance into what she believed was a business partnership with Jago, into a company which were building holiday homes. The potential rental income he'd promised was phenomenal. Until he had told her the pair of them had been duped and that the land hadn't existed. He'd lost his money he had told her, she had no proof, but she was sure he'd taken hers deliberately.

It was hard to know which hurt more – his betrayal of her or the loss of her whole future. How had she not seen his sudden interest began once he had known about the money she had inherited.

Issy, her fingers burning from the smouldering cigarette butt she had forgotten she was holding, shook her head. 'He wouldn't do that on purpose.'

'He bloody did,' Miranda spat viciously, 'I trusted him.' The reality, she knew was she had been drunk with the excitement of his attention.

Issy chewed her lip nervously, 'He couldn't have. He wouldn't do that. I don't believe he'd be so cruel.' Issy gazed across the field towards the house where police cars came and went, large dark vans and the brightly emblazoned patrol cars.

'He stole that money from me,' Miranda said, bitterly, 'My Dad worked all of his life to leave that to me and I lost it. Every penny.' Miranda lit another cigarette. The stone bench, when she put the lighter down was warm from the sunlight. 'How could I be so stupid. So trusting. Naive.' she drew on the cigarette, pulling the smoke deeply into her lungs before exhaling in a long drawn-out sigh.

'My dad, was out working as soon as he left school, he worked in a shop, a small grocery on the edge of town and bought it from the owner when he retired.' Miranda was silent remembering the shop from her childhood, crammed with everything that a corner shop could stock. Her father had long hours building up the business, buying a second shop and then another. 'He worked so hard, with my mum. We hardly ever got chance to go away.' Miranda shook her head, remembering brief weekends on the coast, her father distracted, constantly looking for phone boxes to call the people who he had left in charge of the shops. His hard work had paid off and he had built up a small chain of shops. After leaving school she had gone to work for him.

And then her father had gone, two years after her mother was killed in a car crash. 'My poor Dad literally dropped dead in the middle of a meeting.' Miranda dashed away the tears that were beginning to spill down her cheeks. 'I was working in one of the shops when someone came to fetch me. I rushed to the hospital, but he was already dead.'

Issy put a gentle hand on Miranda's arm. 'I'm so sorry. It must have been horrible.'

'Thanks. My asshole of a brother was working with my dad. I'm sure the stress of dealing with Roderick contributed to his death.'

'He's older than you?'

Miranda nodded, 'Dad was barely cold in his grave before Roderick told me the business was to be sold and I'd be given my share.'

Her job had gone with the sale of the shops. The new owners hadn't wanted any of the original team to continue. Even with years of experience, finding a new role that paid properly had been virtually impossible.

'So soon after losing your dad and everything, you couldn't have been thinking straight when you invested in Jago's business.' Issy mused.

'I thought I was,' Miranda got to her feet and walked across the grass to lean on the fence again. 'I used some of it for a deposit for a house.' Being jobless hadn't mattered, she'd intended to start a business of her own. A small gift shop, perhaps a lovely coffee shop.

She'd bought a small, terraced house in the centre of Marazion. It was filled with the furniture that her parents had accumulated over their marriage, large dark solid practical pieces of wood and delicate ornaments she hadn't got the heart to throw out.

'Then I bought Elite off Jago,' Her voice cracked, betraying the bitterness that lay so close to the surface. 'And invested in his Spanish business idea.' Miranda pushed her fingers against the side of her jaw where the muscles ached with tension. She wanted to shout and rage at the sheer injustice of it, of Jago's betrayal of her. Instead, she bore the pain, let her hatred of him occupy every waking moment.

'He couldn't have known the business would fail. He couldn't,' Issy spread out her arms and opened her palms, 'Jago wouldn't have done that to you on purpose.'

'Don't be so fucking naive,' Miranda rubbed her forehead with her fingertips to try to ease the tension that furrowed the skin. She had to stop feeling so bitter, nothing was going to replace the money. Jago was dead, he had got his comeuppance, he had died screaming and it served him right.

'He knew I'd inherited that money,' Miranda fixed her eyes on Issy's concerned ones. 'Why else would he prey on me?'

'But…'Issy began again,

Miranda was silent, staring into space, trying to frame the thoughts that bounced and jostled in her mind. Were they half imagined truths and skewed facts? She cursed her stupidity and her trust of him. The betrayal hurt like hell. She had really believed that he had liked her, cared even and yet all the time he had been laughing at her, delighted at himself for having taken her money.

Why hadn't she seen through him, known that he was out to con her. He had stolen her future. All of her money had gone. Pride and grim determination had kept her alive. The anger she had felt had been like an uncontrollable animal rampaging inside her.

She'd kept Elite with Jago, determined not to show him how little money she had left. She had wanted him to believe the money he had stolen had been a drop in the ocean of the vast sum she had inherited. Stupid she knew. Pride. All because of her pride.

She'd found a job. It had started through desperation and an article she had happened to read in a magazine. Working at an escort agency had been the answer to her prayers, getting paid to go out for dinner. Then she hadn't even realised what the reality of the job was. She understood now.

'I need to go,' Miranda carefully arranged her face into a bright smile.

Issy got to her feet. 'Going anywhere nice?'

'Just out for dinner.' Miranda linked her arm through Issy's as they walked back towards the stables.

She was glad Jago had suffered before he had died. He was never going to laugh at her again, never going to crow over her trusting nature. He'd got what he deserved.

Chapter Fourteen

For someone who had grown up in the leafy suburbs of Surrey, Simon had an enormous affinity with the sea. He drove his battered pickup high onto the broad grass verge, turned off the engine and scrambled out, drawing sea-scented air deep into his lungs. He locked the vehicle, used to the threat of it being stolen, something that marked him out amongst the locals as an incomer. Shoving the key in his jeans pocket Simon pushed his way through a narrow gap in the undergrowth emerging the other side on a narrow footpath that wound between two hedges. He followed the footpath, the evening light dim beneath the branches that had grown so tall they had twisted together, forming a green arch above him. The soles of his runners padded quietly on the dust-dry earth.

At the far end of the path, he climbed nimbly over a wooden stile and dropped down onto grassland. Cows, huge black and white beasts grazed the land, masking the smell of the sea with their warm, farmyard odour. He paused, unsure of the threat they posed. One raised its head to watch Simon as he nervously skirted the edge of the field. He released a long breath, as he slipped through a gap in the tangled stone and briar clad Cornish bank into a second field, that sloped down to the sea. He slowed his pace, his heartbeat steadying as the ragged gasp of his breathing became more even.

Letting the camber of the hillside take him, Simon began to run, long legs raking over the ground as his feet sought and found purchase on the sheep trails that led like steps down towards the cliff edge. He stopped, close to the edge, the grass ending abruptly as the land fell away to a steep, rocky cliff. Hundreds of feet below the sea surged relentlessly onto the rocks.

With an ease born of practice, Simon swung himself off the edge of the cliff, dropping a few feet onto a path, which led down to the rocky shore below. He picked his way cautiously downwards, wary of the sea slicked rocks and the treacherous waves that pounded onto them. Halfway down to the sea, was his destination, a small, hollowed cave formed from years of storm-force tides lashing against the cliffs. Here, sheltered from the world, he lowered himself to a smooth rock, which made the perfect seat.

Alone he thrust balled up fingers into his eye sockets as if he could suppress the tears he had been holding in. 'Christ,' it hurt to speak, his throat was taut with tension.

He shook his head, trying to rid himself of the image that played itself on a loop in his mind. Jago, stretched on the bed, the coils of intestines looped around his legs, blood slowly dripping from the drenched mattress to pool onto the wooden floor.

Over the sound of the waves breaking on the rocks below him came the buzz of his mobile as a message came in. There was to be no escape, no peace to process what had happened the day Jago had died. 'Yes. Hi.' He brought the phone to his ear.

'It's me, Autumn. When are you coming home? Where are you? Are you alright?'

Simon nodded, levering himself slowly to his feet. 'I'm just down at the sea, I'll be home soon.'

'But *when* will you be home?' He could hear the beginnings of anxiety in her voice. He had the vague sensation of life flashing past while he was stuck in the horrific moment of Jago's death.

He walked back to the pickup, irritated that he hadn't told Autumn of his deep need to be alone for a while. He felt responsible for her, knowing if he was gone too long, she'd have a meltdown yet again.

She flung the front door open as he drove into the yard. While he loved the peace and isolation of the tiny cottage he'd bought, she found the quietness intimidating. 'Hi,' she ran out, flinging her arms around his neck before he had scarcely got out of the pickup. 'I've made dinner.' Autumn linked her arm into his as they walked the short distance to the cottage.

'You're a star, thank you.' Simon wished he had left her in the London suburbs where she belonged. He should tell her to go. Her love for him was claustrophobic.

'What is it?' She busied herself getting plates out of the cupboard as Simon undid the laces on his boots, easing his feet out.

'What?' He dug his fingers into the taut muscles of his shoulders, working at the tightness.

'You've been so distant, the last few days.' There was a needy, whine to Autumn's voice that set Simon's teeth on edge.

'What do you expect?' Simon met her eyes. They were a pale green, in the light from the kitchen window he could see hazel-coloured flecks around the pupils. 'After what happened with Jago, do you think I could be ....' he sought the word, 'normal?'

'Yes, of course, I know it must have been horrific.' Autumn began to ladle casserole into two dishes. 'I wish you'd talk to me about it.'

Simon pulled one of the dishes towards himself. He pushed a spoon into the mixture. His mouth watered with the delicious aroma of meat, wine and herbs. His stomach growled with hunger, but he knew no matter how hard he tried he could not eat.

'I will… just leave me be for a while.'

'I know how awful it must have been,' Autumn continued. 'You must be so upset. What a dreadful thing.' Her voice, filled with sympathy.

Simon glanced at her, seeing the longing reflected in her eyes, like a ghoul wanting to know all the gory details about Jago's death.

'I'm not.' Simon saw her head jerk up as he spoke. 'Not a bit upset that he's dead.'

'What?' her voice took a higher note.

'He was a bastard; the world is a better place without him in it.'

* * * * *

'Issy, don't take on so.' Issy lifted her head and looked at her mother with blank eyes. Catherine put a gentle hand on her daughter's head. The hair was silky smooth, heat radiating beneath her fingertips. 'You'll make yourself ill, crying so much.'

Issy blinked slowly, lowering her eyelids as though they were made of lead. She lay quietly, shivering despite the muggy heat of the late afternoon as her mother fussed around her. Catherine seized a rug that rested on the back of the sofa and draped it over Issy. 'There,' she spoke gently, a habit from looking after the nervous farm animals. 'You'll feel better in a while.' She tucked the rug around Issy's neck, pushing the folds of fabric around her back, lost in the face of the weight of Issy's grief she moved distractedly, driven by a need to keep going, anything other than sit still and face what was wrong.

'I'll make you some hot chocolate.' Catherine straightened up, pushing her fingertips into the small of her back to ease muscles taut with tension.

Issy nodded, her face scratching on the fabric of the sofa. 'Thank you.' Her voice was barely a whisper.

'Or would you prefer tea? Some hot milk?'

'Please, leave me alone. Hot chocolate is fine.' Issy, sat up blinking away tears. 'I'm sorry,' she lay down again as if the movement had exhausted all her reserves of energy. 'Just hot chocolate, please, Mum.'

Catherine busied herself in the kitchen, glad to be out of the oppressive atmosphere in the lounge and her helplessness to do anything to ease Issy's pain.

The pan of milk boiled and there was no choice but to make the hot chocolate and take it back to the lounge.

Issy had sat up and curled in one corner of the sofa, the blanket tucked around her legs as if it were the depths of winter rather than mid-summer.

'Here love, drink this, you'll feel better for getting something inside you.' Catherine handed the mug to Issy. She cupped her fingers around the mug, gripping it tightly as though she were afraid of dropping it.

Catherine lowered herself into an armchair. Long moments ticked by as the women sat in a silence broken only by the sound of Issy sipping the hot chocolate. In unison they glanced up to watch, through the window, as the cows came into the yard for milking. The low-slung farmhouse bordered the cobbled farm yard on one side, the other three sides were made up of buildings fashioned in pale stone which housed the milking parlour and farm buildings.

The sound of Issy's father shouts of encouragement came through the open window, as he drove the huge animals into the pen before they were milked. 'He's getting so he can't manage them on his own.' Catherine commented, her eyes flickering from the scene outside the window to come to rest on Issy.

Issy held her eyes for a moment before she dropped hers to look at the liquid in her mug.

'There's so much to do,' Catherine continued. 'The cows, calves, all the land.'

Issy released a long sigh.

'I know you like working away from me and your dad, but perhaps you'd think about helping out here.'

She shrugged, helplessly. 'I'll think about it. 'I loved my job. Things won't be the same at Park Hall without…,' The word died on Issy's lips.

Catherine's eyes roved over her daughter's stricken face. She was white, grey smudges blurred beneath her eyes where the mascara she had clumsily applied had been cried off.

'Loved Jago more like,' Catherine's voice was barely above a whisper.

Issy jerked her head up to meet her mother's eyes.

'I've been sick of watching you breaking your heart, running after him.'

'Well, I won't be doing that again. He's dead.'

Catherine clamped her mouth shut, her lips disappearing into a taut white line that split the lower part of her face. She had hated seeing Issy suffer at Jago's hands, knowing how much she had adored the man.

Issy dropped her eyes, she drained the last dregs of the hot chocolate and put the mug onto the table beside her. Her mother was right. She had adored Jago and hated herself for behaving like an eager puppy in his presence. She would have done anything for him, did do anything he asked. She had tried hard to get him to notice her, knowing he did not give her so much as a thought other than as a strong, willing workhorse, someone to do his bidding.

She had hated watching the other women, attractive, skinny, wealthy, confident, everything she was not. To them she was sure, she was a figure of amusement, someone who was barely worth acknowledging. Jago should have realised how perfect she was for him. She would never have left him, never nagged at him like Zara did. They had laughed at her, she knew. They mocked her, crouching and wringing their hands in a parody of Uriah Heap.

She had hated every one of the bitches. Of course, she never let on, as far as they knew she laughed at herself along with them. More than the women she had hated Jago. Her love for him, over the years she had worked at Park Hall, had turned from longing and admiration to pure hatred. He had brought his death on himself, though his actions. He should not have taunted her, should not have taken her love for him and used it against her.

She had suffered so much pain, each time he had snubbed her, or looked past her, or ignored what she wanted to say. She was glad he was dead. The world would be a better place without him. She would be happier, eventually. She knew it would take time to forget him, to find someone else to love.

Jago had let her down. He did not deserve someone like her. Someone kind and gentle, rather than the harsh, brittle bitches he chased, or the silly, fragile grooms who he drove away with his constant attention. He had deserved to die.

* * * * *

'Diamond, please stop being naughty.' Cindy Wainwright shook her head in annoyance as her fifteen-hand black and white hairy cob snatched its front leg roughly out of Sam's grip.

'It's a shame you're not a lady. He prefers women to men. Just a minute.' Cindy handed Sam Diamond's pink leadrope. 'I'll get him some of the gingernut biscuits he likes. He can have some for being such a good boy.'

Sam was aware of a tense muscle beginning to twitch under his left eye. Diamond eyed him balefully. He glimpsed Cindy's wide backside disappearing around the corner of the stable block and jerked on the leadrope. 'Stand still, you bastard.'

Diamond shot backwards snorting. 'Mess me around and I'll give you a reason to hate men.'

Cindy reappeared a moment later. 'He loves these. And they'll take his mind off what's happening.' Cindy took the leadrope nervously. Juggling the leadrope and biscuits she began to feed the portly gelding as Sam lifted its front foot again.

Diamond, pushing his not inconsiderable weight into the raised foot, leapt into the air. Cindy shrieked, running backwards out of the way of Diamond's hooves.

'Cindy, if you can't hold him I'm going to have to sedate him.' Sam gestured towards the bottle of horse tranquiliser which nestled amongst his shoeing equipment.

'He's afraid of needles.' Cindy was close to tears. 'The vet had a right job when he came to vaccinate Diamond. He's not being naughty, he's just afraid.'

Sam clamped his mouth shut tightly as if to trap the torrent of abuse he longed to unleash on Cindy and her wilful horse. There was nothing wrong with either of them that a good hiding wouldn't fix.

'Poor Diamond,' he said through gritted teeth, hauling Diamond's hairy leg up again. Not much longer and then he could stop. The life of a farrier was not for him. He was destined for better things. Sam banged the first nail in, his arm and back muscles screaming with the effort of holding the leg up.

Knee deep in mud, getting abuse from horses and their stupid owners was a way of life he had hated for years. He was sick of the dirt, of owners who were bossed and bullied by their horses and of the ache in his back which no amount of painkillers really seemed to get rid of.

Jago had stood for too long in the way of the life Sam wanted. But not any longer. He was gone. It was time for Sam to step into his shoes. Jago had been the king of the castle. A place he no longer held, he had been swept off, in a bloody, agonising tide of blood and guts. Sam was going to take his place. He had seen what he wanted, the path to a better life and had done everything he needed too to make sure he got his way. One day Zara soon would thank him for changing her life.

* * * * *

Zara ran a red tipped finger nail the length of the ice cold champagne bottle, before seizing the cork and easing it gently out. There was a satisfying pop, a whisp of champagne scented mist drifted into the air.

'Let's drink a toast.' Zara pushed chilled champagne glasses towards the four women who stood in front of her. 'One for you,' she poured the champagne. 'Ruth…Issy… Miranda… and Tamara… and for me.'

'Are we toasting Jago?' Issy asked, taking a small sip of her champagne and pulling a face etched with uncertainty.

'Of course,' Ruth said, taking a long swig of the liquid.

'He was a wonderful man.' Tamara smiled, lifting her glass and clinking it against the others.

'Absolutely the best,' Miranda drank deeply, running her tongue over her lips to savour every last drop of the champagne.

'I was so very lucky,' Zara made her way to the wrought iron garden chair and sat down, indicting with a wave of her hand that the others should do the same.

'I can't believe he's gone,' the words had become Issy's mantra, repeated to anyone who would listen.

'Well, he has, dear.' Ruth met Issy's eyes. A faint whisper of a smile turned up the corners of her mouth.

'Funny to think he won't be around anymore, with his charm and sense of humour.' Tamara pulled a long, dark horse hair from the front of her jodhpurs and let if fall to the ground.

'I'll definitely miss that.' Miranda drained her champagne and held her glass towards Zara who refilled it.

'He must have suffered terribly,' Tamara covered her mouth with her hand. 'In those last moments.'

'I can't think about it.' Ruth shuddered. 'What he must have gone through…'

'Poor man. Who could have done that to him?' Miranda wiped at a tear that rolled slowly down her cheek.

'Someone who really hated him.' Zara shook her head. 'Who could have hated him enough to have killed him like that?' Zara looked around the group, her eyes flickering over theirs.

'Why haven't the police caught anyone?' Issy's voice held a strident note.

'Who knows,' Miranda shrugged.

'They must be very clever to have got away with killing him and not getting caught.' Ruth puffed out her cheeks and released a long breath.

'Mustn't they just.' Tamara smoothed back a strand of her blonde hair, tucking it behind her ear.

'They'll have to keep investigating.' Issy swigged the remainder of her champagne as if were lemonade. 'They have to find out who killed him.'

When the reminder of the women were silent, Issy continued. 'They will, won't they? Find out I mean?'

Zara shrugged. 'We'll see. They don't seem to have a lot to go on at the moment.' She raised her glass, meeting the women's eyes, her gaze moving slowly from one to the other.

'No, they don't.' Agreed Tamara.

'Not a thing,' Ruth turned her mouth down and shrugged.

'Terrible really,' Miranda signed.

'Poor Jago,' Zara agreed, draining her glass.

Chapter Fifteen

'Tallis. Where are we with the Park Hall murder?' DCI Steve Cooper unwrapped a stick of nicotine chewing gum and popped it into his mouth. His battle with smoking was ongoing. Every few years he quit and then relentlessly would be drawn back into the lure of smoking. He chewed thoughtfully; his eyes fixed intently on the photographs Pete had pinned up.

Grace pushed herself up from the desk she'd been perched on. She moved to the front of the room, fiddling self-consciously at the stray strands of auburn hair that had escaped from her ponytail. She looked at the gruesome images of Jago Carey. She'd been looking at them for days now and the sight of Jago's brutalised body didn't get any easier. 'We've interviewed everyone at the farm. Apparently. No one saw anything.'

She turned to face Steve Cooper. 'We'll keep digging until we find out who killed him.'

''I want to get this solved,' Cooper tapped the images of Jago Carey's ravaged body. 'I want whoever did this brought to justice.'

'I'm going out today to see Mia Lewis.'

Steve Cooper stopped chewing; his focus directed at Grace.

Grace traced a finger across an ordnance survey map on the board, letting it rest close to Park Hall. 'Blackthorn Farm is next door. Maybe Mia, or Nan Hammett, saw something or know something. Maybe someone had a grudge against Jago Carey.' She studied the map for a moment, 'This is where we found the bodies of three victims of Mia's father, Eddie Hammett. Very close to the boundary of the two farms.'

Cooper rummaged in his jacket pockets, unearthed a shredded ball of tissue and spat the gum into it, replacing it immediately with another piece. 'Mia Lewis.' He spoke as it the words left a bitter taste in his mouth. 'Death and tragedy seem to follow that young woman.'

'What's the story with Mia Lewis?' Max ventured when silence fell over the detectives grouped at desks in the room.

As he watched Grace's eyes clouded, remembering the case. 'Her father, Eddie Hammett, killed her mother, Glanna Pendrick. Mia was born on the farm where he was keeping young women captive before killing them.'

Cooper continued as Grace paused. 'Mia was eight when she found one of the women and let her go. That was how we found out what he had been doing. He was an evil bastard.' He tugged at the knot of his tie, a sheen of sweat glistening on his forehead. 'As soon as he knew we were onto him he killed himself. We found the bodies of his victims at Blackthorn Farm. Other bodies were found some years later.'

Grace broke the silence that fell as Steve Cooper stopped speaking. 'Mia was in a car accident that killed her best friend, her adoptive parents were killed in a fire. She moved down here with her boyfriend to live with Eddie's mother, her grandmother. The old woman served time for covering up his crimes, although she's always denied knowing anything about them.'

Max released the breath he'd been holding in. 'Mia's had a tough life.'

'Oh, there's more,' Pete spoke. 'Her boyfriend went missing. Presumably committed suicide a few years ago. Appears to have jumped off the cliffs near Rosudgen.'

'We found his jeep, parked on the lane that leads to the coast path, and his phone on the path. We've never found his body.' Grace finished the story.

'Come on, Max time to meet the pair of them,' Grace unearthed the Land Rover keys from the pocket of her jeans. 'I want to talk to them, see if they know anything about Jago and what's going on at Park Hall.'

Leaving the detectives to work on the tasks she had assigned them, Grace strode from the briefing room with Max on her heels.

'Tell me more about the Blackthorn Farm case,' Max released a long breath, trying to relax as Grace powered the Land Rover around the narrow Cornish lanes. 'Mia was born in 1989, as Steve Cooper said, her mother was one of Hammett's captives. When she was eight she found Susie Carne, a young woman her father was holding prisoner and let her go. Eddie committed suicide when he realised we were onto him. I'd just been made a detective. Then about four years ago,' Grace's voice trailed off as she remembered the case that had made such an impact on her life. 'To cut a long story short, we found more graves in a field...'

Max braced his hands on the dashboard as Grace slammed the brakes on to avoid colliding with a SUV and caravan coming in the opposite direction. 'The field was close to the boundary between Blackthorn and Park Hall. I wonder why he picked that spot?'

Max shrugged. 'I guess we will never know. Access perhaps? Land that was easy to dig?'

'Strange though...' Grace mused pushing the vehicle into a higher gear.

'This place gives me the creeps,' Grace said a short time later as she steered the Land Rover in between the narrow gate posts that marked the boundary of Blackthorn Farm. 'So many women's lives ended here.'

As she drove into the yard Grace was silent. An eerie sea mist drifted around the buildings.

She wrenched open the Land Rover door and slid out, Max in her wake. In the greyness the old farmhouse and its cluster of low slung buildings would not have looked out of place as the setting for a horror movie.

'The terrible things that happened here.' Grace shook her head. 'Hard to imagine. It feels like the place has soaked up that pain and suffering.'

Max nodded. There did feel as if there were a deep foreboding presence in the very air they breathed.

Grace shuddered involuntarily. She hated Blackthorn Farm and everything it represented. How Mia could carry on living here was beyond her with the woman convicted of helping murder her mother. Mia had believed Nan, her grandmother when she had denied knowing what her son was doing.

Max and Grace stood together watching as a tall, slender young woman crossed the yard towards them.

'Hi, Grace.' Mia Lewis extended her hand.

'Mia,' Grace returned her greeting. Mia's hand as she took it was icy cold.

'You've come about Jago Carey, I assume.' Mia's eyes followed Grace's. The silence lengthened as the two women looked at the black car parked at the side of the yard.

'He's been missing so long now and still I can't bring myself to get rid of Tom's car.'

'You must miss him,' Grace met Mia's eyes.

'Of course.'

An elderly woman emerged from the farm house, her face an angry red, lips turned in on themselves. 'What do you want?' her voice held a hard edge.

'Morning, Nan.' Grace stretched her hand out to the woman, dropping it moments later when it was clear she was not going to take it.

'Nan, Grace has come about Jago Carey.'

Grace nodded. Nan gazed at the vast stone slabs that made up the yard, while Mia's gaze was locked on a spot just over Grace's left shoulder.

'You know of course that Jago was murdered, we're just talking to everyone in the area, in case you saw anything unusual, anyone around that stood out.'

'How would we see anything?' Nan's voice held a note of sarcasm.

Mia put a hand on Nan's arm. 'We didn't see anyone around.' Mia spoke softly, 'Poor Jago, he was such a lovely man.'

'It was a long shot,' Grace shrugged. 'Just in case…'

'That's fine.' Mia's face arranged itself into a smile.

'Any excuse and you're up here poking your nose into…'

'Nan.' Mia's voice was cold, silencing the older woman.

'Well, thanks for your help.' Grace was backing out of the yard towards the Land Rover.

Max nodded his farewell and followed Grace.

'Fuck,' he released a tense breath as the Land Rover bumped down the drive away from the farm. 'The grandmother is some piece of work.'

'Poor Mia,' Grace looked in the rear view mirror. The two women stood side by side in the farmyard watching the Land Rover leave. 'Tom, her boyfriend was so lovely. Her adoptive parents were too. There's been so much tragedy around her.'

Eventually the long and fruitless day drew to a close. At the evening briefing Grace tried to be enthusiastic. She'd hoped the case would have been solved quickly and easily, that a suspect would have been obvious. It was anything but.

'Go on, bugger off, I'll see you all at eight.' She turned away, looking at the board, her focus still on the victim and the people who had surrounded him.

'Night, boss.' Max trooped out of the room with the other detectives.

The countryside made him tense, the openness of it, the wildness, the animals, the silence. How anyone could possibly want to live out in this bleak, open space was beyond him.

He began to relax again once he reached the outskirts of the city where there were pavements, shops, pubs, civilisation. The sooner he could escape from Cornwall and head back to the city, the better in his opinion. The countdown app on his phone was slowly ticking down the days.

He parked the car beside his house, torn again between his love for the vast old house that he could never have afforded in a city and his desire to be back in a metropolis. As he drove into his parking spot he spotted a shadowy figure standing beneath a tree near his entrance. As always alert to danger he clocked the girl. She looked young, about seventeen or eighteen, neatly dressed in jeans with a dark-coloured coat. A wave of long hair hung half-way down her back, from beneath a sloppy hat pulled down over her forehead. 'Hi,' he said politely locking the car and walking towards his house. She smiled, watching him walk past. Probably a local girl waiting for friends he decided putting the girl out of his mind.

He dropped off his bag in the kitchen and then hungry, headed out, back into town. The girl was still standing beside the tree. He wondered momentarily if she had been stood up by her friends.

He began to run as the gun metal grey sky unleashed the rain it had been threatening for the last few hours. One of the reasons he had been tempted to come to Cornwall were the promotional posters he had seen dotted around the train stations in Manchester. They had portrayed endless sunshine. How wrong they had been, in his opinion it seemed to never stop raining.

Soon after his arrival in Cornwall he'd found a restaurant which had become a favourite of his just off the main street. At this time of the evening, it was usually quiet. The students that occupied it for most of the lunch time and the drunks who came to gorge after tipping out time were absent. In the early evening he knew he could get a table and sit in the relative peace with the newspaper, relaxing while he ate.

He ordered a burrito filled with spicy chicken, hot sauce and rice. Gratefully wrapping his hand around the cold can of beer the chef handed him, Max found a table at the back of the restaurant. With a sigh of pleasure, he spread out an abandoned newspaper, crumpled and stained after a day of use and began to eat. A movement made him look up briefly, the young woman from outside his house was standing at the food counter ordering a meal. He looked up as she collected her food, watching as she walked past his table.

Once back at his house he leant against the window, looking out unseen through the wooden slatted blinds. The girl was there again sitting on the bench opposite the house. She sat at one end, covered by an enormous red and black umbrella so big that the rain hit it and trickled off around her.

Why was she there? Was she waiting for a boyfriend or a work colleague? Her presence somehow made him wary. He was a copper for heaven's sake, what threat could a young girl waiting out in the rain pose? Ridiculous, she was just some girl, eating her food, in the rain. But still her presence unsettled him.

Chapter Sixteen

'I imagine I won't be seeing you anytime soon.' Kaden scowled in Grace's direction.

'I know, I'm sorry. It's a big case. I can't just work office hours. You know that.'

Kaden lifted his coffee mug to his lips. There was a damp circle on the surface of the pine kitchen table. He dipped a long finger into it, drawing the spilt coffee into the centre of the circle.

'It's always like this when my work is busy. We've been together long enough for you to know that.' A familiar knot of tension settled in the pit of Grace's stomach. She glanced around the kitchen, letting her eyes rove through the open door into the depths of the house. There was so much that needed doing, walls that needed plastering, old wiring that needed replacing. The task of renovating the house was monumental. It was too much for Kaden to take on the work of supervising the builders when he needed to focus on the stables. The house would have to wait until she was less busy.

Kaden was silent, his lips twisted into the angry expression Grace had become used to over the last few months. Buying the farm had been a mistake. The journey to it had been the dream, now they had arrived the reality was living in a mess, looking at a nightmare of tasks they needed to do before the house became a home, and not being able to have the time, or finances to do anything about it.

'I need to go.'

Kaden shrugged. 'See you later. Whenever you can spare the time. Good job I've got Rachel to help me.'

'Okay,' Grace grabbed her keys from the worksurface beside the front door. Sometimes he was like a sulky child. She loved him but hated the times when he resented her work.

After a moment, when Kaden made no reply Grace clamped her hand around the keys, feeling them dig into her palm, 'See you later.'

She didn't wait to see if Kaden replied, instead hauling open the front door. The old wood had swollen in its frame and when opened dragged against the stone tiled floor. It needed replacing, another thing to add to the list of essentials. Outside she breathed a lungful of fresh, salty air, relieved to be out of the oppressive atmosphere of the house.

'Morning,' Rachel called, hurrying across the yard, hauling fresh haynets towards the stables.

'Hi Rachel,' Grace scrambled into the high Land Rover seat. She watched Rachel enviously. How wonderful it must be to have no responsibility, to fill her day with caring for the horses and to go into her cottage at the end of it all, without shouldering the weight of a murder case.

Grace started the vehicle and steered out of the yard, her mind already filling with the case she needed to solve.

Her first port of call was a small café, tucked into an alleyway at the opposite end of the town to the station. She'd been in such a hurry to get out of Kaden's way that she hadn't had breakfast.

As she ducked into the alleyway she spotted a now familiar figure approaching from the opposite direction.

'Morning,' she smiled, raising a hand in greeting to Max. 'You've found my bolt hole.'

'I was going to say the same thing,' Max grinned, pushing the door open and standing to one side to let Grace walk in.

Grace breathed in the tang of a citrus aftershave. 'Best breakfast in Penzance.'

'Full English please,' Max led the way across the crowded café to the counter.

'Make that two,' Grace caught the eye of the slender woman who owned the café.

'Are you okay sharing a table?' Max glanced towards the solitary empty table.

'Yes, sure.' Grace squeezed between two smartly dressed businessmen sitting on adjoining tables to the one Max had indicated.

She sat down, easing herself into the narrow gap between the chair and the back wall of the café. Max perched himself on a vacant stool.

'Great, they're usually quick to bring out the food.' The table was half hidden from the rest of the café, tucked into a gap between a wall and the rail used for hanging coats. It felt illicit, as if they were hiding from prying eyes.

'How are you settling in?' Grace glanced around the room, it was unlikely anyone they knew would come in.

'Good, thanks.' Max stumbled over the words, hoping Grace wouldn't see the truth that lay behind his words. This morning, striking yet another day off the countdown app on his phone, buying mints in the corner shop he had walked into the girl who he had been sure had been following him the previous evening. The encounter had unnerved him, made a bad start to his morning.

'Do you think we've already interviewed our killer?' Max's voice was hushed as he leant towards Grace.

'They're a tight-lipped bunch,' Grace raised her eyebrows in warning as the waitress came towards them carrying two laden plates. 'We'll see how the alibis check out,' she continued as the waitress walked away. 'Gives me the creeps that Park Hall is so close to where Eddie Hammett lived.'

'This is the sort of case I've always wanted to be involved in. A big murder.' Max reached across the table for the sauce bottle and squeezed a liberal amount on the side of his plate. Grace nodded slowly, savouring a mouthful of the home-cured bacon the café was legendary for. 'I'm glad we've got something interesting to keep you occupied. Shame someone had to die though.' She met Max's eyes, seeing the eagerness that lay behind their kind depths.

Twenty minutes later Max jokingly elbowed Grace out of the way in his haste to get to the till first to pay for the food. 'My treat,' he said, firmly.

'Mine next time.' The words were out of Grace's mouth before she had time to check them. Her cheeks burned as colour flooded into them.

'I'll hold you to that.' There was an invitation in his voice.

'See you at the office,' Grace hurried away from the café, disconcerted by what she could see in Max's eyes, aware for the first time in a long while of a deep longing within her.

'Thanks for coming in everyone,' Grace stood beside the whiteboard, conscious of the gruesome images of Jago Carey pinned just beside her.

She glanced at Steve Cooper leaning beside the door, watching the briefing. As her eyes roved over him he unearthed a piece of chewing gum from the depths of his jacket pocket, popped it into his mouth and chewed rapidly. He was, she knew, struggling again with the urge to smoke. In the twenty or so years she had known him he had tried to kick the habit on countless occasions, each abandoned when the pressure of a case built up.

'Where are we on the case …? Anyone…?' Grace shifted her position slightly, moving so that Max, perched on one of the high stools, his jacket open to revel a blue shirt and smartly knotted tie, was out of her eyeline.

'Boss,' Rowena Lowe was the first to speak. 'I've been checking phone records. Jago's has nothing unusual, no calls that needed to be flagged.'

Grace nodded; it would have been very handy if there had been messages on his system with someone threatening to kill him. Someone immediately identifiable.

'But,' Rowena walked to the front of the room, a printed pile of phone records in her hand, 'What we did find were quite a few saved images, borderline porn, soft stuff, nothing illegal.'

Grace shrugged. 'Nothing none of the boys has got on their phones.' She raised her eyebrows, glancing around the room, grinning at the collective ripple of embarrassed amusement from the male detectives.

'Right, but there is something,' Rowena flicked through the pages, finding the one she was looking for and pushing it in Grace's direction. 'Here,' she ran a finger over a highlighted phone number, 'I doubt it's related but Tamara Grey has been in contact with an abortion clinic.'

'Can you follow that up with her. Discretely of course. Ron. How have you got on?'

'Right boss,' Ron's leisurely strides brought him to the front of the room. 'I've had a look at Jago's computer.' Ron raised his head, staring at the ceiling, hands thrust into the pockets of his trousers. For a moment he rocked backwards and forwards as though framing the words in his mind.

Grace was aware of her foot beating a tattoo on the tiled floor, wanting to hurry the ponderous detective. He had always proved himself to have a great deductive mind and was, she considered to be a fabulous detective, but his mind and body ran at a slower pace than everyone else's, something that irritated the hell out of her.

'And?' she prompted him.

'Like the phone,' Ron dropped his gaze from the ceiling to address his colleagues. 'Nothing on there that needs flagging. A few fairly soft porn, dollybird shots but nothing serious.'

'Fair enough.'

'But,' Ron dragged out the word, 'The tech team are still looking at both the phone and computer just to see if there's anything else we might have missed.'

'Good work.' Grace let her eyes rest on Mike Smith the detective Steve Cooper had drafted in from Truro, to help with the workload.

'I've been looking at police records for everyone connected with Park Hall.' Mike made a move to stand up, then seemed to change his mind and addressed the team from his desk. 'Just the usual, minor offences, parking tickets ...' Mike flicked through the papers in front of him. 'But,' he said, finding the paper he was looking for, 'Sam Green has a conviction for assault.'

'Interesting,' Grace let her eyes flicker over the photographs of everyone who had been on the yard at Park Hall the day Jago had been killed. 'Anything else?'

'Boss,' Pete got to his feet. 'I've been looking at the alibis.' His voice trailed off with a dramatic flourish as if he were a magician about to do an audience stunning trick.

He crossed to the front of the room, buttoning the jacket of his smart suit as he walked. 'He,' Pete tapped the image of Michael Alderton, the vet, 'said he left the yard to deal with an emergency. The farm he said he went to say he wasn't there. They didn't have any emergency.'

Grace raised her eyebrows, glancing at the pleasant looking image on the board. What secrets lay behind his eyes?

Pete, now with everyone's attention, continued. 'Tamara Grey said she was riding in the woods. The other two women, Ruth Watson and Miranda Dawson have collaborated her story.

There was a collective murmur of interest. Pete moved further along the board, tapping another image with a finger.

'Miranda Dawson said she had stopped for ice cream on the coast trail and her horse had been given water by someone who works in the café. No one has any recollection of a horse and rider being outside. However, Tamara and Ruth have both said she was out riding, that she met up with them and they all came back to the yard together.

Grace frowned. All three women were backing one another up. Were they all lying?

'Ruth Watson also said she'd been through the woods.' Pete continued.

'And everyone backs her up.'

Pete nodded. 'Issy Jordan's story seems to check out.'

'About time one of them told the truth,' Ron made a sucking noise through his teeth.

'Go on Pete,' Grace interrupted the hum of noise that followed Ron's comment. 'Sam Green was trimming horses with Issy, so they've provided alibis for one another.'

'Handy,' Mike's voice dripped sarcasm.

'And Simon O'Connor,' Pete tapped the image of the curly haired man, 'He was working in the gardens. He found the body.'

'Is he our man?' Mike asked, glancing around the room.

'We've a bit of work to do yet before we know who is responsible.' Grace released a long breath, contemplating the huge amount of work that lay ahead of them all.

Pete reached the final image. 'Zara Carey seems to have been where she said, one of her shops is in Truro, the staff there have said she came in. Although we haven't checked the police cameras yet to see if we can find her vehicle anywhere.

'So, Grace turned to look at the images, eight faces started back at her from the photographs. 'We seem to have eight suspects, all of whom are lying.'

Chapter Seventeen

'I hate funerals.' Grace released a long sigh. 'I'd better get changed.' Grace shouldered the leather overnight bag she had slid into the space beneath her desk and headed towards the station bathrooms.

Every eye in the office turned to look as she returned a few moments. Instead of her usual jeans, she wore a smart, neatly fitted suit, a dark jacket that accentuated her narrow waist and a skirt that skimmed her hips and fell neatly just below her knees. She had, Max noticed with appraisal, great legs, elegant calves and narrow, finely boned ankles. She'd slid her feet into high dark shoes and piled her hair neatly on top of her head, although stray tendrils of her auburn hair were already escaping and falling onto her face.

Max got to his feet, conscious of a longing to stare at her. Instead, he fixed his eyes at a point on the wall.

'Will you drive?' Grace handed him the key to a pool car, 'I hate driving in heels.'

'Sure, be my pleasure.'

When they arrived thirty minutes later, the area outside the village church was already packed with cars. Max found a parking space, on the grass verge a short distance away. They joined the crowd of people making their way towards the church. Everyone, it seemed had turned out for Jago's funeral. A tragedy always drew more spectators, everyone wanted to witness the drama. Murder victims were always guaranteed a big turn-out at their funerals.

Grace shivered in the biting wind that whipped through the churchyard, setting the long grasses on some of the untended graves dancing. 'Be warmer over here.' Max led the way to a sheltered spot in the leeward side of the church where they could watch the proceedings without their presence being too obvious.

'Be interesting to see who comes,' she whispered, in her high heels Grace's lips were level with Max's ear. Grace let her eyes rove over the faces.

Killers often had a bizarre desire to be involved in the crime as much as possible, whether to gloat, or just to see who far the police had got in their investigation. After a few moments she had picked out the people who were at Park Hall the day Jago died.

Ruth Watson stood alone beside the church gate. Grace watched as she shivered, pulling her coat tighter around her chest, gazing up the road looking for the hearse. She held a long umbrella in one hand which she twirled around in her hand, her feet moving as if she could not stand still.

Tamara Grey clung to the arm of her handsome husband, casting admiring glances at his face which was turned towards her, concern etched in every line. She was elegantly dressed in a long pale grey coat with a fur collar that framed her pretty face. From across the road Grace could see the whiteness of her knuckles as they clutched a very expensive looking handbag.

Miranda Dawson stood amongst the crowds, her face deep in the shadow of the broad brimmed hat she wore. As Grace watched she withdrew a mobile from her pocket, tapping hurriedly on the screen.

On the edge of the crowd stood Sam Green the farrier, his dark hair slicked back from his forehead. The tweed jacket and dark cord trousers sat uneasily on his wiry frame as if he were completely unused to being out of his old jeans and checked shirt. He shuffled from one foot to another as though the ground was boiling beneath him.

'The vet is over there,' Max nodded in the direction of the gravestones.

Michael Alderton stood with a tall, dark haired, sour looking woman whose lips were pursed with distaste as if she would rather be anywhere but here. He was looking at a couple walking up the uneven church flagstones. Grace followed his eyeline the woman was blonde, elegant, eye catching, her husband well built with a mop of dark hair. Grace realised with a jolt the vet was not looking at the woman but instead looking intently at her male companion.

'Hi,' Grace turned to see who had touched her arm. Rachel stood close by, her dark hair scraped back off her face, 'Kaden brought me. He's over there.' She pointed towards a group of people standing on the road outside the graveyard. Grace met her husband's eyes and lifted her hand in acknowledgment.

Rachel fumbled in her coat pockets, unearthing a tattered looking tissue which she used to wipe her nose. 'Such a nice man. So good with horses.'

'Yes.' Grace smiled gently at the younger woman.

'I hate funerals,' Rachel shuddered, 'Not that I've been to many, just my Mum's.'

Grace nodded, distracted, wishing that Rachel would go away, she needed to focus on the gathering crowds to see who stood out as unusual. Somewhere, something in Jago's life held the clue to who had killed him.

It began to rain, gentle drops falling at first, everyone hunched their shoulders, trying to ignore the shower, but gradually the drops became heavier and more insistent. 'Great summer,' a woman's voice complained bitterly.

Max abandoned his post beside Grace and ran to his car for an umbrella. The mourners stood inside the lee of the church, or huddled beneath the shelter of the vast yew trees that were scattered about the graveyard.

'I'm going to talk to Issy,' Rachel touched the back of Grace's hand with icy fingers.

Max returned with the umbrella holding it up over Grace so that she could gaze out and look at the mourners who were still arriving.

She watched Rachel ease her way through the crowd, picking out Issy Jordan who burst into tears as Rachel reached her. Beside her, Simon O'Connor said something to Rachel who shrugged.

'I can hear them coming,' someone said. Grace strained her ears. Above the sound of the howling wind she could hear the sound of horse's hooves faint at first but growing louder as they neared the church. There was an audible gasp of admiration as the funeral hearse came into view, pulled by two huge prancing Friesian black horses, harness jingling, brightly polished, behind them in the hearse, adorned with masses of flowers, was Jago's coffin.

As the horses pulled up outside the church Grace could see that no expense had been spared, even in death Jago had the best of everything. One of the horses neighed, its neighbour tossed its head, long mane dancing in the wind. Behind the hearse, a sleek black funeral car came slowly down the road. It came to a stop beside the church gate.

A sudden hush fell over the graveyard, broken only by the sound of the wind whipping the leaves of the yew trees and the rain falling heavily on the tops of umbrellas.

The driver opened the back door and stood back. Zara emerged, clad in black, complete with a dramatic black hat with a veil that swept over half of her face, leaving only her bright red painted lips visible. Beside her was an older man who Grace assumed was her father, or perhaps an older brother. He looked frail and leant heavily on a stick.

Grace did not recognise any of the pall bearers who shouldered the coffin. One was a younger version of Jago, the others she did not recognise, she watched them carefully. Wondering what secrets they harboured.

Zara walked slowly up the path to the church, turning her head to nod and smile wanly at people. At the church porch she paused, turning to wait, inclining her head slightly in reply to something the older man said to her.

The coffin was brought into the church, the pall bearers walking slowly and carefully up the uneven path. The rain bounced off the coffin, and the bouquets that adorned it.

As the coffin entered the church the mourners began to hurry into the church, eager to get out of the rain.

'Come on. We'll watch the service.' Grace led the way, following the mourners.

It seemed to take forever until everyone had shuffled into the church, their footsteps hushed on the maroon carpet that stretched the length of the aisle. Pews creaked as people sat down. Someone blew their nose loudly, another coughed.

Finally, a relative hush descended, broken only by the sound of Zara's sobbing. Out of the gloom beside the alter, the vicar emerged, and the service began.

As the funeral mass ended the vicar, speaking for Zara, invited the mourners to attend the reception at the house.

Max looked at Grace questioningly, 'We may as well go to the house,' she whispered.

The service came to an end. The coffin was taken to the graveyard, Zara walked beside it, one hand clutching a corner, as if she could not bear to be parted from her husband.

During the service the rain had stopped and the wind died down. The sun emerged from behind the grey clouds. Coats were stripped off and draped over arms as the temperature climbed. ''Summer and winter all in one day,' an old lady complained bitterly, rolling her eyes in the direction of her companion.

Keeping to the periphery of the crowd Grace and Max watched as the coffin was slowly lowered into the ground. Zara visibly sagged, her knees buckling. Two middle aged men, who had shouldered the coffin supported her.

Michael Alderton, Grace noticed was still gazing with interest at the dark haired man. Issy was sobbing uncontrollably, Rachel's arm around her shoulder. Sam Green was watching Zara. Simon O'Connor's face had a grey tinge to it. Grace could see his throat working as if he were battling the urge to vomit. She scanned the faces around the graveside and saw the pleasure reflected in Miranda, Ruth and Tamara's faces.

'Hope there's plenty to eat, I'm starving.' Max said, a short time later, steering the car between the stone pillars that stood at the bottom of the driveway at Park Hall.

The area in front of the house was packed with cars, most of the people who had attended the funeral, were there. Grace and Max followed the crowd into the house, it was the first time they had been inside since telling Zara that Jago had been murdered. The house was filled with flowers and sympathy cards. In the dining room a vast table was spread with food, uniformed waitresses walked around with trays of drinks handing them around to the mourners.

Zara seemed to have very quickly cast off the role of the devastated wife, Grace thought watching her over the rim of her glass as the widow seized a glass of wine from one of the waitresses and took a long slug from it.

The rooms buzzed with chatter. Grace stood beside Max, watching people's faces, as they circulated, groups forming and breaking apart while amongst them all the waitresses dashed red faced and flustered.

An hour later the crowds began to thin. 'We'd better get back,' Grace stacked some discarded plates together on a side table to make room for her empty glass. 'I'll just find the loo.'

Grace made her way slowly up a wide staircase to a large airy landing. A pale green carpet stretched in either direction. Grace wandered down one of the corridors. There had to be a bathroom somewhere. She could hear voices, hushed and low, one male and one female one. Grace tracked the sound getting closer to its source. She stopped outside one of the doors, voices came from behind, one was Zara, the other a man whose voice she was not sure she recognised.

She continued, finding and entering a vast bathroom. As she emerged the door where the voices had been behind opened. Grace stood, half hidden in the doorway to watch. Zara came out, rubbing her lips together as though she had just applied lipstick and running her hand around the collar of her blouse as if to ensure it was laying correctly. Zara went downstairs. As Grace watched bedroom door opened again and Sam emerged. He smoothed down his dark hair, stuffing hands into the pockets of his jacket before following Zara downstairs.

Chapter Eighteen

'Another glass of wine, darling?' Michael got to his feet, taking his wife's empty glass.

'Thank you darling,' she glanced in his direction over the top of her glasses, before going back to the book she was reading.

He poured a generous amount into her glass. One more and hopefully she would drop off to sleep.

'There,' he handed her the glass. 'You look shattered.' He lowered himself into the armchair opposite his wife.

'I really am.' She took a long slug of the wine.

Michael watched her throat move as she swallowed. Soon…

He sipped his own drink, whiskey, with a lot of water. He forced a breath into lungs that were taut with tension, fraught with the need to get away. Just a short time longer and she'd make the inevitable yawn and head up to bed. She slept so soundly now she wouldn't hear him come back, not that she seemed to care anyway. She wouldn't know whether he was out on a call, or not.

He sat back down in the squashy leather armchair, picking up the latest copy of the vet's magazine and stealing a glance at his watch. Almost nine, how much longer would he have to wait until she went to bed and he could head out into the night?

* * * * *

The chill air in her flat lay like a damp blanket around her shoulders, Ruth her hair still wet from the shower shivered. Heat, like everything else at the moment was a luxury, her wages were so little that they barely stretched to food once she had paid her rent. Heating was something that she used only in emergencies. Gingerly she picked up the clothes she had discarded when she had returned from her shift. Holding them at arm's length she carried them into the tiny bathroom and dropped them into the laundry basket. The white short sleeved top she wore beneath her overall lay at the top, the yellow stain uppermost. The carrot and potato puree that Eddie Lambowe had thrown at her had penetrated the nylon overall. She had tried to scrub it off but had only succeeded in spreading it more. The remainder of the day she had completed her duties with a large orange patch over most of her front.

Ruth sighed, what a way to make a living. She moved to the bathroom mirror and gingerly touched her cheek. Already the bruise was coming out, the skin turning from a bright angry red to grey. The old bastard had lashed out as she removed the cloth she'd put around his neck while he ate. He had dementia, they said, he doesn't mean to lash out. Ruth doubted that, there seemed to be real intent in his eyes when he had done it. 'Fuck you,' she whispered, echoing the words Eddie had spat as the back of his hand made contact with her skin. 'Fuck you, Jago.' It was his fault she was in his position. He might be dead and now buried but she could never forgive him.

* * * * *

Sam arranged his face into what he hoped was an expression of interest. It was amazing how easy it was to zone out so he didn't hear Fiona speaking any more. 'And I need to repaint the bathroom, so you'll have to give me money for…' he let her words float away. He took a swig of his beer, savouring the taste of the ice-cold liquid, at least that was one thing she was good at, keeping the fridge well stocked.

He should tell her to shut up. The last thing a man wanted when he came home was to have to listen to a woman going on and on about this and that. He heard enough of them during the day, moaning about their husbands and their horses until he felt that his head was going to burst, stupid bitches.

'So can we go tomorrow afternoon and pick the paint,' her strident voice pierced his thoughts.

'Yeah, of course.' He got up. He had to get out of the room, away from her before he said something he would regret. 'I'll be outside.' He said. 'Got to load the van ready for tomorrow.'

Outside the air was fresh, the faintest tang of the sea blowing into the yard. Sam leant against his van, staring out over the fields that surrounded the cottage he shared with Fiona. On the horizon, its spire just visible above the trees was the churchyard where Jago had been buried. He was gone. Forever. Nothing stood in Sam's way anymore. Soon he would be able to leave Fiona and move into Park Hall with Zara. He'd wanted to be with her after the funeral, but she had sent him away. 'Not yet,' she had said, repairing the lipstick he had tried to kiss away. That bitch of a detective had seen him leave her room, he was sure of that. He didn't care. What did that prove. Let her think what she liked.

* * * * *

'Damn that traffic,' Patrick burst in through the front door, his arms full of flowers, the strap of his leather overnight bag slung over his shoulder, 'What a nightmare of a drive. I'm going to take the overnight train next time.' Tamara went into the hall, her heels tapping on the wooden flooring and slid into his outstretched arms. Even in heels he still towered over her. She breathed in his citrus aftershave, the skin on his cheek was smooth and warm against hers. She leaned into him, loving the feeling of his arm around her waist as he drew her towards him to kiss.

'Those are for you,' he said, pulling away slightly to hand her the enormous bunch of pink roses. 'Dinner is ready.' Tamara led the way into the kitchen, smiling as Patrick breathed in appreciatively savouring the warm, meaty odour of pasta and meat balls.

Patrick pulled out one of the tall stools that stood beside the marble topped breakfast bar and inclined his head in thanks as Tamara handed him the glass of wine. 'I'm worn out,' Patrick's voice held a note that Tamara recognised. He was not in the least tired, but rather was hoping to take her to bed.

'Perhaps you should take the train next time,' Tamara deliberately misinterpreted the implications of his words. The last thing she wanted was to go to bed with him. She had been on tenterhooks hoping he wouldn't want sex. How could she let him see her body? She was still bleeding. She had to keep her body hidden from him, for a while longer anyway.

'I'm not that tired,' Patrick took Tamara's hand and pulled her gently towards him.

'I know, I'm sorry.' Tamara eased herself out of his arms, letting the tears fall. 'I'm still so shaken about what happened to Jago.'

'Of course, you are, I'm sorry.'

Tamara glanced at her husband, seeing the hurt at her rejection in his expression.

Just a few more days, that was all she needed and then she would be free of Jago and his influence on her life.

* * * * *

Miranda tried to ignore the splodge of mayonnaise that had collected at the corner of his mouth, but whatever she tried to look at, his tie, loud and cheap, his shirt, straining at the buttons, his eyes, firmly fixed on her breasts, nothing could hold her attention and she found her eyes drawn relentlessly back to it. She leant forwards, giving him the full benefit of her chest, cleaved together with a Wonderbra, his mouth opened, revealing a row of grimy uneven looking teeth. 'How long are you going to be in town for?' she asked, working her way slowly through a patter she had developed, enough chat to make him think she was interested, not enough to panic him about the family and wife he had left at home somewhere. It helped if she told herself she didn't have to do this, she didn't have to sleep with him, not if she really didn't want too.

The man put down his knife and fork with a clatter against the dinner plate. His eyes raked over her. 'I've got a room here if you'd like a nightcap.'

Miranda swallowed as the silence lengthened. She forced a smile, which he took for agreement.

His chair almost fell over backwards in the man's eagerness to leave the table. Only the swift intervention of the waiter stopped it. 'This way.'

She was aware of his rapid breathing, as he followed her along the corridor. She should leave, take Elite from Park Hall, sell her house, pay off the mortgage. Now Jago was dead there was nothing to prove to him, or anyone else. There was a world of possibility now he was gone. Soon…

* * * * *

Issy crouched beside Jago's grave. The flowers laid by those who had attended his funeral were already beginning to wilt. She let her fingers drift over the handwritten cards attached to the flowers, reading the messages of sympathy. What hypocrites they all were. Pretending to care, pretending they were sorry he was gone, that they were sorry for Zara and her loss. She hated every one of them.

Issy found the flowers she had brought, they were half buried beneath the huge bouquet Ruth had laid on his grave. Her own bunch, delicate blue cornflowers and pale rose heads, mixed with the white dog daisies she had picked from the gardens at Park Hall were his favourites. She pulled one of the roses from her bouquet, bringing the head to her nostrils she breathed in the scent that remained. She stood, holding the rose. She would take it home, press it in one of the scrapbooks she had of Jago's eventing career. She would never forget him. She was the only one who had truly loved and understood him.

* * * * *

Simon stopped. He moved into the shelter of one of the trees and stood, waiting, listening. He had been sure he could hear voices. Once he was sure it had been his imagination he moved on, the soles of his boots making no sound against the thick bed of leaf mould that made up the forest floor. He was so deeply into the forest it was almost dark, the leaves making a canopy that almost blocked out any daylight. Here, the branches grew almost into one another making it impossible to walk upright. He crouched, pushing his way through, the branches scraping loudly on the back of his wax jacket. He lifted an arm to protect his face, wincing as the thorns from a briar tore his skin.

The trees ended abruptly. He stood upright finally. A short distance away was the dark, still water of Foxes Lake, named generations ago for the previous landowners. He listened again, waiting for any sound which would alert him to the presence of anyone around. There was nothing except for the listless noise of the uppermost tree branches, creaking in the breeze. Reaching into the depths of his jacket Simon slowly withdrew a crumpled plastic bag. Bile stung the back of his throat as his empty stomach heaved. With a hand that visibly trembled he opened the bag and peered into its blood-stained depths. There at the bottom, amidst the flaking slivers of dried blood was the knife that had killed Jago Carey.

He withdrew it, looking at the long blade, stained rust coloured with blood. He wiped the handle with a cloth he had tucked into the pocket of his jeans for the purpose and then, swung his arm as far back as he could and released it. The knife arched through the air and landed with a barely audible splash in the centre of the lake. For a moment it was visible, shining through the water until a moment later it sank into the darkness and was lost from view. Simon, barely able to breathe, sank to his knees. What the hell had he done?

Chapter Nineteen

eeks after the funeral Michael's constant feeling of relief was unimaginable. Jago was dead. Buried. The bastard had got what he deserved. Michael closed his study door behind him and took a deep appreciative breath.

This was the room he felt most comfortable in. His room. It looked out over gardens laid out two hundred years ago by a famous landscape designer, whose name always seemed to elude him. The gentle rolling acres of acres of manicured lawns were broken by only lines of colourful shrubs and bordered by a deep, long herbaceous border. Everything was kept in check by a gentle, quiet elderly gentleman who Julia eluded too only as 'The lawnmower man.' His wife, 'Mrs Mop,' who was equally quiet and humble, toiled daily in the house to keep it neat, clean and smelling of lavender polish. Michael sometimes wondered if Julia even know what Jed and Susan's real names were.

Julia's stamp was over the whole house, in the expensive furniture, the paintings he knew cost a fortune. He thought they looked dull and bland. He assumed they had been painted by a notable artist and would undoubtedly appreciate in value. The house was filled with antique furniture and ornaments as if it were the setting for a feature in an interior's magazine. He had no love for the house, his taste would have been for something bright and airy, filled with light. But he'd learned over the years there was no point in arguing with Julia.

This room though was his own, apart from the moments when 'Mrs Mop' came into clean.

His study, as Julia named it, was the room where he could relax. There was a leather wing backed armchair, positioned to look out over the gardens, the perfect spot in which to sit and read. Julia had picked it, but at least it had a masculine air. He loved his desk too, the vast expanse of leather topped mahogany with a modern office chair, this too had a view of the gardens. In quiet moments he marvelled at his good luck.

It was to this room he could escape from Julia's constant carping and be alone with his thoughts and his laptop, password protected of course.

'I'll come and see you soon,' he said, into the landline handset. In the ear piece he could hear the sound of a television, some awful day time show and strident voices, the clatter of crockery, the backdrop to his mother's existence in, thanks to Julia's not inconsiderable money, a very nice nursing home.

'Yes love, I know how busy you are, be great to see you any time,' her northern accent was clear over the phone, one he had worked very hard to lose. They both knew it was a lie, he rarely found the time to visit. It was something he regretted constantly, but it was difficult to get away from work and when he did, he had his own things to do. He ended the conversation, feeling guilty as always.

'Dad, we need to go,' Danny's voice was muffled through the heavy wooden door.

'Just be a minute,' Michael jumped as his phone vibrated in his pocket. He pulled it out, looking at the message on the screen. '*See you later?*'

'*Hope so,*' Michael quickly tapped back before deleting the message and sliding the phone back into his pocket.

Danny was sitting at the bottom of the stairs.

As always Michael was awed by how he and Julia could have created something as wonderful as Danny. He was the best part of both of them, with Julia's perfect oval face, which made him very good looking though certainly not feminine. His eyes were Julia's too, grey, the pupils lined with black that only seemed to highlight their incredible beauty. Danny's shock of dark hair was all Michael's as was his bright, intelligence and love of science. At fourteen he was becoming a man, the first fuzz of soft downy hair beginning to show on his face.

'Come on Dad,' Danny said getting to his feet. His voice was beginning to break, the last stage in losing his childhood.

'Come here,' Michael said as Danny stood up. Standing on the bottom step of the wide staircase he was as tall as his father. Michael looked him in the eye as he straightened the silver and burgundy tie he wore, 'Better make you look presentable.' Satisfied he swept his hands over the shoulders of Danny's burgundy blazer removing imaginary stray hairs.

'Finally. We're ready,' Julia appeared at the top of the stairs, immaculate as always. Her hair, coloured to hide odd the grey strand she had been horrified to find, was neatly blow dried into a bob that framed her perfect face.

Michael hated the heavy makeup she used, but she knew how to make the dark eye liner frame the shape of her eyes. A slash of dark red lipstick highlighted her wide, generous mouth. She was, as always, beautifully dressed, with a bright blue dress that Michael knew she had chosen to accentuate her shape. Over the dress she wore an understated but obviously expensive grey jacket the same colour as her shoes and the handbag she carried. Conservative and discrete jewellery completed the look, making her look elegant and yet up to date. A woman he could be proud of. She came down the stairs towards the father and son, and then, together they walked to the front door.

Mrs Mop was polishing the mirrors, a seemingly endless task that kept her occupied for hours, upstairs and downstairs. Julia said they caught the light and made the house seem brighter. Michael was sure she had bought them so that she could admire her reflection.

'Oh, you do all look lovely,' Mrs Mop crooned, watching as Michael opened the door for Julia, 'Thank you…' Julia inclined her head in a regal gesture. For a moment Michael was sure she was going to say Mrs Mop. The older woman smoothed her overall over puffy knees. Michael wondered if the cleaner had considered curtseying. Julia, he knew, would have accepted this gracefully.

The lawnmower man was not so sycophantic and barely glanced up from the herbaceous border he was half buried in. He glanced up long enough to meet Michael's eye and nod briefly in his direction. Michael wondered, if their gardener could see through the elegant charade they presented to the outside world.

Michael's work car was not considered, by Julia to be suitable transport for the family and so they travelled in Julia's silver Mercedes. Michael driving of course. He swept down the drive, fingers gripping the wheel, waiting for Julia to start emitting small, barely audible gasps of horror at his driving. The first shudder came early as he passed through the stone pillars that marked the end of the drive; in her opinion he had driven too close to the stonework.

Danny, he noticed, looking in the rear-view mirror had his earphones firmly jammed in his ears clearly not wanting to listen to his mother's nagging.

The entrance to Solus school was as impressive as the eye watering fees they charged for the pleasure of teaching the sons of the wealthy and well-connected. Michael steered the car between stone eagle topped pillars and parked in between a brand new Range Rover and a top of the range Porsche.

'Is your phone turned off?' Julia gave a small laugh, as Michael locked the car, 'We don't want to be interrupted in the middle of the prize giving by someone with a dog who has a sore paw,' she spoke lightly, making a joke of it, but her meaning was clear.

'Yes,' God forbid he would do anything to embarrass her in front of the local gentry.

Danny spotted some of his friends and walked away to join them.

Julia slipped her arm in Michael's. Her vision was complete, wealthy vet and his elegant wife. How different the reality was.

They walked together up the low stone steps into the cool entrance hall of the school which smelt of damp stone and teenage boys, overlaid with the school dinner smell of mashed potatoes and cabbage. Julia smiled and waved at acquaintances, Michael did the same, recognising some of his wealthy farmer clients and indulgent pet owners.

Their names, and Danny's had been stuck onto chairs that lined the school hall, their front seats an indication of their standing in the community. No being shoved out the back for them, they were pillars of local society, looked up to and respected.

Danny, having prised himself away from his friends came to take his seat beside them. Julia rewarded him with an indulgent smile, at fourteen he knew that meant he had better not go off again. He was the perfect accessory to complete her elegant charade.

Once all the parents had assembled and silence gradually fallen, the school head took his place on the stage.

'I'd like to welcome everyone here this afternoon,' he said, casting a proud eye over the upturned faces, 'This is one of the highlights of our social calendar, the prize giving where we see who has done well, who has improved, see the stars of the future before they head off to university.' As he rambled, Michael let his mind wander, briefly. Julia would soon dig him in the ribs to jolt him back to attention.

The prize giving began, boys bounding lightly up the steps onto the stage to be presented with awards for academic and sporting achievement, their well-cut suits and smart haircuts a testament to their parent's care.

Danny had won a prize for the best result in one of his exams. He beamed from ear to ear as he ran up the steps to take his trophy, holding it in the air like an actor receiving an Oscar. Michael never failed to marvel at the difference between his education and that of Danny's. His son would undoubtedly attend university, paid for by Julia's parents and then into a glittering career. How different from the rough comprehensive Michael had clawed his way out of. A dingy, leaking flat roofed building, thrown up in the sixties and tired by the seventies, run by teachers who had to be as rough and tough as the children they taught. In the backstreets of a council estate on the outskirts of Leeds it was a dog-eat-dog world, there was none of the refineries that Danny had grown up with, poverty was rife and there was only one way out for anyone with any ambition.

Michael had won a scholarship to university to study veterinary science, meeting Julia at a party while he had just landed his first job at a small animal clinic on the outskirts of London. She had been living in the city, a frippery of a job to entertain her during the hours she was not at parties or some other social occasion, before she married and went home to the family estate and her father's money. For some reason, he never knew why, she had seen something in him and had liked him.

He had seized the opportunity with both hands. Who wouldn't? The lifestyle came with a price, she was an utter bitch, but her money had built him the practice, one of the best in the county, something he would never have been able to do alone. And of course, now there was Danny and the adoration he felt for his son and the pride that he would have everything Michael would only have dreamed of as a child.

As Danny ran back down the steps off the stage Michael felt his telephone vibrate in his pocket, Carl.

Chapter Twenty

'What do you fancy?'

'What…?' Tamara dragged her attention to Patrick. His cheeks were the same colour as the red stripe in his expensive cotton shirt. He'd spent the previous afternoon pottering around in the garden and got burned.

'To eat, darling.' He waved the elegant grey menu in her direction. 'You're miles away.' Under the table Tamara kicked off her shoes. Her feet ached. She felt tired and tetchy. Her hormones were all over the place. She really hadn't been in the mood for trailing around the shops looking for a new dress for one of Patrick's work events.

'Sorry, I'm just tired.' How could she possibly tell him the real reason for her lack of attention?

'You do look peeky,' Patrick leant forwards and took her hand. 'After lunch we'll get the red dress. I like that one, then we'll go home and relax.'

'Thank you.' Tamara ran her fingers over Patrick's forearm. He really was the kindest man she had ever met. She turned her attention to the long and comprehensive menu.

The Snooty Fox was their favourite lunch haunt. It was a small, very exclusive restaurant tucked away down one of the Truro alleyways. It was the haunt of those whose pockets were deep enough to pay for the expensive, but delicious food and drink. The stone flagged floor was uneven, wooden barrels doubled as tables, the lighting dim.

She scanned the menu, the words blurring with unshed tears. She wiped her eyes hastily, no time for emotion now, she was over the worst, she had to be tough and get through this.

'I'll have the Paella,' she said finally. She really didn't fancy anything to eat but paella was the only thing she felt her churning stomach might be able to cope with.

Patrick glanced in the direction of the waiter who came immediately towards him, remembering how favourably he tipped. As Patrick, ordered a family came in, a toddler, laughing holding on to a man's hand and a woman, pushing a pushchair in which sat a beaming child. Tamara's heart skipped a beat. A baby, the one thing she really wanted. How could she have destroyed that life in one quick, cold callous visit to a soulless surgery.

There had been no choice. She could not have kept the baby. Years before he had met her Patrick had undergone a vasectomy.

The family sat at a table close to Tamara and Patrick, the baby in the push chair caught Tamara looking at him and grinned broadly, waving the plastic toy he held in her direction.

Excusing herself she leapt to her feet and dashed to the relative silence of the bathroom. They were at the back of the building, foggy with warmth and smelling of expensive hand lotion. Tamara fled into one of the cubicles and bolted the door, letting the tears flow.

She used the loo, the smear of blood on the paper an accusation, her body still rebelling at what she had done. Her breasts hurt, her body crying out at the injustice she had done to it.

Tamara took a strangled breath. She had to stop crying, Patrick would wonder what was wrong, she could not, would not hurt him, she had come too far now to go back.

Tamara let herself out of the cubicle, grabbing a handful of tissue to repair the damage to her face.

She hadn't cried since driving up to Exeter, on her way to the clinic. She had sobbed all the way there, heartbroken at the cruelty of Jago, and the injustice of how he had found her and after all those years and had used her past against her. He had forced her into a relationship with him. She had been at his beck and call, all in exchange for his silence, something he never tired of threatening her with.

Now he was dead she had peace. No one would ever force her to betray Patrick again. It was unlikely anyone else would ever know who she really was. Her old life was so far in the past. She had thought that before she had encountered Jago.

Tamara rested her forehead against the coolness of the bathroom mirror, she had to calm herself, try to forget what she had done, but she knew it would haunt her forever. The abortion clinic had been horrendous. Polite, kindly nurses, a waiting room where no one looked at anyone. Then there had been a consultation with a doctor, who had confirmed her pregnancy. After the consultation came the bizarre, sordid handing over of a heap of cash to pay for the operation. No credit cards, no cheques. No come back.

In a daze she had left her clothes in a bedside cabinet, changed into a hospital gown, blue and white checked, then with a kindly nurse beside her, had been wheeled on a trolley down to the surgery. She had panicked the whole time, wanting to stop the procedure, the death of her child. And yet she could not, she was silent, waiting as the needle slid into the back of her hand, watching the Doctor's eyes, brown, fading into blackness.

Then it was over. She was back in the bed, a large uncomfortable pad between her legs, a nurse handing her tea and toast. Outside the window the sunlight was shining through the leaves of a tree, casting dancing shadows on the bedsheets, like small angels, the spirits of the babies who had died.

She hadn't been supposed to drive, but had lied, said she had a friend collecting her. She had parked nearby, getting a taxi, to collect her in case anyone enquired about how she was getting home. They did not. The expressionless driver had kept his opinions to himself whatever they were.

No one had mentioned the horrors of what she was doing. Killing a child, a child she already loved and desperately wanted, but a child that could end her relationship with Patrick. Knowing she had betrayed him would have destroyed him and so the pregnancy had to be terminated.

When it was over, during the drive home, she had screamed in torment. The surgery had told her to keep using the pad, but she had switched to a tampon before she got home. Patrick probably wouldn't count the days since her last period, but he would certainly wonder why she was using old fashioned sanitary pads.

Now it was over. Jago was dead. There would be no more phone calls demanding her presence, never again would she have to let him undress her, her skin crawling with revulsion as his slimy tongue forced its way between her teeth. Never again would she have to lie to Patrick about where she was going and when she would be back. No more running into the house ripping off her clothes and plunging into the shower scrubbing at her skin until it was raw just to rid herself of the smell and touch of Jago. His death had bought her freedom. He had deserved to die.

Tamara drew in a deep breath. She reapplied her lipstick and looked at the woman in the mirror, tall and beautiful and finally free. She turned away, back to the restaurant and Patrick.

Mandy, the girl she had once been had vanished, replaced by Tamara. The frightened woman who had been blackmailed, forced into a relationship by Jago had also gone. His death had freed her from the fear of what he could do.

After lunch Patrick had taken her shopping, back to the shop where, he had bought her two dresses. An older lady she had once met had given Tamara some good advice, marry a man who is too proud to let you work, and she had done that for sure. Patrick was kind and gentle and generous, he loved nothing better than treating her like a princess.

They went home, leaving the bags of shopping abandoned in the kitchen. He had tried briefly to take her to bed but when she had whispered something about times of the month, he had left her alone.

'I've got something to tell you,' Patrick said taking her hand, later as they relaxed together on the sofa. 'I'm going to have my vasectomy reversed. I know how much you'd love to have a baby.'

She lay awake all night, staring into the darkness, the feeling of guilt at what she had done mingling with the relief. In the morning she forced the feelings away, it was time for a new start. Without Jago's malevolent presence she could get pregnant, knowing the child would be Patrick's. Jago's death had set her free.

Leaving Patrick working in his home office she stuck to her routine of a morning ride. While she knew that it would hurt like hell every time she saw a baby, or a pregnant woman, Tamara knew that the feeling of relief that Jago was gone would never go away. She had her life back again.

The police operation was still going on at Park Hall, the groom's accommodation taped off with fluttering blue and white tape, a lone policeman standing guard at the door, the forensics vans still in the yard. The horses had been moved to stables behind the main block. They were usually used for isolation when a new horse came.

Issy the groom, hearing her car pull up and came out of the stable she'd been working in. She flung her arms around Tamara, 'I hate being without him,' she said bursting into tears, 'Everything seems so strange without Jago here. I miss him so much.'

Tamara fought to keep her expression impassive. Issy never saw the bad in anyone. She was like a little Pollyanna, always seeing the good in every situation. 'He was so good to me,' Issy hunted for a tissue to wipe her streaming eyes and nose, in the end she gave up and wiped her nose on her sweatshirt sleeve. Tamara handed Issy a neatly folded handkerchief. 'Thank you,' Issy said, blowing her nose loudly before handing it back. 'You keep it,' Tamara said gently.

'I don't know what's going to happen now…' Issy's voice trailed off as she looked towards the big house.

'I'm sure things will carry on, as they were,' Tamara was glad they wouldn't.

'I hope so,' Issy spluttered.

Tamara's horse Lanson stood as always at the back of his stable. He was an incredibly handsome horse but never had been very friendly. He seemed to tolerate, rather than enjoy any human contact. Tamara often wondered if Jago beat him or made him afraid just to torment her. Jago's presence had made life unbearable. Each time she came to the yard he was there, leering, groping her in the stable, arranging meetings, if she stayed away he phoned demanding to know where she was, always with the threat of telling Patrick about her past.

She should, she knew have called his bluff, taken Lanson to another yard, got on with her life, but the threat had felt very real and what she had to lose was too precious.

Today though Lanson seemed more relaxed, as if he knew Jago was gone, and came forward to take a mint from her outstretched hand.

'It's okay,' she ran her hand over his face, and down the long expanse of his black and white neck. 'We're going to survive.'

Issy still sniffling helped her to saddle Lanson and led him out for Tamara to get on.

She rode out of the yard and onto the track that led into the farmland that surrounded Park Hall. They hacked quietly to the far end of the farm where a stubble field still had not been ploughed. Here she let Lanson canter and then pushed him into a gallop, laughing for sheer joy as the powerful horse moved beneath her. Jago was gone. His death meant her life was beginning again.

Chapter Twenty-One

Miranda walked slowly across the field in front of Park Hall. Her horse, Elite was grazing at the far end, the slowly sinking sun against a backdrop of the parkland making him look like a beautiful oil painting.

The handsome black horse saw her coming and with a neigh of recognition lifted his head and trotted towards her. He seemed to skim over the ground, showing off the beauty of his paces. The sight, as always made Miranda feel such pride that he belonged to her. She might have lost everything to Jago, but she still had Elite and would do anything to keep him.

'Hello,' she said, gently as he plunged his muzzle into her hand to take the mint she held out to him. She buried her face in his mane, breathing in his warm horse smell. Drawing away she glanced towards the house, there, in the stone building behind it, Jago had died. She was glad, so very, very glad.

Patting Elite's neck, she led him out of the field and down the long track that led between the lines of neatly fenced fields, back to the stable yard. She spent an hour grooming Elite making his dark coat shine in the late evening sunshine.

She was brushing out his tail when Issy appeared in the yard, shoulders hunched as she struggled with heavy buckets spilling water all over the cobble stones. She opened one of the stable doors and put the buckets inside before walking across the yard to Miranda. 'He looks magnificent,' Issy said in a voice filled with awe, reaching out to touch Elite's dark quarters. As she turned away her shoulders began to shake. Miranda gently turned Issy towards her. Issy's face was taut with grief, she brushed away the tears spilling down her cheeks. 'I still can't believe he's gone.'

Miranda glanced towards the archway at the far side of the stable yard through which she could just see the building where Jago had died. 'Served him right,' she spoke softly, the tone of her voice disguising the venom of her words, 'he did the dirty on too many people. I'm glad he's gone.'

Her hatred of Jago burned brightly, even though he was dead. He had known exactly what he was doing when he had spun her a story about the fabulous business idea. The scam that had cost Miranda everything.

'I need to go,' she told Issy, untying Elite's lead rope and leading him into his stable. She deftly put on his rug and then with a last look, tore herself away.

She drove home with an increasing feeling of dread. It began with a dead feeling in the pit of her stomach and became a feeling of nausea combined with a tight band of tension that locked itself around her forehead. She parked her car in the driveway and sat for a moment looking at her empty house. The silence, when she opened the front door, was a palatable thing, mocking her loneliness and failure.

She had naively assumed Jago had been telling the truth when he had spoken of the fantastic business idea. She had thought how lucky she was he had invited her to join him. How ridiculous it seemed now.

She had been such easy prey for Jago. She had been so flattered that he, the man everyone looked up to and admired had shown some interest in her. He had known how desperate she had been.

* * * * *

Miranda showered, letting the piping hot water run over her body. The evening was her gateway, the end of one life and the beginning of another. Later she would shower again to mark the end of everything she endured and wash the stench of the men away. She shut her mind firmly to the reality of what she was doing. When she had lost everything and hadn't been able to find a well-paid job, there had seemed no alternative. She should have followed her head and put her money into the small café she had thought about establishing, but instead she had listened to Jago and his talk of big, easy money.

She dressed carefully; it was important to look her best. She chose things she hoped the man would like, donning expensive lingerie, stockings, high heels and a dress that clung nicely to her curves, finally, she sprayed herself with scent. The noise of the door slamming as she left the house seemed to mock her stupidity for getting herself into this situation.

She was early, as always, and ordered a glass of wine from the bar; it helped to steady her nerves. Then she sat to wait, positioned in a far corner of the room where, she could make a discrete exit if she needed too. She recognised him instantly, not from his face, as she had never seen that before, but from the way he moved, furtively, looking around the room, scanning the bar. He looked ordinary, dressed in a smart suit, his shirt starkly white, contrasting with a bright red tie. He could be anyone, just a man meeting a friend, or his wife. He was older than she had expected.

She watched him get a drink from the bar, then he turned and caught sight of her looking at him. She held his gaze and smiled. It was important to make him feel relaxed.

She got up, seeing his appreciative look as she walked slowly through the bar towards him. To anyone watching they looked like old friends meeting, not people who were total strangers.

'Mark?' she said, leaning into kiss his cheek, his skin was smooth. At least he had taken the time to shave, and he smelt nicely of a woody aftershave. She wondered if it was his real name, or if he had given the agency a false one. 'Jan?' he said, his mouth moving over the word as if testing it for size. The name she used seemed to put a distance between the character she became at work and her real self.

'Pleased to meet you,' Miranda extended her hand and took his. His grip was firm, fingers hot in her hand.

'I've booked us a table for dinner,' he leant into her cheek, she could smell toothpaste.

'Lovely,' Miranda smiled, that saved her having to buy a burger on the way home, or having a miserable supper of toast when she got home.

He led the way into the restaurant, giving her the time to look him up and down. His suit was smart, well cared for, he was perhaps slightly portly, but not horribly unattractive and at least he had made the effort to be clean and tidy for her.

The waiter found them a table at the back of the room furthest to the door. Did he know what was happening Miranda wondered? Mark made sure that he sat facing the door, so that, presumably, he could keep his eye on who was coming in and going out, in case he recognised anyone.

Eating dinner was a skill itself. Food had to be chosen that would not leave an unpleasant odour on her breath or make her feel bloated and uncomfortable. And then there was the conversation, the words that would fill the space in between now and whatever happened later. Normal conversation, she had realised, was made up of day-to-day snippets of what had happened to one another, hopes, dreams, gossip, but not in this situation, bar the most basic of interaction, anything else was too personal. She made sure she was up to date with politics, business and day to day news, asked him his opinion on the state of the world, and then tried to look attentive and impressed while he talked.

The important thing was to make him feel comfortable and safe as if she were his oldest and most trusted friend, one who admired and adored him. It was not easy.

The waiter brought their main course and dessert, finally coffee was served. The conversation was harder now, more forced. His mind clearly on the next part of the evening, while she battled to keep the conversation going to avoid long uncomfortable silences.

The waiter took their coffee cups, Miranda saw him smirk in Mark's direction, casting a knowing glance. Had he been here before she wondered, with some other tired, afraid, hopeless woman?

The conversation petered out and Mark folded his napkin. If it hadn't been for Jago, conning her out of her money she would not have been in this position.

'I have a room,' his voice was barely above a whisper and his eyes remained fixed on the white linen tablecloth.

'I hoped you had,' she was in full work mode now, a slight smile and a glance at him from under her eyelashes.

He got to his feet, clumsy in his haste and hurried through the restaurant. Miranda kept her eyes firmly on his back and yet was still aware of the smirking waiter watching them go. Mark led the way across the reception area, moving fast, she followed at a more leisurely pace, not wanting it to be obvious they were together. In the lift, she could feel him twitching with impatience and tension presumably from the fear of being seen with her. They stood apart, strangers. The lift doors opened, and he quickly led the way down a long, quiet corridor.

Miranda's mind raced, was she safe? Who knew where she was? He fumbled with the door in his haste, the key card not working the first time. He tried again and this time succeeded in opening it.

She followed him inside, glancing around the room, there was a set of keys on the vanity unit, some small change, a laptop. Amongst the keys she noticed a wedding ring, gold, a thin band he had discarded before coming to meet her. Did he think that made it okay? To take off the mark of his marriage and leave it abandoned on the side?

He took off his jacket, dark circles of sweat stained the underarms of his shirt. Miranda breathed in the smell of his deodorant. He folded his jacket carefully over a chair back and then reaching into the pocket pulled out his wallet, 'Perhaps we should get this over first.'

A wad of notes safely tucked away in her handbag, Miranda turned to him, letting his hands rove over her body as he drew her towards him. His mouth found hers, wet, clumsy, she moved her face, nuzzling his neck, anything to avoid that wetness on her lips. She let him pull off her dress. She moved her hands to undo his trousers, letting them fall in a heap around his ankles, lowering his boxers in a swift movement. She stepped away wondering if he knew how pathetic he looked, his trousers pooled around his ankles, a slug of a penis poking eagerly between the sides of his shirt. He had a condom packet in his hand, she wondered where that had appeared from. He handed it to her, moaning as she undid it, meeting his eyes with what she hoped was a mischievous gaze. She rolled it onto his erect penis, marvelling as always at what she could do when she had to.

He clumsily removed her underwear, groaning with pleasure at her stockings and the pale flesh above their lacy tops. She led him to the bed, letting him push her legs open with his knees.

It was over as quickly as she could have hoped and he rolled away, his breath gradually slowing to a more even tempo after the ragged breaths of his orgasm.

She left, their interaction over. She closed the door softly, hearing him already snoring peacefully.

The waiter was in reception, chatting to a blonde receptionist. He grinned in her direction and nodded knowingly.

And then she was outside in the fresh air, longing for her second shower of the day and knowing that however much Jago suffered when he died, it was not enough.

Chapter Twenty-Two

In the moments before she woke fully, Ruth could imagine that nothing had changed. She would wake thinking she was safely in bed with Neil in their beautiful home. Lying in the darkness in the twilight world between sleep and consciousness it felt as if none of the last year had happened. But then, as this morning, the harsh jangling of the alarm on her phone would bring her back to reality, the lumpy, uncomfortable bed she had squashed against the wall, the only way to get any space in the diminutive room.

Hastily she switched on the lamp beside her bed, in case she rolled over and went back to sleep. She forced open her eyes, shuddering. The first thing she saw each morning was the wall she had painted, very badly. She had never done any decorating in her life before. The experience had not been a good one. At least the paint job had covered up the unidentifiable stain she had not been able to remove no matter how hard she scrubbed. Ruth eased herself into a sitting position, drawing her knees up so her feet were in the warm spot in the bed.

The room was always bitterly cold, a draught blew in through the ill-fitting curtains, cancelling out the pitiful heat the night storage heater released. Ruth let her eyes rove over the room, taking in the cheap, horrible furniture and the threadbare, stained carpet. She closed them again quickly with a shudder. Jago. This was all his fault.

Gingerly she got out of bed, easing down the expensive 200 thread Egyptian cotton sheets that Neil had allowed her to take. Even the sheets and the luxurious pyjamas that were remnants of her old life did not make up for the rotten surroundings.

Already at five am, the street outside was beginning to come alive, delivery vans were parked beside the corner shop. She could hear the driver and his mate unloading the crates of cheap beer and wine that allowed people the escape from the horrendous reality of the grimy backstreets. On the pavement near the shop would be stacks of newspapers, spreading the celebrity culture of wealth and fame that only sought to make the no hopers more aware of their situation. The shops would soon be open, selling supplies to those heading off on early morning shifts and to those returning from nights hoping for a peaceful day asleep.

Ruth slid her feet into her slippers. There was no way she would ever walk barefoot on the grimy carpet. She made her way to the kitchen, pausing briefly in the tiny lounge, to switch on her laptop. It would take a while for it to come to life, the ancient software going through the motions of grinding, churning and clicking until the screen lit up. By the time it did she would have drunk her first mug of tea and showered. The cheap nylon uniform would have to wait for the last moment, she could not bear to wear it any longer than necessary.

The laptop was working by the time she had finished drying her hair and applying her makeup.

Ruth paused; her fingers positioned over the keyboard. As always her breath caught with the pain of looking at her home page. She ought to change her picture, it only served as torture, making her bitterly aware of the reality of the situation she had brought on herself through sheer stupidity. The image was of her and Neil, taken by a fellow traveller on holiday a couple of years ago. Behind them the background was of blue skies and the sea. In the distance was a sliver of golden sand, palm trees bent in the breeze. How happy they had been. There had been nothing to show of the grim future that lay ahead. A future she had created herself.

The laptop deigned to open the internet, latching onto the nearby McDonalds' wifi. With a few deft taps on the keyboard Ruth opened her social media and tapped Neil's name into the search box.

It had become her daily routine, like picking at a raw scab, the pain was immense, but she could not help herself. The social media app opened on Neil's page, his profile page still a shot from that wonderful holiday, a deserted beach, dotted with palm trees and in the foreground a tall glass of beer. Ruth could remember the moment, the taste of the cold beer after they had wandered hand in hand to the end of the beach, sated by early morning love making. That and a few leisurely swims in the sea, all the exercise they would take. Later after a long siesta they had returned to drink beer before dinner, eaten on the beach as the sun went down.

Ruth bit her lip. Below his profile page there was more agony. A new photograph had been put into his social media feed. It must have been taken the previous evening. Neil, grinned at the camera, his arms around a pretty, smiling, young woman, her toned, tanned body pressed up against his. She wore a bright turquoise bikini which barely covered her bronzed flesh. In the background were yachts and a bright blue sky. 'Morning stroll around Porto De la Solos', read his status, beside which were a dozen heart emojis posted by friends. Ruth scrolled through the comments, all from people who had been their friends. Now their allegiance so firmly with him, she, the evil one truly vanquished to the side lines.

She touched the screen, running a finger along the blonde's neck, later after work she would manipulate the image. She would remove the woman, put herself beside Neil, where she belonged. Her veins coursed with hatred for the woman. Ruth wished she was dead. Like Jago.

Ruth wondered when he was going to be back from the holiday.

He'd blocked her telephone number to stop her calling. None of their friends would have anything to do with her.

But it was only a matter of time until he answered one of her calls. The holiday with the blonde had been a respite for him from her determined campaign to get him back. Once he saw how sorry she was, the mistake she had made, what a great team they were and how they belonged together, he would surely come back to her. She would wait until he had been back from the holiday for a while, wait until he tired of the blonde before she began her campaign again. Was the blonde woman one behind the visit Ruth had endured from the police warning her against contacting Neil? He would never have wanted that. Besides, who could stop her parking her car outside what had once been her home, or sitting in a bar where Neil was. It was her right to go where she chose. She would get him back, she would make him realise how much he loved her and then he would forgive her. After all it had been because of Jago. He had led her astray, tempted her away from Neil.

Tension coursed through Ruth's veins. She had to put Neil out of her mind, for now. There was nothing she could do to get him back while he was out of the country. Ruth took a deep breath and logged out of her social media. She turned off the laptop, for the moment she had no choice but to endure this existence until she could get him back. All of this, the way their relationship had imploded, losing her home, the indignity she suffered now had all been Jago's fault.

He had got what had been coming to him. Seeing his coffin disappearing into the damp earth had been the best thing that had happened in a long time. Knowing he was dead, that he couldn't harm anyone else was something that made her immensely happy. He had caused her terrible pain, but in the end she had won. His death and the knowledge that he had died in agony.

Ruth glanced at her watch. The familiar knot of tension knotting her stomach as she saw the time. The bus she needed to catch was due in a few minutes. Ruth collected the container of food she had prepared the previous evening and left the flat.

A few moments later she was joining the bus queue, shuffling slowly forwards. Her ancient car was yet again being coaxed back to life by garage mechanics. The bus was crowded, filled to capacity with other hopeless cases who started early morning shifts in dreary dead-end jobs. Her fellow travellers clung to the support rails, their eyes dead, expressions filled with misery at the day that lay ahead of them. Ruth took her place, wedged between an enormous woman who smelt of body odour and frying, and a man whose breath stank of stale beer.

Once off the bus she followed a line of other healthcare assistants heading to start the day shift at the Happy Haven Nursing Home.

Work, as always, was unbearable. After listening to a brief handover from the exhausted looking night shift she plunged straight into the depressing grind of the end-of-life conveyer belt. After three hours of feeding residents and changing incontinence pads Ruth managed to sneak away from the watchful eye of the domineering staff nurse to what was misleadingly called the canteen. The small, dark room was as depressing as the rest of the building, smelling of ancient bowels and stale urine. The overlay of cheap disinfectant did nothing to mask the smell, instead it clung to everything, hair and clothes. Here, cupping her hands around a mug of bitter tasting coffee Ruth sat to read the local newspaper. Listlessly turning pages of advertisements for clothes shops and cheap beer she found an article about Jago's death. Ruth opened the newspaper fully, spreading the pages wide on the table, savouring that for once the room was empty. She leant over the newspaper, looking at a full page spread about the tragedy. Splashed across the top of the article was the lurid headline, Murder at the Gallops. Ruth rolled her eyes; some journalist had no doubt thought they had done a fabulous job of coming up with an eye-catching headline. They clearly hadn't even known Park Hall was not a racing stables, but in fact a top-class livery yard. At the top of the page was an image of the house, Park Hall and the stable yard. There was another large image, of Jago winning a competition years ago.

Ruth fixed her eyes onto the newsprint version of Jago. 'You're gone.' She pushed her index finger into the image of Jago, the newsprint creased beneath her finger. His death had been the best thing that had happened to Ruth in a long time. Because of him her life had been ruined. He had deserved everything he had got. And more.

Ruth dipped her finger into her coffee and pulled it out, dark liquid dripped onto the paper. Slowly she traced Jago's face, spiralling her finger round and round until his face was soaked. She dug deeper and the paper tore, pulling apart, his face disappearing in a heap of wet newspaper, erased in death as he had been in life.

'There you are,' the canteen door swung open and the staff nurse's moon face appeared around it. 'I've been looking for you.'

Ruth got to her feet, 'Jean, I'm just taking my break,' she told the younger woman, folding the newspaper and shoving it into the kitchen bin.

'Well hurry up, Edward Pearce needs changing.'

Ruth forced the corners of her lips upwards, 'I'll do that straight away.' If only she could erase Mr Pearce as easily as Jago.

Chapter Twenty-Three

S am checked his rear-view mirror for the umpteenth time. The road behind him stretched into the distance, empty. No one was following. He'd been watchful since he'd driven away from his home. The bloody bitch of a detective seeing him coming out of Zara's room on the day of the funeral had spooked him. 'Get a grip,' he muttered under his breath. What did it prove, her seeing him leave Zara. They were old friends; she was one of his clients. Of course, he would have been comforting her on the day of her husband's burial. The detective seeing him meant nothing. But still ever since that day he had been conscious of watching to see who was observing him. He'd kept an eye out when he was driving, half expecting to find a car tailing him to see what he was doing. Even in the little grocery shop in the village he had been watching to see who was in there, and who followed him in. He felt paranoid now, more than slightly foolish. Why would the police have any interest in him? No more than they had any interest in anyone else who had been on the yard at Park Hall the day Jago died. He put his foot on the accelerator and the jeep increased its pace, leaving a snake of deserted road behind him.

A moment later, he swung the vehicle into a wide layby beside a tract of mature forestry. The yellow barrier that prevented cars from entering the forest was down, hauled to one side. He drove as fast as he dared down the forestry track, the light fading as the tall trunks of the pine trees closed in. Above them the sun was beginning to set, turning the sky into a kaleidoscope of purples and oranges. He went too fast around a corner, the jeep sliding on the gravel surface. He took his foot off the accelerator. He mustn't have an accident down here. Most things he could explain away but coming off the track and crashing the jeep in the depths of the forestry wasn't one of them.

Cautious now he focused on the road ahead. The gravel track, at first a wide access, with grass down the centre, narrowed and then split into two, one more frequently used, continuing into the forest, the other, was half hidden with overhanging trees and brambles. He took this option. He was forced to slow further. The track was narrow but made almost impassable by the trees and branches that crashed and swiped against the windscreen and scratched down the sides of the jeep. He was safe now, there was no one to observe what he was doing. If anyone had been trying to follow him, they weren't now. He slowed the pace of the jeep to a crawl, there was no point in risking a broken windscreen.

Two hundred yards further on the track suddenly widened out into a clearing. The end of the track had been a turning circle once for the lorries that had cleared some of the forestry. They had driven in, when the track was wider, the lorries had been loaded by machinery and had then taken the tree trunks off to the lumber yard. Now that work was compete, the forestry thinned out, already slender birch trees and young pine trees had replaced the mature woodland. This would be the perfect spot for drug dealers to meet, or for someone to commit a murder, very few people knew about this place. Except the owner of the car already parked in the clearing.

Sam raised a hand in greeting. He parked the jeep close to the car, turning it so that he could leave without reversing. The air was still inside the forestry. He breathed in cut pine and rotting leaves.

He could see her watching in her rear-view mirror as he walked around the back of his jeep and to the side of her car. He saw her reach across the passenger seat and push the door open.

As he slid into the passenger seat Zara eased herself towards him. She moved into his outstretched arms. 'No one saw you coming here?' there was a tension in her voice.

'Don't worry, the road was clear, no one followed me.' Sam moved away, cupping her chin in his fingers. She looked exhausted; her skin grey, there were lines around her mouth he hadn't noticed before.

'I'm glad the funeral is over.' Zara brushed her lips against his cheek. 'Can we walk?'

'Sure,' Sam let himself out of the car. Zara hurried around to the back of the car and slipped back into his arms. He could feel her ribs, clearly outlined beneath the lightweight sweater she wore. She'd lost weight in the weeks since Jago had died.

'How long will it be until this all dies down?' Her fingers, clasping his, were damp with sweat.

Sam shrugged. 'How would I know?' The taut line of anxiety around the pit of his stomach made him tetchy.

'I'm their number one suspect. Wives always are.'

'You weren't even there when he was killed. You can prove that.' Sam took her wrist, pulling her around to face him. 'Just stick to your story, no one can prove any different.'

'I'm sick of pretending I'm upset,' Zara wrenched her wrist out of his hand. 'I'm not sorry not one bit, I'm glad he's gone. Jago was nothing but a bastard.' She turned away when she spoke again her voice little more than a whisper. 'I hope he suffered, that he took a long time to die.'

Sam made a small noise which he assumed she would take for agreement.

'He deserved what he got,' Zara's voice was filled with bitterness. 'It was only a matter of time until someone killed him. I hated him. I can't feel any grief.'

'You need to act as if you do.' Sam enunciated each word slowly. The most important thing now was to wait until the police investigation died down and then they could move on. 'Don't do anything stupid.'

Zara put her hand on Sam's arm drawing him towards her. 'I won't.' She began to walk away, leaving Sam no choice but to follow her. She glanced at him, 'Will you still want me now I'm free?'

'You don't have to ask that.' The sun dropped lower, sending its last rays shining in through a gap in the trees. They shone directly on her face. The harsh light highlighted the dark shadows beneath her eyes and the lines at the side of her mouth, she looked tired and old. 'Of course, I will.' Sam spoke as much to himself as her. Now that Jago was out of the way there was nothing to stop him moving into Park Hall and to be with her.

'Ten years is a big age gap,' Zara, as if sensing the light did not flatter her, turned away, walking back towards the cars. It was a familiar statement.

'It doesn't matter to me,' Sam's reply was one that always seemed to reassure her he found her desirable.

'I hope not.'

He watched her walk ahead of him up the track. Her dark green jeans hung from her now skinny frame. The curves he had once coveted had gone. Her figure was showing her age, just as the lines on her face were.

With two long strides he caught up with her, slid his arm around her waist and drew her body towards him. She was easy to placate. He just had to tell her what she wanted to hear. The truth was her biggest attraction was her money, the land and property she wholly owned now Jago was gone. That was a lot more attractive than she was, but he was never going to say that. Now they just had to ride out the storm that would follow Jago's death. They had to keep their heads down, wait until it was over and then gradually, he could be seen in her company and then they could be together.

She was going to need help; she would never manage to look after the finances and day to day running of the yard without someone to help her and that someone was him.

Jago's death couldn't have come at a better time. He had been sick of courting Zara, playing the besotted lover for what he could get out of her. Having her in his thrall had been good. She had been generous to him, the jeep he was driving had been a gift from her. There had been new clothes, a stunning, eye-wateringly expensive hunter. And now she was free of Jago everything she owned would come to Sam. Eventually.

'When can we be together properly?' Zara reached her car and leant against the driver's door.

'Soon. I promise. We just need to be patient.' Sam's words were as much for himself as for her. This was the crucial time. He had played her like a fish, capturing her adoration and slowly wooing her. It was clear she would do anything to have him. Now he just had to reel her in.

'You're right.' In the growing darkness her eyes glittered with emotion. 'You know I'll do anything for you. Absolutely anything. Just like you do for me.'

Sam nodded, unsure of what she meant.

'I don't think I said thank you, did I?' Zara gripped Sam's shirt.

'What?' his voice was hoarse with confusion.

'For setting me free.'

'You're welcome.' Sam was conscious of the growing dusk. 'We should go.' In the depths of the forestry, it was almost dark, the last rays of the sun had slipped beyond the tree line. There were only so many lost hours he could explain away to his wife.

Zara nodded; regret etched in the downturned line of her mouth. 'I'll see you soon though?'

'Of course, you will. We just need to be careful, just for a while.'

Sam opened Zara's car door, standing to the side to let her in. He waited as she pulled a lipstick out of her handbag and reapplied it carefully before scraping at a flake of mascara that had become dislodged and come to rest on her cheek. She ran her fingers through her carefully messed bob.

Sam's leg twitched with tension. He needed to be home.

Finally, she blew him a kiss, pulled the car door shut and reversed the car to face back the way she had come.

'Jesus,' Sam flung himself into his jeep, impatient to be away. He followed her taillights down the track, hoping she remembered to turn them off momentarily when she reached the road. It was almost dark, the cars on the main road would have their headlights on, so it would be easy to see and avoid any oncoming cars when she left the woods. They both needed to be cautious not to alert anyone of their liaison in the forestry. It would not do to be seen together. Not now. They had come too far.

The brambles and overhead branches scraped against the jeep. The two cars reached the end of the track and turned onto the main road. Sam let his hazard lights flash on and off a couple of times by way of saying goodbye to her. A moment later he turned off onto a side road in the direction of home and pushed his foot hard on the accelerator. As he reached the outskirts of the village Sam caught sight of himself in the rear-view mirror, illuminated by the first of the streetlights. His eyes were bright with excitement. 'Play it cool boy.' he said to his reflection, 'Just play it cool.'

Chapter Twenty-Four

'Seriously. It's seven thirty on a Saturday morning and you're on the phone to Max Wilton already.' Kaden glared at Grace as she ended the call and shoved her mobile into the back pocket of her jeans. 'You spend more time talking to him than you do me.'

Grace met his eyes and saw the anger burning there. 'This is my job,' she replied, knowing he would hate the patient tone in her voice. 'We have a murder on our hands, a man dead. It's my job to find out who did that. We're together a long time. You know what my job entails.'

Kaden forked the last mouthful of scrambled egg into his mouth and shoved his plate across the table. 'Of course, I do, but we've just bought this place. I thought we were going to spend time doing it up together. Turning the farm into a business, making the house nice.'

'And we will,' Grace crossed the room to stand behind him. She rested her arms on his shoulders and bent to kiss the tangle of curls at the top of his head. 'I have to put in the extra hours at work at the moment. It won't be forever. Just until we find out who killed Jago and then we'll go back to more run of the mill stuff.'

Grace rested her cheek against Kaden's hair, it smelt of the shampoo he used, overlaid with the faint scent of hay. His words had cut deep, he had told the truth. At the moment she did spend more time talking to Max than him, but she had a crime to solve. She needed to bounce ideas off someone and while she had worked with the members of her team for years Max brought a fresh pair of eyes to the case. Max was as invested in bringing Jago's killer to justice as she was. And, although she would never admit it to Kaden, being submerged in a proper crime was far more exciting than spending time scraping paint off one of the many doors in the farmhouse.

'Anyone would think you were jealous,' she teased, gently.

'I am,' Kaden's voice had a husky note. His hands closed around her wrists, pulling her onto his lap. 'Who wouldn't be? It's tough having another man spending quality time with my woman.'

'Neanderthol' Grace grinned, easing his head towards her so she could kiss him. He had never been like this when she had spent time with any other members of her team.

'Go on,' Kaden pushed Grace to her feet. 'Spend the day with your other man. Just make sure you come back to me.'

Thirty minutes later she steered the Land Rover into the car park of a small pub just outside Penzance. The pub opened early and, in her opinion, did the best coffee in the whole of Cornwall. While Kaden was okay with her spending so much time at work, he probably wouldn't be too delighted to learn that she was had arranged to meet Max so they could chat about the case in peace before they went to the office. The quiet time was valuable, the two of them could mull over how the case was going. It was easier away from the distractions of the office where she would have a dozen questions to answer simultaneously as well as countless phone calls, unrelated to the case to deal with.

Max was halfway down a large mug of coffee when she arrived.

At this time in the morning the place was deserted, they could chat without being disturbed. 'Finally found somewhere that serves half decent coffee,' Max waved his mug in her direction.

'See, it's not all cider and Cornish pasties,' Grace pulled out a chair, its wooden legs scraped on the uneven stone floor.

'I ordered you a bacon roll,' Max replied, looking up as the pub landlord, seeing Grace arrive, came out from behind the bar with a laden tray.

'Great, thanks.' Grace hadn't the heart to tell him she had already eaten breakfast with Kaden.

'There you are my lover,' the landlord put down two plates heaped with bacon rolls big enough to feed a hungry builder. Max shot the thickset man a glance, still unused to the Cornish term of endearment.

The mouth-watering smell of bacon made Grace forget the healthy smoothy which had been her breakfast. 'Good call.'

Max, mouth full of roll, nodded in agreement. There had to be some advantages to living in the sticks and this was surely one of them.

'I bet you were expecting Cornwall to be all sheep rustling and tractor theft.'

'No, of course not.' Max lied.

Grace raised her eyebrows in disbelief. 'You certainly weren't expecting a case like this.'

Max took a long slug of his coffee, put the mug down, his eyes locking on Grace's. 'No, I've been involved in plenty of assaults and murders, but nothing to compare to this one.' Max put his roll down his appetite momentarily evaporating as he recalled the horrific scene of Jago's murder.

'We're no further on than we were days ago. No one saw anything. We haven't even found a murder weapon, or a reason for anyone to want to kill Jago Carey.' Grace drained her coffee. 'But this doesn't seem like it was a random crime. It's just so unlikely someone just happened to go into the building and murder him.'

'We just need to keep digging.' Max hoped his voice held a tone that would encourage her.

'It feels very, very personal,' Grace eased herself back in her chair, pushing her jean clad legs out in front of her. There was mud and straw stuck between the ridges of her soles. She'd let her horse into one of the fields before she left. Hopefully Kaden would bring him in and perhaps even ride him for her. They'd planned to redecorate their bedroom this weekend. Before Jago had been killed, when her life had been moving at a far easier pace. Now she felt the pressure to find the answers.

'There can't be many crimes as nasty as this.' Max bit into his bacon roll. He needed food, the days on a major crime were long, heaven knew when he would next get chance to eat anything half decent.

'We get our fair share of crime. The Blackthorn Farm, Eddie Hammett's kidnap and murder spree was a real nasty one.'

'You solved it,' Max glanced at her with admiration.

'Yes,' Grace ran a hand through her hair in a self-conscious gesture. 'No one had linked the missing girls with Cornwall and Eddie Hammett.'

Max watched as a cloud passed over her eyes. Even years later the memory of the crime still made the hairs on the back of her neck stand up.

'One of his victims, Carrie Anderson, was left brain damaged after his attack.' Grace's voice was little more than a whisper. 'I visit her sometimes, she's in a residential unit.' She didn't mention how she hated seeing Carrie. It was horrific to see her glazed expression and to see the weariness on her mother's face. Carrie's heart might have still been beating, but Eddie Hammett had ended her life the night he had attacked her.

'What made you link the missing women to Eddie Hammett?'

Grace shrugged. 'I don't know, something, just a gut instinct I guess.' She did not mention she had so nearly been one of his victims, he had attacked her one night after having damaged the wheel of her car. Without the pure luck of someone coming to help she could have easily ended up dead. Perhaps her broken body would have laid undiscovered like some of the others he had killed. The world was a better place without Eddie Hammett that was for sure.

'His daughter is a pretty woman.' Max met Grace's eyes, trying to judge her reaction. 'The grandmother is an odd fish for sure.'

'She served time for helping him, although she always denied it. She's an unpleasant woman.'

Max nodded, knowing well the hidden meaning behind her professional understatement. Nan Hammett had given him the creeps.

'We should go,' Grace got to her feet. Hauling a bunch of notes out of her jeans pocket.

'My treat,' Max pulled his wallet from the inside pocket of his jacket.

'Cheers. My turn next time.'

Max turned away to hide the broad grin that the promise of a next time had caused.

'I'm sorry to have dragged you all in at the weekend,' Grace told the assembled team in the briefing a short while later.

'Part of the remit,' Pete shrugged. The others in the team nodded in agreement.

'I've a dog handler coming out later, I want to go over Park Hall with a fine toothcomb. We haven't found a murder weapon yet. It must be somewhere, unless the perp took it with them.'

'Hardly want to walk across a stable yard carrying a bloodied knife.' Lowena sniffed.

'Exactly, I think it's been hidden somewhere. Our killer dumped it. We're going to have teams out, underwater divers will be searching the lake and the sniffer dogs will be looking for the knife. Maybe that will give us a break.'

'We bloody need one,' Steve Cooper came into the office. 'Time is ticking and we're going nowhere. No one saw anything, yet someone must have.' He moved to the whiteboard where, beside the gruesome pictures of Jago, Grace had pinned shots of each of the women who kept their horses at the stables, along with the vet, the farrier, plus the gardener and the groom.

'One of them must know something,' Steve Cooper walked slowly along the length of the whiteboard tapping each of the images in turn. 'And we are going to find out who it is and bring our killer to justice.'

'Unless it's all of them,' Lowena commented, 'Like that Agatha Christie film, Murder on the Orient Express.'

'Except, this isn't a film,' Cooper shook his head slowly, wishing smoking was still allowed in the building. 'This is reality, with real victims and someone out there who hated Jago Carey enough to butcher him.'

'Come on team,' Grace stood beside Steve Cooper. 'This is a hard slog, but we need to keep going. We will find who killed him and build a case to make sure they go to prison for a very long time.'

She looked around the room at the team she knew so well. 'What have you found?'

Mike Twelyn was the first to speak 'Gov, I've looked at further into Sam Green's assault convictions.

'Okay?' he had Grace's full attention now, 'Tell me.'

Mike Twelyn read off his computer screen, 'He gave Jem Tremayne a thrashing for breaking in to his house. But apparently on another occasion he found his wife and another man together. He went after her lover a few days later, stabbed him with a kitchen knife.' He scrolled down, reading slowly, while Grace clenched and unclenched her hands, wishing he would hurry up.

Grace released a long breath. She had tangled with the Cornish rogue before.

Pete spoke from the back of the room. 'Got off that one with a stern warning, pleaded diminished responsibility.'

'I saw him come out of Zara Carey's bedroom on the day of Jago's funeral.' Grace frowned. Was that a possible reason for the farrier stabbing Jago? Sam's alibi had seemed water tight for the afternoon of Jago's death, but there was definitely a nasty streak in him. Sam stabbing someone and then doing this, almost ritualistic killing did not seem likely, but then maybe it was not that big of a leap from knife crime to out and out murder.

'Anything else?' Grace raised her eyebrows in askance at the detectives. 'Any alibis come unstuck? Any phone records shown anything up?'

Eyes flickered from her to stare at their desks, papers were shuffled.

'So, we're no further on,' Grace's voice was filled with impatience. Every moment that passed was time the killer was using to cover their tracks. They needed a break, but at the moment it was showing no signs of happening.

Chapter Twenty-Five

Rufus was one of the biggest Labradors that Larry Cashman had ever seen, he was also the most active. There was no wonder that the Guide Dog Association could do nothing with him and no wonder Larry's girlfriend Emily, one of their trainers had recommended Rufus as a sniffer dog.

The enormous, jet black two-year-old dog with paws the size of a wolf's and a gaping grin to match, had quickly found a soft spot in Larry's heart. Rufus was like a gangly teenager, all legs and incoordination. He also had a severe lack of focus, but when he did work, he had an incredible nose and would, Larry was sure, make an amazing sniffer dog one day. Larry was sure there was a role for Rufus. He just needed to mature and develop some concentration, although, listening to the dog throwing himself at the gate of his crate, Larry wondered just when that would be. It would do Rufus good to be out while the more experienced dogs were working.

Larry eased his tall frame out of the car and stood with his fists in the hollow of his back trying to ease his sore muscles. On the beat, his bulk had made him a target for the thugs who seemed to take pride in challenging him. Not many had managed to floor him, although many had tried. The one who did had carried a flick knife which he had unleashed in Larry's stomach, missing, fortunately, anything vital by millimetres. Cornered like a rat, Larry, braced to stop him fleeing had felt a punch. He had been stunned to find himself on the ground and even more shocked to find blood pumping out of his belly, rapidly soaking his white shirt. The fall, onto a tangle of broken breeze blocks damaged his spine, and now, although fit for work, he suffered with chronic back ache. He would never confess though as it would mean the end of his career. After the stabbing he had moved into a role as a dog trainer. He loved seeing the young dogs grow and mature and took great pride in seeing them go from his care into work with their handlers.

'Wait,' Larry raised his hand palm upwards as he opened the back of the car. Rufus bounced lightly, eager to get out, his mouth open, long pink tongue lolling, his thick strong tail spinning rapidly. 'Wait,' Larry repeated, hoping that he might gain the dog's attention. Rufus, sat, his tail still waving furiously, his front paws paddling with excitement.

Finally, Rufus managed to sit still long enough for Larry to undo the wire gate, reach into the crate, hold of his collar, clip on a lead and let him out of the car. Larry was sure that the big dog would become a great cadaver dog one day, his bosses were not so sure, the dog's unruly temperament meant that sometimes they despaired of him ever doing a satisfactory job.

Sitting on the bonnet of her Land Rover, Larry spotted DI Grace Tallis, beside her, watching the search operation of the lake close to Park Hall, was the new detective DS Max Wilton.

Gail, Larry's younger sister, was one of the dive team who were involved in the search for the weapon that had killed Jago. Larry did not envy her the job of delving around in the complete darkness doing a fingertip search through the mud. The thought of being down in the darkness made him shudder. He had once tried diving but the feeling of being cut off from the world had frightened him to death.

Larry had no idea of how long the divers would be under the water, the teams would stay until every inch of the murky depths had been searched, or until the light faded enough to make it dangerous for the surface teams to stay on board the boats. He hated the thought of Gail being down there, exercising Rufus had been a great excuse for him to be present. She might be thirty-three, but in Larry's mind Gail was still his little sister and needed his protection.

With the lead clipped firmly on Rufus's collar Larry began to walk around the field that adjoined the lake. The grass was long in places, grazed short by horses in others. Larry skirted the edge of the field, keeping to the long grass, Rufus for once trotting politely beside him, his tail waving happily, tongue lolling.

In the stable yard beside the field a group of women were grooming and saddling horses, the hive of activity going on despite the police operation.

Sensing the presence of the people in the yard would prove a distraction for Rufus, Larry headed to a quiet corner of the field and released the dog. As he walked Larry, pulled one of the search training toys out of his battered wax jacket. The big dog, eager to play, bounded at Larry's feet, whining, unable to contain his excitement.

Larry gathered all his strength and hurled the toy, containing a specially smelling treat, as far as he could. Rufus bounded after it, scouring through the long grass in search of the toy, his face a picture of delight when he finally found it and galloped back to Larry with it in his mouth.

'Time for a bit of work old fellow,' Larry said, distracting Rufus, he dropped the toy into the long undergrowth. He walked to the far side of the field, away from the trained dogs who were scouring the land closer to the lake, Rufus for once trotting politely at Larry's side. Larry crouched beside the dog and gave him the search command. Rufus bounded away, scouring the field, nose to the ground, big tail waving as he plunged happily into the undergrowth and the long grass. After a short while Larry heard his bark of delight and Rufus bounded back up the field with the toy in his mouth. He held it until Larry took it off him. 'Well done, mate,' Larry rubbed the dog's huge head.

They continued to stroll around the field, Larry dropped dog treats in the grass watching with interest to see how many Rufus could find and hoping he would bring them back uneaten. The dog had to learn to work without getting a food reward and he also had to learn to keep going even if he didn't find a treat. Some of the search dogs suffered with disappointment and would give up easily if they did not find something straight away. Rufus, Larry knew was different. He had an incredible nose, bringing back such delights as dead rabbits and once the corpse of a cat. It was that exceptional nose that had now to be trained and his skill honed.

Watching Rufus gambol around the field Larry shook his head. He hoped the big dog would mature soon as patience wasn't a virtue his boss had. If the dog didn't start working properly soon, he'd be rehomed.

As he watched Rufus began to mark around a stack of wooden show jumps at the far side of the field.

'Rufus,' Larry shouted, the dog had most likely been distracted by a small rodent living beneath them.

Rufus continued to bark, clawing at the ground, making the signal he had been trained that would alert his handler that he had found something. The signal was unmistakable, Larry began to jog across the grass towards him. Rufus had found something Larry was sure.

'The dog isn't even properly trained,' Max complained irritably, a while later, watching the police team mark out a square around where the dog had been barking.

Grace set off walking towards the activity, 'Looks like they are going to have a look anyway, Larry is pretty convinced his dog has found something.'

There was the feeling of dread, mingled with the excitement as always that something might be happening. Larry stood with Rufus stroking the dog's head. 'He's a good dog. He can smell something,' he told Grace, adding with a shrug, 'probably just a dead animal.'

The search team made their way across the field, spades resting on their shoulders. Behind them a mini digger made slow progress in their wake. As the show jumps were moved out of the way Rufus began to bark again, unable to contain his excitement.

One of the search team poked at the ground with the toe of his boot. 'Ground has been disturbed here.'

A forensic tent was erected, the work excavation began, the mini-digger peeling off the top layer of earth and then the team digging gingerly, scraping away the soil where the dog had signalled.

Grace shivered as the temperature dropped, the day beginning to cool. The sun set, streaking the sky with red. Someone brought coffee, Grace cupped her hands around the mug, silent, shivering, glad of the warmth of the coffee. Darkness was beginning to fall. Soon they would have to call both searches off. She looked up as a young constable jogged across the grass towards them, his face flushed with excitement.

'The dive boss said to tell you they haven't found a knife,' his face was etched with disappointment. There was always a great sense of achievement when a search was successful, the delight that they had found something that would help to the case.

'Okay.' Grace tried and failed to keep the frustration out of her voice. 'We're going to have to call it a day with this dig as well soon.'

Grace shivered, pulling the fastener of her jacket higher up her neck.

Steve Cooper arrived, irritable the dive team had not found anything, sceptical about the trainee dog's ability and complaining about the amount of overtime he was spending on the dig.

'Another thirty minutes and I'm calling this off for the night.' Cooper thrust his hands into his trouser pockets and hunched his shoulders against the cold breeze. Grace saw the look that passed between the constables wondering who would get the short straw and be allocated the duty of standing guard over the forensic tent until morning when the dig would commence again.

Grace stood with Max, listening to the sound of the men chattering, the sound of metal hitting rock as stones were unearthed. And then finally the sound of excitement, something had been found.

'Boss,' one of the team opened the tent flap and shouted in Grace's direction.

'Probably a dead rabbit,' Steve Cooper sniffed as Max and Grace donned white suits and foot covers.

'That's not the smell of a dead rabbit.' Grace followed Max into the tent, breathing the unmistakable smell of damp earth and the strong odour of rotting flesh. She shaded her eyes against the powerful arc lights that had been erected in the tent, aware of her heart thundering. One moment they had been searching for the weapon that had killed Jago Carey, now they had unearthed a body.

The corpse was buried some four feet under the ground, covered with a sheet of plastic, the dig had gone down as far as the plastic but the shape of a body beneath it was unmistakable. The police team began to take photographs from every angle while the others measured the plastic bundle.

Grace watched silently, her mind racing. Who lay beneath the plastic sheeting and what, if anything did it have to do with Jago's death. Nothing could be done while the remains were still in the ground, it needed to be taken to the mortuary where the plastic could be removed, an autopsy done and the body identified. One thing she knew for certain, it was unlikely that whoever lay beneath the heavy black plastic had died a quiet, simple death in bed.

Chapter Twenty-Six

No matter how many they attended, the autopsy was always the ultimate test of a police officer's nerve. Clad in a long green gown Grace steeled herself to face the ordeal, while wondering how Max would cope.

They were met in the reception area by the pathologist's assistant and led down a long corridor to the mortuary. She opened the swing door and stood aside to let them pass, the music of AC/DC echoed around the stark white tiled room.

Grace, saw Max visibly change colour as his eyes flickered over the tools used to open and dissect bodies. She took a shallow lavender scented breath. Beneath her face mask the fragrant gel she had applied clung to the skin below her nostrils. The mortuary air was heavily laden with the stench of body fluids, blood, over laid with disinfectant, not something she wanted to willingly breathe.

'Morning.' Mark Lowther turned the music down, the sound of AC/DC fading into the background, an odd backdrop to the scene in front of them.

His assistant, her eyes the only part of her visible beneath a green overall and facemask, wheeled a gurney into the room. A white sheet covered what Grace knew were the remains unearthed from the land beside Park Hall.

Lowther, pausing like a conductor about to give a performance, slowly pulled back the sheet. The skeletal remains were barely recognisable as a human being. Grace was aware of a tangle of bones covered by a dark, oozing substance which had once been flesh. There were long strands of hair and what she assumed were coils of rope. Despite the lavender gel the overpowering stench of rotting flesh hit the back of her throat, Grace fought to stop herself retching. Max shifted position beside her, his eyes fixed firmly on the floor.

'What have we got?' Grace asked, conscious of her words sounding completely wrong, the pathetic bundle of bones, fragments of cloth and rotten flesh had once been a human being, someone's child, someone's friend.

'Well, we have the body of a young adult female,' as Mark looked at the body Grace could see the softness in his green eyes.

'She was about five six in height, what's left of the hair shows she was blonde, with long straight hair.' They looked at the muddy tangled strands, it was hard to imagine someone once washing and brushing them.

'Age?' interrupted Grace.

'I'd say early twenties, perhaps a little younger.'

Cause of death?' she asked.

'Hard to say,' he sighed, noncommittally, 'But there was rope around the first few vertebrae indicating she was probably strangled. The same rope been used to tie her wrists and ankles.'

'Anything from the wrapping?'

'Can't say,' he shrugged, 'Gone to be looked at. We are doing dental records now.'

'So not much to go on yet.' Grace signed, someone had taken this girl's life and she wanted to know who. Grace looked at the remains and vowed she would find out who had done this and get justice for the girl. Who had buried her body in a field beside the scene of another horrific murder? Were the two murders connected?

'Not yet.' Mark Lowther gently lowered the sheet, covering the body.

'How long has she been dead?' Max finally found his voice.

'I'd estimate about six months.'

'Anything else that can help us?' Grace shifted her face mask as a bead of sweat made its way slowly down the side of her nose.

'Yes,' Mark Lowther walked to the far side of the room, his gown swirling around his white wellington boots. He returned with a plastic evidence bag, 'This was on the body,' he held up a tarnished silver chain with half a heart ornament muddied and scratched, dangling from it.

'Any DNA evidence?'

Lowther nodded, grinning with a clearly felt delight, 'Your killer was pretty sure the body would never be found there was a pair of gloves in the grave. I've sent them away to be tested for DNA.'

Two days later Grace was given the news that the dead woman had been identified by her dental records. She watched Edward Farrell cross the room towards her, knowing what the file he held would contain. 'Reported missing about six months ago. No record of who made that report.'

Grace closed her office door, sat at her desk, and looked at the pathetically thin folder which contained all the known information about the young woman and her life. Her name was Catherine Marshall, from Liverpool. Within the folder was listed a string of petty crimes for shop lifting. What was she doing in Cornwall, Grace mused, looking at the photograph of Catherine as she had been before she had been killed. She had one relative listed. Her mother.

'Max,' she said, opening her office door and looking out at her team, all engrossed in their work.

'Yes boss,' Max got to his feet.

'Trip to Liverpool. We'll leave first thing.'

They made the long journey north in one of the pool cars, the motorway snarled constantly. They stopped for coffee and later for something to eat but even with the breaks the journey seemed interminable.

Eventually they pulled into a rough housing estate and parked, Grace wondered about the wisdom of leaving the car unattended. It looked like the kind of place where they could return to find the vehicle propped up on bricks with its wheels missing.

Here she guessed the inhabitants would instinctively recognise a serving police officer, even in plain-clothes. Grace was aware of hostile looks as she and Max made their way to Blair Tower, the last address they had for Catherine's mother. The lift was out of action. They made their way up five flights of concrete steps. The stairwell smelt of urine, greasy food, overlaid with an overlying sense of despair.

'Where's number fifty-three?' Grace asked an aggressive looking woman with bleached blonde hair.

The woman jerked her thumb, indicating the direction, and stood back to let them pass, her heavily tattooed arms folded belligerently across a vast expanse of chest.

Fifty-three was in the middle of a row, the blue front door paint was peeling, a central pane of shatterproof glass, was cracked down the middle. Grace knocked on the tattered wood at the side of the door.

Long minutes ticked by until the door swung open a few inches and a woman's face appeared in the gap. 'Yes?' her voice was filled with suspicion.

'Karla Marshall….?'

'Who wants to know?'

'DCI Grace Tallis and DS Max Wilson,' Grace and Max held up their badges, 'May we come in? We need to talk about Catherine.'

Karla Marshall stared impassively at them.

'Your daughter,' Grace continued as the silence lengthened.

The woman pulled an impatient face, 'I know who Catherine is. What's she done now?'

The door was wrenched open, the wood, rotten with age and swollen with damp screeched against the linoleum floor.

Karla led the way into a small lounge, it smelt of smoke, beer, heavily overlaid with the spicy aroma of curry, an Indian takeaway

Grace guessed glancing at the foil cartons crammed into an overflowing rubbish bin. Karla sat down heavily in a grease-stained armchair; its fabric scored with cigarette burns.

Grace and Max hovered for a moment but when Karla said nothing both sat down on the sagging sofa opposite her. Karla busied herself rolling a cigarette from a packet tucked down the side of the armchair.

'Well?' she said impatiently.

'When did you last hear from Catherine?'

Karla lit her cigarette and took a long drag. She exhaled slowly the smoke pluming from her nostrils. 'Fucked if I know?' Karla shrugged. 'She left here three years ago. She went to work in some riding school somewhere, stupid girl always had ideas above her station.' She drew on the cigarette again. 'Riding school,' she sneered her voice rising into what Grace assumed was her impression of a posh accent. Karla sniffed. 'Heard from her a few times, but then she stopped calling or texting, I assumed she was too high and mighty to associate with the likes of me.'

'Catherine was reported missing about six months ago.' Max said.

Karla leant forwards; her blood shot eyes boring into Max's. 'Not by me.' Karla assumed an expression of impatience. She stubbed the cigarette out in an overflowing ashtray.

Grace spoke softly, 'Karla, we believe we have found her. A body has been identified as that of Catherine.'

Karla looked as if she had been punched in the face, she continued to stare at Grace, slowly shaking her head. 'Fuck,' she said slowly, a single tear sliding down her cheek taking a clump of black mascara with it. 'What happened to her?'

'We can't say at the moment, but we will keep you informed.'

'Sure, you will,' Karla spat, her wide mouth quivered. She struggled to her feet. She crossed the room to a battered set of drawers.

'She sent me this,' she handed Grace a picture of a slender, blonde haired girl, on horseback, leaning forwards, her narrow chin was touching the horse's mane, a broad grin of delight splitting her face. 'I thought she was happy, that she didn't want anything to do with me.'

Grace handed the photograph to Max, their eyes meeting. A silver chair with a half-heart pendant hung around Catherine's neck. In the background were the stables at Park Hall.

Karla was still holding the photo when Grace and Max left the apartment a short time later.

'That photo was taken at Park Hall. Catherine Marshall must have worked there.'

The drive back to the south-west was no better, the traffic especially around Birmingham was snarled and slow. Eventually as dusk fell, the bulk of the journey completed, they stopped in Bridgewater for something to eat and a chance to stretch their legs.

As they walked back towards the car Grace asked Max to drive. Without waiting for his reply Grace got in the passenger seat of the car.

'No problem.' Max glanced at Grace as she reached beneath the seat for the mechanism to make the seat go backwards, giving her space to stretch out her long legs. She looked deep in thought.

'Okay?' Max paused before starting the engine. It was unusual for her not to do all of the driving, she was a notoriously bad passenger.

'Yes, I just want to think,' Grace lowered the back of the seat, resting her head against the headrest. Something about the tone of her voice did not invite further conversation.

Max steered the car back onto the motorway, squinting against the setting sun.

'Jago Carey's next-door neighbour was Eddie Hammett,' Grace said, as the motorway became the dual carriageway that would take them the rest of the way into Cornwall.

'Yes. And?' Max knew his voice held a quizzical note.

Grace sat up abruptly, pushing her seat into the upright position.

'It's just there has to be a link between Catherine Marshall's murder and the women Eddie Hammett killed, there's a similarity.'

'Yes, there is. What are you thinking?'

'Jago and Eddie Hammett must have known each other.'

'They lived on neighbouring farms.' Max did a rough calculation in his head. 'There's years between them though, they'd hardly likely to be friends.'

'You're right,' Grace replied, in a tone that indicated she thought the opposite.

'Jago must have only been, what... eighteen, nineteen when Hammett died.'

'Something like that.' Grace became silent, staring sightlessly out of the window as the countryside slid by.

As they neared Penzance Max leant forwards, easing the tension between his shoulder blades. The last thirty miles had been torture, the traffic painfully slow as holiday makers and commuters alike were funnelled along the narrow road that led them past Truro. Max stifled a sigh of impatience. He was driving past his home to take Grace back to the station and would have to battle the commuter traffic on his return journey.

Grace sat up suddenly, pushing her hands through the auburn strands of her hair. 'What the fuck is going on? Is Catherine Marshall's death related to Jago's? It must be.' Her voice was filled with tension. 'Are we looking for two killers? Her death is so like the victims of Eddie Hammett. Could there be more victims?'

'Okay, so what next, Boss?' Max accelerated the car into oncoming traffic at a traffic island waving an apology at the angry looking driver who had been forced to brake hard.

Grace released a long sigh, 'Trying to get Steve Cooper to come around to my way of thinking.'

Chapter Twenty-Seven

When Max arrived at the station a few days later Grace's Land Rover was already in the car park, squashed in against the wall. Max always admired the way she handled the giant, lumbering beast, he would have struggled to get his own, much smaller car into a similar parking place.

In the days since they had travelled to Liverpool to break the sad news to Catherine Marshall's mother, the dual cases had spun into a myriad of directions. Max didn't envy Grace her job of trying to keep abreast of the mountain of information her team were dealing with.

'Wilton,' Steve Cooper, signalled Max into his office with a jerk of his head. 'Take these to Tallis, more files of missing women.' he gestured at a heap of battered cardboard files on a corner of his desk.

'Thanks,' Grace mumbled shortly as Max came into her office and dropped the pile onto a desk already overflowing with files and papers, 'just what I needed.'

She looked, Max thought, tired and stressed.

'How are you doing?' he asked, closing the door quietly behind him.

She focused intently on the sheet of paper in front of her, 'Fine, thanks. I've wound Steve Cooper up again, making assumptions there might be more victims.' she said, bitterly, bleakly turning over the page in front of her and writing down something on a pad. She shrugged and finally looked up, meeting his eyes. 'As if I don't have enough to do with the murders of Jago and Catherine Marshall.'

'Sorry to interrupt,' Steve Cooper voice was tinged with sarcasm as he came into the room, deliberately leaving the door open. Max hovered uncomfortably, not knowing if he should leave or stay.

Steve Cooper cleared a space at the corner of Grace's desk and propped one buttock on it. He made a gesture with his hand which Max took as a signal to leave. As he began to pull the door shut Steve Cooper snapped, 'Leave it,' he wanted the world to know when Grace was being hauled once more over the coals.

'You're wasting time. Going through old cases. You should be focusing on the live cases, Jago Carey and Catherine Marshall without going off on a tangent.' Cooper raised his hands in a frustrated gesture.

'I just want to satisfy my curiosity.' Grace sat back. 'These files are in a complete mess.'

'This one for instance,' she reached forward and selected a file off the top of one of the piles, 'Missing for three years according to our files, but when I called her home, she had been back for the last two, seems she just went walkabout and when she got fed up with the wildlife she went home.'

Steve Cooper released a long breath. 'Most missing cases are like that,' he inched forward off the desk and stood over Grace picking up a handful of files and waving them slowly in her direction. She felt the breeze from them lifting the tendrils of hair around her face. 'People leave for their own reasons. Just because someone is missing doesn't mean they've been murdered, or that we've got another serial killer stalking the county.'

Grace met his eyes. 'These files have never been updated, let alone transferred to the computer system. There is months of work here.'

Cooper smacked the files down on top of one of the piles and leant over her desk. 'You were the one who suggested looking at other cases to see if there are more missing women who could be linked to Jago Carey. You have enough to do without adding to your workload.'

He swept from the room, Grace watched him go, seeing beyond her doorway the heads of the detectives swivel quickly to their computer screens and files away from watching the action in her office.

Grace felt the muscles at the side of her jaw clench tightly together. He was right of course, but her instinct told her otherwise. She would, Grace decided, give the cold cases another hour and then call it a day. Grace sighed, so many people walked out of their homes never to be seen again, some to start new lives, escaping from domestic violence or family problems. Some came back, often they turned up in a different city, with a new life, new home, new friends, but others simply seemed to vanish into thin air.

She had trawled through literally hundreds of missing person reports, crossing off those who had reappeared and those who had been found dead. Many of the files were a catalogue of misery, bodies found hanging, washed up on the beaches, hidden in sheds with their wrists slit. Some were still missing, but some of course did not want to be found.

Grace stretched to ease the tension in her back. She opened another file, a young girl who had gone missing four years ago. Grace began to read the file. Amber Friday, there was a grainy picture of a pretty, young woman with a cloud of dark hair, grinning cheekily at whoever had taken the image. She was sitting on the gate to a field, dressed in a striped top and jodhpurs a riding hat dangling from her hand. Where was she now? Had she run away from a horrible home? Had she got in with the wrong kind of people and fled to start again?

She tapped onto her computer keyboard to bring it back to life, Amber Friday had worked at Park Hall, Jago Carey's yard. Grace leant forwards, her aching back forgotten. She scanned down the computer screen and then hunted through the files on her desk. There was a pile for people who had returned home or been found, and the files not updated and a now a smaller pile for people who were still missing.

Yes, there it was, a second file another young woman who rode horses and who had briefly worked at Park Hall. The files were full of similar situations, women who had come to Cornwall, worked in local bars, in hotels and restaurants and then moved on, but this was the second one who had worked at Jago's stables. Had she gone onto another job before she went missing? There was no record of who had reported her missing.

Grace began to shift through the piles of folders, quickly hunting though them, opening them and shutting them as she looked through for more like Amber Friday.

'No Ma'am, there is no record of any of the names you gave me,' the voice over the end of the phone was tinny and echoed as if the speaker were sitting in a vast empty hall.

'No employment, welfare, medical, deaths even?' Grace repeated.

There was a sigh from the other end of the line. Grace imagined the woman's impatience at her insistence of checking and re-checking.

'No Ma'am,' she said slowly, as if convinced Grace must be mentally defective, 'No records at all.'

Grace put down the receiver, something did not seem right about the disappearance of Amber Friday. She pulled another file towards herself and opened it.

Hours later she sat back, suddenly aware that she was starving, her head ached with tension. On her desk the missing persons files lay scattered in tilting heaps. In front of her were three thin cardboard files, each containing a single missing person report and a photograph.

Grace splayed out her hand on the files, tapping her fingers, her mind racing. The three files were different from the rest. Three women, all in their early twenties, who had all at some time worked for Jago.

There was too much of a connection to ignore.

'Sir,' she said, walking into Steve Cooper's office and sliding the files onto his desk, 'I've got three files here of women who have been reported missing in addition to Catherine Marshall. There is a definite link between these girls and Jago Carey. They all worked for him and are now missing.'

Cooper pursed his lips, his expression unreadable. 'What are you thinking?'

Grace spoke, aware of not framing her thoughts. 'I'd like to investigate these further. Where are they? Perhaps there are more bodies at Park Hall. Could Jago's death be something to do with these women?'

Cooper's eyes locked onto hers, slowly he shook his head. 'No.' He pulled open the top drawer of his desk, sifting urgently through the papers, withdrawing, with a look of relief, a stick of nicotine chewing gum. Fumbling in haste he took the wrapper off, put it in his mouth and began to chew.

Grace pulled out the chair opposite him and sat down.

Cooper slowly opened the uppermost file. 'The cadaver team are still sweeping the land around Park Hall. No one had expected to find anything more. Surely to God there won't be more bodies…' His voice faded to silence, his eyes moving swiftly over the reports. 'Tallis,' he said finally, closing the files and pushing them back across the desk towards her. 'Eddie Hammett, Jago Carey, neighbouring farms.'

Grace picked up the files. 'Was Jago Carey killing as well as Eddie Hammett?' she said quietly looking at Cooper's pale face.

'Wait and see what the dog teams find. We could be going off at a complete tangent.'

Taking the files she backed slowly out of his office and closed the door quietly.

Grace, glanced around the office, it was half empty, everyone out now, those that remained were engrossed in their work, tapping on computer keyboards. The murders that Eddie Hammett had committed had been horrific. He had taken young women off the streets, held them captive at Blackthorn Farm before killing them. Those he hadn't killed had been irreparably damaged. Her mind swirled with different scenarios about Jago's death and the possibility he could also have been killing young women. There were years between Eddie Hammett and Jago. There was no way they had worked together. But… The need to get out of the station and away from the death and destruction she was dealing with became urgent.

She put on her leather jacket, quietly slipped the files under it and made her way quickly down the stairs and out into the carpark.

Max followed her out. 'Going home?' he asked, catching her up.

'I need a bloody drink. Do you want to come?' she slid into the narrow gap between her Land Rover and the wall, eased open the driver's side door and got into the vehicle. A moment later she was reversing out of her parking spot and shoving open the passenger door for him to get in.

As she drove out of the car park, Grace wrenched the files out of her jacket and tossed them onto his knee. 'Look at those.'

'Shit,' Max said, looking quickly through the files, each one had a connection to Jago's farm and yet nothing had been picked up on.

'These are years apart,' he said flicking though the files as Grace drove through the streets of Penzance, honking her horn and glaring at a group of tourists, cameras dangling around their necks, who were wandering off the pavement, oblivious to oncoming traffic. 'No one was interested in them; they didn't get flagged as they were so far apart.'

Grace nodded, shoving the gear into fifth now that they had escaped the town boundaries and were hurtling down the dual carriage way. 'And with no one asking, nothing had been done anything about them.'

'Could be nothing, just coincidence,' Max added, holding the door handle discreetly to counter the horrendous way the vehicle swung around on the road.

'It's not though, surely you can see that.' Grace steered into a pub car park just off the dual carriageway.

'Yes,' Max agreed. 'All of these women worked for Jago Carey. That was never flagged.'

Grace slid out of the driver's seat and stood facing Max. 'Because they were all young women no one cared about.'

'Fuck,' Grace pulled her mobile from her pocket as the ring tone sounded. 'It's Cooper.' She met Max's eyes.

'Tallis,' Cooper's voice was taut. 'I need you back here. The search team has found more bodies.'

Chapter Twenty-Eight

'Sorry Sir, say that again.' Grace tapped on the screen of her mobile, putting it on loudspeaker so Max could hear. Steve Cooper's voice was filled with a mixture of excitement and disbelief as he repeated himself. 'I just got a call, the team at Park Hall found three more bodies. They were buried close together at the far end of the field closest to the house.'

'On my way, Sir.' Grace spun the vehicle around in the car park.

Max tore his eyes away from the inviting lights of the pub. 'Guess we're in for a long night.'

'Looks that way. I'd better call Kaden.'

Max looked out of the Land Rover window, watching the countryside slide past as she made the tense and awkward telephone call to tell Kaden she would not be home.

'Fine.' Kaden's voice, audible over the phone sounded resigned, and clearly not happy, 'I'll eat dinner on my own again.'

'Look, I'm sorry. You know how it is.'

'Yes, of course. I'll go and see if Rachel would like your share. At least she'll be glad of my company.'

'That's a great idea. Your pasta sauce deserves to be shared.'

Max was aware of the pained note of forced jollity in her voice.

'Always tough for a partner.' Grace said quietly, ending the call and abandoning her mobile on the top of the dashboard.

'Yes.' Max knew how high the divorce rate was for anyone in the force, the hours and the stress were telling on even the best relationship.

The station when they arrived back a short time later, buzzed with anticipation.

'There you are Tallis,' Steve Cooper waved an arm towards an empty chair in his office.

'Yes, Sir,' Grace closed the door and took her place beside him, nodding and passing a taut smile in the direction of the Chief Constable, Mike Fahy.

'Now we're all here…' Cooper's voice dripped sarcasm.

Grace felt her cheeks burning. Cooper always managed to twist a situation around to show himself in a good light. It must look, to the Chief Constable, as if she hadn't been interested in the case, let alone being the one that had tried to alert Cooper to the possibility there could be more bodies. Now he was carrying on like he had been the one to push the search forwards.

'Three more bodies,' the Chief Constable repeated, as if trying to drive home the facts into his psyche. 'It's like the Hammett case all over again.'

'There must be a link,' Grace interjected, earning herself a glare from Cooper.

'Let's not jump to conclusions.' Cooper hissed out of the side of his mouth.

'This is going to be a big case. Finding out who killed these young women, and the murder of Jago Carey on whose land the bodies were found.' Mike Fahy shook his head in disbelief. 'I've every faith in you Grace.' He stood, lifting his arms as he stepped to one side, like a compare announcing the star act.

The meeting with her superiors over, Grace addressed her team of detectives, 'We can't do anything more tonight. Head off home. We'll make an early start in the morning.'

By eight the following morning Grace was at the mortuary, Kaden's sulky cold shoulder in bed and his snappy, 'Hopefully you'll be home for dinner tonight,' forgotten as soon as she got into the Land Rover. Max's cheerful disposition was a welcome change from her husband's surliness.

Mark Lowther met them at the door, his green gown rustling around his white wellington boots. 'DNA has been found on all the bodies.'

'Have you…' Grace began.

'Yes,' Lowther silenced Grace. 'Jago Carey's DNA was present.'

Grace's mind spun with Mark's words. It hadn't come as a surprise. Where they were buried made it highly likely he was the one that had killed them. Lowther's words just confirmed what she had been thinking.

'Any identification yet?' Max asked as they followed Lowther down the corridor.

'Not yet.'

Lowther held the mortuary door open for them to walk in.

The familiar mortuary smell of death hung like a low fog in the chilled atmosphere.

It was hard to look at the three corpses, their bodies laid side by side on trolleys. 'A total of four women, similar ages, all wrapped in the same type of black plastic, tied with rope that appears to have come from the same roll.' Lowther's voice was hushed. 'I think this is the first,' he eased a sheet from the first trolley, revealing a jumble of yellowed bones. 'Seems to be at a greater stage of decomposition.'

Silently they looked at the remains, a pathetic jumble of bones that had once been someone young and vibrant with their whole life ahead of them. The same type of rope that had been wound around Catherine Marshall's wrists and ankles had been used on this body.

'Something else,' Lowther slid the sheet back over the tangle of bones. 'There's another DNA on this one. On the quilt the body was wrapped in we found the DNA of our friend, Eddie Hammett.'

'You're joking, surely.'

Lowther shook his head. 'Nope. There were two samples found. Jago Carey and Eddie Hammett.'

Grace released a long breath; it was hard to comprehend the implications of his words.

He lifted the sheet from the next body. 'This would have killed her pretty quickly, I imagine,' he said, touching the rope, wound around the woman's neck with a stainless steel probe. 'There seems to be a couple of years in between her, the first and the second one,' he pulled back the covers on the other bodies, again the rope was present.

'I found three missing women as well as Catherine Marshall. Amber Friday, Susan Lawrence, and Danielle Brown, all worked for Jago Carey. I'd lay money on these bodies being Amber, Susan, and Danielle. We'll know more when we've got dental records to confirm their identities.' Grace shivered, 'There has to be some connection between Jago's death and these girls, surely.'

The air outside the mortuary was warm, the mid-summer sun already high in the sky. It was a welcome relief from the sights and smells they had just witnessed. Max drew in a lungful of clean air, hoping his stomach would settle before he had to travel with Grace again. 'Get me a search warrant for Park Hall,' Grace's first call when she left the mortuary was to Pete. 'And I want to bring Zara Carey in for questioning. She has to know something about these women.' She flung herself into the high seat of the Land Rover. 'We'll meet you at Park Hall.'

A short while later they were part of a police convoy speeding up the driveway to Park Hall. The police presence had been removed and the house and stables looked peaceful, a stranger would have no idea of the trauma that had happened here so recently.

At either side of the drive, in grassy paddocks, horses grazed, one looked up, ears pricked as the convoy of vehicles passed by. Park Hall was idyllic, the old house slumbering within a patchwork of green pastureland. It was hard to imagine the horrific crimes which had been committed. Jago Carey had been murdering young women and then someone had murdered him.

They drove past the archway that led into the stable yard and on towards the main house. Pete's car was already parked beside the house.

Simon O'Connor was running a ride on lawn mower around the acres of grass in front of the house. He glanced in their direction before resuming his work, his eyes averted from the proceedings beside him.

Max rang the bell and after what felt like forever Zara Carey answered the door. She looked coldly at Grace, before lifting her gaze to flicker a disdainful glance over the assembled team of police and detectives.

'Yes,' Zara said coldly, in that voice that indicated she had quite enough of the police.

'Can we come in please,' Grace asked, extending her arms to include Max and Pete, 'we'd just like to ask you a couple of questions.'

Zara let out a pained sigh, clenching her lips tightly together before drawing back the door and inclining her head to indicate they were to enter. She closed the door firmly, glancing coldly at the assembled police team who stood beside their cars. 'I suppose I don't have much choice.' Her eyes swept over Grace and Max as if they were something she had just scraped off the sole of her shoes. 'Do come in.' Her voice dripped venom.

The hall smelt of furniture polish, horses and damp stone. They followed Zara, head held high, her back stiffly erect, down a long corridor into a bright airy room at the back of the house where they had broken the news of Jago's death to his widow. A tall window looked out onto acres of pristine grassland dotted with ancient trees.

'Have you found out who killed Jago,' Zara smoothed her skirt over her hips before sitting down on an armchair, indicating Grace and Max were to do the same.

Grace shook her head, 'We are here about something different.'

'Ah,' Zara inclined her head. 'I imagine you're here about the collection of bodies we seem to have.'

'That's right.'

Zara shrugged, waving her hands as if shooing an over attentive waiter away. 'I know nothing about them. I had no idea. How could I?'

'I doubt that very much,' Grace struggled to keep her temper in check.

'Records show they all worked here at some stage. Surely you must have noticed they had gone. Did you not wonder what had happened to them?'

Zara turned down the corners of her lips and glared at them in disbelief. 'I can assure you I have nothing to do with the stable hands, I've no idea who they are and where they come from, or when they leave.'

'These young women,' Grace said, holding the photographs of the missing women as they had been in life, young and vibrant, grinning at the camera, 'They all worked here at some stage before they went missing.' She fanned them out and handed them one at a time to Zara whose eyes flicked with disinterest over the photographs before she passed them back to Grace. 'No idea,' she said coldly, 'there's always grooms here – they come and then they go, they don't seem to want to work half of them.'

'This is a warrant to search the house.' Grace fought to keep her voice impassive in the face of Zara's utter hatred. 'And while that's going on I'd like you to go to Penzance for a quick chat with one of my officers.'

'Do I need a solicitor?' Zara glared at Grace.

'You're not under arrest, we just want to have a chat about the women that have worked for your husband who have now been found dead. '

'I see.' Zara's voice was icy cold. 'Seems I have little choice in the matter.'

'Would you like to get a coat and your handbag?' Max's voice was filled with barely disguised sarcasm.

'Make sure they don't do any damage.' She grabbed the coat her housekeeper held out, 'You'll have to stay here until I get back,' Zara flung instructions at her, angrily shaking Pete's hand off her arm as he guided her towards the front door.

'I want this place taking apart,' Grace said, as her officers came in through the door. She leant in the doorway watching as the car transporting Zara vanished down the long driveway. 'Did we miss something to link Zara to Jago's death. Is there anything here that relates to the bodies we found.'

Grace and Max walked around the house watching the police team as they searched, going through shelves and cupboards, feeling at the back of wardrobes and lifting rugs to see if anything was hidden.

Just before midday one of the officers came to find Grace, holding an ornate wooden box. 'We found this in a concealed compartment in Jago's office. Looks like it belongs to Jago.'

Grace opened the box, inside were hair clippings, a heap of neatly folded lacy underwear, and a gruesome set of grainy images of terrified young women, tied to the bed on which Jago had died. The women whose bodies now lay in the mortuary.

'I'm going back to Penzance.' Grace pushed the box into a large evidence bag.

When she got back to the station, Zara was in an interview suite where she sat, looking uncomfortable, upset and angry.

'Am I under arrest?' she challenged Grace as soon as she sat down, 'My husband is killed by some maniac and I'm the one that is under arrest for the deaths of those women.'

Grace kept her face expressionless and her voice as calm and quiet as possible, not wanting to inflame Zara further. 'No, Zara. You aren't under arrest; we just want to ask you some questions.'

Zara sat back in the chair, glaring at Grace, her lips pursed, deep lines circling her mouth which was white with tension. Ask then,' she seemed very afraid at being in the police interview room, but that was normal, not many people had ever been in this situation.

Grace decided that there was no point in skirting around the question, 'Did you know that Jago had killed the women we found buried in the fields.' She placed Jago's box on the table, opening the lid and slowly removing Jago's trophies, now in sealed evidence bags.

Two red spots appeared on Zara's cheeks, her eyes widened in horror as she looked at the contents of the box, 'What?' she spat, 'What do you take me for? Do you really, seriously think that I would have known what Jago was doing and would have ignored it? Do you think I helped him, is that what this is all about?'

That was a good opportunity for Grace, 'So did you? Help him?'

Zara began to scratch at an already reddened piece of skin on the underside of her wrist, 'Of course I didn't. I had no clue what he was doing? You think I'd have a part of this?' She leant back as though to distance herself from Jago's trophies.

'So, you never wondered where he was at night, when he must have been with those young women, killing and burying them?'

'No!' Zara spat. And then her shoulders seemed to sag, she leant forwards and looked Grace in the eye. 'Truth is I was glad when he was out, it suited me, we've never had much of a relationship.'

She was silent for a moment considering what to say before she continued, 'We lived our own lives. I did my own thing.'

'What thing would that be?' Grace raised her eyebrows.

'I was seeing someone, Jago and I, well our relationship was over long ago, we stayed together for the business. I didn't care what he was up too, nor he what I was doing.'

'Is there someone who can collaborate that for you?' Grace asked, wondering if Zara would admit who her lover was.

'Do I have to answer that?' Zara glared at Grace.

She pulled a wry face, 'You had better, we are going to need to know who you were seeing otherwise you can't prove you weren't part of this.'

Zara signed, 'I didn't know he'd killed anyone. I wasn't involved in their deaths. And I had nothing to do with his death. I've been having an affair with Sam for years. When Jago was killed, I was with Sam. We both lied about where we were.'

Grace was aware of Max writing furiously on his pad. She frowned, Zara had lied about her alibi so had Sam, both would now need to be re-interviewed about what they were really doing the afternoon that Jago was killed. Zara knew nothing about the dead women, she had no interest in who worked on the yard, to her they were just grooms who just came and went. And she knew nothing about the sexual predator she was married to.

Chapter Twenty-Nine

'**S**hit. Shit.' Zara hissed under her breath as she ran down the steps at the front of the police station. The bastards had offered to drive her home, but after spending the past few hours in their company, the last thing she wanted to do was to waste another second breathing the same air as those supercilious bastards.

She hurried across the car park at the front of the building, her cream coat swirling around her calves. Zara darted through the front gates and out onto the street beyond, hoping no one she knew would see her. At once her pace slowed, her shoulders dropping as the tension slid from her body. No one seeing her would know that she been questioned about Jago's nasty little side line, his unsavoury taste for young women.

She had vomited when after his trophies, they had shown her the images they had found in Jago's office desk. Grace's side kick had deftly pushed a waste bin under her nose as she heaved. She was sure she had convinced them she had known nothing about what he was doing. Nothing about the women who had worked on the yard and then gone away. And nothing about who had killed him. They had broken up the interview, giving her time to rest.

Zara could smell the foul odour of the plastic mattress on her clothes. She hadn't slept, instead tossing and turning trying to get comfortable and trying and failing to keep the image of Jago and what he had done out of her mind. His death had done the world a huge favour.

She hurried down the High Street, relieved as she finally joined the late-afternoon shoppers and could mingle with them unseen and unrecognised. She telephoned the local taxi office and was told there would be a wait of up to an hour. They'd pick her up near the chemists.

Coffee, she needed coffee, strong coffee to revive her after the ordeal of being questioned about the dead women. Before the interview began again after the break, they had offered her a cup of tea, it had been the colour of parchment and served lukewarm in a plastic cup.

The café was crowded. She moved past the wooden tables, the wooden floor ancient, and protected with a series of faded rugs, was uneven and creaked beneath her feet.

There was a poster on the wall, with a picture of a cream tea notifying customers the cream tea belonged to Cornwall, not Devon as the rival county often claimed.

The room hummed with the sound of chatter, a large group of Americans were crammed into one of the booths, their plates heaped with delicately cut triangles of sandwiches and scones piled with clotted cream and jam.

Zara found a table at the back of the room, there was a small alcove popular with those who knew it existed, because of its glorious views over the harbour. She was glad to find it was empty. She sank down into the seat gratefully and picked up a menu, staring sightlessly at it while her mind whirled. A waitress, clad in an old fashioned black dress and white pinafore came to the table and took her order. 'Coffee, please,' she watched the young woman walk away and tried to relax, she was out of the police station now, no more questions for the moment, but still her head was spinning.

One of the American women on the adjoining table glanced at her sharply, Zara realised she had been subconsciously tapping her finger nails on the table, unable to contain the tension that lay within her. Had that sharp eyed detective, Tallis been able to see through her mask, see beyond the image of the heartbroken wife she had portrayed?

Jago's death had been one thing but the last thing that she had wanted was for her relationship with Sam to come out. She'd hoped the police hadn't any clue about. Clearly, they now had. It was very awkward and embarrassing for it to be known that, while Jago was torturing and killing young women she was lying in Sam's arms. Somehow that prying detective knowing made the relationship seem even more sordid. The thought of it becoming public knowledge was something that revolted her. Now Jago was out of the way her use for Sam was over.

Zara pulled her mobile out of her handbag, turned it over in her hand, toying with the notion of calling Sam. Would he be suspicious if, yet again she reminded him to not say anything to Fiona about their affair even though the police knew. The last thing she wanted was for Fiona throw him out. He would undoubtedly come to her expecting to continue with the relationship. Now was the perfect time to end her dalliance with Sam, time to move on. She just had to find the right moment. She put the phone down on the table. She would tell him later; she was too exhausted now.

The waitress brought her coffee. Zara, added two spoons of sugar and stirred the dark liquid, a small smile tilting the corners of her mouth. Stupid Sam. She had played him like a fish.

In a few years' time, once the hoo-ha had died down she would sell the house and yard and move abroad to live comfortably in the sun. Hopefully buyers would forget about Park Hall's blood-soaked history. She smiled as her phone pinged with an alert to say a text had arrive. Zara picked it up, opening the message, before tapping out a quick reply. Her future suddenly looked a lot brighter.

* * * * *

Sam pulled a wry face as his telephone vibrated, in his jeans pocket, yet another text message from his wife, wondering where he was. Fiona was not a fool.

He parked his jeep in the pub car park, he needed, more than anything, a drink to calm his nerves while he decided what to do. The pub was crowded, the bar area packed, over which the television showed coverage of the land at Park Hall where more bodies had been discovered. He ordered a pint and took it to the furthest side of the pub away from the noise. He needed to get his head around the fact that the bodies of four young women had been found. They had to have been killed by Jago.

Fiona could wait, he reasoned, he may as well be hung for a sheep as a lamb, she would be no angrier if he went home in an hour or two than if he arrived home now with a guilty expression.

He found a seat and called Zara, wondering what she had told the police about their relationship. Her phone went straight to voicemail. He left a message asking her to call him. He spoke quietly, his voice devoid of the anger he felt, after all he had done for her, she had the insolence not to answer his call.

He drained his pint. Perhaps it was time he confessed to Fiona, brought his relationship with Zara out into the open. Zara had said telling Fiona was something they should talk about. It was earlier than she had wanted, he knew that. She had said they should wait for a reasonable time after Jago's death before being seen together but what was there to lose by letting the world know about them now, especially if she had told the police about them. They were bound to be asking questions about the bodies that had been found. It was only a matter of time before they came looking for him.

There would be a scandal, when he left Fiona. She would half kill him when she found out that he had been having an affair behind her back, especially with an older woman. But, he mused, fetching another pint, his relationship with Fiona was dead in the water. Her father had brought them the cottage where they lived, that had been the main attraction in dating her in the first place, but once he was with Zara, he could give the cottage to Fiona and move onto better things.

Another pint later he had everything straight in his mind. He knew exactly how to deal with the problem. Head on, that was the best option.

He drove home, leaving the jeep at a crooked angle on the driveway. Fiona stood in the doorway as he walked towards the house.

'The wanderer returns,' she said coldly, folding her arms over her ample chest, which was one of the things he liked the most about her.

He nodded, he wasn't going to start a fight out here, outside the house.

She moved aside to let him pass, her lips pressed tightly together, an expression he knew meant she was furious. 'Where have you been?' Fiona's words hung in the air. 'Do you know anything about the bodies they've found?'

He walked through the cottage. The difference between it and Zara's house was marked. Zara kept the big house immaculate, although admittedly she was helped by a housekeeper who came in every day and Simon who did the gardens, but still she had to supervise them. Fiona didn't have a big house to look after. Fair enough she had a full-time job, essential to ensure they had money coming in when his farrier business was slow. More and more people were saving money and riding their horses barefoot instead of having shoes put on every six weeks.

But even with a full time job Fiona had the time to keep the place clean, but instead she spent her time painting in the loft space her dad had built for her when they had moved in.

Sam pulled out a kitchen chair, letting the legs scrape on the tiled floor something he knew she hated, and sat down heavily.

'So?' she came to stand in the doorway, glaring at him.

'I don't know anything about the dead women. I'm assuming Jago…'

'Where have you been until now?'

'I went to the pub,' he said, raising his eyes to meet her stony glare.

'But you said that you were shoeing a horse over Filston way.'

Sam was silent, trying to garner the courage to speak the words that were bubbling at the back of his throat. Finally, he spoke, 'I lied.'

She rolled her eyes, drawing in a deep breath and letting it out like a sigh that a dragon would make. He hated this, hated the way she treated him like some guilty schoolboy who had been caught miching off school. Suddenly he wanted nothing more than to really hurt her.

'I want you to know something.' The words tumbled out of his mouth, 'I'm leaving you for Zara Carey.'

'Zara Carey?' Fiona mouthed. 'Did she kill her husband so she could have you?' She gave a snort of derision.

'I've been seeing her for a long time now, in hotels, the back of your car.'

He had, briefly the satisfaction of seeing her face crumble before a teapot, full of tepid black liquid shot past his left ear and shattered on the wall behind him.

An hour later, his left shoulder damp and chilled from the cold tea that had exploded over him, he was standing on the cottage doorstep. His beer buzz now turning relentlessly into a headache that sat just behind his eyebrows, at his feet were his clothes, shoved rapidly, by Fiona into three bin bags.

She slammed the door loudly behind him with such force that the ends of the plastic bags rattled.

So that was stage one of the plan he had mulled over in the pub. He had told Fiona about him and Zara, now it was time to tell Zara he was a free man. He was sure that she would be thrilled when she got over the shock. This had not been their plan. They had intended to wait, but what the hell. They'd face all the shit about Jago's death and the questions about the dead bodies together.

He drove over to Park Hall, feeling that sense of pride as he turned off the lane in between the stone pillars and continued slowly down the drive towards the house, that would soon be his home. The fluttering police cordon tape marking off sections of the field beside the stables was a brutal reminder that there was a long way to go until life went back to normal.

As he drove into the courtyard he frowned, a strange car was parked beside Zara's. An expensive looking Mercedes. He wondered if the police had returned to question Zara, for a moment he paused, contemplating turning his jeep around and leaving. That would look worse if he had been seen, parking at the opposite side of the courtyard he walked towards the house.

A moment later the front door swung open, and Zara came out, looking very smart in a plain tweedy coloured skirt and black roll necked sweater.

She let the door close behind her and stood with her back to it. The doorway was the first place he had kissed her, when Jago was away buying horses in Belgium.

'What are you doing here?' she hissed, through clenched teeth.

'I've told Fiona,' Sam met her eyes. He opened his arms wide expecting Zara to walk into them.

'What the fuck did you do that for?'

'I know what we agreed,' Sam said, 'but I thought it was time we were together properly, why wait?'

'You stupid man,' she said angrily.

Sam felt as if the ground beneath him were shifting, he put out a hand to steady himself. As he did the door behind her opened and a tall, beautifully dressed man came out.

'Is everything alright?' he said, putting a smooth looking white hand on her arm.

'Yes, thank you darling,' she said, 'Just the farrier here to arrange to shoe the livery horses next week.'

Chapter Thirty

An insistent buzzing noise woke Tamara from a fitful sleep in which she dreamed of corpses and Jago. The relief he was no longer a threat sent frissons of delight coursing through her veins. She'd spent the previous evening, with Patrick, reeling from the shock of the police finding more bodies and that Zara Carey had been taken in for questioning and later released. Had Jago been responsible for their deaths? What was Zara's involvement? She had gone to bed with her emotions churning, finding it hard to come to terms with the fact that the bodies of murder victims had lain in the ground beside the stables.

She sat up, Patrick slept on, his breathing deep and regular. The buzzing stopped, but something had to be wrong for her phone to ring at three in the morning. She slid gently out of the bed and padded across the floor, crouching beside a set of drawers. She gradually inched the top one open, barely daring to breathe.

When the gap was big enough Tamara slid her hand inside, reaching between the slippery folds of her silken underwear until her fingers touched what she was searching for. She curled them around the mobile handset and drew it towards her. She tucked it against her stomach to hide the light from the digital face and left the bedroom. She padded swiftly along the hall to the bathroom where she closed the door behind her, and finally switched on the light.

She sat on the closed toilet lid and tapped her password into the telephone. There was a text message. For a moment Tamara gazed at it.

'*Hi Mandy,*' Tamara frowned as she saw her birth name on the screen. '*Please can you call me as soon as you can, Mum's sick.*' Janice, her steady, plump, bovine sister believed Tamara worked abroad.

Tamara put the phone into her lap, unable to comprehend why on earth Janice had chosen to text her in the middle of the night. Their mother was always sick, always suffering from some minor ache or pain, which she usually blew up out of all proportion. Janice thought Tamara was working somewhere exotic, anywhere but the depths of Cornwall. Tamara had told Janice she was a busy tour guide, living an exciting life, travelling the world, living in five-star accommodation.

Tamara got slowly to her feet and padded downstairs, slipped her feet into icy, clammy feeling wellies put on the fleece jacket she wore for riding and let herself out of the house. She crossed the lawn, lifting her nightdress off the wet grass. Outside it was cold and very dark, the air smelling of damp soil and faintly of fox.

She made for the shelter of the wooden summer house. The door swung open silently. Inside it was warm, yesterday's sunshine had heated the wood. She breathed in air that smelt of dust and earth. The summer house was the perfect venue for late evening drinks with friends or for rainy Sundays when she and Patrick squabbled gently about who was going to make the next mug of coffee.

Tamara closed the door and got onto her favourite window seat, curling her legs underneath her and wrapping them in her night dress for warmth. Finally comfortable she pulled out the mobile phone and dialled Janice's number.

'Hello,' it was answered after a couple of rings, something that made Tamara's heart sink, what on earth was Janice doing up and about in the middle of the night?

'Janice it's me, I just saw your text.'

'Thank goodness.'

Tamara could picture Janice, her face, made even rounder by the awful, old fashioned black rimmed glasses she wore. Even before she had escaped her much hated roots Tamara had nothing in common with Janice who had wanted nothing more than to live amongst the dank rows of terraced houses, and marry a man who worked in a factory and spent his evenings in the pub, as their mother had.

Tamara could never understand why Janice wasn't filled with a desire to better herself, to break away and find a better life. She had left home as soon as she had been able to, abandoning Janice to the task of caring for their mother. Tamara tamped down the pang of guilt that surfaced occasionally.

Briefly she pictured the house where she had grown up, she had hated the noise and the oppressive atmosphere, everyone squabbling, their mother often in bed listless and constantly ill.

'What's wrong with Mum,' Tamara whispered, despite being sure Patrick couldn't possibly hear her. He slept so well that there was no way he would wake.

'She was rushed into hospital yesterday; she couldn't breathe properly.'

Tamara tuned out, annoyed that Janice had woken her for that bit of news, their mother was always ill, constantly looking for new things to have wrong with her.

'Anyway, they did a scan and an MRI and its cancer, stage four, that means its terminal.

I'm still at the hospital, I didn't get chance to call you before, things have been moving quickly today. She's going downhill very quickly. She is being moved to a hospice in the morning. I thought you'd want to know. Can you get back to England, so you can see her before it's too late.'

Tamara was silent, mentally aligning her two selves, Tamara, the glossy girl who had everything and Mandy the girl from the rough street. She couldn't imagine going back there, becoming Mandy again, even if for a short while and yet it was impossible not to go. The last time she had visited was when their father had died, some three years previously.

'I'll come, of course,' she said, talking fast, anything to stop Janice prying into her life. 'I'm in England now anyway. I'll be there tomorrow.'

'Come straight to the hospice, it's the old Prospect Hall,' Janice told her.

Tamara couldn't disguise the snort of amusement at the ignominious fate the old house had suffered. When she was a child Prospect Hall had been the home of the family who owned the local factory. It was set on a small hill above the rows of terraced houses as if to remind the workers of their position in life. Even at home the factory workers could not escape the sight of the people who provided their very existence.

'See you tomorrow.' Tamara ended the call and sat in the silence of the summer house, thinking, dreading the next few days, and yet knowing that there was nothing she could do to avoid them.

She slipped back into the silent darkness of the house, halfway up the stairs she could hear Patrick's peaceful breathing. She returned the phone to its hiding place and got back into bed beside him.

Sleep did not come, her mind raced, remembering her past and dreading seeing her mother and Janice. It was last thing she wanted to do, but she knew she had to. Her mind flitted over the excuse she would give Patrick, and what she could tell Janice about her life. She had found on a few occasions the problem with being a liar was you had to have a good memory and hope you could answer any awkward questions.

Eventually she slipped into a deep sleep, exhausted mentally. She woke to find the bed beside her empty. Patrick, she remembered had a meeting in Exeter. He must have left early. It was already mid-morning, and the room was filled with bright sunlight. Tamara showered and dressed, threw a few clothes and toiletries into an old, battered weekend bag.

Finally ready, she sat on the edge of the sofa, looking around the lounge, longing for the day when she would be back here. She wished she knew how long her mum's final, and real last illness would take.

Eventually there was nothing left to do, she couldn't delay the inevitable. She picked up her phone and dialled Patrick's number. 'Morning darling, I left you to sleep you looked so peaceful,' he said, as the call connected.

'Thank you, how is the meeting going?'

'Good, we've just come out for an early lunch, some finances to go through afterwards and then I'll be on my way home. Do you fancy going out for dinner when I get back?'

'Thing is darling, I just had a call,' Tamara hated how easily she lied to him. 'An old school friend, Hilary, is very sick in hospital. She's terminally ill. Doesn't have long. I'm going to go and visit her for a few days. I hope that's okay with you.'

'Of course,' Patrick's voice was so quiet she struggled to hear him. In the background she was aware of voices, the clatter of cutlery. ''It's kind of you to do that. Where does she live? I've never heard you mention her before.'

Tamara was ready with her answers, telling him that another old school friend had called with the news. Over the years she had lost touch with Hilary, that was why she had never mentioned her. Tamara had thought the world of her friend and wanted to go to the midlands where she lived to see her before she died.

She finished the call and sat for a while, the weight of her lie settling on her shoulders. Finally, she stood, picked up her bag, clicked the house lock alarm system into place and left.

Six hours later she drove off the motorway into the warren of narrow backstreets where she had grown up. It was as if she had never been away. The streets were the same, except some of the shops were boarded up, others had changed hands, an Indian restaurant stood in the place of what had been the local chip shop. Her primary school was still there, the red brick structure had another generation of pale faced grubby looking children clustered in the playground.

Tamara turned the car into a narrow side street, drove to the end and up a treelined driveway to the front of Prospect Hall. Tamara remembered the owner of the house, a tall, slender, elegant lady who drove a sports car rapidly down the streets as if she could not get out of there fast enough. Tamara had modelled her new life on the woman whose parents had owned the factory and employed most of the locals. Now the factory was closed, and the old house turned into a hospice for the sick and dying.

Janice was sitting in the foyer as Tamara walked in, her bovine face red with crying. Seeing her older sister walk in Janice heaved herself to her feet her plump body a lumpen shape in an unsuitable pair of dark leggings and long top. 'Mandy,' she breathed. She enveloped her in a hug that Tamara struggled to reciprocate. 'Funny to be in here, isn't it.' Janice voiced Tamara's thoughts. 'Remember when we used to sneak across the grass and look in through the windows.' Tamara remembered well, her lounge at home, the one she had decorated when she had moved in with Patrick had been modelled on the very colours they had gazed at.

'Mum's this way,' Janice led the way through the foyer, pushing open a glass door that led to a long corridor.

Tamara followed Janice's wide backside down a series of corridors into a bright sunny room at the back of the house. Through the window Tamara could see the gardens they had trespassed in as children.

The room was painted yellow with bright, cheerful, curtains in a floral print, a single hospital bed was positioned opposite the window.

Tamara felt her breath catch in her throat. Her mother was barely recognisable, she was tiny, shrivelled, her skin pinched and yellowed, her eyes closed, cheeks sunk inwards.

Janice pulled up a chair for Tamara and squeezed her bulk into another, she took the woman's hand, 'Mum, open your eyes, look who is here,' she said softly.

Tamara waited, but there was no response.

Chapter Thirty-One

For Miranda, normally the early morning was the best time of her day. Whatever she had endured during the long hours of the previous night was in the past. During the daytime she had time to herself. She enjoyed the peace, having the time to watch people doing normal things, like going to work, or taking their children to school. The café near her apartment was her favourite place to relax.

She had finished at three in the morning and returned home. She had leant against the door with gratitude, finally safe in her own surroundings. Stripping was the first thing, shedding the short tight skirt, the low-cut top, lacy underwear and leaving them where they fell as she hurried to the shower, scrubbing at her skin to erase every trace of their touch. It was her fourth of the night, but the best, ridding herself of her life out there and becoming herself again.

Emerging from the shower she picked up the clothes with her finger tips, wrinkling her nose at the male smell which lingered in the fabric, before shoving them into the washing machine. Then, with every trace of her night-time existence erased she curled up in pyjamas and socks, warm and cosy with the electric blanket on and fell into a deep sleep.

She woke before eight, the habits of a life time hard to erase. Her life, before Jago messed everything up had been one of routine. Before she had been sucked into a nightmare of Jago's creation, she had would have risen at eight, before dressing in a smart suit to head out to work. Now that life was over, but still her body clung to the routine.

Once awake there was no way she could sleep again hence her routine of a trip to the café. Later, she would nap so that she was ready for whatever the night time would bring.

She stood back in the queue to let a harassed looking middle-aged woman go in front of her, she looked like she needed coffee more. Miranda smiled sympathetically at the woman who thanked her before putting a top on her coffee cup and hurrying out of the café.

'Morning,' Janey, the owner of the Nice Cuppa café Miranda frequented daily gave her a cheery smile. Would she be so pleasant, Miranda sometimes wondered, if she knew how the large tip she usually left had been earned?

'The usual, love?' Janey followed Miranda to a vacant table at the far side of the café. She ran a damp cloth over the wooden surface. 'I'll bring it over. Fancy a Danish too? I've some nice Apricot squares.'

'Lovely, thank you.'

Miranda sank thankfully down on the wooden chair. At the table beside her a man was flicking through the news on his phone. Miranda glimpsed the headlines of the article he was reading. Miranda tore her eyes away from the mobile phone, horror spreading through her body like a jolt of electricity. Three more bodies found at Park Hall. The information wasn't new to her, but since Ruth had rung to tell her, Miranda had avoided thinking about the other bodies that had been found.

During the night, she'd managed to keep her thoughts away from what had happened at the farm. She couldn't afford to let her imagination stray towards the young women whose bodies had lain in the earth above which she had ridden her horse. The assumption that Jago had to have killed the women was not hard to make. He had been all charm when he was persuading her to buy Elite and talking her into giving him money for the business idea, but she had seen another, darker side to him when the situation had changed. Jago had deserved to die, she was glad. However long it had taken and however much he had suffered it was not enough. What had those young women suffered at his hands?

To think about what they had gone through and how easily she could be a victim did not help her. She knew how vulnerable she was. But the harsh truth was she had to earn a living, and during her working hours her body belonged to the series of men she gave it too.

Now though that part of her life was over for the moment and her mind raced. How long had the bodies been in the ground? How many times had she ridden close to where the corpses of those young women lay?

'Here you go my lover,' Janey put a steaming mug of coffee and a plate with a Danish pastry on the table. 'You just missed the rush, couldn't move in here half an hour ago.'

'That's because it's so nice in here. You do a great job.' Miranda smiled at the dark-haired woman.

'Thanks, I could do with some help now though, it's hard doing everything on my own. I'm shattered.'

Miranda smiled in sympathy. It had been a long night. Now it was over it was hard to imagine what she had gone through and that this was her life. It was incredible she mused sometimes that the human mind could blank out things so effectively. She should have felt revulsion and fear of course, but somehow she was able to switch off from everything she did.

It was a remarkably easy way to make money, most of her clients were sad old men, lonely souls who wanted nothing more than to have female company. But still, she hated the smell of them, the feel of their clammy hands on her skin and the sadness that seemed to reverberate off them. It had not been a career move she had ever imagined. Thanks to Jago and her naive stupidity she had lost everything. She felt tarnished as if she glowed with failure.

Back at her apartment she changed, pulling on a pair of jodhpurs and a sweatshirt. She drove the short distance out of the town, into the countryside to Park Hall. She stopped her car on the driveway to the stables, watching the activity in the fields where the police were still busy. Sections of land had been divided by tape that fluttered in the breeze. Blue forensic tents covered, what she presumed were the places where the bodies had been buried. At the far side of the field a man walked with a dog. The jet black Labrador feathered the land, its nose inches from the soil, looking, she assumed for more bodies.

The horses had all been moved into another field down the drive from the house, away from all the police business. She pushed her car into gear and drove on. Park Hall looked empty. Was Zara still with the police, Miranda wondered. What had happened to her? Ruth had said Zara had been taken in for questioning. Surely, she hadn't been the one who had ended Jago's life? Had she known about the young women who had been killed and given him what he deserved? If she had Miranda thought she should congratulate her. Someone had done the world a favour when they had ridded it of Jago Carey.

Miranda parked her car and got out.

Issy walked across the yard pushing a wheelbarrow laden with manure. 'Hi,' Miranda called in greeting, seeing Issy's stricken face as she turned to reply, before hurrying away. However hard it had been for her to lose Jago, her hero, it must have been agonising for her to discover that he wasn't the person she had worshiped.

Miranda grabbed Elite's headcollar from the tack room and walked down the drive. Away from the police activity life in the stables seemed to go on normally.

Her horse was beside the fence, grazing, his head down. Elite was the most beautiful horse she had ever seen, tall and powerful and yet filled with elegance. His head, as he raised it to look at her was utterly perfect, the muzzle finely shaped, his dark eyes huge and wide beneath sharply pricked ears.

Miranda sat down on the bench beside the field, letting the sunlight play on her face, the ancient stone warm at her back. This had been the place where so many dreams had been created, where in triumph she and Jago had sat discussing the promising future he had used to con her. It had all been lies, he knew there was no future. He had known all the time he was taking her money and robbing her not only of her dreams but also her very existence. Miranda turned to gaze up the drive towards the stone buildings that made up the stable yard. From here she could see the groom's apartment window behind which Jago had met his end. It was an end that he had deserved.

What kind of man had he been beneath the slick exterior. He had charmed her, conned her into believing he was a wonderful man. She'd laughed with him, flirted, been glad of his attention. He'd sucked her into his web of deceit. Had he done the same with women whose bodies the police had unearthed? Had she been lucky not to end up there too? Would that have been her resting place if she had kicked up more about the loss of her money?

Miranda picked up the headcollar and walked into the field. Elite was the perfect gentleman, standing quietly as she put the head collar on, buckling the leather strap at the side of his ears. She led him from the field back into the yard, Elite walking politely beside her. She tied him outside his stable and groomed him, letting the brush slide slowly over his glossy black coat.

She put the saddle and bridle on Elite and led him to the mounting block. He stood politely while she pulled down the stirrups, stepped onto the mounting block and then eased herself gently into the saddle.

The yard was deserted. No one else had wanted to come, Miranda assumed none of them could face the place where their hero Jago Carey had died and where, now the myth of the wonderful, charming man he was had faded as the bodies were unearthed.

She nudged Elite with her heels, turning the big horse towards the woods, down one of the many lanes that crossed the Park Hall land. The route took her past the fields where the forensics team were working. Elite raised his head, ears sharply pricked to gaze with interest at the fluttering police tape and then confidently strode on.

It was cool in the woods. Miranda breathed in the peaty air, letting the tension slide from her shoulders. Elite's hooves were silent on the paths that led through the trees. She jumped him over a fallen log, feeling the horse's immense power as he flew over the fence. Through the trees she saw, far below her, a vehicle speeding down the driveway towards Park Hall. She rode Elite to the edge of the forestry and stopped him. She watched as the Land Rover, belonging to Grace Tallis came down the drive. It stopped in the yard beside her car. Grace Tallis, tall and slender, her long red hair escaping from her ponytail got out, Max, her assistant, walked at her heels, like a faithful puppy. As Miranda watched they walked across the field, deep in conversation. Once Miranda would have envied Grace her partnership with Max Wilton. He was an attractive man. Now she hated men, she'd seen beyond their façade to the very depths of the depravity they were capable of. And Jago had been the most depraved at all.

Chapter Thirty-Two

Ruth switched off her car. It juddered and spluttered to a halt beside Miranda's Mercedes as if relieved it could finally stop. The police were still busy. As Ruth watched, she saw Grace Tallis and Max walking across the fields. All the police activity seemed to be focused around the house and the fields near the main stable block. According to the phone messages that bounced backwards and forwards between the horse owners, the police seemed to think Zara was responsible for Jago's death.

It was hard to imagine what horrors the police had unearthed from the fields where the horses had once grazed. Ruth remembered Catherine Marshall. She had been good with horses, they seemed to like her calm, quiet manner. Ruth had been sorry when she had left. Except she knew now she hadn't left, she had been at Park Hall all the time, buried in the field, the last of a series of women. Had Jago really been responsible for those deaths? It was hard to imagine the charming man she had once been so fond of could have been capable of murder. Still, Ruth mused, slipping off the shoes she wore for driving and putting on her riding boots, it was amazing what a person could do when they had too. She threw the shoes into the boot of the car and headed to the stables.

This, the time she spent with Badger, was when she could be herself. The self she clung to despite everything in her previous life crumbling to dust. All because of her stupidity. This was the place, where she could forget about trying to get her husband back, forget about her horrible apartment and forget the crappy car she now drove. At Park Hall she could focus on the horse she was so determined to keep and feel like her old self.

Badger, her gorgeous grey gelding was housed away from the main yard, in the less luxurious stable block where the DIY liveries were housed. The move had been an incongruous one, away from the luxury of the main stables where Issy had done all the work, to an ignominious stable yard where she did all of the work, driving out every morning to feed, ride and muck out Badger's stable. At first, she couldn't believe how heavy the work was. Shovelling horse manure into a wheelbarrow, and filling haynets was almost as hard as the hours of slogging she did in the nursing home. At least during the summer the horses lived out in the fields so she was spared the daily stable cleaning routine.

She lifted her saddle and bridle out of the boot of her car, there was a tack room but it was often left unlocked and Ruth did not trust anyone. Her beloved Stubben saddle was far too precious to be left unattended.

Badger was an easy horse to do, kind and gentle, Jago for all his failings had found the perfect horse for her. Ruth caught Badger, brought him into the stable yard where she brushed the gentle gelding, saddled up and then headed out into the shade of the forestry, her favourite spot. The gelding walked calmly away from the yard, along the farm lane, his ears pricked. Ruth turned Badger off the lane into the shade of the trees, planning to ride to the far side of the forestry plantation. There she could go down wide, soft tracks that circled the woods. The route would bring her to a point near Jago's yard where, concealed in the trees she planned to look out across the fields to watch the police activity.

She urged Badger into a trot and then into his comfortable rocking horse canter.

'Hello,' Miranda sat astride Elite at the edge of the forestry watching the activity in the fields below them. Ruth brought Badger to a halt beside her and from here she had a grandstand view of Park Hall, the stables and fields.

'Did he kill those women?' Ruth broke the silence.

Miranda turned to face her. 'It looks like it. And it looks as if they think Zara is guilty of his murder, although apparently she's home now, but no one has seen her.'

'Who'd have thought it?' Ruth tried but failed to keep the wry note out of her voice.

'The police have found Catherine Marshall's body.'

Ruth shuddered. 'Horrible to think of what he was doing. He seemed so charming, so kind…'

'Yes.' Miranda lent forwards to swat a fly away from her horse's neck. 'Looks like he fooled us all.'

'Certainly fooled me.' Ruth tore her eyes away from the horrors that lay in the field. It was hard to imagine what had gone on behind the walls at Park Hall. Jago. The man who had wrecked her marriage, the man who had been an insatiable lover. What had he been thinking when he had seduced her? Was he planning a similar fate for her as the one the young women had?

Ruth leant forwards in an effort to ease the band of tension that clutched at her stomach muscles.

'He got what he deserved though.' Miranda met Ruth's eyes.

Three hours later Ruth took a deep breath, savouring the cold, clean fresh air for one last moment before she pushed open the nursing home door for her afternoon shift. The wave of heat and the familiar smell of disinfectant, cooking overlaid with a hint of stale urine hit her as the door closed behind her.

'Ooo, been shopping before work, have you? Nice. Look at this posh body lotion.'

Sandra, one of the other care assistants grabbed the plastic shopping bag out of Ruth's hand and peered in at the contents before she had the opportunity to stash it in her locker.

Ruth clenched her teeth into a forced smile, silently seething as Sandra seized the bag and looked in, her ham like fist almost dwarfing the delicate bottles. 'Must be a special occasion,' she said, pulling an impressed face, handing the bag back to Ruth.

'Present,' Ruth said shortly, there was no point in even getting into a conversation with Sandra, whose idea of luxury was a takeaway curry after a night in the local pub.

'Oh, right.' Sandra was not in the least phased by Ruth's shortness. 'Will you give me a hand to change Lavinia White when you're ready.'

Ruth nodded, sighing as she hurried along the corridor to the locker room where she changed into her uniform before locking away her toiletries and her day clothes. She slid the key into her uniform pocket and hurried to find Sandra.

Her life outside of work became a distant memory as she helped Sandra with the first of many urine soaked incontinence pads they had to change. This, Ruth sighed, smearing antiseptic cream onto Lavinia's bottom, was not how her life should have been. She detested herself for being so stupid to fall for Jago, but she hated him with a passion that went beyond the grave. If only she hadn't been so bored with Neil. If only he had wanted children as she had. If only, if only, the reasons were so many. If only she had been happier with him, she would never have been interested in Jago. She had imagined they would be together, that Jago would leave Zara and they'd marry and have children. What a fool she had been.

The afternoon flew by, shuffling the patients from their dozing positions in the television room where the heat almost took your breath away, into the dining room for their afternoon tea, after which they were guided back to the television. The resident shuffling done Ruth and Sandra spent the rest of the afternoon hurrying along the rabbit warren of corridors answering call bells and dealing with an endless conveyor belt of incontinence pads.

At seven o'clock, the handover done as the night shift came on duty, she fled to the locker room, pulled off her uniform, grabbed her bag of toiletries and let herself out of the building. The cool air felt wonderful on her skin as she sucked in a lung full of fresh untainted air that smelt of summer flowers.

The ancient car hesitated and then fired into life. Ruth patted its steering wheel. 'Thank you,' she said, putting it into gear and steering out of the car park.

Once at her apartment Ruth unpacked her precious treasures and ran the shower. The water took forever to warm up as the thermostat was unpredictable, finally though the water was warm. She stripped off her clothes, even with the protection of her uniform she felt as if the smell of the nursing home pervaded her hair and skin. She stepped under the water, relief flooding through her as she letting the water soak her hair, smelling the familiar scent of the expensive shower gel and shampoo she had brought. They had cost almost a day's salary, but hopefully the expense would be worth it. Neil, she knew would remember the smell. They might be meeting to discuss their divorce, but Ruth wasn't going to miss out on an opportunity to get him back. Once dry, she lathered her skin in the body lotion, carefully dried her hair and applied her makeup.

She put on a dress and boots. The dress fit her beautifully, she had lost weight since she had last worn it, the long days at the nursing home had toned her body. The dress she was sure, looked fabulous. Once ready Ruth sprayed herself with some of the precious scent she had left over from her old life, picked up her best handbag, good coat and let herself out of the apartment.

Once at street level she slid out of the doorway, not wanting anyone to see her coming out of the dingy building. On the pavement, away from the apartment she could be anyone, from anywhere, well dressed, smelling lovely, no one would question her buying the expensive potions now.

The restaurant Neil had chosen was a short walk away. She was glad not to have to drive, she would have hated him to have seen her arrive in the battered old car. She arrived just on time to see him parking his sports car in the car park, she hurried across, touching him lightly on the arm as he pressed the buzzer to lock the car.

'Hi,' she could see the appreciation in his eyes as he looked at her, perhaps recognising the dress from another occasion.

'You look good,' he smiled, holding her at arm's length. Ruth wondered later if he had held her so that she could not kiss his cheek, perhaps he knew if she did, he would crumble.

'Shall we go in?' Ruth asked, linking her arm into his before he had time to do otherwise.

'Of course.' Ruth knew Neil had asked her out for dinner so they could discuss their divorce on neutral ground. Ruth was confident once she got him talking, once he saw how beautiful he was he couldn't leave her. He would see how sorry she was, and now that Jago was well and truly out of the picture, surely he would want her back. He would give her another chance, he just had too.

The restaurant was quiet, they were guided a table at the back of the room. Neil, through force of habit ordered the gin Ruth preferred. 'Thanks for staying away from Gilly. I'm glad you've seen sense. Time for us both to move on.'

'You know I'll never want to do that.' She looked at the menu, unable to decide what she wanted, until finally she said, 'I can't decide between the pasta or the fish. We used to get one of each and swop.'

He frowned, 'Not now Ruth.'

The waitress took their order, Ruth sat back, seductively crossing her legs, and giving him a smile. He was so happy to see her, she could tell, they would leave together, she was sure of it.

'How have things been?' he asked.

'Rotten,' she gave him a sad smile, turning her mouth down at the edges, 'I miss you so much.'

'I'm so sorry you do Ruth.' Neil said with a gentle smile. 'It's been a hard time for both of us. I'm glad you came tonight, there is still a lot to discuss. I think it's great we can do that in a mature way without all the fighting people seem to do. We can start to put our old lives behind us and move forwards.'

'I'm not sure I want too,'

'Bit late for that!' Neil gave a wry shake of his head, 'I've something to tell you, I've asked Gilly to marry me as soon as our divorce is through.'

Chapter Thirty-Three

'Right, Jenny, that's the last one.' Michael pulled the last thread, knotting the final stitch closing the wound that had stretched across the shoulder of the young female cat. She had come off worse in an encounter with a car. Gently he lifted her limp, unconscious form, carried her into the adjacent room where he laid her gently on a thick towel in one of the recovery crates. Jenny ran a hand softly over the slumbering cat.

Michael adjusted one of the towels beneath the cat. 'She should start and come around in an hour or so. I need to go. I've more calls to do. Jenny, do you mind letting her owners know they can collect her this evening.'

'Don't worry, I'll look after her,' Jenny ran a gentle hand over the cat's soft fur. She closed the pen door. 'I hope your afternoon calls don't take too long.'

'Right, I'm done.' Michael washed his hands, rolled down the sleeves of his cotton shirt, pushed his arms into his jacket and with a brief smile in Jenny's direction, hurried out of the surgery.

A moment later he was reversing his car out of the tiny carpark and onto the streets of Penzance. Michael stretched back his shoulders and lowered his chin onto his chest in an effort to ease the tension that made the muscles of his neck taut. As always he had fought to compartmentalise his life, shutting off everything while he focused every bit of his attention on his work. Yet still he knew, from the tautness of his muscles he had only succeeded in momentarily pushing the stress to one side.

'I'll be twenty minutes,' Michael spoke into the telephone microphone situated beside the rear-view mirror.

The work call that was to occupy his afternoon was a simple one, taking just moments. He pulled his car onto the grass verge beside a long driveway that sloped down a long valley. He pushed an envelope containing a pack of antibiotic injections for a lame cow into the farm letterbox and got back into the car. His duties were finished for the day.

He drove back down the lanes, turning the car onto the bypass where he pushed his foot hard on the accelerator. The powerful car ate up the miles and a short time later he was turning off onto a country lane where he had sped uphill, through narrow lanes bound by hedges until finally he emerged at the top on the moors. The urgency pushed him faster, swinging the car around corners, powering it up the inclines.

He had stopped as soon as he could, scrambling from the car, dashing to the back where he vomited, losing all his lunch and the three coffees he had drunk. He leant against the side of the car letting his head clear, sucking on a polo mint to take the vomit taste out of his mouth. He stared blankly at the horizon his mind filled with images of Jago. Gradually Michael's breathing returning to normal. Jago had gone. Push someone too far and eventually they would snap. He would no longer be able to intimidate Michael with his snide remarks, amused glances and always, the inferred threat of what he could do to wreck Michael's life if he chose too. He was glad Jago was dead. He deserved everything he had got. He needed to have suffered. He died terrified and in pain just as those poor women had done.

In the beginning Michael had spent countless sleepless nights worrying about Jago and what he havoc he could potentially reek. And all of the time Jago had his own secret, one far worse, far more depraved than being involved with someone of the same sex. While he had been tormenting Michael, Jago had been hiding the fact he was killing young women in the most horrific way possible. Nothing Jago had suffered during his death was enough. No one deserved being discarded in a field like some piece of rubbish as Jago had done to the women whose bodies had been found in the fields around Park Hall.

Michael took a deep breath of clean, cool air, trying to calm himself. It was magnificent up here, the moors stretching into the distance, bordered by agricultural land, a patchwork of small fields and hedges. In the distance, blue like the tropics was the hazy horizon of the sea where it met the azure sky.

Zara being held for killing her husband was a just reward for the two of them. Jago for his vileness, Zara because in her own way was as rotten as he had been. She might not have killed young women, but she was, Michael was sure, aware of what he was doing. She had to have been.

Michael ran a hand through his hair and straightened his shoulders as he heard the sound of a car engine, coming fast along the country lanes.

He released a long juddering breath he hadn't realised he had been holding in as the car came into view. The sight of Carl's face in the windscreen made Michael's heart thump a rapid tattoo.

'I thought I'd never get here.' Carl switched off the engine and pushed open his car door.

'Well, you're here now.' Michael hurried to Carl's side, leant in and kissed his lover. He straightened up, glancing in both directions down the lane, his ears alert to the sound of any other vehicles approaching.

Even though he was dead, Jago still seemed to manage to influence Michael's day to day life his foulness there tainting every hour. He might be gone but someone else could easily take his place, Michael knew that. It would only take someone to see him with Carl and the whole thing could start again.

'Shall we walk?' Carl shrugged on a thick sweater and blue quilted jacket.

'Good idea.' Michael fell into step beside Carl, letting his fingers brush gently against the other man's. The strode along the moorland path, for all appearances just two men out for a hike on a warm summer afternoon.

'I saw in the newspaper that Zara Carey had been brought in for questioning about Jago's death. Could she really have killed him?' The breeze whipped the words from Carl's mouth as he spoke.

'She's been released so probably not, unless the police don't have enough evidence yet.' Michael focused on staying upright as the path turned sharply downhill, the well-trodden grass slippery beneath the soles of his shoes. He should have changed into walking boots instead of the old shoes he wore for getting in and out of the car on farms before he changed into wellington boots.

'Are the police any closer to finding out who killed Jago? Carl glanced at Michael; his eyes filled with curiosity.

'Doesn't seem like it. They were happy to accept my alibi anyway.'

'Of course, they were.' Carl bent to break off a long strand of grass which he stuck between his teeth.

'They can't prove otherwise.' Michael spoke as much to reassure himself. He glanced at Carl, seeing the understanding in his eyes. 'Jago Carey got what was coming to him.'

'He was an animal.' Carl grabbed Michael's arm to steady him as his soles slid on the grass.

'Who could do that to another human being. But not even once, but what, four times that we know of.'

'I don't want to think about him,' Michael's voice held a stern warning that he didn't want to continue the discussion.

'Maybe this is something you could think about.' Carl tucked his arm under Michael's and pulled him into the shelter of a low, stunted, wind bent tree. Beneath the tree the ground was bare, dusty after the long rainless summer, the grass worn away by the hooves of the ponies, cattle and sheep who had sheltered beneath its branches. He eased his hands around the back of Michael's neck pulling his face gently downwards to lock lips in a kiss. Michael felt his breath catch at the back of his throat as his body responded to the touch of his lover.

'It's okay,' Carl sensed the apprehension as Michael drew away. 'Jago's gone. He's not going to torment you anymore.'

'Maybe we shouldn't. Not here.' Michael cast an anxious glance to the path in either direction. 'Someone might…'

'Someone might what for heaven's sake.' Carl's voice was filled with exasperation.

'See us,' Michael said shortly, easing another step away from Carl.

'Oh okay. You're happy to be with me behind closed doors where no one can see, but to admit to anyone that you love me is a different thing.'

'You know it's not like that,' Michael's voice was low, filled with emotion.

'What is it like then?' Carl took a stride away, kicking a small rock in an angry gesture.

'We have to wait.' Michael, filled with tenderness for the younger man moved closer, putting a gentle hand on his shoulder.

'Make sure no one can see you.' Carl said bitterly.

'I must wait until my son is older. So he can understand how I feel, make his own choices about if he wants to remain in my life.' As he spoke Michael looked past Carl to the line of blue, where the sea met the sky on the distant horizon. He couldn't imagine life without his son. But neither could he imagine being without Carl. The two were inexplicably linked.

His wife he felt nothing for, neither love nor hatred. She was just there, on the fringes of his life.

'And what about the poor woman you're deceiving?' Carl's voice was filled with bitterness. 'And me, left on the outside of your life while you have everything your way.'

'It's not like that.' Michael could hear the tension in his voice as he protested, yet he knew Carl was speaking the truth. He couldn't imagine walking away from his wife and Danny, nor could he imagine life without Carl. It was impossible for them to be together. Not yet. His son would suffer terribly if he discovered what his father was. Michael had seen what Jago was capable of when he thought he could lord over Michael, taunting him with the guilty secret he had discovered. There was no way he would expose Danny to that kind of torment just because of something his father had done. Carl, he hoped, would wait, understand. With Jago gone there was a respite from the tension, he just had to bear being with his wife for the time being, until their son was old enough to understand.

'I'm not going to wait forever.' Carl's voice had a steely edge.

'Please, trust me. This is all for the best.' Michael laid a hand on Carl's cheek, feeling the smoothness of his skin. 'I love you.' He drew away, unable to prevent himself glancing at the path to make sure they were alone.

'Fuck's sake, you make me feel like you're ashamed of me.' Carl pushed Michael's hand away and brushed past him, stalking back up the slope towards the cars.

He rushed after Carl. 'I'm not, I promise. But just for now things must stay this way.'

'I'm sick of this Michael.' Carl's long legs ate up the ground as he strode away.

Michael left him for a moment and then hurried in his wake.

'Leave me alone,' Carl snapped as Michael caught up with him.

Michael put his hand on Carl's arm to stop him. 'I told you when we started this, things just have to be this way. I can't, I won't just walk out on my son. Not now.'

Carl's mouth twisted down into an angry, bitter line. 'How do I know you won't find some other excuse when he is older. Another reason to keep me hanging on.'

'I won't. I promise.'

Carl took Michael's face between his hands, kissing him gently on the lips. 'You know Michael, one day I'm going to make you choose.'

Chapter Thirty-Four

'Boss?' Max glanced at his watch. It was almost six, both had been at work since before eight. 'Time for us to get out of here.'

Grace nodded, stretching her arms over her head to ease the tension in her shoulders.

'Drink?' Max asked, she looked like she needed one.

'I think that's a bloody good idea,' she agreed, stacking her files together, 'I've had enough of this job for one day.'

She stood up, lifting her jacket from the back of her chair, 'Actually, I've had enough of this job for a lifetime.'

Max glanced sharply at her, but there was no sign on her face of whether she meant it or not. It would be a shame if she left the service, she was a bloody good copper, although he knew her maverick tendencies to follow her instincts instead of protocol sometimes got her into deeper water than she deserved to be.

It had been a long day, but a productive one. They'd gone back to Park Hall. Grace had got Steve Cooper to authorise a further search of more land in another effort to find the knife that had killed Jago. A team were doing a further search of the farm buildings, divers were searching another lake further away from the buildings. Grace could imagine how indignant Zara would be by being invaded by the police yet again.

She'd followed Max up a path and over a stile into the woods. The forestry, usually peaceful and silent was filled with the sound of police trampling over the bracken and crushing dead twigs beneath their boots.

At the far end of the forest was a lake, larger than the one they had previously searched. Grace and Max stood on the edge of the water, watching the dive team work.

The underwater search unit were a specialised bunch, doing what Grace felt was the worst job in the force. Their day to day duties usually involved dredging for missing bodies and body parts, not something for the faint hearted. Someone had estimated where, if a knife was thrown from the bank, it would land. The search was then coordinated to search backwards and forwards from that point back to the lake shore. It was a fairly unprecise art, as the throw of a person could vastly differ. The divers once down connected by a rope to the boat had the job of slowly swimming along the chosen area dredging with their fingertips in the deep mud.

Grace admired their fortitude, she could not imagine anything worse than being under water.

Occasionally a diver would surface, holding something they had found on the bottom. A few hours into the search a gruesome plastic bag was brought to the surface which was found to contain the remains of a litter of kittens.

Moral was flagging with nothing being found and the senior office recalled everyone to break for lunch. The divers slithered back onto the boat, like grey seals as they were brought back to the shore.

After lunch a second team went down. A skull was brought up but found to be a sheep, the bones of which were brought up later, the poor animal must have got out of its field and wandered into the lake where it met a horrible end. The team were about to wrap it up for the day when one of the divers resurfaced holding a hay knife, they had found the murder weapon.

'I think we need to celebrate. Let's get away from this lot,' Grace tossed her head in the direction of the open plan office which still hummed with quiet activity. 'Kaden's gone to Exeter to deliver a horse he's sold. He's staying overnight, Rachel's doing the horses, so I'm not in any rush to get home.'

'The Sand Bank?' Max mentioned a rough and ready beach bar frequented by surfers and hippies, not often discovered by tourists. The food at the Sand Bank was known to be very good and it had a terrace, covered by a wooden roof where they would be sheltered from the worst of any wind. He had found it when he had been learning to surf, an activity he felt was perhaps not for him.

'Perfect,' Grace agreed, hurrying down the stairs and out into the sea-scented air of the car park.

She had driven out of the car park before Max had chance to manoeuvre his car out of the tight spot some prat had blocked him in to. The road was deserted once he cleared the outskirts of the town. Grace had driven so quickly away from work he knew he stood no chance of catching her, so drove steadily, enjoying the late summer sunlight on his face.

The Sand Bank was down a narrow single-track lane off the main road, the turning almost hidden by overhanging trees.

Grace was already in the terrace bar, a half empty pint glass in front of her, a full one on the table beside her for him.

'Good idea,' she said, raising her glass in salute to him and taking another long pull of cider. 'I hope finding the knife will solve this case. With any luck Lowther's team will find DNA and prints, and we'll know who killed Jago.'

'Let's hope so.' Max clinked his glass against hers.

They sat companionably in silence, watching the brave, hardy surfers who were enjoying the wild surf, churned up by a recent storm.

'Looks so easy,' Max commented, watching one wet suited, long haired, slender lad ride a wave into the shore before flipping off his board and paddling back out to sea.

'Practice,' Grace said, nonchalantly, 'You'll get there,'

Max, snorted in derision, 'Like I have so much time to practice in this job.'

'You could have come and practiced tonight, instead of bringing me for a drink.' Grace raised her eyebrows and looked at him quizzically.

He could have, Max mused, but somehow this was more appealing. 'I wanted to do this more.' He glanced at her, half expecting her to make some witty comment, but she was silent, staring out to sea, watching the surfers as they ploughed through the waves in perfect balance.

Their drinks finished Max fetched another half, they both had to drive, and neither dared to risk their precious licences. The beat bobbies and traffic officers would not have any sympathy for anyone in the force found to be over the limit.

'Fancy something to eat?' Max asked, he knew he ought to go home. 'There's a good Chinese near me.

He half hoped that she would decline his rash offer, but instead she nodded, 'Yes, why not. There's nothing spoiling at home.'

They drained their drinks and got into their respective vehicles and made the twenty minute journey to Truro. Grace followed Max and parked behind his car outside his house. She smiled, noting his look of pride as he glanced at the building he called home.

They walked in companionable silence up the road towards the Chinese. Max scowled, the bloody girl was sitting on the bench again. Every time he came home she was there, every time he had breakfast in the café up the road she would come in.

'What?' Grace asked, sensing his discomfiture.

'Nothing,' Max replied, it seemed too irrelevant to mention.

'What do you fancy?' Grace said, looking at the menu. The steamy Chinese smelt of frying and spices that made Max's mouth water, he looked hard at the menu, the obvious answer dancing on his lips.

'I'll have my usual,' he said, as the waiter came to take their order. The young man gave Grace a once over and nodded approvingly at

Max who pretended not to notice, 'Boss?' he said, hoping the waiter would get the message that this was not a date, and he should not leer at Grace. Perhaps it had been a mistake to bring Grace somewhere he was so well known.

'Chicken Chow Mein,' she said, putting the menu down.

They ate in companiable silence. 'I'd better go home.' Grace stretched, aware now of how tired she was. They stood to leave, Max ignored the cheery, 'Good night Mr Max,' from the Chinese waiter.

'Looks like you are well known in there,' Grace met Max's eyes.

'I like to eat healthy,' Max grinned.

'I don't fancy driving all the way back to the Lizard.' Grace yawned as they walked back towards her vehicle.

'Stay if you want,' the nonchalant words hung in the air.

Grace moved to face him, 'Might not be a good idea.'

'Might not,' he said gently.

'Coffee? To help with the drive.'

'I ought to go…' Grace considered for a moment. 'Oh, but what the hell.'

Max led the way up the stone steps to his house, swinging the front door open, relieved that it was tidy.

'Come into the kitchen.' It felt a safer option than the lounge.

As the kettle boiled Grace prowled around the kitchen, running her fingers over his cookery books.

A moment later the doorbell rang, a loud insistent note that went on for a long time, someone pressing the buzzer and keeping their finger on it. Grace turned to face him. 'You'd better get that.'

Max flung open the door and looked outside, in the light from the doorway he saw the girl who had been sitting on the bench outside the house when they had arrived.

'Hi,' he said warily.

'Hi,' her accent was familiar, from Lancashire he surmised. Close up he estimated she was about eighteen, dressed in the red coat he was now familiar with, her hair dark and curling softly around her face, brown eyes looking intently at him.

'Yes,' his voice was harsher than he meant it to be, annoyed at the disturbance, shocked at the fact she was here, set on edge by her presence.

'I'm Tara Lloyd,' she said, as if that should mean something to him, 'My mum was Clare, Clare Lloyd.'

His brain worked overtime trying to catch up with what she was saying. Clare Lloyd? An old girlfriend he had not seen for a hundred years, what relevance had she got? 'So?'

'I think you are my dad.'

'I'm going to leave you to it.' He was dimly aware of Grace walking discretely down the steps, leaving him alone in a thick silence, looking at the girl who had just announced she was his daughter.

'Obviously we'd have to do a DNA test,' Tara gave a small half smile.

'Yes.'

There was a long silence. Over Tara's shoulder he looked down the street, watching as Grace pulled herself nimbly into the Land Rover, giving a cheery wave in his direction, her face spilt in a broad grin.

Max tore his eyes away from her to focus on the girl standing in front of him. Without thinking he pushed back the front door, and she walked in.

'I always knew you were my dad,' she said, sitting uneasily on the edge of the sofa. He wished his mind were clearer so that he could properly process what she was saying.

'Mum told me you had broken up before I was born, she had pictures of you. And this from the paper.'

Tara handed him a battered looking clipping cut neatly from a newspaper, it was the local one from where he had grown up, a small piece about him. He had just joined the force and had saved an old man from drowning. He had wandered out of a nursing home and fallen into the canal. The rescue had not been as dramatic as the newspaper painted it, the old chap had only been in up to his waist in water and had merely had to be helped to the side of the canal. Someone else had pulled him out. After the incident the old man had been brought to hospital and presumably back to his nursing home, but the newspaper had made it out to be something spectacular.

'I saw you sitting in the park.' Max's mind spun with her revelation.

Tara nodded. 'I didn't know what to say to you. I've been staying in a bed and breakfast down the road trying to pluck up the courage to talk to you. Now Mum's dead and I don't have anyone else but you. I came to find you. It was what she told me to do.'

Chapter Thirty-Five

Grace was never a morning person until she joined the police. The late nights and parties she loved were replaced with early morning starts. There was no more staying up past midnight, it was necessary to be in bed early so she was alert and responsive for a morning shift.

Now she had worked her way up through the ranks, early mornings and late nights were often the order of the day, especially when there was a big case to deal with. Usually, she left Kaden asleep and made a habit of getting up early and heading out to the stables before work.

Some of her colleagues ran, some went to the gym. It was vital to have some time just to unwind, to free the mind from the turmoil of a case. She found that time spent riding made her time to focus on the horse and often the machinations of whatever case she was working on would be clearer afterwards.

This morning she had woken, chilled, unused to Kaden being away. She'd slept badly, the events of the previous evening whirling around her mind.

The yard was deserted, but brightly lit. Installing powerful arc lights had been the first thing Kaden had done. There was enough light in the yard for her to be able to see in the sand arena. She pulled her saddle and bridle out of tack room, unclipped Comet's rugs and tacked him up. Then she rode him in the arena, his movement her whole focus. Later she brought him back into his stable, pulled off his tack and put his inside rugs back on.

'Hi,' a voice made her jump. Rachel moved out of the darkness to lean on the stable door. 'Sorry, I didn't mean to scare you.'

'No problem,' Grace buckled the final strap, 'I've just finished, dashing to get into the shower. I'm going to be late.' She smiled, softening her shortness, hoping Rachel would appreciate she did not have time to stand and gossip.

'I'll put Comet in the field in a while. I'm just going to do the morning feeds first,' Rachel said, holding the door open so Grace could come through with her tack. How long had Rachel been standing somewhere in the shadows watching? The thought flickered in Grace's mind and then was gone. 'Thank you, Kaden should be back soon.'

'Can I talk to you about the bodies that were found at Park Hall?' Rachel said, walking beside Grace, her voice was cold, odd sounding.

Grace nodded, 'Yes, of course.' The deaths were all over the media. There were lurid headlines in the newspapers, there was nothing to hide, very little she could not tell Rachel.

Rachel's eyes locked onto Grace's. 'Catherine Marshall and some other girls.'

'Yes.'

'Did Jago kill them?'

Grace sighed, the momentous unimaginable horror drawn into one single word, 'Yes. It looks that way. Why bring this up now Rachel?'

As Grace watched Rachel's face crumbled, 'I may as well have killed

Catherine,' she said, her voice cracking as tears began to flow. 'I got her the job with Jago.'

'I didn't know you knew Catherine.' Grace glanced at Rachel.

''Not well. Not at all really,' As they reached the tack room Rachel stood back to let Grace go ahead.

'You didn't know he was going to do that,' Grace said, sliding her saddle into its place amongst the others.

'But she died because of me.'

Grace shook her head. It was a reaction she saw countless times, a form of survivor's guilt where people who knew the victims thought they had unwittingly led them to their doom. The truth was perhaps they had, but the reality could not be changed. They had to come to terms with that and realise they did not kill the person; it was not their fault.

Grace found a tissue in her jeans pocket and handed it to Rachel, who took it, and blew her nose loudly.

'What is going to happen now?' Rachel asked, her eyes searching Grace's face.

Grace drew Rachel gently into her arms, feeling the girl's body heave as she began to sob. 'Look, I have to go to work now, but I'll come and see you later, we can talk properly then.'

Rachel drew away, nodding wordlessly.

Grace slammed the Land Rover door shut cursing herself for heaping more work onto her already busy schedule. Now she had added counselling to her list of jobs. The last thing she wanted to do was to spend the evening listening to Rachel's outpourings of guilt. But she had known Catherine. Could she have known the other victims?

* * * * *

An hour later Grace, showered and changed, walked into the station. Steve Cooper, when she passed his office looked pale and tired. After the Blackthorn murders of Eddie Hammett this was the biggest crime to have ever crossed his desk. He preferred Penzance quiet, with rural crime and the odd bit of smuggling thrown in for excitement.

'Interesting night?' Grace asked as Max came towards her.

'You could say,' Max stuffed his hands deep into his trouser pockets. 'Is she…. the girl… your daughter.'

Max met Grace's eyes. 'We have to prove it, but probably.'

'Wow,' Grace could think of nothing else to say.

The daily briefing took place a short time later. Grace addressed the team while Cooper stalked up and down at the front of the room, as if he were unable to contain his energy.

'Bad news is there's no DNA or finger print evidence from the knife. We're no closer to finding out who killed Jago Carey or why. Are those dead women the key to this?' He stopped and glared around the room as though he was going to see the answer written on one of their foreheads.

'Could we be looking at him working as a team, with another man if Jago originally killed with Eddie Hammett as looks to be the case…' Pete leant forwards, his chair creaking.

'Could he have been killed in a falling out of partners?' someone else suggested. 'Have there been any signs anyone else is involved in the killings or burials of the girls?'

Grace shook her head, 'Eddie Hammett and Jago's DNA was on the quilt the first body was buried in. We haven't found any other DNA on any of the girls other than Jago's, that doesn't mean to say he didn't have help, just that perhaps they were very forensically aware and didn't leave any trace.'

'Do we know where any of the girls were killed?' Max asked.

Nope,' Grace replied, the questions being thrown at her, combined with those running through her mind were making her head spin. 'We aren't likely too now. We'd never find any proof of anything now unless we were very lucky.'

Grace tapped on the whiteboard, letting her fingertip rest briefly on the images of each of the people who were at Park Hall the day Jago died.

'We've checked and rechecked the alibis, They all lied. Let's have another chat with all of them.'

'Shit.' The small word encompassed a mass of work, delving into the lives of everyone who had a connection to the yard at Park Hall. Cooper remained adamant a man had to be responsible. Grace's opinion was a woman could have also committed the crime.

'I know you don't see a woman doing this,' Grace said to Steve Cooper, her tone deferential. She had learned in her years working with him the best way to challenge his train of thought was to make him believe you weren't doing that.

'I don't. This,' Cooper shifted through the crime scene images laid out on his desk. 'This,' he repeated, 'has been planned, executed coldly.'

'And you think a woman isn't capable of such a crime. That we're essentially cuddly creatures that only kill as a last resort.'

He scowled at her choice of words. 'Something like that.'

Grace shook her head, 'We're just as capable of murdering in cold blood as any man.'

'Where are we with the suspects. There's enough of them.'

'We found the murder weapon. The knife seems to have been one that was used on the yard, so anyone could have picked it up.'

'That seems to indicate a spur of the moment crime.' Cooper began to rummage through his jacket pockets, his fingers searching and finally finding a discarded pack of nicotine gum. He wrestled the gum out of the wrapper, shoved it in his mouth and chewed gratefully.

'I don't think so, Sir. Issy the groom said it had been missing for a while, she had got a new one from Jago.'

'What about Sam Green, the blacksmith? He's got a record, assaults, petty theft, put someone in hospital. He was lucky to not get time for that.'

Grace shook her head, 'He caught Jem Trevayne breaking into his house. He chased him out and in the process ended up hurting him pretty badly. He probably deserved it. But he also badly beat up a man he thought was flirting with Fiona, Green's wife.'

It was hard to have sympathy for Jem, the man who had once threatened her and Kaden while they were in a local pub for a night out. Grace took a deep breath, even years after the event she still had vivid memories of the man's malice. That same night she had been attacked by Eddie Hammett. If it hadn't been for a car coming down the road she could quite easily have become one of Hammett's victims. She forced her thoughts away from the terrifying event. Jem had been in hospital for a while after the assault by Sam Green and had left the area afterwards. No one missed him and she was sure many had breathed a sigh of relief when he had gone. Petty crime around the local farms had certainly gone down since he had left.

'Show's Green has it in him to be violent.'

'That was spur of the moment stuff, he was threatened, frightened by someone breaking into his house, and by someone coming onto his wife. He hit out in anger. Jago Carey's killing was cold. Calculating. Someone thought long and hard about that murder. Planned it carefully. Sam Green is having an affair with Zara Carey, that gives him a motive.'

'Was,' Pete interjected. 'She's just moved Roddy Eden into the house.'

'Roddy Eden the owner of the Cliff Hotel?'

'Could he…?' Cooper turned to look at Pete who shook his head. 'Already checked. He was in Rome on business.'

Cooper stuffed his hands irritably into the pockets of his trousers and stalked around the room. 'What about the gardener, Simon O'Connor, and the vet, Michael Alderton. What have you found?'

'Nothing on either.' Pete shook his head.

'The vet is slicing things up every day. Was Jago shagging the vet's wife? The gardener… he's a tough strong man.'

Grace waited until Cooper paused for breath. 'No sir. We've found nothing to link Michael Alderton with Jago. He got a speeding ticket five years ago, but that is the only brush he's ever had with the law. Seems to be a very law-abiding citizen.'

'What about his wife? Was she playing away?'

'No sir, she's very involved in the Women's Institute, all the usual Parent Teacher committees at school. Nothing to suggest she's anything other than a very ordinary wife.'

'The gardener then?'

Grace again shook her head. 'There's nothing. Witnesses on the yard have reported they could hear his ride on lawnmower in the grounds around the time of Jago's murder. Plus I can't find anything in his background that would suggest a reason for him killing Jago.'

'Doesn't mean there isn't one.' Cooper said, sagely.

'The women…'

'I can't see any of them for this.' Cooper said, cutting off Grace mid-sentence.

Grace paused, clearing her throat, waiting for Cooper to justify his statement. When he said nothing further, she continued. 'So on the yard there were the vet, groom, Issy, Sam, the farrier, Simon, who found the body, Ruth, Miranda and Tamara. They all said they were there, yet it seems all of them lied.'

'Issy?' Cooper shifted through the photographs. 'She looks like she's the right age for Jago to be interested in her.'

Grace shook her head. 'She's from a stable family background. Very middle class. Doesn't fit the profile of the women he'd be interested in. They're needy, vulnerable. She's neither of those.'

Cooper sat back in his chair, smacking his lips together in a frustrated gesture.

'The others, what do we know?'

'They've all got a motive for killing him.' Grace leant forwards to slide the photographs apart. 'Ruth,' she found the image she had been looking for and turned it to face Cooper. 'She got involved with Jago.'

Cooper made a noise that was a cross between a tut of annoyance and a sigh of frustration. 'Why can't they just keep their knickers on?'

'We don't know all the circumstances, Sir,' Grace told him patiently. He was very quick to jump to conclusions about people. 'Seems her husband found out and threw her out. She lost everything. She's working in a nursing home now.'

'Poor cow,' Cooper sifted the image of Ruth to one side, tapping lightly on it with his index finger. 'How can people be so dumb.'

'Trusting, Sir.' Grace heard the irritated note in her voice.

'And the rest of them?'

'Miranda.' In the image she pushed towards Cooper, Miranda glared at the camera, caught in the moments after Jago had been killed before they were interviewed by the police. In the image her hair was plastered to her head, sweaty from being crushed beneath her riding hat. 'She was got involved in a business idea with Jago. Lost all of her money on a dream. I don't know if it was a scam or just bad business.'

'And Tamara,' Grace looked for a moment at the photograph. Tamara, it seemed, could not take a bad photograph. In the image, even caught on the hop she seemed perfectly composed, her gaze towards the camera steady, lips painted a perfect shade of pink.

She saw Cooper's expression of approval as his eyes flickered over the image.

'Tamara doesn't actually exist.' Grace felt a stab of satisfaction seeing his face change from out and out approval to confusion. 'She changed her name by deed poll years ago. Looks as if she reinvented herself completely. The real Tamara is a woman called Mandy who comes from County Durham which coincidently is where Jago grew up.'

''You think he knew her?'

'Oh, I'd say so. Gives her a reason to kill him. Just like the rest of them.'

'I still don't buy it.' Cooper pushed the images back towards Grace.

'I think you could be blinded by the motives of these three women, Tallis.'

'Right, you're the boss.' Grace hoped her voice had the right mixture of deference and obedience.

'And don't you forget it.' Cooper's mouth twisted into a wry grin.

Pete came into the office, a reem of papers fluttering in his hand.

'I think we might have something.'

'Go on then,' Cooper snapped impatiently as Pete paused.

'Michael Alderton, the vet.' Pete paused, letting his words sink in. 'I've been going through his phone records just to see if there was anything of interest.'

'Yes…' Cooper drummed his fingers on his desk.

'I think he could be having an affair…'

'Oh, so what. Him and every other red-blooded male.'

'I agree,' Pete's voice was filled with a curious mixture of amusement and triumph. 'But I think it could be with another man.'

'Right,' Cooper's eyes swept over Grace. Meeting hers. She dropped hers first.

'Oh, for fuck's sake, Pete, give up the punchlines. I just want the information.' Cooper rounded on the detective.

Pete's cheeks flushed.

'Two men with motives to kill Jago. And heaven knows how many women.' Cooper's voice echoed with satisfaction.

Grace grabbed her jacket, 'Max, let's go. We need to visit all our suspects for a chat.'

Chapter Thirty-Six

Sam threw a horseshoe across the shed. It landed with force, clattering against the pile of others. 'I don't know what you expect me to say.' There was a taut line to his mouth.

'We are looking for the truth,' beside her Grace was aware of Max straightening his shoulders and pulling himself up to his full height as if to discourage any further aggression from the angry farrier.

'You weren't shoeing horses at Park Hall the whole of the afternoon Jago died.'

Sam made a noise of agreement. He slouched against the wall, stuffing his hands deep into the pockets of his jeans. 'I wasn't. You are quite right.' There was a sarcastic tone in his voice. His eyes flickered over Max as if sizing him up, wondering if he could beat him if it came to a serious row.

'So, were where you? Grace did nothing to disguise the note of impatience in her voice.

'Look,' Sam ran a hand through his hair. 'I'll tell you, but this can't get back to my wife. We're just trying to patch things up. We had a row. I left. Then I went back. As you can imagine, things at home are frosty to say the least.

'We'll do our best to keep your private life that way.' Grace said quietly.

Sam shrugged in a gesture of resignation. 'There's a woman… I was with her. She will vouch for me.'

* * * * *

'Zara, were you with Sam the afternoon Jago was killed?' Max's voice was impassive.

Zara Carey gave a snort of amusement.

'Guilty,' she threw her hands in the air. 'But that's all.' She continued.

Zara got to her feet and paced the length of the room, her heels tapping lightly on the ancient wooden floor. At the far end she paused and stood in the bay window looking out over the carefully tended gardens. Sunlight streamed in around her, making it impossible to read her expression when she turned and began to speak again. 'Sam and I have… had a bit of a thing. Something to keep me amused. I think it meant more to him than me. I've moved on since.'

Grace saw the coldness in her eyes she had seen before, on the day Zara had been told Jago was dead.

'Where did this take place.' Max swallowed, clearly uncomfortable about asking anyone the intimate details of their life.

Zara met his eyes, a slow smile spread slowly over her face, her amusement at his discomfiture obvious in her expression. 'It's alright sergeant it's a perfectly normal thing to do when people have needs that aren't met.' She was silent, one expensively shod foot tapping lightly on the floor.

'We have a hotel we liked. I rented a room. Sam paid for lunch. We'd spend the afternoon in bed. We'd go home. No one was any the wiser. His wife didn't know, although she does now. Jago didn't care what I did.'

'So, what you told us before about visiting one of your shops wasn't true.' Grace struggled to keep a professional tone in her voice, faced with the spite of Zara Carey. No matter what she had thought about her husband, he had died an horrific death.

'Shocking, wasn't it?' Zara smirked, 'I wanted to keep my dirty little secret.'

* * * * *

Ruth's face flooded with colour as she pulled back the front door and saw who had been knocking on it.

'May we come in?' Grace had no intention of chatting to Ruth in the entrance hall of her apartment, especially not with the sharp faced elderly lady hovering at the bottom of the stairs, trying very hard not to look like she had the slightest bit of interest in Ruth's visitors. 'Yes,' Ruth shrugged, a studied effort to appear nonchalant.

She led them into a small, very neat and clean, but clearly very battered and shabby lounge. Grace's eyes swept the room. Ruth had clearly tried to make the place look as nice as she could, a vase of flowers was situated in the middle of a coffee table, throws disguised what she guessed was the sorry condition of the sofa. Ruth leant uneasily on the edge of the sofa, indicating with her hand they should sit down.

Max and Grace lowered themselves onto the sagging sofa. 'Do you know why we're here?' Grace studied Ruth, seeing her uneasy expression. 'No.'

'Do you remember what you told us about your movements on the day Jago died?'

'Yes.' Ruth's eyes flickered over Grace and Max before she stared at the bunch of flowers as if they were the most interesting thing she had ever seen.

'I think,' Grace said softly, 'what you told us wasn't quite correct and wondered if you would like to change your account.'

Ruth lowered her head. 'You know anyway, I'm sure. I wanted to see my partner's new woman. I've been charged with stalking her. I can't stay away.'

* * * * *

Issy changed in front of Grace's eyes. Altering from the naïve country girl she had come to know, to one who was filled with hatred and resentment.

I'd gone mad,' she shook her head, staring fixedly at her work worn hands, which rested in her lap. 'Mad with jealousy.'

Grace watched her, silently, letting Issy frame the words that were so clearly bursting inside her.

Issy met Grace's eyes, she twisted her mouth into a wry grin. 'I wanted to be like the women Jago was attracted to. I wanted to be one of them.'

'You were lucky not to be.' Max reminded her gently.

'I was so angry at him for not wanting me.' Issy continued, ignoring Max. 'I couldn't tell you that,' Issy leant forwards so her knees were almost touching Grace's. 'What would you have thought if you had known how much hate I had inside me. I didn't want you to think I might have killed him.'

Grace shook her head. 'You should have told me the truth. You could never kill anyone; I can see that in you.'

Issy screwed up her nose. Shaking her head. 'I could. I hated him so much and everyone he was messing around with. I don't know. I can see I just went a little bit mad. He'd hurt Rachel so much too. I wanted to protect her so she wouldn't get in trouble. I lied for her.'

Issy pushed her hair behind what Grace noticed were tiny, delicate ears, studded quirkily with a row of different coloured studs.

'Why did Simon go up to the flat?'

Issy paused, 'Rachel told Simon that was where Jago was.'

* * * * *

Simon buried his face in his hands. Grace was aware of Max's eyes widening in horror as Simon began to sob. 'I should have told you lot the truth in the first place.' He looked up, his normally pale cheeks reddened with tears. 'But then I realised if you knew the truth you would think I'd killed Jago.'

Grace was silent, waiting for him to continue. Autumn stood, white faced, beside the kitchen sink where she had been washing up when they arrived.

'If you knew why I'd gone to talk to him you'd have been certain I'd killed him. I had the opportunity, you knew that. I was in the loft where he died. But I thought if you didn't know the reason I went there you wouldn't think I'd done it.'

'Perhaps you should enlighten us.' Max shifted in his chair, the wooden legs scraped on the tiled floor.

'My sister has been missing for three years. I knew she had been in Cornwall. I knew she'd worked for Jago. He laughed at me when I asked him about her.'

'You thought he had killed her,' Grace probed gently.

Simon looked up, meeting her eyes, his face etched with pain. 'That's right. But he let me think that. I think he enjoyed hurting me.'

'So, you lied so we wouldn't know you had a motive to kill him.'

Simon nodded. 'Oh God,' he buried his face in his hands once more sobbing loudly. Autumn crossed the room and put her arm around his shoulders. 'I'm so sorry.' Simon said, looking up and facing Grace. 'I found the knife. I thought if you found it with my prints on you'd assume it was me who had killed him. The knife was one I'd often used. I took it and threw it in the lake.'

* * * * *

Miranda took a large swig of her gin, 'Just like everyone else, I had a motive to kill him.' She pushed herself to the back of the plush hotel armchair and crossed her legs slowly. Grace noticed her glance at Max, wanting to judge the result her actions had on him. She was pleased to see there were none. Max, professional as ever, was completely unaffected by Miranda showing off her toned legs and trying to flirt with him.

'Like Ruth and Tamara, you weren't riding together. You all lied to cover for each other.'

'So, it would seem.' Miranda's voice had a cold edge to it. She was, Grace realised, completely unafraid of her authority.

'What were you really doing?' Grace forced a light-hearted tone into her voice, realising if she pushed Miranda, she would get nowhere with her. There was a hardness to the woman that was not natural, something she had built around herself as protection.

'You know what I do?' Miranda met Grace's eyes. 'Do you know why I do that?'

'Tell me,' Grace said softly.

'I was so stupid,' Miranda said after regarding Grace solemnly, looking at the detective to see if she wanted to trust her. 'I fell for Jago's charms. I gave him virtually every penny I had. I was left high and dry. No job. Bills to pay. What's a girl to do. Apparently, it's the oldest profession in the world,' Miranda drained the last of her drink. 'It must have started because some poor woman lost everything because of a man and had to earn a living.'

'Why didn't you tell us in the first place.' Grace asked.

Miranda gave a slight shake of her head, sighing bitterly. 'Because I'm too embarrassed to tell you I was on my back having sex for money when Jago died.'

* * * * *

Michael closed the surgery door, glancing anxiously towards it, as if judging if his voice could be heard by anyone in the waiting room.

'We won't take a minute.' Max's fingers toyed with an array of shining silver implements. If he didn't know otherwise the vet could be someone who could have carried out Jago's murder. He had all the right tools.

'I just want to know why you lied.' Grace leant against the work surface that spanned the length of the surgery.

'Ruth, Miranda and Tamara helped each other, they all had reasons for lying, for wasting my time. I'm sure you have a reason too.'

'The old reason. Love.' Michael pushed his fingers into the bridge of his nose, smoothing the tension tightened skin.

'Another woman. We'll have to chat to her, to check out what you've said.' Max told him.

A small smile flickered briefly over Michael's face. 'If only it was that simple. I'd have told you that.'

When Grace and Max were silent, Michael released a long sigh. 'I'm gay. I love another man. How could I possibly tell you that. Risk my secret coming out. The country vet is queer. No, I couldn't have told you that.'

* * * * *

Tamara brushed her horse, long rhythmic strokes over his body. She continued brushing, ignoring Grace's words.

'Tamara,' Grace's voice held a note of irritation. It had been a long day, filled with sorting out the time wasters who had sent the case off in completely the wrong direction, given Jago's killer time to escape. She had no patience to wait while Tamara ignored her. 'I know you all covered for one another. I know the reasons why. And I want to know is why you were part of that.'

Tamara turned, rubbing a metal curry comb against the soft bristles of the brush to rid it of hairs and dust. 'Jago got what he deserved. He hurt too many people, me included.'

'Why did you lie? Tamara what are you hiding?'

'A whole life,' Tamara turned and threw the brushes roughly into the box on the floor, her horse jumped back, startled.

'Can you explain that.' Max met Grace's eyes and raised his eyebrows quizzically.

'I'm not even Tamara. My name is Mandy. I thought I'd hidden my past. Jago by some mad coincidence recognised me. Charming individual he was, he thought he would use that to his advantage.'

'Blackmail,' Grace spoke quietly.

Tamara sniffed, 'If only it was that easy. Blackmail yes, but he wanted me not money. Unfortunately, I got pregnant. My husband had previously undergone a vasectomy so it would have been fairly obvious to him what I had been doing.'

Grace winced, imagining what she must have gone through. 'The afternoon he died I was arranging an abortion to get rid of the baby.'

Chapter Thirty-Seven

'**K**aden! You need to move.'

Faint, competing with the roar of wind and the sound of rain thundering on the roof, Grace made out the odd word. 'Barn…tarpaulin…' The call ended abruptly. Grace stared at the telephone. 'Shit, shit, shit.' She dialled Kaden's number, sighing as the call went straight to voice mail. No point in leaving him a message as he never listened to them.

A moment later her phone rang. Kaden. 'I came inside. I'm soaked, even in my waterproofs.'

'Thanks, I can hear you now.'

She imagined him standing in the kitchen, wet weather gear dripping, the water pooling on the recently laid slate tiles. 'How long are you going to be?' There was an irritated edge to his voice.

'I don't know,' Grace knew she was failing to keep the shortness out of her voice. 'It will be hours before I get home.'

The discovery of the weapon used to murder Jago had been little help. There had been no fingerprints or DNA evidence on it. The general opinion seemed to be that a man had to be responsible, someone who would have the strength to restrain Jago and also the strong stomach necessary to cut someone open from chest to navel. It was not, Steve Cooper insisted something a woman would be capable of doing.

'This is a big case,' she continued. 'I've so much to do.'

'So have I.' Kaden's irritation had turned to resignation. 'I need to get a tarpaulin over the hole in the barn roof.'

One of the tin sheets had blown off the ancient roof in the last storm. They had meant to get it repaired. It was one of the many things on the to do list that somehow never got done. When they had looked at the farm they had fallen so in love with the place and its potential that neither of them had truly seen the problems that lay ahead. The surveyor and builder had presented them with a long list of issues that needed to be addressed, but such had been their confidence neither of them had really paid it the attention it needed. They both realised that now. Every problem they tried to fix just uncovered more issues. A delivery of precious winter hay had been stacked into the now leaking barn. If it got wet their winter feed would be ruined.

'I can't do it on my own.'

'I understand that, but I can't leave here. Could you ask Rachel?'

'I'll have to, she's bloody got enough to do without that.'

'I know, I'm sorry.'

'What about dinner?' Kaden's voice softened.

'You have yours when you can, there's a shepherd's pie I made, it just needs putting into the oven when you're ready.'

'What about you?'

'I'll get something here. Max was going to get something from the Indian. I'll probably go with him.'

'You spend more time with Max than you do with me.' The irritated edge was back again. Grace heard the roar of the storm as Kaden went back outside.

'You know I…' Grace listened, the storm noise was gone, the phone silent against her ear, the phone coverage could be poor out at the farm, especially when the weather was bad.

'Great.' Grace shoved her phone into her back pocket. As if she didn't have enough to deal with, the last thing she needed was a sulky Kaden when she eventually got home. Her job, and more recently any mention of Max seemed to provoke Kaden more than anything. 'Boss,' Pete got to his feet as Grace went back into the office. 'We've got confirmation of identification on the bodies.'

A knot of tension slowly tightened in the pit of Grace's stomach. Having names somehow made the deaths of the women more real. There were families somewhere missing them, who would soon have the news that their loved ones were no longer missing, but were dead. Murdered. Before they were given that news, no matter how much they suspected what had happened to them, there was always hope that someday they could walk back into their lives with feasible explanations as to what had happened to make them disappear.

He crossed the room with a piece of paper in his hand. 'You were right Boss. Danielle Brown, 23. She was from Birmingham. Went missing after coming to Cornwall to work. The other body is Amber Friday, she was 20, came from Newcastle. She was an orphan, had been in care. Reported missing by a Terry Nicholl, no relative, just a friend, he thought she'd come south to work. The other is Susan Lawrence.'

Grace stared at the names Pete had scrawled on the piece of paper. Names to go with the crumpled heaps of bones that had been unearthed from the ground near Park Hall.

'Thanks, Pete.' There were addresses beside the names. Danielle Brown's parents and presumably that of Terry Nicholl who had reported Amber Friday missing. At least Danielle had parents to mourn her. What sadness they had gone through, losing her and then discovering she had ended up discarded like a piece of garbage into a cold, damp field. Susan had no one. 'Max, we'll be making a trip up country, tomorrow.' She needed to interview the parents of Danielle and the friend of Amber Friday. Already it seemed obvious what had happened to the girls, but she needed to clarify everything.

That Jago had been part of their deaths was not in doubt. The girls had come to Cornwall to work, undoubtedly filled with excitement about the wonderful jobs and new life they were going to have in the county. Whatever Zara knew about their deaths she wasn't saying.

'And there's something else.' Pete's voice brought Grace's attention back to the office where the detectives were looking at her expectedly. 'All the women were wrapped in duvets as you know, and there's more DNA evidence.'

'Jago Carey?'

'Jago Carey and we've already got Eddie Hammett present on Amber Friday's body.'

'I fucking knew it.' Grace turned away, looking at the whiteboard where the newly posted images of the additional dead women now looked down, beautiful in life, broad grins splitting their faces, unaware of the horrors that lay ahead of them. Hastily she wiped a tear from her cheek, disguising the gesture by running a hand through her hair as if she were pushing it off her face. What had they gone through, in their final moments.

Eddie Hammett. His name had been ever present throughout her career, even though he had died soon after she had started in the force. There seemed to be no end to the damage he had inflicted. And now the knowledge Jago Carey had been his partner in one of crimes and had then continued killing. The thought of the two of them made her feel sick, repulsed by the thought of them acting together, selecting a victim and killing her.

Steve Cooper threw his arms skywards in a gesture of despair. 'Jago Carey and Eddie Hammett working as a team? We can't link Carey to any of Hammett's bodies, but they were working together to kill one of the women we found buried at Park Hall. Are we going to find more?' Cooper eased himself into his chair. It creaked in protest as he sat back, leaning his head wearily against the headrest. 'I'm struggling to get my head around it. Filthy bastards.'

Grace nodded, she rested her arm on the filing cabinet beside the door, resisting the urge to lay her aching head on it.

The two men had been neighbours. They had both taken part in the killing of Amber Friday. Had Jago had any part in the deaths of the victims at Blackthorn Farm. Eddie Hammett's home? It had always been assumed that Eddie Hammett had acted alone, only his DNA had been found on the bodies buried on his land, or in the cellar where he had kept his victims. When had they become partners? Grace tried and failed to imagine a conversation between the two men that had set them on the course to working together. The thought was unbearable. Even more so was the fact that Jago seemed to have been inspired to carry on what he had started with Hammett.

Grace's thoughts spiralled. How had Eddie Hammett created such a lovely daughter as Mia? She had been lucky to escape when he had died. The girl had grown up with a loving foster family, although tragedy had seemed to stalk her every move. Nan, Eddie's mother had been part of her son's crimes, even though she had always denied it. The jury, at her trial had thought differently and she had served a prison sentence. Mia seemed to have believed her innocence because she lived with her grandmother in the isolated farm where the crimes had been committed. The tragedy that stalked her had struck again with the suicide of her boyfriend. Grace's thoughts flickered briefly over the handsome young vet who had accompanied Mia when they had moved to Cornwall. His struggles with his relationship with his father seemed to have pushed him over the edge and it was assumed he had killed himself, although his body had never been found.

Nan had to know about her son's relationship with Jago. 'Get uniform,' Grace said to Pete. 'Max, let's go and pick up Nan Hammett, see what she knows about her son's relationship with Jago Carey.'

'What do you fuckers want?' Nan Hammett spat an hour later as Grace stood in the doorway of the farm.

'Mrs Hammett we just want to have a chat with you about your son's relationship with Jago Carey.'

'They were neighbours.' Nan shook off the hand of the uniformed officer who led her towards the patrol car. 'Get your bloody hands off me.'

'We just need a few minutes of your time.' Grace smiled tightly, turning to face the young woman who was crossing the yard towards them.

'What's going on?' Mia Lewis was a stunning young woman,

tall, willowy with a mane of dark hair. She was, Grace knew from photographs, the image of her mother, Glanna Pendrick, who Eddie Hammett had imprisoned and eventually killed.

'We just need to have a chat with your gran about Jago Carey and his relationship with your father.'

'Jago Carey?' Mia looked surprised. 'They were neighbours. I don't know about any relationship between my father and Jago. I never met my dad as you know.'

Grace met Mia's eyes, seeing the confusion in their depths. 'We'll just have a talk to Nan. I'll make sure she won't be long. It's easier to do it down at the station.'

Grace held Mia's gaze until she dropped it, focusing on the surface of the yard at her feet. 'I'm sorry.' Grace shrugged, feeling a surge of sympathy for the young woman. It wasn't her fault that she had been born into such an awful family.

Side by side they watched as the patrol car, carrying Nan swept out of the yard. Nan stared fixedly ahead, her mouth set in a grim, tight line. 'I'll get Nan back to you as soon as I can.' Grace said gently.

'Fine.' Mia fixed Grace with a cold stare.

Once they arrived at the station Grace addressed Pete. 'Caution Nan Hammett please, I want this conversation recorded. Get the duty solicitor to stay on for a while longer.'

'I've arranged for some tea to be brought in.' Grace sat beside Max. The duty solicitor, engaged to tend yet again to the legal needs of one of Penzance's more prolific petty criminals, smiled gratefully.

'Stuff your fucking tea,' Nan Hammett, pushed herself as far away from the table as she could, folding her arms across her ample bosom.

An hour later Grace stopped the interview. She stood up, stiff with tension.

'Thanks Mrs Hammett. I'll arrange for a lift home for you.'

Nan glared at Grace, aggression oozing from the taut line of her body and her harsh, bulldog face.

Grace left the room, leaving Nan to the care of the duty solicitor and Max. The air in the corridor felt cleaner. She leant against the wall, gasping the cooler air into her lungs. Nan, as she had guessed, had told them nothing. She had denied all knowledge of any relationship her son had with Jago Carrey other than that of farming neighbours who helped each other out if there were issues with straying livestock or broken machinery.

Grace kicked angrily at the wall beside the interview room. She knew Jago and Eddie had worked as a team. At some stage they had realised that they shared the same perverted need to torture and kill young women. They had begun to work together, joining forces to kill and bury Amber Friday. The thought of them discussing their crimes, of each other witnessing, or acting together was too horrific to even think of. The thought of one serial killer in the depths of Cornwall was hard to contemplate. But two. Working together. How could anyone have known those things were going on and done nothing. Nan Hammett had to have known. She had always denied knowing what was going on at the farm, but she had. And now, it was certain she had known of her son's relationship with Jago Carey. She had known what the two of them were doing. But Grace could not prove that. And Nan knew it.

Chapter Thirty-Eight

If he could ever be granted a superpower Michael often pondered, he would like the ability to stop time. That is what he wished he could do right now, to freeze this perfect moment and keep it forever.

The room was darkening, the curtains closed, the light coming in through the tiniest of chinks casting a pale, yellow glow over the room. A single strand of the late summer sunlight lit on a painting that hung on the wall the furthest side of the room from the bed, bringing the moorland scene to life, making the river look as if it were alive with light.

It was warm in the bed, the mattress beneath his back was soft, the pillows plump beneath his head, but the best of all was the gentle sound of Carl sleeping beside him, the warmth from his body against Michael's side. In the half-light Michael could just make out the bedside table and the half full glass of wine Carl had brought from the dining room where they had eaten lunch. He had never got around to finishing the wine.

If they could stay safe like this forever, life would be perfect, away from the eyes Michael saw looking at them assuming, condemning, sniggering. The pressure to stay with Julia and his love for his son were at odds with the deep abiding love he had for Carl.

The hotel was one they often used. Carl would stay the night after Michael had gone. He would drive away feeling guilty, guilty for leaving Carl, guilty for the betrayal of his family, guilty at sneaking off from work. The staff were quiet and discrete, if they wondered at the relationship between the two men, they never gave any sign, the service was always courteous and friendly.

Lunch as always had been perfect, a glass of gin from the vast selection of tempting bottles that they had gradually worked their way through, sampling each on different occasions. Monkey 47 had been a favourite although Carl preferred Hendricks to anything, served perfectly in the hotel in a chilled glass with a long thin slice of cucumber curled around the inside of the glass. Then lunch, in the dining room with the high ceiling and beautifully starched linen tablecloths. The hotel was expensive and lunch times were very quiet, the hotel was way off the normal tourist trail and the only guests were those who wanted and could afford the luxury and peace that the price afforded.

After lunch they had walked in the gardens, chatting companionably, Carl was intensely knowledgeable about garden plants, and they had discussed the various ones they had seen as they wandered around. Until finally their stroll took them back towards the building and upstairs to their room.

Carl stirred, yawning and stretching pleasurably as he woke. He slid out an arm and snapped on the bedside light, casting the room into dark shadows. He turned and seeing that Michael was sitting up, propped against the mountains of pillows, pushed his back and sat up.

'I ought to be going,' Michael said, it was a familiar end to their afternoons. The breaking of their golden bubble of pleasure, the time they spent together.

Carl sighed, 'Of course, back to the wife. Leave me on the side-lines yet again while you continue with your lie.'

Michael was silent. The last thing he wanted was to row with Carl again over their relationship, or what Carl perceived as the lack of it.

'It's getting late,' Michael slid out of bed, reaching for the checked shirt he had discarded so hastily earlier on in the afternoon.

'Michael,' Carl's voice was quiet, with a hard tone that Michael did not recognise. 'I'm not going to keep doing this.'

Michael shoved his arms into the sleeves of his shirt, suddenly uncomfortable about his nakedness.

'We are happy together, aren't we?' Carl continued, reaching for and putting on his glasses. His eyes were sad behind the lenses, his chin now had a blue haze of stubble on it that had not been there earlier.

'Of course,' Michael itched to be away, it was getting late, he would find it hard to explain to his wife if he was terribly late. Periodically Carl would demand Michael left his wife, he wanted them live properly and openly. The row would blow up seemingly out of nowhere. Carl often said they should move to London and make a new start. Michael could set up a practice in the city, there was no need for him to be out at all hours of the day and night tending farm animals. Usually, Michael was able to sidestep his demands, promise one day they would be together, when his son was older, when he was able to understand about his father. One day.

'I'm just not going to keep doing this?' Carl had a hard edge to his voice now, he had thrown back the quilt and was sitting on the edge of the bed. Michael glanced at him and felt a surge of desire for Carl, he was in great shape, kept so by daily running and gym sessions.

'I've had enough of being your bit on the side,' he half turned to glare at Michael, 'And I'm not going to do it anymore. You need to decide what you want, me or Julia.'

Michael moved to put his arms around Carl's shoulders. 'You know that's what I want.' He rested his face against Carl's skin, breathing in the smell of his skin, body wash and aftershave, 'I just can't do it yet.'

'That's fine then.' Carl got hastily to his feet, brushing off Michael. 'You stay living your lie with Julia. I'm not going to be alone for the rest of my life.'

'Let's talk about this.' Michael slid off the bed and took a stride towards Carl who held out his hands palms upwards in a gesture designed to stop him coming any closer.

'There's nothing to talk about,' Carl said, 'I'm done.'

The row was nothing unusual. Carl often got upset by their separation and Michael's apparent lack of commitment. He would come around, he always did. Michael was slightly disconcerted as he drove home by the fact Carl would not answer his telephone, but Carl often would sulk for days after they had rowed. Eventually he would call or answer his telephone as if nothing had happened.

Dinner was a silent affair, as it often was, especially when Danny was staying with one of his friends. Julia served dinner. She made it a rule they always ate at the dining table, no meal in front of the television with trays on their knees, which Michael would have preferred. But it was what she wanted and so he went along with it. Julia had asked him about his day, he had answered, suspicious as always, she had found out about his other life, about Carl, but she did not seem interested in catching him out. He had asked about her day and her replies had been stilted. He put it down to tiredness and was not concerned, it was easier not to have to talk to her, there was little they had to say to one another apart from banal day to day topics.

'I'm sorry Michael,' Julia said suddenly, breaking the silence.

Michael looked up, his fork halfway to his mouth. 'What?

Julia was looking at him with an intense stare. He waited, with a feeling of dread, as she struggled to compose her words. He was aware of the grandfather clock ticking in the corner of the room, the fire crackling, the light dancing on the walls reflected from the fire.

'I have something to tell you.'

Michael put down the food he had halfway to his mouth.

Julia met his eyes. Her voice was cold when she spoke, 'I want a divorce.'

He felt his mouth drop open, it was the last thing he expected her to say, she was always so particular about the face they presented to the world, she the perfect wife, keeping an immaculate home, he the local vet, pillars of the community.

'I am so sorry; I've been having an affair with someone. I've fallen in love, and we want to be together,' she paused, her eyes wide. Spots of red had appeared on her cheeks. 'I'm moving in with him. I want to sell this house. Take Danny with me.'

Michael opened his mouth to speak but couldn't form any words. He couldn't imagine Julia having an affair, she was dull, passionless. After everything, all the time he had spent trying to present the perfect façade to the world, she was going to shatter that illusion and go off with someone else. He was going to lose everything, Danny, their life together, all he had tried so hard to preserve.

He woke up alone. He had slept in the guest room. He shivered, from cold and shock in the unfamiliar bed. He had wanted their marriage to end, but when the time was right, when Danny was older. Now she had brought everything to a head. All the time he had been hiding his affair from her she had been doing the same.

By the evening he knew what he would do. It was time to change his life, forget about the façade he wanted to present to the world, Julia had made the decision for him. He would go to Carl, live life with him as Carl had wanted. Who cared what people thought about two men living together? Why had he been so stupid and waited so long?

He packed a small bag; told Julia he would be back for the rest of his things in a few days. She promised to tell Danny about the end of the marriage, assured him she would let him see their son. Their separation she said would be amicable. Michael didn't care anymore. Her words had lifted an enormous weight from his shoulders. He didn't know why he had waited so long, why he hadn't been brave enough to make the break before.

He found Carl's road easily, parked his car and walked back along the pavement. There seemed to be a buzz of excitement in the air, a newness that he relished, he could start again here with Carl.

The house had a newly painted black door with elegant tubs of plants at either side. Michael rang the bell, from within the house he heard footsteps coming towards the door. He swallowed, his mouth dry with excitement. The door was flung open and a handsome young coloured man stood in the doorway. 'Yes?' he smiled. From deep within the house Michael heard Carl voice, 'Who is it Reggie?'

Reggie looked at Michael, his eyebrows raised quizzically.

Michael backed away, 'I'm sorry, wrong house.'

Chapter Thirty-Nine

Filthy old bitch. Ruth wrung out the washcloth once more and scraped it across the brown stained wall. 'That wasn't very nice Mary, was it?' she sat back on her heels and looked at the woman who was lying in the narrow hospital bed beside her. The old lady smiled at the sound of her voice but did not seem to associate the sound with the person in the room. What was the point of keeping someone alive when they were so far removed from having any kind of normal life?

Mary had advanced dementia and did not recognise anyone, she existed in some kind of parallel universe, the only time she ever seemed to come to life was when she soiled the thick incontinence pads she wore. She would then wriggle her tiny, claw like hand between the folds of her wrinkled flesh and the thick fabric and scooped up whatever mess she found there and with a nifty jerk of her wrist splatter it all over the wall beside her bed. Ruth had just spent the last half an hour cleaning the brown, evil smelling mess from Mary's hand, where it was firmly stuck beneath her neatly trimmed nails. Her bed linen was changed, yet again and she now lay peacefully dozing while Ruth got to work clearing the rest of the damage off the wall beside the bed. She had changed the bowl of water three times already and even though she was clad in long rubber gloves and an all-encompassing plastic apron she still could feel the stench soaking into her skin.

It felt like forever until she was finally keying the code into the exit security panel and stepping out of the oppressive heat into the cold night air. She breathed deeply, sucking clean air into her lungs. She had been waiting for her shift to finish for hours, today she was going to challenge Gilly Blackwell, the woman her husband wanted to marry. Ruth had to make Neil see sense, had to get him back and Gilly was the one standing in the way. If only she could talk properly to Neil again, the old spark was there, she was sure, it was just that Gilly was distracting him from realising where his true future lay. Ruth was determined to warn Gilly off, to get her out of the way so that she could get Neil back. She realised she had to do something to make Neil realise once and for all he belonged to her. She had made a mistake, but she knew Neil would forgive her. He'd had nothing to do with getting her charged with stalking, that had all been Gilly.

Ruth drove across town. She parked on the street where Gilly lived, got out of her car and paused, standing on the street opposite the house. Ruth had spent hours standing in the same spot until the police had arrested her for stalking. Gilly's curtains weren't drawn, and Ruth could see into her living room, it looked neat, lined with books, shadows from a fire cast a red glow on the wall. Gilly was curled up in the corner of a leather sofa, the smug bitch looked like she was very happy with her lot. She didn't need Ruth's husband, she could find someone else, Ruth was sure of that. Gilly would let Neil go once she knew how desperate Ruth was to have him back.

Finally, Ruth marched across the road and knocked on Gilly's front door. After a moment it was eased open, a security chain safely in place.

'Hello, Gilly,' she smiled, 'I'm sorry to disturb you. Do you mind if we have a bit of a chat.'

The woman stood uncertainly. 'You're not supposed to be here, you know that.'

'Please,' Ruth implored.

'Is something wrong with Neil?' Gilly's voice was filled with concern, she drew the chain back letting Ruth into the warmth of the house.

'Yes,' Ruth said, there was no point in beating about the bush, 'He wants you to leave him alone. He doesn't want to marry you. He wants to come back to me and you are in the way.'

The woman made an exasperated noise. 'Get lost,' she said, putting her hands on Ruth's shoulders and beginning to shove her in the direction of the door.

Ruth furious pushed back.

Gilly stumbled, falling backwards, onto the carpet. 'I'm going to have you for that.' She rolled onto her feet, scrambling up slowly. 'You stupid cow. I'll have you done for assault. That will go well with stalking. You're heading to prison.'

'I'm sorry. I'm sorry.'

The sight of Gilly tumbling to the floor had brought Ruth abruptly to her senses. Shocked Ruth backed away; she opened the door. The night was silent, the streets surrounding the terraced house deserted and still. She drove home imagining Gilly reporting her for what she had done.

She didn't care, let the police find her, without Neil she had nothing to live for.

Later, at home, she lay in the bath, it was hard to imagine what she had done, she'd lost everything and then been stupid enough to attack Gilly. She had been wrong, having an affair with Jago, blaming Gilly when everything had been her own fault. Now she had to face the truth there was no one else to blame but herself.

Later, as she curled up on the battered couch her telephone rang, it was her ex-husband. 'You do that again and it will be the last thing you do. Gilly said she won't report you. You're lucky she's so understanding.'

'Neil, I'm sorry.' Ruth closed her eyes, she had wasted so much time dreaming about getting Neil back when she should have been moving on with her life, meeting someone else, putting the past behind her. Jago had been the catalyst of their breakup, but he hadn't been the reason, things had been wrong long before Jago had come along. It was time she faced that and got on with her life.

* * * * *

Tim was nice, or as nice as any man could be who used the services of a prostitute. Miranda felt safe with him. Some of the men she, as the agency termed it, 'escorted', felt uncomfortable to be with, she was nervous of them from the moment she met them until she finally bolted her apartment door and stripped off her clothes at the end of the night. But Tim was different, he was as Sally at the office said, an older gentleman, smartly dressed. His wife had died, from cancer, a few years previously. He found it hard to be with another woman as he felt he was betraying her, somehow, according to the twisted logic men seemed to put onto their use of prostitutes, using one was completely different because he was paying for it.

Miranda had dated Tim a few times, having dinner, making polite conversation, something she had become used to over the last year since her association with Jago had wrecked her life.

The first occasion they had just had dinner, he had been kind and courteous. Had the circumstances been different Miranda would have imagined she was on a date with him. Tim was a handsome man, tall, elegantly dressed. One their second meeting he had booked a room in the hotel where he was staying and had politely asked her to join him. She had felt safe enough with him, the agency knew where she was and he did seem gentle and friendly, just a lost soul mourning the loss of his wife.

The sex been gentle, almost loving before they had parted, him giving Miranda a large tip, always a big help after the agency had taken their cut of her earnings.

Tim had arranged to meet her again and had suggested that they bypass the agency, what was the point he'd said, of Miranda giving them half her wages. Put like that it had seemed logical, he was nice, she was safe and so she had arranged to meet him at his house.

It was a soulless looking house, set up a long drive. 'I bought us a bottle of wine.' Miranda waved the bottle. 'Brilliant,' he said, looking around the kitchen for a bottle opener. The house was free of any clutter nothing to signify his dead wife had ever existed.

He opened a couple of cupboards and found wine glasses. That was when his telephone rang. 'Yes, yes, I'll be home this evening.'

Miranda felt the air change imperceptibly as he looked at her while he spoke on the telephone. She realised with a jolt, he was not a widower, he was talking to a partner, this was not his home and no one had a clue where she was. It was not until he ended the call she found movement in her legs, dashing from the kitchen.

He was faster than she was, grabbing her by the hair as she reached the door and slamming her head against the wall. She fought with all of her might to free herself, but he was so strong. He pulled her by the wrist, 'Stop fighting,' his whole demeanour had changed, he was no longer the quiet, well dressed, softly spoken man but was instead a terrifying monster, his face, red with rage, contorted with anger.

Somehow, she found the strength to push him away from her, unbalanced he fell clumsily. Miranda took her chance, grabbed her coat and bag and hurtled from the room, wrenching open the front door and dashing back to her car. She opened the car door, throwing herself into the front seat. She locked the doors, terrified as Tim ran after her. Miranda started the car, shoved her foot hard on the accelerator, feeling the wheels spinning, trying to get purchase. In the rear view mirror she could see him standing on the drive watching her go. He knew she could not report him.

She was still trembling when she woke the following morning, she was still wrapped in the towel she had dried herself on after scrubbing herself clean in the shower.

Miranda grimaced as she rolled off the bed, every fibre of her body ached. Her arms, when she gingerly lifted the towel, were covered in livid red bruises. This madness had to stop. She was risking her life every time she went out to work. She had begun to hate herself for being so stupid as to lose everything to Jago. Selling her body had been a way to punish herself for being such a fool. She had to be kinder to herself, stop putting herself at risk. She had made a mistake, she had lost everything, but there had to be another way. She had more to offer than just her body and more to lose than just her life.

Moving slowly to ease the ache in her muscles, she tore two black rubbish sacks off the roll in the kitchen drawer and scooped all her silken underwear into one of them. The next she filled with all her work uniform of low-cut tops and short skirts.

She showered again, blow dried her hair straight, put on a pair of jeans, a white shirt, and a baggy sweater, she completed her outfit with a pair of clumpy boots. She left the flat, walking along the pavement to the Nice Cuppa café.

'Hi,' Miranda leant on the counter, smiling as Janey, the owner came towards her. 'You know what you were saying the other day about a job…'

Chapter Forty

'Can you stay here for a while?' Janice asked as the two sisters sat outside the hospital. 'Until mum…' Their mother still clung to life and showed no signs of deteriorating further. Janice was munching her way steadily through a burger, brought at the fast-food joint on the edge of the town.

Tamara had bought herself a falafel wrap, which her sister had looked at disdainfully. 'Well of course I'll try,' Tamara lied, she had to get home, there was no way she could explain her absence to Patrick much longer. 'Couldn't you get a job near here?' Janice said, through a mouthful of burger, 'There are plenty of firms on the industrial estate, I'm sure you could find a receptionist job.'

Tamara swallowed hard; the food felt like lead in her throat. The last thing she wanted was to be here permanently, she had tried hard enough to get away. Why would she ever leave her lovely life with Patrick, Janice was mad even to suggest that. It was sad she could not be there for her mother, but that was how things were.

It was with a feeling of great relief, a couple of hours later that Tamara turned her car southwards and pushed her foot hard on the accelerator, the further the distance between home and the world she had grown up in the better. She had said her goodbyes, wondering how there could ever be any connection between her and the frail looking woman in the hospital bed, or the vast lump that was her sister. It was unlikely Tamara would ever see her mother alive again.

The car ate up the miles, hurtling down the motorway and then onto the smaller minor roads and finally turning with relief into the driveway of home.

Patrick's car stood in the driveway, she parked her car beside it and sat for a moment savouring the silence as the powerful engine ticked quietly as it cooled. Home. The feeling of relief was immense.

The house enveloped her with its feeling of peace, the smell of fresh, clean air, the gentle ticking of the grandfather clock.

Patrick was in the lounge, his legs crossed, surrounded by files and paperwork.

'Hi,' Tamara crossed the distance between them, kissing him softly on the cheek.

'Hi,' his voice was distant. 'How was…I forget what you said her name was…'

'Hilary. She's not well at all.' Tamara almost convinced herself she wasn't lying.

'I see.' There was a coldness to his voice she did not recognise.

'Patrick, what is it?' When he was silent, she tried again, 'Patrick?' louder.

Slowly he lowered the papers he was holding and looked at her, his eyes were cold an expression she did not recognise.

'Yes, Tamara,' he said, 'Or is it Mandy?'

She felt her mouth drop open. It was the last thing she ever expected him to say, she had covered her tracks so well, she had become Tamara so fully she could barely remember being anything else.

Patrick picked up one of the files, 'I thought that you were having an affair,' he said, opening the file and looking through it, 'But this…' he was silent, not looking at her. 'You aren't even called Tamara, I don't know who you are.' He spat coldly.

Tamara's legs felt as if they would not support her, she put out a hand to hold herself up and walked to the arm chair opposite him and sank down, her head spinning.

'I was ashamed of where I came from,' she said quietly, looking at him but he did not meet her eye. 'I wanted to be someone you'd want to have with you.'

She felt her cheeks burning, wondering if he knew about Jago and the abortion, if he had been following her, delving into her life he had to have discovered that.

'So many lies,' he said, 'I can't get my head around it.'

'He was black mailing me.' She said, beginning to cry, 'He said he'd tell you if I didn't do what he asked.'

'What are you talking about?' Patrick's voice was barely audible. Seeing the shock on his face, Tamara's breath caught in her throat. She opened her mouth to speak but no words came out.

* * * * *

Simon paused as the police station door swung shut behind him. There was a finality he hated, as if he may never get back outside again. 'Can I help you Sir?' the desk sergeant, paused, his pen poised over the form he was filling in.

Simon stopped, his feet felt as if they had been glued to the tiled floor, halfway between the door, his escape to the outside world, and the sliding, glass hatch behind which the grizzled Policeman was looking at him his face pushed into a quizzical expression.

'I… er…' Simon considered the wisdom of the whim that had seen him hovering outside the station for the best part of the previous hour and that had kept him awake for most of the night.

'Sir?' Simon watched the policeman take a stride away from his desk, opening the door and coming towards him.

'Sorry,' Simon threw up his hands in a gesture of helplessness as he finished his journey towards the desk, arriving at which he seized the wooden surface with both hands. His heart was pounding, his breath coming in short bursts.

'How can I help you?' The quizzical look had been replaced by one of great interest.

'I need to talk to someone, urgently.'

'Oh, right.'

'About the Jago Carey murder. I... er... I just need to talk to someone please.'

'You'd better come this way,' the grizzled policeman opened the office door and took Simon's arm as if to stop him fleeing. The grip was firm. Still holding his arm, the policeman punched numbers into a keypad beside a door and pushed it open. 'Wait here please.' The door closed with a dull click, locking behind him. Simon turned slowly, it was as he had imagined. Grey paint, harsh strip lights, in the centre of the table stood a wooden table, four plastic chairs stood at in pairs.

He turned again as the door opened behind him. The detective, Max Wilton came into the room an A4 pad under one arm. The men sat at opposite sides of the table. 'You wanted to see someone about the Jago Carey murder. Is there something you need to add to the statement you gave.' Deliberately Max wrote the time and date on the top of the pad and then waited, pen poised, his eyes locking onto Simon's face.

Simon managed to emit a strangled noise through a throat that seemed to have closed up completely. 'Yes.'

Max watched him, his face impassive, giving Simon time to frame his words.

Simon closed his eyes, seeing Rosalind's face. The search for his younger sister had driven him since the day she had gone missing, ten years ago. 'My sister. She vanished. I knew she'd come to Cornwall.' Now Simon had managed to start talking it was impossible to stop the torrent of words that poured from his mouth in a relentless tide. 'I traced her to the Ligavessy, she worked in a pub there. She loved horses, the closest stables were at Park Hall.'

Max's pen flew over the pad.

'I moved down here to look for her. Got a job at Park Hall. When I asked Jago if he remembered her, he…' Remembering Jago's laugh and look of amusement, Simon paused. 'He was a filthy bastard. Told me she'd been there. Working. That he'd screwed her.'

'Yes,' There was an impatient note in Max's voice.

'The day he died I'd gone to the stables to have it out with him. Find out what had happened to her. He laughed at me. Said it was a joke and that he'd never seen Rosalind.'

Simon traced a circle on the surface of the table with a trembling finger.

'When I went up to him, I found him dead. I picked up the knife. I don't know why and then I panicked, thought you lot would think it was me. My prints on it and that… I took it with me and threw it in the lake. I messed up your investigation.'

'Yes, we've covered this before.' Max sat back, folding his arms.

Simon shrugged, his mouth twisting into a wry grin. 'Well, my sister turned up at our parent's a few days ago. Seems she got involved with a man, who knocked her about, she was too embarrassed to come home before. I just wanted to say how sorry I was for what I did.'

* * * * *

Issy shredded a tissue between her fingers. 'I miss him so much, Rachel.' Issy swung her legs, letting her heels bang on the wooden cabinet doors of the units above which she was sitting.

'Oh Issy,' Rachel pushed herself off the work surface and crossed the kitchen to stand beside the distraught young woman. She rummaged in the pocket of her jeans and found a tissue which she handed to Issy.

'What will I do? I can't get over knowing he died like that.' Issy shoved a balled fist into her mouth to stop the moan of pure horror that escaped from her mouth. She closed her eyes. 'There must have been so much blood.'

'You'll forget. It will get easier,' Rachel spoke with more confidence than she felt. She put a gentle hand over Issy's ice cold fingers.

'How could anyone do that to him? He was such a lovely man, so kind.'

'I don't know.' Rachel drew Issy's head towards her. Issy let her face rest on Rachel's shoulder, feeling the fabric dampen as her tears flowed onto Rachel's shirt.

'He must have been in such pain.'

'It was over quickly,' Rachel's voice was decisive.

'How can you know that?' Issy spat. 'To be tied up, have your stomach cut open…' Issy drew away, using the tissue to blow her nose.

'What on earth are you so upset about him?' Rachel held Issy's face in her hands, locking her eyes onto the younger woman's.

Issy twisted her face into a wry expression. 'Rachel, didn't you see…'

'See what?'

'How I felt about him. I would have done anything for him to want me.'

'Issy no. He wasn't the man you thought he was. The bodies they found; he was killing women who were working there. Can you not understand that?'

Issy ignored Rachel's words. 'I knew he had gone up to the groom's accommodation. I wanted to see him. I thought if I could get him on his own in the right place, he'd see me as someone he could be with.'

'Issy,' Rachel pushed Issy away, moving to stand at the kitchen sink, staring out over the farmyard. At the far side of the yard Issy's father was following a line of black and white cows who were walking slowly towards the milking parlour yard. 'You had a lucky escape.'

'I don't believe he killed those women.'

'Issy for heaven's sake. The police found his DNA on the victims.'

Issy shook her head violently. 'Someone could have put it there. The police could have planted it.'

'Issy, grow up.' Rachel turned to face Issy. Her face was reddened, raw with the tears she had shed. 'He was a killer. He's been killing young women, and you were throwing yourself at him. He wasn't interested in you. He only wanted those who weren't willing. He'd have never looked at you in a million years.'

'Why not?' Issy thrust her chin out in an aggressive gesture, glaring at Rachel.

'Because you are not the type he went for.'

'How can you possibly know that.' Issy's voice was filled with sarcasm.

'I do know.' Rachel leant back against the sink, thrusting her hands deep into the pockets of her jeans.

Issy scowled, looking at Rachel, silently before she whispered, 'How do you know how long it took him to die?'

Chapter Forty-One

'My first early finish in ages and you're going out.'

'Yes, well, I don't see you arranging your life around me very often.' Kaden's voice held more than a challenge. He had become increasingly grumpy about the hours she was having to put in on the dual challenges of the murder of Jago Carey and the young women. Long frustrating hours. Nothing seemed to be moving. Everyone felt as if they were banging their heads against a brick wall. Jago's DNA linked him to their deaths, and more horrifically Eddie Hammett's DNA linked him to the murder of Amber Friday, but they were still no closer to finding out who had killed Jago.

'I'll stay in Hayle at Rob's.'

'Okay,' Grace replied, there was no point in saying anything else.

Grace leant against the frame of the open front door as Kaden drove away.

There seemed to be an ever-widening rift between them. The stress of her job and then at home being constantly reminded how much work had to be done on their property. They had been stupid, carried away on a dream, completely bowled over by the romance of the old house and its amazing views. Now the dream had become a nightmare, they were both painfully aware of the vast amounts of money the old farm needed spending on it and how little progress they were making.

'Hang on I'll give you a hand.' Grace spotted Rachel struggling to bring in three of the young horses, leading two in one hand and the other in her free hand. She had been waiting for a chance to talk to Rachel about knowing more that was going on at Park Hall than she had mentioned.

'I'll take this one.' Grace took one of the lead ropes from Rachel and led the big youngster towards the stables. The three horses had come from Ireland as part of a batch Kaden had bought. Grace knew Kaden and Rachel had spent hours gentling them and getting them ready to be ridden. Grace understood his love of training the youngsters, but while they had a house that needed making habitable, it did not seem a good use of his time.

'You've done a great job of handling these three.' Grace smiled at Rachel.

'Thanks,' Rachel beamed. 'They were tough enough, I wouldn't say they'd had much handling before they came here. Kaden is hoping to start riding Murphy, the one you're leading, next week.'

'He's fabulous,' Grace put a hand on the massive shoulder of the horse she was leading. She prickled with irritation; she knew darn well what the horses were called. She spent enough time listening to Kaden talking about them. It had become the one safe subject they had to discuss now. Venturing onto work or the non-existent progress of the house restoration took them onto ground which shifted constantly and led them into the potential for an argument.

Together they put the horses into the stables, rugging them against the chill air.

'Give me some of the feed buckets,' Grace said as the last horse was rugged. 'I'll give them to the horses.'

'Thanks.' Rachel scooped feed into the buckets handing them to Grace with instructions as to which horse they were for.

A while later, the horses all fed, water buckets and hay nets topped up Grace pushed her fingertips into her aching back muscles. 'Hard work this,' she smiled at Rachel. 'You must be tough doing this every day.'

'I guess so,' Rachel shrugged. 'I don't know any different.' She paused for a moment before turning away. 'I'll head off, see you tomorrow if you're not gone to work when I start.'

'Fancy getting a takeaway?' Grace asked, not wanting Rachel to go before she had time to talk to her. It was a conversation she wanted to ease into, rather than ask blunt questions. 'You must be starving.'

'I am for sure,' Rachel took off the cap she wore and shook out her dark hair, 'I was just thinking that all I have in the cupboard is some manky bread and some beans, not very inspiring after the long day I've had.'

'Come on, let's get a Chinese, my treat.'

With Rachel in the passenger seat Grace drove back into Penzance where they ordered a takeaway and then headed back to the farm. They chatted companionably about the horses and the work Rachel was doing.

'Saves us cooking,' Grace led the way into the farmhouse kitchen.

'I'm all for that,' Rachel lifted the packages out of the carrier bag while Grace found a bottle of wine in the fridge she and Kaden had started and not finished, 'This will be perfect.'

Rachel grinned, 'Brilliant, thank you, now you can have a drink too and relax.'

Grace dished up the food and took it into the lounge, while Rachel lit the fire. They sat with their plates in their laps to eat.

'I love this place,' Rachel said, fork of food halfway to her mouth.

'Have you always worked with horses?' Grace realised how little she knew about Rachel, Kaden had given her the job, a few months after they had moved into Long Meadow Farm, Grace had the impression he had known her for years.

Rachel nodded, 'Yup,' she said in between a mouthful of food. 'I was homeless, I'd run away from home, the usual story, Mum died, I got shuffled between grand-parents and aunts until I eventually had enough and upped and left. I ended up in Penzance, the end of the line the destination for everyone who is escaping from something.'

She took another mouthful of food, chewing thoughtfully before she continued, as if she was not sure how much of her story she could trust with Grace.

'I met Jago in a pub, I was sleeping rough on someone's floor at the time. He gave me a job and somewhere to stay. I'd always liked horses, when Mum was alive, we had ponies.' Grace looked at her wistful expression.

'I didn't know you'd worked for him. You never said.'

Rachel met Grace's eyes; her face expressionless. 'It never really came up. I was the groom at Park Hall for a while.'

'Did he ever make you feel afraid?' Grace's eyes roved over Rachel's face. Jago seemed to have targeted young, rootless women.'

Rachel gave a snort of laughter. 'Look at me,' She waved her hands over her body. 'I'd hardly be his type.'

A silence fell between the two women broken only by the crackling of logs in the fire as they burnt and settled.

'I can't get my head around Jago killing those women though.' Rachel's voice was little more than a whisper. Grace had to strain to hear what she was saying. 'I thought they had just gone away, got different jobs. Horse work is tough, not everyone can stick it. There were always people coming and going. Grooms, people with horses, they'd get a bit of money, buy a horse and then realise how hard it is, riding in all weathers, paying for a horse. And grooming, girls think it's a bit of fun, just riding and galloping around. They soon realise it's not easy at all, its tough work, dirty, heavy, you get wet and cold, horses bite and kick and throw you off.'

'So, you just assumed they'd left.'

Rachel shrugged her shoulders. 'What else would I think?' There was an irritable edge to her voice. 'You wouldn't think that someone you liked and admired was going round killing people and burying them in the fields, would you?'

Grace shook her head, her eyes never leaving Rachel's which glistened with tears. 'No, of course not.'

Rachel took a gulp of her wine, the noise of her swallowing loud above the sound of the fire.

'I should have said something. Told you I'd worked there, it just never seemed to be relevant. I didn't know anything about what he was doing.'

Grace nodded. 'Was Jago nice to work for?'

'He was fair,' Rachel said shortly, 'If you did the work everything was fine.'

'It's a lot to do on your own though.' Grace commented.

'I wasn't always on my own,' Rachel said, putting down her plate, with a look of regret, she looked as if she could have eaten the same again. 'There were often others there helping, starting and then going away again,' Rachel said, collecting up the plates and taking them into the kitchen.

Grace thought of the files on her desk, the women that had worked at the yard before they had disappeared and the ones that had been found buried in the field. How many of those women did Rachel know? Had she known what was going on at Park Hall despite her protestations she did not.

'Grooms often came and went,' Rachel said sitting back down, she held the wine bottle and topped up Grace's glass, 'No one stayed there too long,' she added.

'Did you get to know anyone well?' Grace asked.

'Some but I didn't get to know anyone too well because I knew they'd always move on again. I know now, some of them hadn't moved on. Some were still there. Under the grass I was walking over every day.'

'That must have been a shock, finding out what he was doing.'

Rachel's mouth turned down, a muscle below one of her eyes twitched. 'How could he do that? She released a long sigh. 'Killing people and then appearing to everyone else as such a nice person.'

'That's often how it is.' Grace said, before repeating her question. 'Was there anyone you got to know well?'

She paused, taking a long sip of wine before laying it down on the carpet beside her feet. 'I was friends with Catherine Marshall. We were good friends. I met her in Penzance. I got her the job I was hurt when she wasn't on the yard anymore. I thought she had gone without saying goodbye to me. I was angry at her.' Rachel said sadly, 'I really liked her.'

Grace waited, not wanting to speak, or move or do anything which would break the spell that seemed to have come over Rachel as she spoke.

Rachel shrugged bleakly, 'One day she was there and then she had gone. Jago said she'd left.'

Grace was silent, letting Rachel talk. 'Then I found out she was dead. Why did he kill Catherine?' Rachel asked, taking a big gulp of her wine. 'And the others.'

Grace put her glass down on the low wooden coffee table. 'Because he could. Because they were there, easy targets for him. They were all lost, alone with no one looking for them, vulnerable and Jago took their trust and used it to kill them.'

Rachel got unsteadily to her feet. 'I'm so pissed.' Not used to drinking.'

'Come on, I'll walk you across the yard.' Grace fought to keep her voice expressionless while every nerve jangled. Rachel knew Jago and Catherine Marshall. Rachel put her arm around Grace's shoulder, laying her head in the space between her shoulder and head.

She led the stumbling Rachel across the yard and into her cottage, Grace guided Rachel through the cottage to the bottom of the stairs. 'Stairs. Bed.'

'You'll have to help,' Rachel giggled.

Grace hauled her up the stairs, stopping frequently as Rachel swayed. At the top of the stairs there were two rooms. One door stood open into a small bathroom, the other, she remembered from looking at the property before they bought it was a bedroom. The room was dark, lit only with a couple of bedside lights which glowed on the red walls.

Grace guided Rachel into the room. As she helped Rachel onto the bed, she spotted a jewellery box on the dressing table. A tangled mass of chains spilled from the half open lid. Something familiar caught her eye. It was a chain with the half heart, just like the one that they had found on Catherine's body.

'Gonna be sick, bowl…' Rachel flung herself on the bed.

'Hang on,' Grace hurried to the bathroom. The battered carpet desperately needed replacing and a stiff breeze blew in from the direction of the window. More work for her and Kaden to do.

The bathroom was brightly painted in a bright purple, the ceiling littered with hanging florescent stars. They'd discussed repainting the cottage when they'd first looked at it, but they hadn't got around to it yet. There was no sign of a bowl. Beside the bath was a cabinet, Grace opened the door and found the bowl Rachel had requested, as she drew it out something at the back caught her eye. A box full of latex gloves, perfect for a murder. Grace crouched to look further in the cupboard at the back tucked away there was a small bottle of horse tranquiliser. She closed the door, frowning. Grace shook her head, she was tired, her thoughts rampaging like wild horses.

Chapter Forty-Two

Grace spent the night tossing and turning, the bed felt cold and very empty without Kaden. She spent the night wondering intermittently what Kaden was doing and then trying to imagine Rachel as Jago's killer. There was no reason for Rachel to kill Jago, what would the motive be? Something nagged at her. As the first light of dawn lightened the gap between the curtains, she remembered what it was. The necklace. Rachel had a half heart necklace, the same as the one found on Catherine Marshall's body. Were the girls closer than the good friends Rachel had said they were?

She arrived at the station, irritable, her eyes gritty. She grabbed yet another coffee and pushed open the office door. Her team were already in the office, Grace looked at the faces of her team, all turned in her direction. She could see the frustration in their eyes and knew moral was low. Nothing was happening.

The alibis of all the people who had been at the farm and who had any connection with Jago had been checked and re-checked. Everyone who had been on the yard that day had all lied, as she had known from the beginning, but it now appeared, none of them were linked to the crime, they all had their own reasons for lying and now all had to deal with the consequences. Whether they would be charge or not was something Steve Cooper would decide. Wasting police time was a serious offence.

While the teams had been busy trying to check alibis, watching hours of CCTV footage, trawling through telephone records, the true perpetrator had been unwittingly been given days in which to cover their tracks.

The cold fact of the matter was they may never discover who killed Jago. There were no clues to lead anywhere in the direction of who was responsible. Getting nowhere with a case sapped the motivation out of the detectives. Trawling hopelessly through blind alleys and dead ends, like sand shifting through their fingers with nothing in return.

It was hard to keep them motivated, and eventually she knew budgets would begin to come into force and her team would gradually be reduced as the trail became colder and colder and then eventually the murder would be shifted into the realms of cold cases. There was no doubt that Jago had worked alongside Eddie Hammett, killing the first of the women whose body they had found. After Hammett's death it seemed Jago had carried on his work, adding his own twist to the deaths of the women that came into his clutches.

'We've established that everyone who was at Park Hall the day Jago died had alibis. They all lied to us, for various reasons, like idiots, but they aren't suspects.' Grace said, trying to put a positive spin on the workload, 'So we've a heap of suspects who we can write off. So we move on, keep sifting through Jago's life, and something will turn up, it is just a matter of keeping moving stones and eventually we will get a result.' Grace concluded her briefing, she hoped she sounded more convincing than she felt. The truth was they were getting nowhere.

'Pete,' Grace leant on his desk. 'Have a look at Rachel for me would you.' She felt uneasy about Rachel, but knew she was too close to the woman to be able to see clearly.

It was later during the morning Steve Cooper called Grace and Max into his office.

Cooper looked as if he could barely contain his excitement, he beamed as they walked in.

'Sit down,' Cooper said, drumming his fingers on the wooden surface of his desk. 'Big news,' he said, taking a long drink from the coffee his secretary brought in. After she left, he looked up, 'We've got our murderer.' Aware of the stunned silence he continued, 'Jago Carey's killer.'

'What?' Grace frowned, her voice taut with disbelief.

'We've had a report from an informant, about a low life, Tony Ferris, someone overheard him bragging about Jago's murder.' Cooper looked like the cat that had got the cream, he had found something out before the team, something that was going to be the key to unlocking the crime and solving it. 'My informant called me this morning. He said Ferris was talking about how he was the one that killed Jago Carey when he scored some drugs.'

Grace shook her head. 'I don't get it. Tony Ferris has no connection to Jago Carey.' She remembered the scrawny, pale faced small time crook. She had arrested him on countless occasions for petty crimes around the area. Everyone had been glad when he had moved out of the area. 'Boss, he's a small-time drug dealer and petty thief. Why would he kill Jago. It's not his thing at all.'

Cooper drummed his fingers on his desk. 'He's been in Bristol for a couple of years now. Could be he's moving in different circles, got new skills.'

'He's not our man.' Grace met Cooper's eyes. Steve Cooper shrugged. 'We are going with this, Tallis. He's confessed. We'll get him down here and see what he has to say.'

Grace shrugged. Not convinced.

'And, what now? 'Max asked.

'We've picking him up and are bringing him back here for questioning.' Cooper turned to face Max, 'He's in Bristol so it is going to take a few hours to get him down here. I arranged a dawn raid on his home, unfortunately he's not there, but we'll get him.'

'Okay, fair enough,' Grace said, barely disguising the sceptical tone in her voice. Tony Ferris had not shown up as knowing Jago. From what she remembered of Ferris he was just a nasty piece of work who did nothing much more than threaten people. Why would he kill Jago?

'I'm going to suggest you knock off for the day, enjoy what's left of the weekend. Grace, you can draw up an interview strategy and we will get to work see if we can't get this put to bed as soon as Ferris is found and delivered here.'

Grace walked out of the police station with Max. 'I don't buy this at all,' she ran her hands through her hair, pushing it back off her face.

'Cooper thinks he's out man. He has confessed.' Max was delighted to have the time off and was planning to take Tara his daughter to Exeter for the day. It would be good for the two of them to spend some time together.

The rest of the detectives hurried out of the building, except those who had been rostered to work.

Grace drove home, trying to ignore the leaden feeling in the pit of her stomach. Perhaps she had got this all wrong. Maybe it was as simple as Tony Ferris killing Jago, maybe he had reasons that would become apparent when they interviewed him.

'Kaden's been back and taken one of the young horses to the new cross-country course near St Ives.' Rachel said, appearing out of one of the stables as she heard Grace's Land Rover pull into the yard. 'How come you managed to get off work?' Rachel, her continued, her fingers deftly untangling the leadrope she was carrying.

'Someone has confessed to Jago's murder,' Grace replied. 'They're bringing him in now.' She met Rachel's eyes seeing her blink slowly once, before shifting her focus to the land beyond the farm buildings. 'Wow, that's great, so the case will be closed soon.' Rachel turned towards Grace, her face devoid of all expression. 'Was it one of the liveries? Or Michael, the vet, Jago was always taunting him.'

'I can't say yet.'

'Oh, yes, of course not.' Rachel shrugged, 'I guess it will come our eventually.'

'Yes, it will.' Grace was still not convinced that Tony Ferris could have anything to do with Jago's death. Nothing about him committing the crime made any sense. 'Looks like Kaden will be gone for the day. How about I treat you to a bite of lunch.' The nagging curiosity she had about Rachel and her life would not let her go. She needed to know once and for all the connection Rachel had to Catherine Marshall and Jago, lunch would be the perfect chance to get her talking.

'Oh, that would be great,' Rachel said, offering Grace a cigarette, when she shook her head, Rachel lit hers climbing eagerly into the front seat of the Land Rover, unwinding the window so the smoke blew out. 'I've just started smoking again.'

'Hard to get off them once you start.' Grace smiled at Rachel, thinking of Steve Cooper's battle to stop smoking.

'Are you allowed to say anything about the case?' Rachel said, drawing deeply on the cigarette and letting the smoke plume out of her mouth.

'I can't,' Grace steered the Land Rover out of the yard, 'If we've got someone it will all come out eventually.'

'I'm so pleased you've sorted it out,' Rachel continued, 'So you'll have more time off once this is finished?'

Grace snorted with laugher, 'I doubt it, there will always be something happening, even here.'

She hoped there wouldn't be a case as horrible again for a long time, that she would be able to go back to investigating stolen bikes and cattle rustling, rather than gruesome murders. 'How about The Cat's Whiskers?' Grace loved the quirkily named pub.

'Perfect, the food is lovely there, it's a great atmosphere.'

'Let's go.' Grace smiled. As she drove Grace was aware of Rachel, sitting with practiced stillness her eyes fixed on the road.

The Cat's Whiskers was on the coast road, sited high on a clifftop above the sea.

The pub was already busy, with lunchtime trade. The white painted, thatched building with its traditional interior of slate floor and wood panelled rooms was popular with walkers and locals alike.

'My round.' Rachel fetched the drinks and joined Grace at a table at the far end of the bar.

'Hiya,' a man came to stand beside Grace and Rachel. He wore baggy trousers and the gaiters popular with walkers.

Grace smiled, tightly, the last thing she wanted was to be hassled by some lecherous drunk.

'Come here often,' he grinned, taking a sip of his cider, 'Not a great chat up line, but I'm a bit lost for words with you two beauties.'

Grace picked up her drink with a sigh, drunks, they were the bane of her life.

'You are especially beautiful; how come you are out on your own?' he was drunk enough not to get the message from their lack of response. 'Why haven't you got a man with you keeping an eye on you.'

Grace sighed patiently. There was nothing to be gained by losing her temper, drunks were an occupational hazard.

'She isn't on her own,' Rachel slid off her chair and came to stand in front of Grace between her and the man. Her eyes blazed with fury. She stood toe to toe with the man. Grace glanced at her, seeing how tall and broad she was. Her chin jutted aggressively, her face inches away from the man. 'She's with me.'

'Ah love,' the man said, putting down his drink and leering into Rachel's face, wobbling slightly as he tried and failed to meet Rachel's eyes. 'What's the harm in a bit of company?'

'Rachel, it's okay, he's going back to his friends now.' Grace took Rachel's arm, trying to draw her away from the man. With a jerk Rachel pulled her arm away.

Grace watched as Rachel changed from being mild and kind to suddenly being filled with barely suppressed anger, she took a stride forwards, forcing the man to stride backwards.

'We don't want any company,' she snapped, 'I suggest that you fuck off back to your mates and leave us alone.'

Grace could see that her face, normally so sweet was unrecognisable, contorted with rage as she pushed her fingers into the man's chest. The violence she could see there was so unexpected.

'Rachel, it's okay,' Grace could see the undisguised surprise in the man's face.

Rachel continued to glare in the direction of the man who for a moment stared at her and then, as if afraid of what he saw in her eyes, he held up his hands palms outwards in a gesture of surrender and turned away. 'Dikes,' he snarled, walking back to his friends.

Rachel glared at his back before dropping her eyes and picking up her pint. Her face was smoothed again, all trace of her anger had vanished. Where on earth had that come from, Grace wondered, why had she never seen this side of Rachel before. It was frightening how quickly she had changed.

Chapter Forty-Three

The following morning Grace was still shocked at change she had seen in Rachel. She'd spent a sleepless night thinking about Tony Ferris, while at the back of her mind Rachel's behaviour nagged at her. Rachel had gone from mild mannered to full on aggressive in the blink of an eye. That and the unlikely suspect made for a mind that refused to settle.

Tony Ferris had been found during the night in a squat on the outskirts of Bristol and had been driven down to Penzance. After a rest, and breakfast he was ready to talk.

Tony Ferris sat in the interview room glaring across the table at Grace and Max. His dark coloured sweatshirt and jogging bottoms hung in folds around his skinny frame.

'Hello Tony,' Grace said, ignoring the way he was trying to exude aggression. She'd worked around enough villains not to be intimidated by another small-time low life. 'Thank you for coming in for a little chat,' Grace continued.

Steve Cooper was convinced Ferris was the man who had killed Jago. If that was the case, it was her job to find the evidence get him out of society for a very long time. She remained unconvinced he was anything to do with Jago's death. He hadn't come up in any of the searches of Jago's acquaintances or had any connection to Park Hall.

He was, she knew, a career criminal, a truly nasty piece of work who had started his career mugging old ladies and relieving them of their handbags, usually after they had collected their pension. His first conviction was for knocking over a seventy-year-old disabled lady when she had left the post office in Penzance. He had grabbed her bag and made a run for it. The police had eventually caught up with him in the pub drinking the proceeds of his haul. They had also arrested the barman for serving an underage drinker.

Ferris had progressed to house breaking, mostly the homes of vulnerable old people, relieving them of any cash they had left lying around.

There was nothing in his charge sheet history that would suggest he was likely to suddenly kill someone but still, as Grace knew only too well, that did not mean he would not. Stranger things had happened. There must have been some reason behind him bragging to the man who had turned him in.

Ferris inclined his head in a cocky gesture. The duty solicitor let out a sigh. Grace could imagine how hard it was to have gone through years of university, feeling you were going to change the world, fighting tough legal battles, and then ending up here, the back of beyond, supporting wasters like Ferris time and again. There was no wonder the young solicitor who looked like he was barely old enough to be out of school, looked fed up and jaded already beyond his years.

'I wanted to talk to you about the murder of Jago Carey.' Grace rested her long fingers on the desk, 'Is there anything you'd like to tell me?'

'I did him,' Ferris leaned back on his chair and regarded Grace through eyes that shone with glee.

Grace could imagine that someone like Ferris who had no hope of any life would find it better to be in prison, there he would be warm and fed. He would have a certain kudos amongst the prison community. Owning up to such a gruesome crime would be a way to get respect there.

Grace had seen it many times before, people who had mental problems, or who had other issues would own up to crimes they had never committed. It was her job to ascertain if he had committed the crime or not.

'Why did you kill Jago Carey?' Grace asked. Ferris looked straight at her as if challenging her to believe him.

'Jago deserved to be taken out,' Ferris spat, 'He was a filthy fucker, he killed, so he got back what he gave. Bastard.'

Grace could not argue with him there. Jago was slime, but he did not deserve to be killed, he should have been brought to justice and made to pay for his crimes.

Grace was silent, listening to the sound of the tape recorder whirling, letting his words sink into her consciousness. Ferris leant forwards, his eyes locking onto Grace's. His eyeballs were a yellow shade with red and black smudges on the skin beneath them. His skin had the tallow shade of a drug user who rarely saw the light of day. 'I enjoyed killing him.'

'How did you kill Jago Carey?' Max asked.

Grace watched for his reaction, Ferris seemed to know everything about the crime, but still she was unconvinced. Perhaps there was something he did not know, and she could trip him up, get him to admit he was lying.

'I threatened him with a knife. Tied him up,' Ferris went on in detail to say what had been done to Jago, there was nothing he did not know.

'Why did you cut his penis off?' Max asked. He was as unconvinced as Grace, but still Ferris did seem to be the one for the crime. 'He deserved it,' Ferris said loudly, 'I wanted to make sure he would never hurt any woman again.'

'What happened the day you killed Jago?' Grace asked, sitting back as Ferris began to speak about the murder.

Finally, his words faded into silence, and he sat, expressionless, his eyes flickering from Grace to Max. 'And the knife?' Grace asked, 'What did you do with that?'

'I left it there.'

Grace sighed. She could not see Ferris as the killer, and yet he was admitting the crime and seemed to know all the details. Ferris was charged with the murder of Jago Carey and taken away to the cells.

After the interview Grace and Max sat with Steve Cooper. 'I can't believe he did it.' Grace shook her head.

Max agreed, 'It was like he was reciting a passage he had learned. Like listening to a performance.'

Cooper shrugged, 'He's admitted it, he knows exactly how the crime was done. He knows about the knife and what was done to Carey'.

With Ferris charged and, in the cells, there was nothing more they could do. They should have been celebrating, but Grace was not convinced by Ferris's performance. 'He didn't do it, I'm certain of that,' Grace said, leaning across the table to turn over the pages of the file.

Max shrugged, 'I don't think so either, but he said he did, and he knows everything.'

'Let's look at this again,' she said, 'Let's have another chat to Zara, see if she remembers him being around Park Hall, or with Jago.'

Something just did not make sense. Ferris had admitted the crime, but still something was wrong.

They headed for Park Hall. Zara answered the door, her face closing in on itself in anger as she saw who was there. 'Tony Ferris?' Grace asked, 'Do you remember him? Did he ever work here.' She showed Zara the crime photo that had been taken of Ferris earlier, before the interview had started. In the image he was glaring aggressively at the camera.

Zara took the image and sat at the kitchen table. The house was silent apart from the ticking grandfather clock and smelt of furniture polish. Far away in the depths of the house they could hear someone hoovering. 'Not at all,' she said, pushing the photograph towards Grace, 'who is he?'

'Just someone we are talking to about Jago's death.' Grace said.

'We are just trying to find out if there is any connection,' Max added.

Zara shook her head, 'Never seen him before.'

They left, Grace had no reason to think she was lying, she had nothing to gain from it. Jago did not seem to have employed men on the farm he preferred young women, which gave him easy access to a ready stream of vulnerable women he could abuse and kill at will. A man around the place would have been competition and would have given them some kind of protection too.

It was, Grace thought, unlikely that Jago would have encountered Ferris during his normal day to day life either, the two men were poles apart, and yet apparently Ferris had known what Jago was doing and was so incensed he was driven to kill. The more she knew the less sense everything seemed to make.

They went back to the police station and re-interviewed Ferris, 'How did you know Jago?'

Ferris visibly faltered; the first time they had ever seen him be fazed by any of the questions.

'I just knew him from town, out and about.' Ferris said, his eyes locking onto Grace's as though he were challenging her to prove he was lying. He seemed pleased with himself for thinking up the answer.

'Okay and how did you know he was killing women, Tony?' Max asked, 'It's just we can't seem to place you with Jago to have known what he was doing.'

'Well, I just did.' Ferris snapped, 'I knew Jago from in town, everyone knew who he was, and I knew what he was doing. He told me.'

'I don't think you knew him, or that he told you anything,' Grace said, 'I can't understand why you would have killed someone you didn't know, and then gone to so much trouble to cover up your tracks.'

'Well, I did know him,' Ferris snapped, 'And you can't prove I didn't,' he added triumphantly.

With Ferris back in his cell Grace explained her fears to Cooper who brushed them off brusquely.

'Forget it, he's confessed, he knows every detail about the killings. He's the one, get him charged and close the case for heaven's sake.'

Ferris was brought to the front desk where Max read out the charges and formally charged him. Ferris as if he suddenly realised the seriousness of what was happening became visibly pale and a sheen of sweat broke out on his forehead, but still he stuck to his story and after being charged was taken back to the cells. Since it was a murder charge, he would be remanded in custardy until his court date.

As Grace and Max walked back into the office a rousing cheer went up, the whole force was delighted the case had been solved.

'Drinks are on you tonight boss,' grinned one of the detectives.

'Yes, of course,' Grace nodded, 'Thank you all for your hard work, but now let's get this wrapped up, get the case notes all in order and make sure everything has been done right so that we get our conviction, the last thing we want is for him to wriggle off the hook because one of us hasn't done their jobs properly.'

She looked out over the room, seeing the nods of agreement, each of them had at one time or another seen a criminal get away with something because the solicitor had found holes in the way the case was brought to court.

Grace sat down at her desk, normally with a case successfully closed she would feel on top of the world. Someone who was guilty had been brought to justice. But something was not right with this case. Ferris might tick all the right boxes, but something was not right, of that, she was sure. She opened her computer system and typed Anthony Ferris into the police database. She investigated Ferris's background, nothing showed up there. She sat back, easing the stiffness in her back. Rachel often complained about having a sore back. Grace dug her fingers into the muscles as she had seen Rachel doing.

On a whim she tapped Rachel's name into the computer. The system whirled. Rachel's name came up with a warning for an assault, many years ago at a children's home against the man who was in charge that day. Grace read through the details. Rachel, it appeared had attacked the man, no charges had been brought even though he had been brought to hospital with a nasty cut to his hand from taking a knife off Rachel. As Grace read through the report, she saw a name she recognised, someone who had been at the children's home and who had been present when the offence had taken place. Anthony Ferris.

Chapter Forty-Four

Rachel and Kaden were feeding the horses when Grace arrived home. The sky was already dark with the promise of a storm. The wind was already blowing in from the Atlantic, whipping across the fields, the salty air bitterly cold.

Grace, head bent against the wind hurried across the yard towards them.

'Just the hay to do,' Kaden, his mood improved by his night out, and the fact he had a buyer for Murphy, one of the Irish horses, which would improve their finances, enfolded Grace in a hug. She pressed her lips to his stubble darkened cheeks, breathing in the familiar scent of horses and hay. They'd made up since the night they'd rowed, promised they'd make more of an effort to find time for one another.

Rachel, her face flushed was hurrying across the stable yard, her arms piled high with feed buckets, 'Please could you open this door,' she asked inclining her head in the direction of the stable beside her.

Grace unclipped the door and swung it open, at the same time taking the top bucket off Rachel's pile and putting it down in the corner of the stable. Comet who had been standing at the far corner of the stable, came forwards eagerly and buried his nose in the bucket, his love of food more urgent than his fear of the storm.

The two made their way around the stable block, hauling open doors against the power of the wind, putting feed buckets into the stables. While the horses ate, they took shelter in the feed room, listening to the increasing noise of the wind. The first squalls of rain hit the roof, drumming against the slates.

'Just the waters to top up and then I'm done,' Rachel said, extinguishing the cigarette she had been smoking as they waited for the horses to finish. Her voice had an unfamiliar tense tone.

'Come up to the house when you're ready I owe you some wages,' Kaden said, hurrying across the yard, one hand holding the collar of his jacket shut to prevent the rain running down his back.

'The other night you asked who we had in custardy,' Grace said as Rachel stood to grind her cigarette out. 'It's someone called Tony Ferris. He was at Joseph Howatch House with you.'

Grace heard Rachel's sharp intake of breath. 'Oh, yes. I remember the name.' She recovered her composure quickly.

'Did you have much contact with him since you left there?' Grace, now she had started, couldn't stop questioning Rachel.

'No,' Rachel snapped, 'I haven't seen him. I don't know him well.'

'Okay,' Grace held her hands up, aware Rachel was becoming agitated. 'Sorry.'

The wind was screaming around the isolated farm as they crossed the yard in Kaden's wake.

'Bloody hell, it's a wild night.' Kaden came out of the kitchen, three cans of cider balanced in his hands. 'Here, you deserve this, both of you.'

'Thanks.' Rachel grabbed one off Kaden. Her eyes narrowed as she glared at Grace. 'Who told you I knew Tony Ferris?'

Her hand, Grace noticed, was shaking so much she struggled to pull the ring pull.

'It just came up in the investigation. You were in the same children's home as him. I just assumed you'd have been friends.' Grace shot her a small smile. "I'll nip and get you some money. It's in my bag upstairs.' Grace put her cider down on the hall table and hurried upstairs, an uneasy tension growing in the pit of her stomach.

She pulled some money out of her purse and headed back downstairs.

'Rachel, I'll…' Grace went back into the kitchen, freezing as she entered the room. Kaden lay on the floor, blood pooling around his head. Behind her she was aware of the door swinging shut.

'You stupid bitch,' Rachel's voice, quiet, was filled with malice, her eyes blazed with fury above cheeks that were reddened with rage. 'Why couldn't you just leave me alone.'

Grace was aware of Rachel moving like lightening across the room and of the pan in her hand before there was a searing pain and the floor rushed up to meet her.

* * * * *

The rain and wind brought Grace abruptly back to reality. Rachel's hand gripped her arm tightly. 'Get in,' Rachel ordered, shoving Grace roughly into the passenger seat of the Land Rover, Grace was aware of her moving away, the door being slammed and then a blast of wet air as Rachel climbed into the driver's seat and started the vehicle.

'Great things these,' she said conversationally as she turned the key, 'Go anywhere.'

Grace felt her eyes widen with horror as Rachel brandished the handcuffs she must have unclipped from her belt. She dangled them in front of Grace taunting her with them. 'Just in case you were thinking of getting out and making a run for it.' She clipped one onto Grace's wrist and attached the other end to the door handle

Grace rested her head against the coolness of the passenger window, watching bleakly as the dark landscape flashed by, the rain sending great sheets of water over the vehicle.

After a while the Land Rover slowed, bumping over a rough surface before it came to a halt. Rachel got out; Grace peered into the darkness trying to make out where Rachel had gone. She was exhausted. Grace fought to keep her eyes open, but couldn't. She was cold, every part of her body seemed to hurt. She had been dreaming that she was swimming in the sea and seaweed was tangled around her face. Grace groaned, some instinct to survive making her fight to wake up. Her hair was draped over her face. Grace remembered she was in the passenger seat of her Land Rover, her hands tied to the door handle. Her head and the side of her face throbbed, she explored the inside of her mouth with her tongue and tasted blood.

A movement beside her made Grace turn her head. She was not alone. Rachel sat in the driver's seat looking at her. Grace squinted in the dim light aware of something that Rachel held in her hand, something that kept catching the light. It was the necklace Grace had found in Rachel's bedroom.

'You just couldn't leave things alone could you?' Rachel said, her voice was quiet, toneless. She had become someone Grace did not recognise.

Grace tried to speak but she could not frame the words, everything seemed so blurred and far away, talking was such an immense effort.

'Yes, this is the same as the one that Catherine was wearing,' she said. Grace watched as she held the necklace up to the light. 'We had matching ones, the pair. That was what we were. A pair, together forever.'

She was silent, Grace shifted, trying to ease the agonising ache in her hips and ankles from the way she had been sitting. Her legs were tied, she realised with a jolt, at the knees and ankles.

'Jago spoilt all that,' Rachel continued. 'He took her away from me. He thought she was just another of those lost girls he could take up to the loft use and then kill. He didn't know Catherine was mine, that we were together, that she had someone who loved her.'

'How did you know he hurt her?' Grace forced the words out through lips that felt dry and cracked. She tried to lick them, but her tongue rasped over them like sandpaper.

'I knew she was meeting him,' Rachel said, her voice harsh at the memory, 'he said he wanted to chat about giving her a full-time job instead of the part time shit he had her doing.'

Grace pulled as far away from Rachel as she could, afraid of the expression in her eyes.

'I put two and two together, when she didn't come home. I knew what he had done but I couldn't prove it and who would believe me against someone like him.'

Grace whimpered involuntarily as Rachel suddenly moved, shoving open the Land Rover door, letting a blast of cold air into the interior. She watched warily as Rachel passed in front of the Land Rover, awake now. Rachel wrenched open the passenger door 'Prison was going to be too good for him even if I could have proved it, I wanted to give him my own justice.'

The cold air was bringing Grace around, more and more with every passing moment, she had to get out of here, Rachel was going to kill her, she was certain of that.

Rachel began to check Grace's leg bindings. She contemplated briefly trying to kick out at Rachel, but knew it would do no good, she had no strength. Rachel would only be antagonised, she had to engage her and try to stay alive as long as possible and hope that someone would find her, or she would manage to get away.

'He cried like a baby when he knew what I was going to do with him,' Rachel smiled at the memory, her eyes distant as she thought of killing him. 'It took a long time,' she told Grace, in a dead matter of fact tone. 'Oh yes, and I enjoyed every single moment.'

Grace could feel the edges of her consciousness beginning to blur, she was going to pass out again, she shook her head, forcing herself to stay focused, 'But you let Tony Ferris admit the killing for you.'

Rachel straightened up, her whole stance filled with aggression, 'He owed me, he bloody owed me. I saved him when we were in the children's home. The fucking supervisor picked him out to be one of his favourites and Tony knew what that meant. I followed him home one night.'

Rachel's mouth twisted into a lopsided grin. 'He's still missing. That pervert will never be found I made sure of that.'

'What did you do to Kaden.' Grace's stomach knotted with tension, remembering the still form lying on the kitchen floor. The blood spreading across the tiles.

'You're the copper, you know what happened to him.'

Panic made Grace jerk at the bindings, succeeding only in tearing her skin.

'What are you going to do to me?' Grace asked, hoping that she would be able to talk some sense into Rachel. Perhaps she could make her realise how futile it was to try to get away with everything, 'They will find me eventually,' she continued, slowly realising no one knew where she was. 'You won't get away with this.'

'Can't I really?' Rachel asked conversationally, 'No one knows where you are. Your phone is gone, they can't track it.'

Grace felt as if a bucket of ice had been thrown over her. There would be no way anyone could trace where she was, even when they finally realised she was missing. She was not due back on shift until Monday afternoon and it was Friday evening now, two whole days before anyone even noticed that she was missing. Could she survive that long, she doubted it, not with the mood Rachel was in.

'Anyway,' Rachel said, conversationally, 'I'm going to leave you now.'

'Just let me go,' Grace was aware of how pathetic and desperate her words sounded.

'Sure, I will,' Rachel said. She undid the handcuffs holding Grace's hand to the door handle, hauling her roughly out of the Land Rover. 'Don't even try it,' she hissed in Grace's ear.

Grace felt the blood rush back into her hand. It had been positioned at an awkward angle for so long, pins and needles jolted like fire through her limb in agonising heat. She knew she was powerless, no matter how much she wanted to fight her limbs had no co-ordination, she was helpless.

Rachel pulled her easily to her feet, her strength was incredible, like she was a rag doll she hauled Grace from the vehicle, the blood rushing back into her feet, making each shuffling step agony.

Grace, her legs tied, had no way to balance herself and crumpled to the ground as Rachel pulled her forwards. The air was filled with the roar of the sea. Grace gasped with the pain that shot through her body, tasting the briny tang of the salt water.

'Shame you're a copper. We would have made a great team,' Rachel hissed, her voice close to Grace's ear, 'We could have rid the world of a whole heap of perverted bastards and no one would have been any the wiser, everyone would have thanked us.'

'You are bloody mad,' Grace was beyond fear now, there was no negotiating with Rachel.

Rachel let out a long heart felt sigh, 'Sorry to have to leave you, my dear,' she said, bending over Grace. She twined her hands into Grace's hair twisting her face upwards. Slowly Rachel lowered her face so that she was inches away from Grace. She could smell Rachel's perfume, the minty toothpaste on her breath, then slowly Rachel lowered her head, still holding Grace's hair until her lips locked onto Grace's. She stroked Grace's face softly. Grace wrenched her face away hating the touch of Rachel's icy fingers on her skin.

'I'm going to leave you now,' Rachel said, drawing away, 'Try not to miss me too much, I wouldn't waste your breath screaming, no one lives up here, the nearest house is miles away and it such a bad night no one will be out.' She began to drag Grace across the grass. Her strength making it impossible for Grace, barely conscious, to resist. She felt thorns scraping against her legs and then the noise of wood breaking and with a jolt of panic realised they were close to one of the abandoned mineshafts on the headland.

'Bye Grace,' Rachel's hand was on her back, propelling her forwards. 'By the time they find you it will be too late. I'll be at your funeral to play the part of a devastated friend.'

Grace, driven by some instinct to survive dug in her heels. She felt mud and grass, beneath her shoes, the dampness seeping in through the fabric of her jeans and then there was nothing, she was falling, bouncing off protruding rocks, tumbling until with a jarring thud she landed on her back.

She was dimly aware of the Land Rover driving away, the engine noise swallowed up by the roar of the storm before she slid into the darkness of unconsciousness.

Chapter Forty-Five

Tony Ferris sucked his teeth, the noise loud in the silence of his cell. He wiped at the film of sweat that prickled on his forehead with the sleeve of the police issue grey sweatshirt.

Being held on remand wasn't as he had imagined. In here no one cared he was a killer, that he had confessed to killing Jago Carey. In here everyone was a killer, or a violent thug with a reputation they wanted to maintain. In the remand centre the walls seemed to echo with the hatred that seemed to run in the veins of those who were trapped. He'd been in the police cells plenty of times, stood in front of a judge often enough too. Always there had been a stern telling off, a warning not to repeat whatever crime he'd been caught for.

He had thought being convicted of killing Jago Carey would finally make him a big man, revered because of what he had done. Confessing had seemed a good idea when Rachel had rung him and suggested it. At the time he had been glad to hear from her, happy to do what she asked. He'd even been prepared to do time for her, he owed her after all.

The reality was no one cared. Inside it was dog eat dog, no one cared who had done what. All that counted was who was the hardest and most violent amongst the inmates. And Tony Ferris couldn't count himself amongst their number. The thickset tattoo covered men made him quiver with fear. He was not like them. The worst thing he had ever done was rob houses and push old ladies to the ground, the last thing he wanted was to confront someone bigger and angrier than himself.

He lay awake at night listening to the sounds of the remand centre, the screams, men sobbing. His bed was narrow, the sheets stiff and uncomfortable, the pillow like a piece of rock beneath his head. He daren't sleep in case someone came in, in case one of the screws deliberately left his door open and some of inmates came in, like before. Confessing to killing Jago didn't impress anyone in here, rather they took it as a challenge to see how tough he was. When they had sussed out what a chicken he was, he'd been pushed way down the pecking order, the harder inmates taking pleasure in tormenting him. His rape, while a circle of them watched and jeered had been the end for him. He couldn't, wouldn't spend a life in fear. Rachel had prevented that happening to him before, but inside there was no one to protect him.

All night the warders walked up and down the metal gangway outside the doors, watching in case any fights broke out, constantly on alert in case anyone tried to commit suicide, determined no one would get away without serving their time. That was, except for when the shift changed, then, Tony had discovered, there was half an hour when no one supervised the cells. The screws who were finishing for the day were presumably chatting to those who were starting.

Ferris listened for the sound of the shift change, the screw's footsteps getting fainter. Then finally alone, he got up, took off his pyjama bottoms, fastened them into a noose, put it round his neck, tied it to the bed and let himself fall forwards.

* * * * *

Max stretched luxuriously, Saturday morning and no work, that was something unusual in itself. Time off. He took a deep breath, the air was filled with the delicious aroma of frying bacon, Tara had promised she would cook him the full English to celebrate his day off.

He popped his head around the kitchen door, she was busy with the frying pan, standing with an expression of great focus as she moved bacon and sausages around in the pan. 'Smells lovely,' he came into the kitchen to hug her gently, it felt strange to have this kind of relationship with someone who he could easily be dating, were she not his daughter. But the DNA test hadn't lied. Tara was his, something that filled him with awe. It was hard to imagine a short relationship, with someone he had barely got to know could have produced someone as incredible as Tara.

'Ready in about ten minutes if you want to take a shower,' she smiled at him. She'd moved in with him soon after their relationship had been established. What father could allow his daughter to be on the streets? They'd muddled along, politely skirting around one another, the bond already strong between them, it was just the mechanics of being a father and daughter he found hard. Normally people had a lifetime to adjust to becoming a parent. He'd had a few short weeks to get used to the idea.

He showered, wondering how to fill the day, relaxing with the newspapers after breakfast, perhaps a walk on the beach with Tara and then lunch in a pub somewhere. Tara loved Cornwall. Having her there made him miss city life a little less, hopefully soon he'd break it to her they would eventually move away, back up north. But he needed to take things one step at a time.

As he dressed his telephone rang, his heart sank, his instinct was to ignore it, he was not on the rota to work, let someone else get called in and deal with the problem, but still relentlessly his hand picked up the telephone and accepted the call.

'Max Wilton.'

'Max,' he recognised the voice as Edward Farrell, the desk sergeant, 'Sorry, I know you are off today, been trying to get hold of Tallis, I just thought that you should both know Ferris committed suicide last night in Dartmoor.'

'Okay thanks for letting me know, Tallis was out last night, she's probably sleeping it off. I'll let her know.' He ended the call. Suicide in prison was an ignominious end for Tony Ferris's sad life. He'd try calling Tallis later.

Tara had dished up the breakfast when he went into the kitchen. The window was open letting clean fresh air into the room. The storm had passed over, sky now a clear blue.

They ate, in companiable silence. It was a luxury not having to work and to have breakfast cooked for him. Max pressed redial again and again, listening as the phone went straight to voicemail. It was unusual Tallis wasn't answering her phone.

After they had washed the breakfast things Max said, 'I need to nip and tell Tallis about this suicide, I won't be long and then we'll go for a walk on the beach if you like.'

Tara nodded, 'Okay Dad,' she grinned, picking up the book she was constantly reading, with a sigh of pleasure she curled up on the sofa, tucking her long legs underneath her.

Max drove up to Tallis's Long Meadow Farm. The yard was ominously silent as he turned off the car engine. The only sound was the breeze lifting a plastic sheet that covered what he assumed where building materials and cry of gulls as they wheeled in from the sea.

'Tallis,' Max called. There was no sign of her. He redialled her number, again it went straight to voice mail. Max felt the first prickle of annoyance, she must have gone out last night, perhaps she had let her phone run out of battery. She must be asleep. Still though the silence had an unearthly feel. There should be activity at this time of the day. He circled the stables, calling out for Grace, or Kaden, or Rachel.

There was no sign of anyone at the stables. The place was deserted. The horses, in the stables watched him. One neighed, the other banged on its door. Max remembered them doing that when he had been in the yard before, waiting as Grace hurried to give them their feeds.

Max felt the first prickle of fear. He left the yard and went up the path to the farmhouse, tried the doors, they were locked. Unsettled he circled again, peering in through the windows. The lounge was deserted, the television on. As he pressed his face against the kitchen window, he saw a pair of boots and jean-clad legs sticking out from behind the table. A moment later he was battering his shoulder against the door, already calling for back up and an ambulance.

* * * * *

'Kaden,' Max finally succeeded in getting the front door to yield and half fell, half stumbled into the hall. He ran down the hall into the kitchen. Kaden lay on the kitchen floor, dried blood had pooled around his head. 'Hurry up with that ambulance,' Max yelled into his phone.

'It's on its way,' came the calm tones of the dispatcher. Max crouched beside Kaden quickly checking and finding a pulse. 'Wake up Kaden,' his tone was insistent.

Kaden groaned, his eyelids fluttering and finally opening. He blinked, trying to focus.

'Who attacked you? Where is Grace?'

Kaden attempted to move, winced and lay still, 'Rachel, she's got Grace.' His voice sounded faint as if it were an enormous effort for him to speak.

'Rachel, why would she…?' Max grabbed a sweater that had been discarded on the back of a chair and put it under Kaden's head, covering him with a coat that he dragged from a hanger behind the door. 'I've got to find Grace.'

'Grace was asking her about Tony Ferris and Jago.' Kaden's face was pinched with fear. 'Leave me. Please find her.'

Max hurried around the cottage, shouting Grace's name. There was no sign of her or Rachel anywhere. The Land Rover had gone.

'Get a trace on Tallis's number,' Max leant beside the cottage door, faintly, in the far distance he could hear sirens. Help was on its way.

'The last ping from the phone puts her at home that was at six last night,' Pete said.

'She's not here.'

'Might be nothing,' Pete continued, 'but there's been a report of a vehicle being abandoned near Hedford Beach. Caller said it was a Land Rover.'

'Hedford Beach?' Max was filled with anxiety something was very wrong. 'What's out there.'

'Nothing just the beach, cliffs, old mine shafts…' Max could hear the fear in Pete's voice.

'Send back up. I'm going straight there.' Max yelled, already running to his car. He passed the ambulance on the farm drive. 'He's in the kitchen,' Max let down his car window, driving off before the ambulance team replied.

Hedford Beach was along the coast from the farm. Max swung his car around the tight corners, hoping he wouldn't meet anyone driving in the opposite direction. Fifteen minutes later he skidded to a halt in the deserted car park. There was no sign of the Land Rover, or Grace. He parked his car, the tech must have been mistaken unless Grace's phone was here, but there was no sign of her, or Rachel. In the distance he could hear sirens coming towards him.

Max stood for a moment, listening to the sound of the sea breaking on the cliffs, he took a deep breath of salty air. 'Grace!' his throat hurt with the effort of shouting as loud as he could. There was no reply except the cries of the sea birds, he scanned the skies looking for the birds and saw nothing. When the cry came again, he realised it was not sea birds he was hearing, but a faint cry for help coming from the ground itself. It was unmistakably Grace.

'Grace,' Max yelled, turning a circle, trying to orient himself with the cry he had heard. He glanced in the direction he had driven in, as a movement caught his eye. The emergency services were on the way. Along the lane an ambulance and two police vehicles were approaching.

'Grace!' Max ran along the cliff top, listening for the sound of her reply.

'I'm here.' Her voice was faint and tremulous, but close by somewhere.

He skidded to a halt, there was nothing around him except grassland and far below the cliffs the surging sea.

'I can't see you,' Max's voice held a note of desperation.

'Help me.'

'Over here,' Max yelled, his voice taken away by the wind. The rescue service personnel were running towards him. He was aware of a rocky outcrop, covered in bushes, that was where her voice was coming from.

He shoved his way through, wincing as the sharp thorns scratched against his skin through his jeans. In the centre of the bushes there was a wooden cover, he grabbed it, slinging it out of the way. Under the cover was a gaping hole.

He peered over, giddy as his eyes adjusted to the darkness below him. Grace lay on a narrow rocky ledge some ten feet below him, her ankle bent at a sickening angle.

'Hang on we're going to get you out of there.'

'Please hurry up… Is Kaden…?' Max could hear the panic in her voice.

'He's on his way to hospital.'

'Is he…?'

'I think he's okay, Grace. Where did Rachel go?'

'I don't know. She's gone. Max it was her that killed Jago. Catherine Marshall was her girlfriend. She killed him in revenge.'

Beside Max, the coast guard team working quickly, rigged up a sling, lowered it into the hole.

'Grace, can you put it around your shoulders.'

There was a faint murmur of agreement. A short time later Grace's wind tossed red hair appeared in the gap followed by her head and shoulders.

The coast guard rushed to grab Grace, hauling her to the surface. She emerged, her skin deathly pale, teeth chattering. Someone wrapped a blanket around her shoulders.

'Get her to hospital, quickly.' One of the rescue men commanded.

'Max,' Grace said, weakly, her hand seeking and finding Max's. 'Find Rachel.'

'Yes Boss,' Max grinned. Even in her weakened state her priority was her job. 'Max' Grace gripped his hand tightly, 'Something else. There's a body down there, a murder victim I'm sure, the skull was caved in.'

'Body? Another woman?' Max hurried to keep up with the rescue services as they sprinted towards the ambulance.

Beneath the mound of blankets Grace met his eyes and shook her head. 'A man, I'm pretty sure I've found Mia Lewis's boyfriend, Tom.'

Thank you for taking the time to read this book. I hope you enjoyed it, I certainly enjoyed writing it. Each time I sit down to write – and that is every day – I realise just how lucky I am this is my job. I can only keep this job because people like you enjoy my books and buy them. No words can express how grateful I am for that.

If you would like to find out more about my other books, please visit my web site.

www.louisebroderick.com

I love to hear from readers so please feel free to contact me on via Facebook, Instagram or email. The details of these are all on my web site.

I hope you enjoyed this book and would like to help me carry on living the dream, writing for a living. If you would like to help, please take the time to leave a book review on Amazon. Positive reviews really do help to sell a book, so if you would do that for me you are helping me to continue creating my books and continuing as a fulltime writer.

I would like to give a huge thank you in advance to anyone who takes the time to do this for me. I know very well how precious time is and am hugely grateful for anyone who cares enough to spend some of their valuable time helping me. Thank you.

www.ingramcontent.com/pod-product-compliance
Lightning Source LLC
Chambersburg PA
CBHW011032190726
48290CB00011B/2815